BORDERLINE
TERROR

Best Regards

Bob Clark

1

3

PROLOGUE

Six months earlier

An Iranian fish factory ship, The Nargess, of Liberian registry docked at an obscure side pier at the port city of St. Pierre in the tiny French island of Miquelon located on the Grand Banks South of Newfoundland, six hundred and fifty miles east of Montreal. St. Pierre and Miquelon are actually a cluster of islands off the coast of Canada, a hold-over from the sixteenth century when France held sway over much of present day New England and the Province of Quebec, only to be beaten by the English during the Seven Years War. As a result of the Treaty of Paris in 1763, France ceded most of its territorial rights in North America to England save for these nine tiny islands in the Gulf of St. Lawrence.

The crew of the Nargess had been busy processing its load of codfish for transport back to the French port city of Concarneau, but first they had transferred a special cargo to another vessel specially outfitted to receive it. There was no manifest. The captain was only aware that it was to be transferred as soon as his ship docked in St. Pierre and that he would be paid handsomely when he returned to his Iranian homeport of Chabahar on the Indian Ocean. Because he was not offloading cargo directly onto the Island, the French Customs officers, or Douanes, were not particularly interested.

The receiving vessel, disguised to look like a fishing trawler complete with nets, outriggers, electronic depth and fish finders and even a "wet" fish hold, was tied up alongside the Nargess. Three lead-lined pallets, each weighing several tons and wrapped tightly in a shroud of thick gray canvas were individually lowered into the cavity beneath the wet fish hold of the trawler. The cargo boom of the factory ship strained as it lowered each pallet into place. When the transfer was complete, the cavity was sealed and seawater allowed to flow into the wet fish hold. A quantity of live cod fish were also added to the fish hold to convince any prying fisheries' officer of its legitimacy as the vessel made its three day voyage up the St. Lawrence River to Chambly, Quebec.

THE DAY BEFORE

"Hello doctor," Marc LaRose whispered as he spotted the black Mercedes SUV passing him in the opposite direction headed toward downtown Plattsburgh.

Veering into the state college parking lot to facilitate a quick U-turn, he caught the upright middle finger of a startled college coed pressing a cell phone to her ear. With tires screeching, Marc wheeled his Ford Explorer back onto Broad Street in pursuit of the Mercedes; only to discover two other vehicles had gotten between him and his quarry. He pushed hard on the accelerator, exceeding the thirty mile an hour city speed limit, gambling he would not attract the attention of the local constabulary in a determined effort to keep the Mercedes in sight.

When the Mercedes first passed him, Marc got a glimpse of the driver, Dr. Alan Simpson, an elusive sort who had been the subject of Marc's attention lately. Simpson's spouse, Marietta, a forty year old blond with a body that still retained an outside chance for a Hustler Magazine cover, had contacted Marc two weeks before, complaining that her husband was keeping longer hours than usual at his very successful ophthalmology practice. She also complained that on several occasions he hadn't come home for days at a time, often seemed distracted, and, when confronted about his unusual behavior, gave no excuses, indicating only that he needed more time away because of the increasing demands of his business. Without putting too fine a point on it, she suspected her husband was fucking around on her.

Marc LaRose is a licensed private investigator and, although the detective business is often slow during the winter months in the Northern tier of New York State, he detests matrimonial investigations. Peeking into windows, trying to catch a cheating spouse in some kind of compromising position is work that Marc has not bonded with. But Marietta Simpson was persistent and, with things as slow as they were, he relented. Besides, Marietta was offering a nice monetary bonus. Fitting fashionable eyewear to the visually impaired pays well.

Simpson's Black Mercedes Benz G Class SUV is easy to spot with its subtle elegance and boxy shape, and along with its hundred thousand dollar price tag, is the only one of its kind registered north of Albany. The Mercedes' signal light indicated a right-turn onto South Catherine Street. One of the cars between them continued straight on Broad, but the other, a white Ford Taurus, also turned right and remained between Marc and the Mercedes.

Just as well. The Taurus will help provide cover, Marc thought as he also made the turn, and continued to close the gap between them.

The small caravan continued south out of the city and onto a long straight stretch of State Route 22 past the runway of the former Plattsburgh Air Force Base, now the Plattsburgh International Airport. The day was clear, and despite the snow banks, so were the roads, but it's freezing cold. January is always cold in the North Country.

Getting a whiff of engine fumes, Marc instinctively glanced to his left toward the runway, thinking it could be from another planeload of Canadians just taking off for Myrtle Beach for a week of golf, tasteless American beer and cruising the "titty" bars along the board walk.

Odd, not an airplane in sight.

Returning his gaze toward the Mercedes that, a moment ago, was just ahead of the Taurus, he discovered the distance between them had suddenly grown to a full quarter-mile, and was increasing fast. Dr. Simpson is a retired Air Force fighter pilot who loves speed, whether he's on the ground or in the air.

"Shit," Marc yelled, as he passed the Taurus in a frantic effort to keep the Mercedes in sight. Up ahead, the brake lights of Simpson's car came on just before it disappeared around a left hand curve in the road. A long twenty seconds later, Marc's Explorer took the curve.

Marc pressed on at seventy-plus miles per hour, oblivious to the forty mile per hour speed signs that whizzed by. Being a retired State Trooper has its perks. Another mile and again he caught a glimpse of Simpson's SUV disappearing over a rise in the road. Marc knew that the hamlet of Peru was just ahead.

Marc has spent the past two weeks keeping tabs on Dr. Simpson's whereabouts. Consistent with Marietta's information, his routine was to depart their custom built home on the outskirts of Plattsburgh around six thirty a.m., and, traveling in his Mercedes SUV, he usually went straight to his modern suite of offices on Upper Cornelia Street.

The ten thousand square foot complex with its myriad of rooms offers state-of-the-art eye care for everyone ranging from pediatrics to geriatrics. Northern Eye Care employs more than fifty people, including Ophthalmologic surgeons, technicians, greeters, telephone operators, bookkeepers, insurance specialists and customer service personnel.

Marc found Simpson's work routine fairly consistent. After working a twelve hour day, he would return straight home, confirming his claim of working long hours. But it's those rare days Dr. Simpson doesn't report for work that interest Marc.

Peru, New York, is a hamlet of a thousand people surrounded by hay fields and apple orchards. Of course, in January, the fields are snow covered and the trees are bare.

Marc again caught site of the Mercedes' brake lights as it entered the more populated section of the hamlet. He had slowly closed the gap between them to a couple hundred yards, a comfortable tailing distance, not so far behind where he would lose sight of the pursued vehicle, but not so close that he would arouse the target's suspicion that he was being followed.

The Mercedes continued south out of the hamlet and again picked up speed. The flatter terrain at the foot of the Adirondack Mountains offered Marc the opportunity to tail the Mercedes from a distance. The brake lights again illuminated as the car turned right onto another two lane county highway that Marc remembered as the Harkness Road.

"Where the fuck are you going?" Marc muttered, knowing that if Dr. Simpson intended to elude him, his Ford Explorer was no match for the powerful Mercedes with its massive 5.5 liter V8 engine. But as Marc made the turn seconds later, he was bewildered to find the half mile stretch of roadway ahead of him completely empty. Not a car in sight.

"How did that son of a bitch disappear so quickly?" Marc asked himself as he strained to catch a glimpse of the Mercedes that, just a moment before, was well within sight, the Ford's engine screaming at full throttle. Accelerating past a farm house off to his left, a flicker of movement failed to distract him as he focused on the road ahead, frantically looking for any sign of the Mercedes. Fifty seconds and another fast mile later, Marc maneuvered around a long bend in the road and was again disheartened to find that this stretch of highway was also completely empty.

"No fucking way," he muttered in exasperation, slowing his

vehicle as he coasted into the hamlet of Harkness, a cluster of forty dwellings, mostly dated manufactured homes and older house trailers with permanent additions, carports and garages displaying a variety of mismatched painting schemes. Peering down each driveway, he searched for any sign of the Mercedes. It didn't take long for Marc to realize that Simpson's vehicle was not there.

Lost him.

Recalling the flicker of movement that he had discounted just minutes before, he concluded that his only hope in relocating Simpson was to retrace his route.

Was it a one story farmhouse or two? Was it red brick or white clapboards? Was it a mile before Harkness, or a little further? Things happened so fast.

Evening comes early to the North Country in January, and though it was only a quarter to four in the afternoon, the shadows were lengthening and the few cars that were on the road already had their headlights on. As he retraced his route, the setting sun was partially covered with a layer of thick dark clouds, hastening the onset of darkness.

Now, which one was it? He asked himself, carefully scanning each driveway.

Passing the Harkness Cemetery, he noticed its one lane access road had been recently cleared of snow. A dark mound of earth on top of the snow indicated a fresh grave had recently been dug. "A little early for spring planting," Marc muttered, smiling at his own private joke, knowing most cemeteries in the North Country do not inter the dead after the ground freezes, unless the relatives wish to pay a premium.

The long section of country road ahead looked deserted, except for a single vehicle coming toward him with its head lights on and turn signal blinking. Marc instinctively slowed, and as he passed a driveway off to his right, he spotted the boxy tail end of Simpson's SUV parked behind a two story brick farm house.

"Son of a bitch," he exclaimed, as he continued past the oncoming sports car. Marc watched in his rear view mirror as the smaller vehicle turned into the same driveway where the Mercedes was parked. Continuing on for another quarter mile, Marc made a U-turn and headed back toward the farmhouse with his own vehicle lights now extinguished. Coasting past, Marc made a right turn down the cemetery's freshly plowed lane, and pulled his Explorer around the back of the pile of dark earth.

His digital camera at the ready, he aimed its 300mm lens out the driver's side window and focused in on the smaller vehicle parked behind the Mercedes on the opposite side of the road. Through the camera's powerful lens Marc could see a tall man in his early thirties sporting a neatly trimmed goatee, wearing a ski jacket and a pair of sunglasses stylishly pushed up over his forehead. Standing at the rear of his sleek Chrysler Crossfire sports car, the man peered into the vehicle's open trunk.

Using his partially opened driver's side window as a support to prevent his camera from shaking in the diminishing light, Marc took a series of photos as the man retrieved a small suitcase before closing the trunk, allowing him a close-up of the vehicle's license plate. It was then that Marc noticed a second man approaching from around the rear of the farmhouse. Continuing to snap photos, he could clearly see the second man was none other than Dr. Simpson. The newcomer approached Simpson and the two men enthusiastically embraced for a long moment before the younger man's hands slid downwards, and with a buttock cheek in each hand, pulled Simpson's loins toward his own, simultaneously, planting a wet, hirsute kiss on the doctor's lips. After a passionate few moments, Simpson broke the embrace, furtively glanced toward the highway, grabbed the suitcase, and led his goateed friend by the hand, around the rear of the farmhouse.

"Oh Marietta, looks like your husband's pinch hitting for the opposing side," Marc whispered as he started the Explorer's engine for the trip back to Plattsburgh, taking note of the number on the mailbox as he passed by.

For Marc, it had been a long cold day, hell, a long cold two weeks of doing the kind of sleazy investigative work he disdains.

Marietta's report will wait until tomorrow, Marc thought, as he relaxed his grip on the steering wheel and headed for home. For now, his sole intention was to return to his condo, reheat the accumulated remnants of foam-covered takeouts stacked in the fridge, wash them down with a Bud Light or two, then hit the covers for a full night's sleep, the first since ringing in the New Year.

DAY ONE

It was 7:30 a.m. and the bank thermometer at the corner of Margaret and Cornelia Streets in downtown Plattsburgh read 15°. Marc parked his Explorer and gingerly picked his way over the crusted snow bank piled along the curb to get to his office, located in a second floor walkup over an empty store front. The cold outline of a now-defunct restaurant's neon sign, "Happy Family Chinese Takeout," was barely visible through the grimy plate glass window.

For the past five years, Marc has shared the office with an old work mate, Norm Prendergast, who has slowly built up his own process-serving business.

There are no professional titles or names pasted on the door. Marc only advertises his private investigative business in the yellow pages, since most of his clients are either attorneys or insurance companies, and Norm, well, he's just cheap.

Marc flipped the light switch and the overhead fluorescents buzzed to life. For the moment, he ignored the red blinking light on the answering machine on his desk. The small electric space heater near the lone window would take a few minutes of snapping and buzzing to warm the office to at least somewhere above freezing, so Marc left his hat and coat on and muttered to himself, "First things first".

There was a stained coffee maker perched atop an apartment-sized fridge, both precariously held off the floor by a garage-sale end table in the corner of the office. The fridge housed an outdated container of orange juice, a few creamers skimmed from the local coffee shop, and the remains of an onion bagel that could double as a Chia Pet with its full growth of green moldy fuzz.

Marc refilled Mr. Coffee with grounds and water drawn from the bathroom sink. With an asthmatic gurgle, it soon began spewing its scented nectar.

Seated at his desk, he punched the number for the local flower shop into his desk phone. Shirley, Marc's ex-wife of five-plus years, should be preparing the morning's shipment of fresh flowers. Although divorced, they stay in close contact.

First true flames die slowly; however, the split was inevitable. She became annoyed with him continually being called to duty at odd times of the day and night, first as a police investigator, then as a PI.

And, she too, was a competitive workaholic, toiling away most weekends and every holiday in her flower shop. Although married for fourteen years and sweethearts long before that, the pull of their individual careers eventually won out.

Shirley picked up on the first ring.

"Shirley's Flowers."

"Hey, lady, are your roses fresh?" It's Marc's pat opening.

"Figured it was you. How have you been, hon?"

"Same-old. You got the shop ready for Valentine's Day?" he asked, attempting some small talk.

"You kidding me? We're still trying to get the place cleaned up from Christmas. Why do people have to wait until the holidays to die? Soon as we get one load of funeral flowers out the door, another order comes in," Shirley lamented.

"Woe is the life of a florist. People fall in love, you make money. People die, you make money. Poor you," Marc countered, good-naturedly.

"Yeah, but I can shut the door and put out the closed sign and go home like most sane people."

"Like you'd ever do that. But look, I didn't call to argue. How's Ann Marie?" Marc asked, referring to their 19-year-old, sometimes rebellious, daughter.

"Sore subject. She was late coming home again last night. I think she's seeing someone, but whenever I broach the topic, she ignores me."

"She still got that black lipstick and fingernail polish thing going on that I saw her with at Christmas? Along with those green and red streaks in her hair, it's a wonder they allow her in to her classes."

"Have you been past the Plattsburgh State Campus lately? I swear they're all in some state of identity crisis. Anyway, she's not wearing that so much anymore; I think her new boyfriend had something to say about that."

"I'm beginning to like him already," Marc said with a chuckle.

"At least she was helpful over the Christmas break. She has an aversion about coming to work on time, but once she gets started, she's really a big help. I'm thankful for that."

"Sounds like everything's pretty much under control then."

"Well, OK for now, I guess. Hey look, anytime you want to stop by, the coffee's always on."

"Thanks, I'll keep that in mind," Marc said without conviction.

Marc could hear the heavy scuffing of footsteps coming up the stairwell. "Look, Shirley. Someone's coming. I should go."

"OK, I guess. Take care of yourself, Marc," Shirley said, sounding disappointed.

"Hey, I have to. Tell Ann Marie her Daddy says 'Hi', and don't work too hard."

"Later," Shirley said as she ended the call.

The office door opened as Marc hung up the phone. Although Norm is freshly showered and shaven, Marc can still detect the remnants of last night's alcohol as he brushes by.

"Morning," Norm grumbled.

"Hey, top of the morning to you too, Mr. Sunshine."

"Fuck you! Coffee made?" Norm growled as he unbuttoned the front of his winter jacket.

Without waiting for Marc to answer, he poured himself a cup of the fresh brew, added two of the pilfered creamers, then grabbed the pile of mail and sorted out the advertisements. A large manila envelope from a local attorney caught his attention and he carefully tore it open. Inside, there were two summonses that needed to be personally served by the day's close of business which immediately sent him into one of his mini tantrums.

"Malone! Aw, fuck me. Don't those assholes know it's a hundred mile round trip? And today, of all days, with these icy roads, they gotta be kidding."

Marc chuckled, knowing that despite these well-practiced antics, nothing would stop Norm from doing his job, not only because of the timeliness of the judicial issue, but because this particular law firm was a good customer, one he couldn't risk losing.

As Norm settled into reading the particulars regarding the summons service, Marc decided it would be a good time to find out what's on the answering machine as the red number two continued its rhythmic blinking. Positioning his pad and pen, he hit the play button.

As Marc suspected, the first message was from Marietta Simpson, looking for an update on her husband's investigation.

"Be right with you sweetheart," Marc said as he hit the cancel button and listened for the next message.

The second was from someone named Lateesha who identified

14

herself as a caseworker for an insurance firm located downstate. Lateesha's message indicated that her firm had received notification of an apparent accidental death involving a client and would Marc be available to make some inquiries.

"Yes, anything besides another matrimonial," Marc whispered.

He dialed the number left by Lateesha and was connected to the Humbolt Insurance Company's computerized telephone directory. After navigating through the list of names and numbers, he was eventually routed to Lateesha, who informed Marc that their client, The Saranac Mountain Inn and Resort of Lake Placid, had contacted Humbolt the day before to report that one of their registered guests had died while cross country skiing the previous Friday.

In an accent Marc could only guess was from somewhere south of the Tappan Zee Bridge, Lateesha related that, according to the Inn's manager, the deceased was taking part in a guided cross-country ski trip which was part of a package of events the resort offered its guests.

Lateesha inquired whether Marc would be available to talk to the Inn's general manager regarding the circumstances surrounding the deceased's visit to the Inn, his cause of death and any further involvement that the Inn had in arranging the cross country ski trip.

Over his five years as a private detective, Marc had investigated plenty of slip and falls, and he knew that Humbolt needed to determine the extent of exposure the Inn and the insurance company may have in any future law suit the deceased's next of kin might place against them.

After acknowledging his availability and exchanging contact information, Marc set the phone down just in time to bid Norm good hunting as he headed out the door, manila envelope tucked under his arm and a full coffee cup in hand.

"Screw you," Norm retorted good naturedly as he pulled the door shut with his foot, sloshing coffee down the front of his coat as he did so.

"Poor bastard," Marc muttered, smiling to himself.

Before starting today's new assignment, however, he used the next few quiet moments to tie up some loose ends from the surveillance of Dr. Simpson. A computer check of the address he had noted on the mailbox outside of Simpson's love lair the evening before led him to a colorful website titled, "A Private Getaway Set in

15

the Scenic Splendor of Apple Valley. Perfect for that Special Someone." The asking price for a week's rental was listed at eighteen hundred dollars.

"Hope he was worth it," Marc whispered with sly grin.

Marc placed the call to Marietta Simpson and for the next ten minutes recounted the details of his surveillance. As he systematically ticked off his findings, Marietta's comments were limited to a few disinterested, "Uh-huhs" and "Mm-hm's", until she was informed of the fairly innocuous revelation that the "Lodge" where Doctor Simpson was found to be holding private audiences with Mr. Crossfire rented for $1800 a week.

"Eighteen hundred bucks a week?" Marietta screamed into Marc's receiver before continuing her verbal onslaught.

"That limped-dick son of a bitch is too cheap to take me out to dinner but he's got eighteen hundred bucks to literally blow on some frigging fruit fly? LaRose, I want those photos, all of 'em, along with your report and your bill. I'm gonna fix that two-timing bastard once and for all."

Marc was holding the receiver at arm's length which lessened the impact of the sharp click he heard at the end of the tirade.

"Sure hope the good doctor has a comfortable couch to sleep on," Marc said to his coffee cup before draining its remnants.

An hour later Marc finished e-mailing Marietta the documents she had so colorfully requested. Refilling his cup for the third time, he got to the task of conducting some preliminary work on this new investigation involving the Saranac Mountain Inn and Resort.

His long familiarity with the high peaks area of the Adirondacks could be traced to his previous employment as a state trooper. Marc found the thought of returning there to work on an investigation not only nostalgic, but intriguing as well.

A perusal of the Inn's website highlighted a few of its amenities: boat rides on a private lake; hiking the Inn's trail with gourmet meals and chef provided; overnight guided excursions to the top of Cascade Mountain, and guided downhill and Nordic skiing trips. It listed the Inn's manager as Noah Emmanuel and provided his photo and a brief bio. There were a few photos of the Inn and a rate sheet for the individually custom-decorated rooms starting at twelve hundred dollars a night. Curiously, however, there was no indication of exactly where to find the Inn. A footnote indicated that directions would be provided to first-time guests pending a reference check and payment in advance. At the end of the website, Marc noted a mailing address using a PO Box number in Lake Placid, along with a phone number.

Marc conducted a computer background check on Noah Emmanuel that confirmed the bio listed on the Inn's website. He'd been employed in the hospitality industry for the past ten years, after graduating from the prestigious Beauregard Culinary Institute in Charleston, South Carolina and, apparently, his present position was his first as a head innkeeper. A database check of the Saranac Mountain Inn and Resort revealed that the Inn is actually a subsidiary of private holding company called 'The McKenzie Group, Ltd.', which also owns other inns that cater to the well-heeled in Canada and the U.S., and has its corporate headquarters in Montreal, Quebec.

After perusing the local newspaper, *The Plattsburgh Standard*, for any mention of the incident, Marc found an obscure piece at the bottom of page six. It read, "Man found unresponsive on the Jack Rabbit Cross Country Ski Trail off Route 73 in the Town of Wilmington, Essex County, Friday afternoon. The Lake Placid rescue squad responded. Attempts to resuscitate the victim as he was transported to the High Peaks Medical Center in Saranac Lake were unsuccessful. The Coroner's physician, Dr. Wilber Gadway, pronounced the victim dead on arrival at the Medical Center."

The article went on to explain that the State Police from the Ray Brook barracks were investigating and the identity of the deceased was being withheld pending notification of next of kin. An autopsy was to be conducted by the Essex County Coroner's office on Saturday.

Marc clipped the article from the newspaper and retrieved a new manila file folder from a desk drawer. Using a black felt pen, he inscribed a unique case identifier on the folder tab and secured the clipped article inside. All bits of information regarding this case would ultimately find its way to the folder which Marc then slipped into his 'active' file drawer.

He then scanned the remainder of the paper, but, before he got to his favorite section, the crossword puzzle, the computer dinged indicating the arrival of the expected e-mail message from the Humbolt Insurance Company.

From the information Lateesha provided, he learned the Inn's manager, Noah Emmanuel had notified Humbolt Insurance of the incident on Monday, January fourteenth. The deceased guest had registered under the name of Jamal Al-Zeid, and had checked into the Inn on Thursday, January tenth, with a planned stay of four nights. According to the Inn's records, Mr. Al-Zeid listed his address as 44981 Sherbooke St. NW, Montreal, Quebec.

Lateesha's message further indicated that the cross-country ski trip Al-Zeid was taking part in at the time of his death was part of the Inn's outdoor activities package, which included transportation to and from the event, further strengthening Humbolt's reason for concern for a possible future law suit, should the heirs of the deceased hire an attorney.

At the end of the e-mail Marc noted that Lateesha had made an appointment for him to meet with Noah Emmanuel the next day, at ten a.m. at the Inn. Also at the meeting would be the assistant manager, Walter Barris and the events coordinator, Lucy Welch.

"Thank you, Lateesha," Marc whispered.

With the rest of the day to kill, Marc figured it would be a good time to reconnect with one of his old buddies at the Ray Brook State Police Station, Senior Investigator Jerry Garrant, and find out what he knew about the case. He remembered the hamlet as a small cluster of private homes and independently operated motels and restaurants on Route 86 about midway between Lake Placid and Saranac Lake. Its major claim to fame is that it is the headquarters for Troop B of the New York State Police, as well as the NYS Department of Environmental Conservation offices next door.

Marc put a call through to the Ray Brook barracks (state troopers refer to their assigned stations as a barracks, a term dating back to when their predecessors ate, slept and lived in a military style dormitory). He was advised by the desk trooper that Jerry was out of the office, but was expected back around one o'clock. Marc left Jerry a voice message saying that he expected be in the Ray Brook area later in the day and hoped to meet up with him there.

Before heading out to Ray Brook, Marc stopped by his condo to pick up a few things whereupon, he found his two kittens, Brandy and Rye, laying on their backs in a corner of the kitchen next to their bubbling "kitty fountain".

With Marc's penchant for the occasional taste of hops and barley, one could rightly ask how he came to name these two previously feral felines after cordials. It just so happened that while watching the 1980 Lake Placid Winter Olympics on TV, there was an episode involving

Randy Gardner and Tai Babalonia, leading contestants in the pairs figure skating category. Unfortunately for them, sometime during their warm-up practice routine, Randy fell and suffered an ankle injury.

The ABC sports commentator, Dick Button, himself a past Olympian, proceeded to lament about 'Poor Randy and poor Tai's unfortunate incident on live network television, to the point that Marc was forced to change channels and watch a rerun of Mutual of Omaha's, *Wild Kingdom*. So, in honor of this singularly momentous occasion of sports boredom, he named his recently acquired pets, Brandy and Rye, in honor of Randy and Tai and their unintended early exit from the annals of Olympic skating history.

Searching his closet, Marc located his fur-lined hooded parka, wool trousers, and a pair of insulated "shooters" mittens that have an open slot for the trigger finger. He also dug out a pair of dust-laden cross country skis complete with poles and boots that had been stored away in the attic above the closet since his breakup with Shirley. It took two trips to load his gear into the back of his Explorer.

Marc's vehicle preference provides another digression.

An important part of being successful in the private detective business is trying to be the veritable fly on the wall. You have to see things, but you don't want to get caught looking. It's bad for business, and possibly one's physical well being.

Federal and state narcotics agents often use specially equipped vehicles, from which they can observe and film their surveillance targets with built in periscopes and portals that are virtually impossible to detect. However, most small town PI's lack those resources and must rely on less elaborate gear, a little experience and lots of common sense. But whatever vehicle a PI uses, it has to be dependable to drive in various road and weather conditions, and it absolutely has to be what's best described as non-descript. No flashy sports cars, monster trucks, Hollywood mufflers, bumper stickers, or anything else that would draw undue attention.

Marc prefers his basic dark green Ford Explorer. The side and rear windows are slightly tinted so he can see out, but people have a hard time seeing who's inside, oftentimes as they are being photographed. The dark green color attracts less attention and people usually don't remember it if he needs to return to the same location for more surveillance. And the SUV gives him more room to store stuff and move around inside. Marc also has a tan Honda Civic that he keeps as a backup for those repeat trips. So, with the Explorer loaded, he grabbed his tape recorder and digital camera for the interview with Noah Emmanuel.

Marc was never big on handguns, or weapons of any kind for that matter, but does own a Heckler and Koch P2000, 40-caliber handgun that he purchased when first going into the PI business. He slid it under the front seat of the Explorer.

It was 10:30 a.m. by the time Marc left Plattsburgh for the hour's drive to the Village of Lake Placid. As he followed the winding road along the Ausable River through the hamlet of Jay known for its quaint covered bridge, he took time to think about this new assignment and the prospect of seeing his old friend, Jerry Garrant.

Marc made the turn onto Route 86 and a short distance later, as he glanced to his right, he could see the brightly colored ski jackets worn by the skiers that filled the slopes on Whiteface Mountain.

The view reminded him of the last time he and Shirley had gone skiing together, when Ann Marie was in the sixth grade. Where have the years gone? He thought to himself as he continued upward, through the narrow, windy section of road known locally as the Notch, that continues alongside the river for the last ten miles to the Village of Lake Placid.

Marc felt a pang of nostalgia as he drove past the Lake Placid Golf Course and entered the mountain village known as the Alps of the East, filled with hotels, motels and restaurants adorned with a Bavarian motif. He passed the old Olympic arena, originally built for the 1932 Olympic Games, situated next to the "new" Olympic arena built for the 1980 Olympics.

It was almost noon when Marc pulled his Explorer in the parking lot of Ruthie's Restaurant, a favorite of the local police, known for its home-cooked food and friendly atmosphere. Local patrons were often good sources of information.

As he entered the restaurant, Marc found, to his pleasure, that the tables were still covered with red and white vinyl table cloths and the day's lunch specials were scrawled out in cursive on a black chalk board mounted on an easel.

Change comes slowly in the Adirondacks.

Marc slid into a booth and asked for a "Ruthie's Special Burger", with fried onions, spicy coleslaw and coffee. As he was waiting for his order he noticed Ned Barnes, the sometimes cantankerous chief for the local volunteer rescue squad sitting alone at one of the tables. Marc motioned for Ned to join him, and without hesitation, Ned picked up what was left of his blue plate special and slid into Marc's booth.

After bringing each other up to speed since the last time they saw each other, Marc got around to inquiring about the incident that brought him to Lake Placid.

"Ned, do you happen to know anything about that skier they found down on the Jack Rabbit trail last week?"

Ned looked up from his plate. "Thought you were retired from the police business."

"Working for myself these days. Private investigator."

"Oh, I see, so that's what brings you all the way back up here," Ned said as he shoved in a forkful of meatloaf.

"The Inn's insurance company is getting a little nervous. I guess they want to know what they're up against," Marc said.

Ned laid his fork down and, while he finished chewing his last mouthful, starred at an unseen spot on the side of the booth over Marc's head.

"Well, the original call came in from county dispatch about 3:00 p.m. Saturday afternoon. I was over in Saranac Lake visiting my daughter and her two boys, when I heard the call on my portable. I'm afraid those two little shits might grow up looking like their grandfather. Tough break. Anyway, by the time I got back to Lake Placid and headed out to the Craig Wood Golf Course, my first responders were already there. We've had calls out there before, so they knew to bring the station's ATV with them. They met up with a few skiers who directed them to where the victim was, down on the Jack Rabbit Trail, not far from the golf course. They were pulling him out on a sled tied to the back of the ATV."

"Did you see the victim?"

"Of course. Just as they were getting ready to load him into the back of the ambulance." Ned said, scooping up a forkful of mashed potatoes.

"How'd he look to you?"

"Looked tanned, in a foreign way, like he was from someplace near the equator, and kinda young too. Of course, when you're 67 years old, everybody looks young."

21

"No, I mean, what was his physical condition?"

"Jesus, hold your horses, Marc. You got some kind of deadline, or something?" Ned said, wiping his moustache with the back of his hand.

"Sorry."

"Like I was saying, I could tell right away he wasn't too well off. He seemed kinda pasty looking, and his breathing was labored too. His heart rate was around 150 and he wasn't responsive. Sure signs of hypothermia, I figured. Made sense with the temperature being around 20 degrees and all. Plus, he didn't appear to be ready for the weather either. I mean, for someone who's on a cross-country ski trip, he was dressed kinda skimpy. A light jacket with no liner, flimsy lightweight pants, no hat, real thin gloves. Just thought that was kinda peculiar," Ned said, then bit into a slice of bread, leaving a line of butter sticking to his moustache.

"Ned, I understand that there was a guide present."

"Yeah. My guys talked to him. You remember Larry Corbet, don't you?" Without waiting for Marc to answer, Ned continued, "Anyway, Corbet told Jimmy that the victim apparently got separated from the rest of his group because it was snowing so hard. Said he didn't realize he was gone until they reached the pick-up point at the toboggan run. That's when he took a head count and came back up the trail looking for him. But look, Marc, don't quote me on any of this, you know how the privacy laws are these days. It's not like when you were patrolling back in your state police days."

"Ned, if I thought anything you're telling me would get you in any trouble, I'd certainly wouldn't say who I got it from."

Marc felt that he needed to change the subject.

"So, what's this rumor I've heard that the village is in the running for another winter Olympics. Do you really think Lake Placid can handle another Olympics?"

"Yeah, well, this new mayor's got some big plans and I wouldn't doubt he's the source. Another Lake Placid Olympics? Christ, didn't we learn anything from the 1980 Olympics? Spectators freezing their asses off waiting for a bus to take them to a venue. We just didn't have the infrastructure back then and it's not much better now, but don't get me started."

Marc chuckled, looked at his watch and scooped up the lunch checks. "Been good talking to you Ned, but I should be getting along.

I've got an appointment in Ray Brook."

Ned started to protest, "Marc, you don't pay for my lunch."

"It's on the insurance company, Ned. Besides, you earned it."

"Well, seeing the company's paying, OK, but, remember, you didn't hear anything from me, OK?"

"Mum's the word, Ned. Thanks," Marc said reassuringly as he headed for the cashier.

Five minutes later, he was headed south toward Saranac Lake for the ten-minute drive to Ray Brook.

At the Ray Brook barracks, he asked for Investigator Jerry Garrant. Having worked with Jerry in the past, he remembered him as the kind of guy you could set your watch by. He wasn't surprised when the desk trooper advised him that Jerry was waiting in his office.

Jerry met Marc as the trooper buzzed him in, sporting his boyish grin, and grabbed Marc's hand for a vigorous handshake and motioned him to his office located at the back of the station.

Without asking, Jerry poured two cups of coffee and offered Marc a chair. "So, what brings you up to this winter wonderland? Can't be the golfing this time of the year and I've never known you to be a big skiing enthusiast. Wait, I bet I know," Jerry continued, his voice raised an octave or two feigning an enlightened revelation. "Could it possibly be that guy who died on the Jack Rabbit Trail Saturday?"

"Busted," Marc replied.

Jerry slid a box of powdered creamer across the desk, "There's really not a lot I can tell you right now. Of course, you know, I shouldn't be telling you anything, seeing as you're just a civilian these days," he continued, retaining his patented smirk.

"Whatever you're comfortable with," Marc said, trying not to sound too pushy as he took a swallow of the stale brew. "About the only thing I know is his name, Jamal Al-Zeid. He lived in Montreal, and was a guest at the Saranac Mountain Inn and Resort. Other than that, anything else would be a bonus."

"Well, let me see," Jerry said as he flipped open his pocket notebook. "According to the Inn's records, Al-Zeid arrived there Thursday night and planned to stay until Monday morning. He was driving a new Lexus SUV with a Quebec registration. His date of birth is February 2, 1985. He wasn't married, as far as we know. Apparently he was a carpet importer in Montreal and this is his third visit to the

23

Inn. Other than that, we think he's a Canadian of Iranian descent, but we didn't find a passport. As for a cause of death, it appears he died of exhaustion and hypothermia, but that's preliminary pending the lab results from the samples taken during the post mortem. So far, this looks like an accidental death with no criminal intent. But, like I said, we're still waiting for the lab results."

"Have you had a chance to speak to the pathologist?"

"Well, I attended the post mortem, so I guess I probably did," Jerry said, feigning offence, then again referred to his notebook. "Neither the pathologist nor I saw anything too far out of the ordinary. He appeared a little thin, but he had a smallish stature anyway. He weighed 135 pounds, 5'6" tall, dark complexion, no tattoos or other physical anomalies. About the only thing that looked a little weird was the presence of a few sores, some on his back and chest and a few on his legs."

"Sores?" Marc asked, his eyebrows raised a fraction.

"Yeah, they weren't bruises, more like ulcers. Not big ones, mind you, but big enough to notice. We took a few pictures of them, just for the record. One other thing, he wore a toupee, black, and he didn't seem to have much body hair, no chest or facial hair, and no hair around his privates. Didn't look like he'd shaved it off, he just didn't seem to have any.

"Yikes, too much information," Marc said jokingly, but he was puzzled by the ulcers that had been found on Al-Zeid's body.

Jerry produced a large envelope from his desk drawer with the word "EVIDENCE" stamped across it. "We have his wallet with his Quebec driver's license and credit cards," he said, producing a black folding wallet from the envelope. "We haven't been in touch with the relatives yet. The Montreal police are trying to run down the names of next of kin for us."

Jerry opened the wallet, removed Al-Zeid's drivers license and handed it to Marc. The photo showed a male, with dark hair and eyebrows, strong pointy nose, very intense eyes with a dark moustache. The issue date on Al-Zeid's drivers license was over three years ago.

"I suppose a photo of the body is out of the question, but any chance of getting a copy of this?" Marc asked, holding up the driver's license.

"Hold on a minute. There are a few more cards we found in his

24

wallet," Jerry said as he produced the documents and laid them on his desk.

Marc pick up the cards and shuffled through them.

There was a small stack of business cards that read, "Global Rug Importers", listing Jamal Al-Zeid as the "Manager", with an address on Sherbrooke Street NW, Montreal, along with a phone number. There was also a gold American Express card and a Master Card both issued to "Global Rug Importers" with Al-Zeid's signature in the back of each card.

Marc noticed that the address on Al-Zeid's driver's license matched the one on his business cards. At the bottom of the stack was a partially faded black and white photo of a man and a woman, somewhere in their mid 60's. Judging from the man's likeness to the photo of Al-Zeid, Marc guessed they could be his parents.

"We also found this in his coat pocket," Jerry said as he produced a disposable cell phone from the envelope."

"Have you checked to see what's stored on the phone's address book?" Marc asked.

Jerry gave Marc a look, "Not yet, haven't had time, besides, like I said, this is not a criminal case."

"Would you mind?" Marc said, reaching for the cell phone.

As Jerry shrugged an assent, Marc activated the phone and accessed its address book. He notice there were a few numbers listed with the local upstate New York 518 area code, but what caught his attention were a batch of sequential numbers with a Montreal area code and an unusual prefix number, the same as the phone he was holding. Marc suspected that these were numbers were also for pre-paid phones, probably all purchased with cash at the same time. If they were, Marc knew it would be very difficult, if not impossible, to track down the owners.

Continuing to peruse the address book, he noticed that each phone number was assigned a one-word name that appeared to be of Middle Eastern origin.

"Mind if I copy down these numbers and names from the address book?" Marc asked as he pulled his pad and pen from his coat pocket.

"Knock yourself out. But look, you didn't get them from me, OK?"

"Don't ask, don't tell," Marc said and began copying the

25

information from the address book.

"Look Marc, take your time, I have to run down to the evidence room for a minute. I'll be back shortly."

There were about a dozen phone numbers and Marc carefully copied them down along with their associated names. Hamid, Arash, Kouros, Sanjar, Naveed. Not your typical French Canadian names, Marc thought to himself.

Marc was beginning to get an uncomfortable feeling in the pit of his stomach. Could it be the after effects of the Ruthie's Special Burger? Got to be the burger, Marc thought.

When Jerry returned a few minutes later, he said. "So, what do you think, got everything you need?"

"Yeah, I guess, unless there was something else that you haven't mentioned?"

Jerry grabbed the evidence envelope and emptied the remaining contents on his desk. "Let's see, you've already seen the wallet, credit cards, drivers license, car keys. His clothes are in a bag in the evidence locker. But I can tell you, I've been though the pockets, nothing there, except a pair of reading glasses.

"Is Al-Zeid's car still at the Inn?" Marc asked.

"I assume so, but I haven't taken the time to look through it. Like I said this…"

Before Jerry finished, Marc added, "Yeah, I know. This is not a criminal case, yet. But has anyone interviewed the guide or the people who found Al-Zeid on the trail?"

"Trooper Greg Farrel had the initial investigation. He's been off duty over the weekend and is scheduled to work evenings later this week, but, according to his computerized blotter entry, he took a written statement from the guide, Larry Corbet. Farrel's report is still incomplete. He should have it finished in a day or two."

Marc felt that there was not much more to learn at this point, so he slid the documents along with the cell phone back across the desk, then reached for his coat hanging off the back of his chair.

"Say Marc, when are you heading back to Plattsburgh?"

"Probably not tonight. I have an interview with the Inn's management tomorrow morning at 10:00 a.m."

"Great! Look, if you don't have any other plans, why don't you spend the night at our house? I'll call Becky. I'm sure she would love to see you again."

Marc remembered Becky well as he was the best man at their wedding eighteen years before. God, how time flies, he thought.

"I don't know, Jerry, this is sort of last minute and I don't want to be a bother. Besides, you know the insurance company would pay my room and meals if I needed to stay over," Marc said not too convincingly.

Marc's meek resistance to Jerry's offer was all the excuse Jerry needed. Without saying another word, he dialed his home phone to advise Becky that Marc was staying overnight.

A minute later, he turned back toward Marc. "It's all set then, we'll see you later? Five-ish?"

"OK, Jerry, but before I go, just one more small favor."

Jerry braced himself in anticipation.

"Any chance I could take Al-Zeid's car keys with me? I'd like to take a peek inside. I'll get them back to you as soon as I'm finished, promise."

Jerry again gave Marc one of his suspicious looks. "You must really think you're onto something."

"Not really. Just trying to cover all the bases."

Jerry reached back into the envelope, shook out the car keys and tossed them to Marc. "OK, but look, no joy riding! You get into an accident with that thing and it'll will be my ass!" He said half jokingly.

"Not to worry, I'm good with my Explorer."

Jerry gave another nervous laugh. "See you around five," he said as Marc headed out the door.

As Marc had no agenda for the afternoon, he reacquainted himself with the village of Lake Placid and took in the familiar sights of the Olympic venues.

After dinner, Marc and Jerry spent the evening in front of the TV, paying little attention to the basketball game while sipping beer and reminiscing about their times spent together riding patrol as uniform troopers, arresting drunks and playing tricks on the station sergeant. It was after midnight when the TV was finally turned off.

It was just after 9:00 a.m. the following morning, when Marc made his way downstairs to the breakfast table. Becky had already left to start her day at the elementary school and Jerry was enjoying the paper and a cup of coffee.

"I'm lousy at breakfast, got time for coffee?" Jerry asked.

"I really should be going. I have that interview this morning and

I'm not exactly sure where the Saranac Mountain Inn is." Then, retrieving Al-Zeid's vehicle keys, he held them up with a jangle, "I'll leave these with the desk trooper on my way out of town."

"OK, but look, if you come up with something, you'll let me know, won't you?" Jerry had too much respect for Marc's cops sense to ignore the possibility that he could have possibly missed something.

"You can count on it," Marc said, and with a wave, he made his way out to his SUV.

Marc climbed onto the Explorer's frozen seat and turned the key. After a few reluctant turns, the engine popped to life. While letting the engine warm, he wrestled his brief case from the back seat and located the directions to the Saranac Mountain Inn and Resort.

Five miles later, Marc felt the first trickle of heat coming from the vehicle's air vents as the film of frozen condensation slowly began to clear from the windshield. There were few cars on the road to disturb the trailing plume of white exhaust that streamed behind the Explorer as Marc made his way to his morning interview.

Following the directions, Marc headed east on Route 73 toward Keene in the direction of the Olympic Bobsled Run. Keeping one eye on the frozen road ahead and the other on the odometer as it clicked by two and a half miles, Marc arrived at the Cascade Lakes area of Route 73 where he spotted the landmark he was looking for. A stained wooden marker with carved yellow letters, half buried in a snow bank next to a narrow two-lane road off to his left that read, McKenzie Properties – Private.

An odd way to welcome hotel guests. Oh well, whatever works.

Marc turned onto the recently-plowed, two-lane road, and after passing a few more "Private Road" signs, spotted a guard shed in the center of the roadway. There was a barrier arm across the incoming lane apparently operated by the guard Marc could see sitting inside the booth. As he approached the shed, the guard stood and slid open a small side window. After exchanging "Good Mornings," the guard, probably a retired cop, Marc figured, asked if he had a reservation.

"I have an appointment to meet with Mr. Noah Emmanuel.

From his demeanor, Marc suspected the guard had been forewarned of his impending arrival as he produced a clipboard seemingly out of nowhere. "Oh, you must be Mr. LaRose."

"In the flesh," Marc said.

"May I see some identification, sir?"

Was that a Quebec accent I just heard?

Marc handed the guard his ID.

After what appeared to be a perfunctory glance at Marc's driver's license, the guard handed it back. "OK, Mr. LaRose. When I raise the gate, please drive straight ahead for about quarter of a mile until you come to the first building on your left. You'll see a sign that says 'Guest Check-In.' Mr. Emmanuel is expecting you."

"Have a good day, officer," Marc said, and waved as the gate went up. Through his rear view mirror, he saw the guard pick up a phone.

He's probably notifying someone that I've arrived.

It took him a few minutes to locate the guest check-in building. Having not passed any other buildings, he assumed the main lodge and guest quarters must be further beyond.

Marc found an empty parking space next to the Inn's three new silver Yukon SUVs. Marc parked his Explorer, grabbed his leather notebook and headed for the guest check in.

The building appeared to be a new, but modest structure. The natural, cedar-stained siding was trimmed in dark brown. A wrap-around porch would have suggested a homey, friendly place, if it weren't for the absence of a few chairs, or possibly a hammock. But of course, this was wintertime, Marc thought to himself. From somewhere he could detect the fragrant smoke of a fire burning nearby.

As he opened the door Marc, heard a faint chime announcing his arrival.

An attractive young female seated behind the counter, wearing a dark green blazer with the Inn's name discreetly embroidered over the pocket, stood and, with a pleasant smile, said, "Hello, Mr. LaRose. I see you found us." Before he could respond, she motioned him to a seating area. "Please make yourself comfortable. Mr. Emmanuel is aware that you've arrived and will be with you shortly. In the meantime, may I offer you a refreshment, coffee perhaps?"

"Yes, coffee would be nice. Just cream, please."

After delivering the coffee, the receptionist disappeared through the doorway behind the counter, giving Marc a moment to inspect his surroundings.

The reception area was spacious enough to hold the oversized leather couch where Marc sat, plus three chairs of the same material and green color. The natural hardwood floor and pine walls had a varnished appearance and the room carried the scent of pine mixed with the aroma of the apple-wood logs burning in the fieldstone fireplace that was set against the side wall.

The small sitting area felt larger than its actual size, helped by the cathedral ceiling and the oversized windows on either side of the fireplace. It was still early in the day and the warmth from the log fire felt comforting.

A flicker of movement from behind the counter caught Marc's attention. A tall man appeared and, judging by his dress and demeanor, Marc assumed was the Inn's proprietor. Marc unconsciously estimated this new arrival to be in his late 30's, six foot three and in fairly good physical condition. He was neatly groomed and wore a bulky ski sweater, corduroy slacks and ankle high LL Bean leather-top boots. His skin had the ruddy tanned complexion someone gets in the winter from spending lots of time on the ski slopes. His fashionable looks were accented by curls of blond hair that hung just over the neckline of his sweater. Marc had the feeling that he was looking at the cover of a men's mail order fall fashion brochure.

He pushed past the counter with his right hand extended, "Mr. LaRose, Noah Emmanuel, so nice to meet you." After a vigorous, but somewhat soggy handshake, Marc suppressed an urge to wipe his hand on his pant leg, but made a mental note to pick up a bottle of hand sanitizer.

Emmanuel continued, "I'd like you to meet a couple members of my staff. We have set aside a room where we can talk in private. Emmanuel's manner seemed courteous enough, but Marc detected an edge to his voice.

What's this guy so nervous about?

Emmanuel guided Marc back around the front counter, past the receptionist, and down a short corridor to a door at the far end. Entering the room, Marc noticed it appeared to have been previously used as a storeroom, apparently hastily rearranged just for this meeting. There were rows of five-gallon water jugs along one wall and a cluster of folded tables and chairs along another.

As the two men rounded the stack of folded chairs, a man and woman, who were seated around one of the set-up tables, looked up at Marc. Emmanuel introduced Walter Barris, the Inn's assistant manager, and Lucy Welch, the events coordinator, then motioned Marc toward an empty chair between the two.

Odd that we shouldn't have this meeting in the Inn's office.

Marc guessed Barris to be slightly older than Emmanuel, with a receding hairline and the tell-tale signs of a paunch pushing out from his midsection. Flakes of dandruff speckled the collar of his well-worn brown twill coat. His red and white striped shirt, orange bow tie with pink pocket hanky accent gave him a clownish appearance, but despite his obvious lack of business habiliment, Marc was soon convinced that Barris was the Inn's behind-the-scene's manager and chief number cruncher.

Ms. Welch, seated to Marc's right, appeared to be closing in on her forties, slim, with just a streak of gray in her jet-black hair, and understated in a gray pants suit.

After perfunctory greetings, Emmanuel quickly directed the conversation to the business at hand.

"First off, Mr. LaRose, my staff and I are at your disposal to assist in any way we can with your investigation of the untimely death of Mr. Al-Zeid, so long as it does not interfere with the privacy of our guests."

"Thank you, Mr. Emmanuel, I'm sure The Humbolt Insurance Company also appreciates your cooperation."

"So then, how can we help?" Emmanuel asked.

Marc opened his note folder and perused his list of items to be discussed, "First, I will need a copy of the Inn's guest registry showing Al-Zeid's arrival and anticipated departure."

"I think this should do," Barris said, apparently anticipating the request as he retrieved a sheet of paper from the folder in front of him and handed it to Marc. It was a copy of Al-Zeid's guest registration, which also served as an invoice.

Marc scanned the document. It showed Al-Zeid had arrived on Thursday, January 10, with an intended departure of Monday, January 14. There was also a notation to reserve a place for him on a guided cross-country ski trip. The registration/invoice showed that Al-Zeid was booked into the "Mount Marcy" room at $1450 per night and, on Thursday evening, he had ordered a bottle of Spanish Tempranillo at a $129. *"Ole"* Marc thought.

He then asked, no one in particular, "Whose duty was it to set up the guided cross-country ski trip that Mr. Al-Zeid participated in?"

Lucy Welch cleared her throat and said, "Ah, that's my department."

"Could you give me the name of the guide the Inn used, Ms. Welch?"

"Actually we just started using a well-known local guide, Mr. Larry Corbet, as of the first of the year," she said, then hesitated, apparently expecting a response. She continued, "You may have heard of him. He competed in the 2002 Winter Olympics in Salt Lake City and won the bronze medal in the men's fifteen kilometer free style cross country skiing event. It was all over the news for about a week or so. He was like a local hero."

"That name sounds vaguely familiar," Marc lied, feigning recollection while trying his best not to appear too uninformed regarding events of local importance.

Welch again hesitated. "In any event, Mr. Corbet is not an actual employee of the Inn, but was hired as an independent contractor on an 'as needed' basis."

"Is there a copy of Mr. Corbet's business insurance policy available?" Marc asked.

Welch glanced at Emmanuel before answering, "The Inn has requested one from Mr. Corbet, but, we have yet to receive it."

"Has anyone from the Inn spoken with Mr. Corbet about the incident?" Marc asked, throwing the question up for grabs, while scribbling notes on his pad.

Barris chimed in, "Not to my knowledge, but I understand the State Police have. Have you checked with them?"

Marc ignored the question and directed his next inquiry toward Welch, "You wouldn't have Corbet's business address and phone number by any chance?"

"I believe that Mr. Corbet operates from his home," she said, removing a photocopy of a business card from a folder and handing it to Marc. He glanced at the photocopy and asked, "May I keep this?"

"Of course, I made it for you."

Marc slipped it in his folder with the rest of the notes.

"Is Mr. Al-Zeid's room still vacant?"

It was Walter Barris' turn again.

"Mr. Al-Zeid's room has since been cleaned and is presently occupied by another guest. The few personal belongings left in his room have been placed in storage, pending the arrival of someone to claim them."

"I see. And what became of his vehicle?"

Barris gave his collar a tug, causing his bow tie to turn at an angle, "I believe his Lexus is still where he left it, in the Inn's parking lot. We haven't moved it because we are not in possession of the vehicle's keys."

Marc, having noticed Emmanuel's lack of participation in the forum, turned to face him directly.

"I happen to have the keys to Mr. Al-Zeid's vehicle on me. After we're finished here, would you mind showing me to his car?"

Emmanuel shifted in his seat, recrossed his legs and glanced at Barris." Would you mind escorting Mr. LaRose to Mr. Al-Zeid's vehicle after the meeting, Walter?"

Barris replied with a nod.

Flipping to a fresh page on his pad, Marc asked if there was anyone else on the guided ski trip with Mr. Al-Zeid.

Again it was Lucy's turn. "Yes, actually, there was another couple from New York City on the outing along with Mr. Al-Zeid. Phillip and Bianca Huber. They are also guests of the Inn."

Marc stayed with Emmanuel and asked, "Are the Hubers available for an interview?"

Emmanuel didn't respond immediately, but glanced toward Barris who had suddenly become mute. Then, just before the pregnant pause was about to enter the crowning stage, Emmanuel spoke up. "Actually, the Hubers are still guests of the Inn, but I believe they are scheduled to check out tomorrow. Right, Walter?"

"Uh, yes, sir. I believe that is correct. Tonight is their last night."

Why had Emmanuel seemed to tense up at the inquiry about the Hubers?

"Would you mind arranging a meeting with them for an interview? It would be most helpful and should expedite my investigation," Marc said.

Emmanuel fidgeted for a moment, annoyingly clicking his retractable pen, shrugged his shoulders and said, "I, uh, don't see why not. Provided they give their consent, of course." Pausing again before continuing. "However, I believe they have left the Inn for the day to tour Lake Placid, but should be returning later this afternoon. I could ask them then, I suppose, if you really think it's necessary."

"Thank you Mr. Emmanuel. I'm sure the insurance company appreciates your cooperation," Marc again said while he retrieved a few business cards from his shirt pocket and passed them around.

"Try my cell first as I intend to remain in the area for another day or so. I know cell coverage can be tricky here in the mountains, so if you can't get through, please leave me a message at my office number."

Emmanuel studied the card for a long moment as if lost in thought, laid the card on his desk, looked up and said, "As soon as I speak to the Hubers, I'll call."

Wonder why Emmanuel is so protective of the Hubers?

Emmanuel then turned to Marc.

"Tell me, Mr. LaRose, have you learned what Mr. Al-Zeid actually died of.

"Tentatively, hypothermia is suspected. As you probably know, there was an autopsy performed, but until the test results are returned from the lab, nothing is for sure."

"I see. Well then. If there's nothing more, Mr. LaRose, we have an inn to run, and it looks like you have work to do as well," Emmanuel said, rising from his chair, an apparent signal that the meeting was over.

Emmanuel motioned to Barris, "Walter, would you please show Mr. LaRose where Mr. Al-Zeid's vehicle is parked?"

"No problem Sir," Walter Barris said, who nodded toward Marc, "Right this way, Mr. LaRose."

As Marc rose, he faced Emmanuel, "I look forward to speaking with you again," he said, allowing himself another soggy handshake before bidding goodbye to Lucy Welch.

With his coat in hand, Marc turned to catch up to Walter Barris who was already halfway down the hallway. He followed Barris out of a side door and across the parking lot toward one of the new Yukons.

With a chirp, the Yukon's door locks released. Barris said, "Hop in, Mr. Al-Zeid's vehicle is parked in the guest lot up by the main lodge."

Away from the Inn's manager, Barris suddenly became chatty and his tone friendlier as he made small talk about the recent snow and cold weather.

Could it be that he had to watch what he said when he was around Noah Emmanuel?

As Barris steered the Yukon up toward the main lodge, he explained the Inn had eighteen guest rooms in all, twelve in the main lodge plus stand alone "camps" near the lake, about a hundred yards in front of the main lodge.

The trip to the main lodge took only a couple of minutes and as Barris maneuvered the Yukon around the final turn through the tall pine trees that lined both sides of the road, they emerged onto a clearing where Marc saw the Inn—an immense three story log structure overlooking a frozen lake and the forested valley below.

The size of the Inn reminded Marc of photos he'd seen of Adirondack Great Camps built in the late 1800's by big city robber barons such as Alfred Vanderbilt, but this was much larger.

Big Al would have been impressed, Marc thought.

Barris continued around the side of the Inn to the guests' parking lot that contained about a dozen vehicles and stopped in front of a mound of snow in the middle of the lot. As the two emerged from the Yukon, Barris said with a chuckle, "It's somewhere under this pile of snow. If we had had the keys, we would have moved it to allow the plow to clear around it."

Marc began clearing the snow from the area he calculated to be in the proximity of the driver's door with his gloved hands. He looked over at Barris and said, "I'll probably be a few minutes. I just need to take a look inside."

"Sure thing," Barris said as he started to leave, then hesitated. "Look, if you have time when you're finished here, come on inside and I'll show you around before I take you back to your car."

"Yeah, I'd like that," Marc said as he continued pawing through the heavy layer of snow.

Barris turned and padded back toward the Yukon, his leather dress shoes sliding on the thin layer of snow.

That boy could use a lesson on how to dress for North Country winters.

After a few minutes of brushing and scraping, Marc cleared away enough snow to get the driver's side door open enough so he could squeeze onto yet another frozen car seat, his third so far today. Not a good day for polyester pants, Marc thought, comfortable in his wool trousers.

As he inserted the vehicle's ignition key fob into its receptor, the dashboard display lit and was accompanied by a faint chiming sound indicating the driver needed to fasten the seat belt. "If I buckle myself into these frozen seats, I might be stuck here till spring," Marc whispered.

A check of the odometer showed a little over 3500 kilometers, roughly 2500 miles, and despite the frigid temperature inside the vehicle, Marc noticed the Lexus smelled like it just came off the show room floor.

A glance around the vehicle's interior revealed little had been left behind. The ashtray was empty, which seemed a little odd, knowing that Canadians, especially immigrants from Europe and the Middle East were often heavy smokers. A check of the glove box revealed the owner's manual as well as a folded up new car window sticker. It showed that the vehicle, a Lexus LX570, was bought at a car dealership in Laval, Quebec, but nothing else.

Marc found the vehicle registration and insurance card in the center console. Lying beneath the insurance card was a small notebook. As he flipped through its mostly blank pages, Marc spotted a notation for the Saranac Mountain Inn and Resort with the Inn's phone number followed by a three digit extension. Underneath the phone number were another set of numbers, "10/01 to 14/01". Marc recognized this configuration as a typical European format for writing dates, tenth day of January to the fourteenth day of January, the days that Al-Zeid had reserved the room. On the next page and in the same handwriting, there was an address and phone number for a residence in nearby Willsboro—Box 1492, Shore Road.

Strange, who would this guy know in the tiny burg of Willsboro, of all places?

Looking again at the vehicle documents, Marc saw that Al-Zeid had registered the vehicle in Quebec the previous October.

New high end vehicle, 2500 miles in what, three months. Sounds about right for a working guy. The carpet business must be doing pretty good to afford the payments on this baby.

Marc checked the front and back seats.

Strange, nothing left behind. No extra pair of gloves, hat, or extra jacket. Not even an empty Tim Horton's coffee cup.

The SUV's voice activated navigation system probably explained the absence of a map, provided that the onboard computer understood French, or Farsi or whatever language Al-Zeid spoke.

Sitting in the muted light of the vehicle's snow-covered windows, Marc casually flipped the sun visor down and a folded piece of paper fell into his lap. As he unfolded the paper, he noticed it contained a handwritten note in the same writing style as the notation in the wire bound notebook. It was in French and basically, it translated to, "Hubers, 15 January, and below that, "Board meeting".

Marc stuffed the note along with the address book in his inside jacket pocket. He located the rear-gate lift button and pressed it to open, but the weight of the snow and ice would not allow the power door lifter to operate. Marc squeezed back out through the driver's door, went to the back of the SUV and as he brushed the snow away from the vehicle's rear gate, it began to slowly open. Marc gave it a final assist by pushing up on the gate allowing him to inspect the vehicle's rear cargo area.

With the vehicle's third row of seats folded down, there was plenty of open cargo space in the rear of the SUV, but like the cabin of the vehicle, this also appeared empty, as were the side compartments.

As Marc was about to hit the rear gate's closure button, he noticed what appeared to be a ripped corner of grey canvas material that had been caught in the space between the second row of seats and the folded down third row. Examining the small swatch of material, he saw the letters, "TA" written in block form. If there was more, it had been torn away, when whatever it was attached to was removed from the vehicle.

Carpet wrapping, perhaps?

Marc slipped the scrap of material into his jacket pocket along with the notebook, and closed the rear hatch.

Satisfied there was nothing more to learn from the vehicle, he again squeezed back behind the steering wheel, started the engine and slid the driver's window down. With the shifting lever in drive, Marc gunned the engine. Then, while peering out the open side window, he maneuvered the vehicle to the cleared section at the end of the row.

After securing the vehicle, Marc felt it was time for that tour that Walter Barris had mentioned.

Walking through the main entrance, Marc found himself in the Inn's lobby and the overstated opulence of a modern grand hotel.

Like the outside, the lobby was finished almost entirely of varnished logs, from the floor to the sixteen-foot high ceiling. Should a guest forget they were in the wilderness of the Adirondacks, the walls were decorated with the heads of numerous mounted trophy deer and bear, a couple of moose, as well as raccoon, lynx, bobcat, a great horned owl, several common loon and even a bald eagle caught in flight with a struggling rainbow trout in its talons.

Two expansive plate glass windows looked out over the frozen lake that Marc had observed earlier. A massive fieldstone fireplace between the windows crackled with a log fire. Again, dark green leather chairs, couches and reading lamps were scattered around the room, with several positioned in front of the fireplace. The window casings, picture frames, coffee tables, even the table lamps were all accented in natural white birch bark. Lush beige carpeting covered the floor, and from somewhere above Marc could hear the lilting strings of a Mozart sonata that he remembered from a music class he once took as a college class elective.

At the far end of the room, Marc observed the Inn's concierge desk that was presently being attended to by an attractive woman with short brown hair who was presently speaking with someone on the house telephone. As Marc approached the desk, she glanced up and ended the call.

"Mr. LaRose, I presume," she said, with what Marc guessed was an Australian accent.

"That's me," Marc said with a playful smile.

"You must be looking for Mr. Barris."

Marc took note of the clerk's name tag.

"Correct again, Sophie."

At the sound of her name, Marc noticed her fair skin reddened, as the lids covering her green eyes flickered.

"Please, this way Mr. LaRose," she said returning his smile, and led Marc through an archway connecting the lobby with the main dining room. He guessed Sophie was probably in her early thirties, and stood rather tall in medium heels. Like the girl at the welcoming desk, Sophie wore dark green slacks, matching jacket with a white blouse and a pale red scarf loosely tied around the collar.

Managing the short flight of stairs with the athletic agility of a figure skater, Sophie stopped at an office door with Barris's name on it, tapped lightly, and not waiting for an answer showed Marc inside where Barris was seated behind his desk. She held the door open and as Marc entered he caught a glimpse of her glancing back at him before retreating to her post.

Was that an approving grin?

"That didn't take long," Walter Barris said and motioned to a seat in front of his desk. "What do you think of our little Inn in the

38

wilderness?"

"Who would've known this place was even here?"

"That's the idea. We like it that way, keeps out the tourist crowd and the gawkers. We cater to a different class of clientele here, as you might have gathered by now."

"I figured as much, but how do you attract new business?" Marc asked, remembering Shirley complaining about the cost of advertising for her flower shop.

"We really don't do much in the way of advertising, per se. Most of our clients are repeats. New ones are usually by word of mouth. Oh, we do run a few lines in the Fortune 500 quarterly. Any new prospects are of course vetted to insure they meet our standards. There is a certain element that we would rather not be bothered with. I'm sure you understand."

"I suppose," Marc said, thinking back to last week's surveillance job and Marietta Simpson.

"Find anything of interest in Mr. Al-Zeid's car?"

"Nothing, really. He had a nice taste in vehicles."

"Mr. Al-Zeid was a good customer and always behaved himself while he was a guest here at the Inn. He actually brought in a few new clients, the Hubers for example."

"So, the Hubers were a referral from Al-Zeid?" Marc asked.

"Well, yes. Actually that's kind of confidential, but given present circumstances, I can tell you that new clients usually have to have a referral. Mr. Al-Zeid, an especially favored guest himself, provided a nice one for the Hubers. They've proved to be very acceptable guests for the Inn. Very discrete, punctual, not overly fussy, if you know what I mean. They also get along well with the other guests, and with their good looks and Austrian accents, they're a nice fit."

"How appropriate." Marc retorted, and then quickly added. "How about that tour you promised?"

"Sure thing!" Barris said, pleased to change the awkward topic of guest qualifications. "Let's start with the dining room."

As they exited his office, Barris motioned down the long hallway and pointed to the far end. "On the left is Mr. Emmanuel's office and across from his is the Executive Chef's." Turning back toward the stairwell, he continued, "Directly across from my office is Ms. Welch's and next to hers is our general accounting office."

Continuing the tour, Barris led the way, up the stairway to the main dining room.

As Marc stood at the top of the stairs, he could only marvel at the grandeur of the dining room that contained a few staff that were busy setting a table in the center of the room.

Barris motioned upwards toward the cathedral ceiling and pointed to a massive spherical shape hanging well above the center of the room. "Custom made for the Inn by North Country artisans. All the antlers are from whitetail deer, taken right here in the Adirondacks. Isn't she something?" Barris said, again, almost too proudly.

Marc felt his jaw drop as he gazed upwards. A heavy black chain was attached to a large hewn timber at the highest point of the room's vaulted ceiling from which this object, made from untold dozens of deer antlers had been somehow intricately woven together and formed a massive interlocking cluster that he estimated to be at least twelve feet across. On the tip of each antler was attached a small white LED candlelight, of which there had to be a least a thousand. As this tangled mass twisted ever so slightly in the air currents of the room, it gave off a twinkling effect, as though one were looking out at the northern sky on a clear cold winter night.

"Amazing," was all that Marc could muster as this giant pronged mass continued to hold his gaze.

"Now before you get the idea that someone actually shot and killed a herd of Bambi's so their antlers could become part of our hanging collection up there, let me assure you that no deer died simply for that purpose," Barris explained. "Whitetail deer naturally cast off their old antlers late in the winter and regrow larger ones the following summer. These particular antlers came from a licensed deer farm not far from here that raise wild game for the commercial market. They simply collected them as they fell off and gave them to our contractor who fashioned them into the chandelier," Barris said with a schoolboy's grin, his bow tie twisted around to five minutes to six.

Despite the unusual chandelier, or possibly because of it, Marc could not help but be impressed with the surroundings as he let his gaze take in the rest of the room. The massive bridgework of hewn logs overhead angled in from the four corners and formed the structural framework for the room. Like the main lobby, the ceiling and walls were finished with varnished pine siding, giving the casual guest the feeling of "roughing it" in a mountain cabin, while sipping

Dom Perignon from a crystal glass. On the far wall, Marc noticed a series of four large windows overlooking the lake, separated in the middle by another oversized field stone fireplace. Along the sidewalls were several curtained booths, each with an hefty wooden dining table and matching chairs. The dining booths were separated by hanging tapestries of forest scenes to give the diners a sense of privacy.

Barris continued, "Ordinarily, we plan for our guests to spend up to three hours at dinner. We want them to relax and not feel rushed. The dinner and lunch menu is provided each guest the day before, then, before the meal, we prepare a sample plate replicating each offering—appetizers, salads, entrees, deserts as well as the recommended wine pairings, all set out on that table in the center." Barris pointed to the table in the middle of the room that was attended to by the wait staff in anticipation of lunch. "This way the guest can preview just what he or she is ordering. The menu also provides a list of the ingredients in each dish in case a guest has a particular health concern, say with dairy, eggs, nuts, wheat, or shellfish. Naturally, if a guest prefers something that is not on the menu, they are encouraged to order whatever they want, provided we have it, and we usually do."

"Just like home," Marc quipped, catching quick glance from Barris, as he continued, seemingly unfazed.

"At breakfast, the guests simply inform the staff what they would like, pretty much anything they want. However most of our clients like to keep breakfast simple and healthy, as many of them are athletic, cross country and downhill skiers, hikers, and the like."

It was getting close to the noon hour and Marc noticed a few of the guests were beginning to straggle in, and with menus in hand, they began to circle the display table in the center of the dining room, deciding what to have for lunch. Kenny G's "Breathless" could be heard softly echoing from somewhere above the antler chandelier.

Barris asked, "Would you like to see one of our guest rooms, Mr. LaRose? I believe we have a few that are still empty as the guests have yet to arrive."

"I'd like that." Marc answered, curious to see what a $1400 dollar a night room looked like.

Barris led the way up the main stair well and around the lofty walkway that overlooked the dining room, then down a wide, dimly lit hallway with doors on each side. Marc noticed that above each door,

41

was not a room number, but the name of one of Adirondacks High Peaks. They passed rooms named, Giant, Algonquin, Haystack, Whiteface, Iroquois, Gothic, Saddleback, Big Slide, as well as one named, "Marcy", that Marc remembered from the Al-Zeid's invoice as the one he had stayed in just a few nights before. Barris took out his master card key and opened a door to a room with the name "Iroquois" above it.

The space was the definition of a suite, with a generous entry, a sitting room with a large flat screen TV, and a spacious bedroom with an adjoining bath. The walls and ceiling, like the lobby and dining room were done with the varnished pine and white birch bark accents. Barris pulled back a curtain, revealing a large bow window overlooking the lake and boathouse below. Between the window and the bed was yet another field stone fireplace, a smaller version of the one in the dining room.

Marc asked, "I assume, this must be one of the upper end rooms?"

Barris matter-of-factly replied, "Actually, Iroquois is mid range, $1650 a night. The higher end rooms have a larger sitting area, an extra Murphy bed and two baths. The cabins have two bedrooms, sitting area and a fireplace with their own private dock and canoe. They go for $2150."

"Whew, my credit card's convulsing just thinking about it," Marc said.

Barris chuckled, then led the way out of the guest room and back down to the dining area.

"I'd take you on a side tour of the kitchen, but with lunch in progress, I'm afraid we'll have to skip that. We can cut through the spa, then return to the lobby from there."

"You're the guide."

Barris showed Marc the spa area with its sauna and adjoining heated indoor pool, then it was back toward the lobby where they passed through a dimly lit cocktail lounge. The bar area was fairly simple, cozy and attractive—small, with a few tables and stools, more glassy eyed mounted fauna adorning the polished pine walls, all surrounding yet another fireplace.

As Marc could sense the tour was coming to an end he wanted to ask a more pertinent question. "Mr. Emmanuel is the manager, but I assume he is not the owner. Who does he answer to?"

"Like the sign out by the road says, McKenzie Properties. Actually, it's really the McKenzie Group Ltd., in Montreal. They own several properties in Canada as well as Europe, China and the U.S. Angus, uh, I mean, Mr. McKenzie contacts the Inn personally every day or so. He likes to be involved in the daily operation of all his properties."

"So, this Angus guy is aware that I'm here looking into to this matter?"

"Oh yes. I'm quite certain Mr. Emmanuel will make a full report directly to him."

"I see," Marc said, then added, "Before I forget, what time is guest checkout?"

"Usually it's 11:00 a.m., however, if you're wondering about the Hubers, I believe they asked for a late checkout for tomorrow. They mentioned something about doing some last minute shopping in Lake Placid right after breakfast, then returning to the Inn before heading back to New York City."

"You wouldn't know what kind of vehicle they're driving?" Marc asked.

"I don't, but let me ask Sophie Horton, our concierge. I think you met her earlier."

"I did, but if you don't mind, I'll stop by her desk and ask her myself," Marc said as they reached the lobby.

"Fine with me. You can find your way out then?"

"Oh, I believe so. Thanks again for the tour Mr. Barris. It's been a pleasure."

"Anytime Marc, and good luck with your investigation."

With a wave, Barris turned in the direction of his office while Marc continued into the lobby where he saw that Sophie was still at her post behind the concierge desk.

She glanced up as Marc approached.

"Mr. LaRose. Are you finished with your inquiries already?"

"Almost. Actually I have a couple of questions for you. Walter Barris said you would be the best person to ask." Without waiting for Sophie to respond, Marc continued, "Can you tell me what kind of car the Hubers have?"

"I think so," she said as she tapped a series of commands into her computer.

"According to the guest registry, they have a white Jeep Grand

Cherokee, with a New York State registration, although from the license plate number, I believe the vehicle is a rental because the plate number begins with 'Z'. We see a lot 'Z' plates here as you can imagine."

"You don't miss much," Marc said, more flirtatiously than he meant.

Sophie smiled as her cheeks reddened again before she returned her gaze toward the computer.

"Now for the tough question," Marc said, continuing to admire Sophie's soft features, "It looks as though I might have to stay in the area for another day or so. Can you suggest a reasonably priced motel in Lake Placid? I understand that the Inn is booked up, and besides, the insurance company I'm working for would never compensate me at these rates."

Ignoring her computer screen for a moment, Sophie looked off toward one of the mounted deer heads and, while tapping her pencil on the counter, appeared to give Marc's query some thought before answering.

"Actually, I think your chances of getting a room tonight are better in the Village of Saranac Lake, that's just ten miles west of Lake Placid. It's not quite as touristy as Lake Placid and the rates there are usually less. As you know, this is ski season. Everything in Lake Placid is pretty full."

"Saranac Lake would be fine, I guess," Marc said, feigning his ignorance of the area. "Can you suggest the name of one in particular?"

"Well, you could try the Miss Saranac Inn, I hear it's pretty nice, and not too pricey. I guess it depends on what you're looking for," Sophie said coyly.

Marc noticed the redness in her face had not subsided. "Actually, the Miss Saranac sounds great. Would you have the address?"

"I can do better than that. Here's the address and the phone number, and, seeing as you've been so nice, I'll even include some directions," Sophie said, still grinning while she scribbled the information on a sheet of the Inn's stationary and handed it to Marc.

"Just curious, do you memorize the phone numbers to all the area motels?" Marc asked.

"No, just the ones owned by my dad," she said, her face in full bloom.

"Oh. And here I had you pegged for an 'Aussie', hired on by the Inn as a temporary worker.

"Actually, I grew up in New Zealand, but my dad's American."

"Whoa, strike two." Marc said. Guess I'd better quit while I'm ahead.

"No harm. Happens all the time."

"Well, thanks for the tip on the Miss Saranac. I'll give her a try." Marc paused before continuing, "Look, I plan on returning tomorrow morning to meet with the Hubers. Will you be around?" Marc asked.

It was Sophie's turn to hesitate.

"Well, yes, I expect so." She said meekly, then quickly added, "Oh, I almost forgot, Mr. Barris asked me to give you a lift back to your car. I guess you left it parked down at the guest check in?"

"That would be nice, if you're not too busy," Marc said, welcoming the chance to talk with her some more.

"Go on ahead. I'll get my coat and meet you in the parking lot. Look for a green Saab in the employee parking area."

"OK, see you there," Marc said as he turned back toward the lobby entrance and made his way down the pathway to the parking lot where he spotted a small sign off to one side that read "Employee Parking". He quickly located the only Saab in the parking lot. A minute later Sophie came bustling down the path, her car keys jingling in her gloved hand.

As they were leaving the parking lot, Marc asked, "You've met the Hubers. What do you think of them?"

"Not much to say really. I believe this is their first visit to the Inn. They keep pretty much to themselves, although they seemed to be friendly with Mr. Al-Zeid. I know they speak French as well as English because I overheard them talking on their way through the lobby Friday morning heading out for that cross country ski outing."

"Do you speak French?" Marc asked.

"No, not really, just a few words. We get quite a few guests from Quebec, so it's not unusual to hear French spoken. Of course it's Quebecois French that I hear the most, not the Parisian French the Hubers speak."

"Oh, you can tell the difference?"

"Not being a francophone, I really have to listen, but the Parisian French seems more soft and 'nasally' if you know what I mean." She said, wrinkling her nose.

"I wouldn't know. I grew up speaking French at home and at the Catholic school I attended. The nuns were brutal and I've got the scars to prove it," Marc chuckled as he exposed the backs of his hands.

As they were approaching the guest check-in, Marc pointed out his Explorer parked at the end of the row.

"Anywhere here is fine, Sophie. Thanks for the lift and the info. You've been a real help."

"No problem," she said hesitantly.

As Marc was about to close the passenger door, Sophie gave a nervous cough and Marc looked back, "Uh, Mr. LaRose, Marc. Forgive me if I sound presumptuous, but there's not a lot going on tonight, and if you decide to stay in town, I know of a neighborhood bar about a block away from the Miss Saranac. I just have to get Zoe, my daughter off to bed around seven."

"Yeah sure, why not?" He said, surprised.

"I'd just have to check with my dad, but I'm sure he wouldn't mind babysitting for an hour or so."

"Sounds like a date then," Marc said, immediately regretting using the "D" word, then quickly added, "As long as it's not problem for your dad. What's the name of the place?"

"The Side Car. It's not far from the old rail yard. But don't worry, they took the tracks out long ago," she said with a light giggle.

"Seven it is. See you then," Marc said as he closed the car door and trudged off toward his waiting SUV.

With a toot of her horn, Sophie waved and turned the Saab back toward the main lodge.

Marc navigated his SUV past the security guard shack and back down the narrow roadway to Route 73.

Marc glanced at his watch, one p.m., still plenty of daylight. He figured now would be a good time to check out the scene where Al-Zeid was located. He remembered Ned Barnes saying he was found on the Jack Rabbit trail, not far from the Craig Wood Golf Course. Marc also remembered the golf course, not without some frustration, trying to break ninety while playing there some years before.

The Craig Wood Golf Course, named after the 1941 Masters Tournament Champion, is one of several Adirondack golf courses cut out of the wilderness during the early 1900's as a compliment to the grand hotels built during that era when tourism in the North Country

46

was just beginning to take hold. Because of the intensive labor involved in building and maintaining a seasonal golf course in the untamed wilds of upstate New York, they are distinguished by narrow fairways, radical changes in elevation and small greens. Thus providing a challenge for the week-end golfer during warm summers and a perfect trail for cross country skiers during the harsh Adirondack winters.

Marc turned onto Route 73 toward Lake Placid and five minutes later located the narrow road leading to the golf course. Although snow covered, the road had been kept open to access the ski trail and a half mile later, he was at the club house parking lot. Although the parking area was covered with a foot of powder snow, he could still see the faint outline of the partially filled-in tire tracks, several, no doubt, left there by the emergency vehicles called to help rescue Al-Zeid the past Friday.

Marc parked his SUV, donned his cross country ski boots, clamped on his skis, slid into his thermal ski jacket and pulled his toque over his ears. He quickly located the trail, and using his ski poles, pushed off and followed the directions provided by Ned Barnes.

The first part of the trail sloped downward and was easy going. Marc skied down the 9th fairway away from the clubhouse and around the snow covered 8th green to where trail leveled off, then turned away from the golf course into the forest. The thick pine woods with snow-laden branches seemed to close in on both sides as Marc propelled himself onward, driving forward on one ski while pushing down with his opposite ski pole. A couple miles of this kind of exercise will surely burn off the calories I accumulated from Becky's lasagna dinner, Marc thought to himself.

Fifteen minutes later, Marc located a spot on the trail that appeared to have been trampled down, and having followed the faint outline of the ATV tracks that ran along the trail, he figured this must have been the area where the first responders had located Al-Zeid. After catching his breath, Marc took a few photos of the area for his report and noted the distance he had travelled from the clubhouse before heading back. Returning to his SUV, he decided to continue westward, down the 18th fairway, across to the 16th, toward the Village of Lake Placid, the direction that the Hubers and Al-Zeid had come from.

With ample daylight remaining, Marc decided to continue on as the trail crossed Riverside Drive to the outskirts of the village of Lake Placid. Off to his left he could see the 90 and 120 meter ski jumps, visible with their lighted beacons flashing. The west branch of the Ausable River was frozen over and Marc skied across it with ease.

A quarter a mile further he passed what at first appeared to be a small pond. The road leading from the pond was plowed, and he observed a Lake Placid Water and Sewer Department truck pass by as he crossed the narrow snow-covered road.

By then, however, the shadows were lengthening so Marc decided it was time to head back to the golf course. By the time he got back to his SUV, the sun had slipped below the snowcapped mountainous horizon.

Although Marc hadn't learned a whole lot from this little outing, at least it gave him a picture of where Al-Zeid was and what he endured during his last moments. Besides, fresh air and exercise were two things he had seen little of in the past few months.

Shedding his skis, Marc left Craig Wood, and turned his SUV west on Rte. 73 toward downtown Lake Placid's Main Street. He observed that the sidewalks were cluttered with skiers fresh from the slopes of Whiteface Mountain in search of entertainment at one of the many local establishments.

Marc slowed the SUV to a crawl, watchful for people darting across the narrow main street and noted the inns "No Vacancy" signs. Sophie had a point about trying to get a room for the night around here, Marc thought.

He continued out of town and headed toward the Village of Saranac Lake, ten miles distant. About midway Marc passed the Ray Brook State Police barracks and thought of stopping in to see if Jerry was still working, but not seeing his car in the parking lot, continued on and referred to Sophie's note with the address for the Miss Saranac Inn. It wasn't hard to find, right on Route 86, just inside the Village limits. The lighted motel's sign in front had a "Vacancy" notice dangling from it and he found a parking spot near the office door.

The gentleman behind the check-in counter was friendly and, from his physical appearance, Marc suspected he could be Sophie's dad.

"Hope you're not too fussy mister. We only got one room left, and it's one of the more expensive ones. Cost ya $69 a night."

48

"I'll take it." Marc said.

By the time he settled into his room it was almost six o'clock. Marc tried out the TV and caught the local, then the national news, and was watching the weather forecast for the next day when his cell phone ring tone sounded.

"Mr. LaRose? It's Noah Emmanuel from the Saranac Mountain Inn. I trust this isn't a bad time."

"Not at all. What's up?"

"Just wanted to let you know that I caught up with the Hubers. They seemed a little surprised to hear that a private investigator was looking into the matter with Mr. Al-Zeid. I guess they figured the police had handled it. Anyway, they said they would meet with you, but it would have to be late tomorrow morning as they're leaving right after to return to New York."

"Sure, what time would be good for them?"

"10:30 in the main dining room. I'll let the main gate know you're coming."

"That should be fine, thank you for setting this up."

"My pleasure," Emmanuel said a little too smoothly, and without waiting for Marc to respond, broke the connection.

I guess I know where I'm having breakfast tomorrow, Marc thought to himself, and jotted down a list of questions he had for the Hubers.

The eight-mile cross country ski hike had left Marc hungry. Abruptly, the prospect of tomorrow's meeting with the Hubers was pushed out of his mind while he tried to think of a place nearby for a bite to eat.

Marc left the Miss Saranac and walked the quarter mile to the Side Car Bar. Peering through the front window, he saw that it looked friendly enough, about half full of patrons, probably locals, he figured, drinking beer and talking among themselves. He continued on for couple of blocks and came to a small deli that he'd passed on his way to the motel. The place looked clean and most of the tables were empty.

After a hot Rueben sandwich with coleslaw and a bag of chips, Marc left the deli and sauntered toward the downtown area as he figured he still had a few more minutes to kill before his rendezvous with Sophie.

Strolling past the Lake Flower Park, Marc stopped to admire the ice castle that had been recently constructed, the centerpiece for the annual winter carnival that was just a few weeks away. The reflection of the red, green and blue lights embedded inside the blocks of ice cast an eerie glow in the cold evening air. Who will be crowned king and queen this year, he mused, absentmindedly.

It was closing in on eight o'clock and Marc figured it was time to head back to the Side Car to see if Sophie would keep her word and meet him there as promised.

The Side Car was a typical neighborhood bar, off the main drag, so the tourists have to stumble on it, or be directed to it. Once inside, Marc noticed it was quite cozy with a horseshoe-shaped bar, booths along the windows and a couple of tables in the center. The flat screened TV behind the bar was airing a hockey game, Montreal vs. Boston, but the few patrons at the bar didn't seem too interested.

Marc chose a booth, a more intimate place to talk, he figured.

"What'll you have, buddy?" The bartender called over.

"Bud Light, in a mug."

Just as the bartender was bringing Marc's beer, he caught sight of Sophie coming through the door. Marc waved. As she made her way over to the booth, she slipped off her ski jacket and knitted hat, then slid across from Marc. Out of her business attire she looked comfortable, wearing jeans, and a bulky white wool sweater with a rolled collar. Her short brown hair curled around her ears gave her a youthful appearance.

"I see you took my advice and booked into the Miss Saranac Motel. What do you think of her?"

"So far, so good. The heat and the TV both work. Sheets look clean. What more can a dislocated PI want? Thanks for the tip. Now, what can I get you?"

"A beer, whatever you're having," she said, nodding toward Marc's mug.

Marc waved at the bartender and pointed at his beer. Marc nervously rubbed his hands together.

Whoa, why are my palms sweaty? Marc thought to himself.

After the bartender left, Sophie took a long swallow.

"So, how do you like working at the Inn?" He finally asked.

God, how lame was that?

"I like it a lot. I've been there almost four years now. Started at the night desk, then, about two years ago I was moved over with Lucy

Welch as the Inn's concierge. Lucy's been great and despite my accent, people think of me as a 'local'. I'm familiar with the area which helps me to communicate well with the clientele."

"Living here must a big change from New Zealand, especially with a young child and all," Marc said, still trying to loosen up.

"Well, actually, yes it has been," she said hesitantly.

Marc sensed that Sophie might be uncomfortable talking about her personal life.

"Sorry, I didn't mean to pry," he said, apologetically.

"It's not that, just not that exciting. Kinda boring actually."

"OK, I'll shut up then."

"No, don't do that. Please, pry away," Sophie said and took another swig.

"I was just thinking, it's a big leap from New Zealand to Saranac Lake, and was wondering how you landed here."

"OK, but don't say I didn't warn you," she said, taking another sip. "About five years ago, my mom passed away. Cancer. That's when my dad told me he needed help running the inn. At the time however, I had other obligations. My husband, his name's Ian, his job took him away from home, too much. I was working and didn't feel I could leave just then. But things changed and now, here I am."

"Wow, sounds like you've had some tough choices to make along the way," Marc said.

"That's not the half of it. After school, I attended college in Auckland, majoring in biomedical engineering. Hard to imagine, I know. Anyway, that's where I met my husband, at Auckland U. We got married before I graduated. Big mistake. He had a law degree and worked for a big firm, seventy plus hours a week. He made good money, but it wreaked havoc on our marriage. At the same time, I was studying my butt off trying to get through my final year at Auckland and before I knew it, I was pregnant with Zoe, our first and only child."

"I thought stuff like that only happened in the U.S." Marc said in an attempt to lighten her mood.

Undaunted, Sophie continued. "After graduation, I decided an engineering career was not for me, and took a job with the New Zealand Customs Service in their Intelligence branch. We monitored imports suspected of containing nuclear components. New Zealand is strictly anti-nuclear, to a point where they're practically schizophrenic about it."

Marc sat, transfixed, gripping his mug.

Sophie stopped to take another sip, looked over the rim of her beer mug, and said, "OK, I know, boring."

"No, no. Actually, it's quite fascinating. Were you ever involved in athletics? I mean, forgive me for saying this, but you appear quite fit," Marc said.

Marc could see Sophie blush again as she stared into her mug before answering.

"No, I didn't have time for sports in college. But since I was a child, I would go to the beach on weekends. We lived near the ocean then and as a kid, surfing was like soccer or basketball here in the states. Of course we had that too, but growing up, surfing was the big thing."

"With Whiteface Mountain so close, I'll bet you're a natural on skis," Marc said.

"Not really. I can't get the hang of standing on two separate skis, one going one way and one the other. But snow-boarding, now that's something else. Snow-boarding and surfing are a bit alike. There's hardly a week during the winter that I'm not on the slopes at Whiteface. Sometimes I even make the trek over to Stowe, Vermont."

A shout from someone sitting at the bar interrupted their conversation. Apparently someone was paying attention to the TV. Boston had scored a goal.

"So, how about you, Mr. LaRose, do you snowboard?" Sophie asked.

"Not really, and please, it's Marc. 'Mr. LaRose' sounds so formal, besides, it makes me feel twenty years older."

"OK, so Marc, do you like winter sports?" Sophie asked, looking up from her near empty mug.

"I can ski, but it's been sometime since I last hit the slopes, or should I say, the slopes hit me." This raised a chuckle from both of them. Marc lifted his empty glass and said, "Got time for one more, compliments of Humbolt Insurance?"

Sophie gave her watch a glance and said, "Sure. One more, but then I really should be getting back."

After the beers arrived, Sophie asked, "So, how long have you been in the investigative business?

"Most all of my life, Marc said. "I retired from the New York

State Police after working there twenty years, then five years ago I opened up my own PI business, and here I am."

"Sounds like pretty exciting work."

"Oh, it has its moments. Some cases are interesting, and some are pretty mundane. Mostly I do Workers' Compensation Insurance surveillances, you know, watching people who are rumored to be working 'under the table' after claiming disability working for someone else. Sometimes they really are laid up, but often they are not. Not very exciting, huh?"

"Actually, sounds kinda fun. Snooping around, catching people up to no good," she said with a sly grin.

"Then there are these kinds of cases—accidental or suspicious deaths, and with the possibility of future litigation, the insurance companies like to know what they're up against."

"You really think the Inn has something to hide," Sophie asked.

"Don't know. But I've found that sometimes, things aren't what they first appear to be. My job is to keep an open mind and keep asking questions."

Both sat silently for a few moments, taking in the bar atmosphere before Marc asked, "Sophie, you mentioned that Mr. Al-Zeid had stayed at the Inn before. What do you remember about him?"

She thought for a moment. "If memory serves me, I believe he's been a guest of the Inn once, maybe twice before. If you think it's important, I could check and let you know for sure. He was the kind of person you don't think too much about. Quiet, stayed mostly to himself and never caused trouble."

"Can you remember if he participated in any of the Inn's activities on his previous visits, skiing or hiking, anything like that?"

"Now that you mention it, I don't think he did. Again, I'd have to look back at his activities' history, but I don't remember him being much of an outdoorsman."

Sophie took another sip and seemed to think about Marc's question. "One thing I do remember is that this last time, before he, you know, died, I was thinking that he didn't look so good."

"Oh, how do you mean," Marc asked.

"I don't know, I just thought he looked sort of, gaunt, you know, run down, and tired from the first day he arrived. Actually, I was a little surprised when he signed up for the cross-country ski trip. I mean, he didn't seem the athletic type to begin with and with the way he looked…"

"Hum, interesting," Marc replied, while studying the bubbles rising from the bottom of his mug.

"The initial report from the pathologist was that Al-Zeid died from hypothermia and exhaustion. The exhaustion part would go along with what you just said regarding his physical description. But, there are a few other things about this that don't fit."

"How's that?" Sophie asked.

"Well, first of all, given his physical appearance and the name, I'd guess, that our friend Al-Zeid is…was…a first generation Canadian who immigrated from somewhere in the Middle East. He decides to vacation in upstate New York, and wants to go skiing, a sport that he probably didn't know much about and wasn't prepared for. He didn't even have the right clothing or equipment. Sophie, you mentioned that Al-Zeid spoke French as well as English? Could you detect an accent other than French?"

"That's hard to say. He had an accent, for sure, but I just assumed that it was French, seeing he was living in Quebec."

"I know what you mean. Sometimes it's hard enough to understand a person with an accent when they are speaking English, let alone trying to determine the exact origin."

"Are you making fun of my accent?" Sophie asked with a teasing grin.

"Oh no, not at all," Marc said, now, his turn to blush. "I enjoy listening to people with an Australian, or in your case, a New Zealand accent. I'd say, they both sound pretty much the same."

"Don't tell that to a New Zealander, actually, the Aussies make fun of our accents and we laugh at theirs. Kind of a friendly rivalry." Sophie quipped as she nursed her beer.

"Sort of like the Americans and the English speaking Canadians?"

"Something like that, hey." She said with a chuckle.

Marc laughed at her humorous imitation.

"Seriously though, we get plenty of people at the Inn that come from other countries, all with different accents, so after a while you don't think too much of it."

"Have you had a chance to speak to the guide, Larry Corbet?" Sophie asked.

"Not yet, but I intend to, hopefully tomorrow."

"I heard Larry's pretty sick about the whole thing. I think you'll find him over at his house, he lives just outside of Lake Placid."

"I know. Lucy gave me his address and phone number at the meeting today."

Sophie glanced at her wristwatch. "Hate to say this, but I should be going. I have to get up early tomorrow to get Zoe ready for school and help dad. Then I have to be at the Inn by nine."

"OK, but let me walk you back to the motel. I know it's not far, but..." Marc let the request trail off as he arose from his seat.

"I can take care of myself, besides, this is a small town and you know how people like to talk. But look, if you're around the Inn tomorrow, stop by my desk."

"See you around then," Marc said.

Sophie slid out of the booth, pulled on her hat, wrapped her scarf around her neck, donned her coat, and made her way past the bar towards the door.

Marc heard the bartender yell over, "Hey Sophie, good to see you again, don't be such a stranger."

Sophie waved, grinned, and effortlessly glided out the door.

The bartender looked back at Marc, "Hey buddy, you ready for another?"

"Sure, why not."

When he brought Marc's beer, he said, "So you know Sophie?"

"Yeah, well, sort of. We actually just met today."

"She's a great gal. First time I've seen her here in a long time. You must have really impressed her to get her to come out this time of night."

"Oh, actually it was mostly business," Marc said.

"That's what they all say," he said with a laugh and then yelled over to another patron before disappearing back behind the bar.

The hockey game was still on, but as Marc stared at the screen, he thought about what Sophie had said regarding Al-Zeid's physical condition when he arrived at the Inn.

Was he ill? If so, why would he go on an strenuous skiing trip knowing he wasn't up to it?

Marc finished his beer and gave the bartender a wave. When he stepped out into the cold night air, he found the streets were empty. The only sound he heard was the crunching of ice underfoot as he trudged towards the motel. Marc thought of the questions he would pose to the Hubers: What did they know of Al-Zeid's death? How long had they known him? What was their relationship?

Marc arrived back at the motel, quickly undressed and slid into the queen size bed, pulling the thick down comforter over him. As soon as his head hit the pillow, Marc's thoughts of the Huber interview faded and were quickly replaced by the prospect of seeing Sophie again.

DAY TWO

The following morning Marc was up at six thirty. Although his exercise regime had been inconsistent as of late, he set out for a brisk two-mile walk around Lake Flower, across to Bloomingdale Avenue, down Pine Street and back toward the Miss Saranac. Marc was surprised to see a few other crazies out doing the same thing, even though it couldn't have been more than ten degrees above zero. With little wind, the puffs of white smoke from the brick chimneys of the clapboard houses seemed to linger in the morning air. It appeared to Marc that every other vehicle on the street was a pickup truck with oversized tires and a snowplow mounted on the front end.

Must be standard equipment up here in the woods.

By the time he returned to the motel, it was just after seven. Marc decided to give Shirley a call, knowing she would be at the flower shop. He informed her he was working in Saranac Lake, that he had had dinner with Jerry and Becky Garrant, and that Becky had asked about her. Shirley was pleased and told Marc she'd give Becky a call. Shirley added that Ann Marie was fine, but was still making noises about moving out on her own.

"Sounds like everything's about normal," Marc quipped.

"How long are you going to be up in Saranac Lake?"

Suddenly Marc felt a wave of guilt about meeting Sophie at the Side Car the night before.

"Huh, I…I'm not sure yet. I guess as long as this investigation takes, probably another day or so."

"Well, be careful, and call me when you can."

"Will do. Talk to you soon," Marc said.

As Marc closed his cell he was bothered by how he felt. It wasn't that unusual for Marc to see other women or for Shirley to date other men, for that matter.

So why the feeling of guilt?

After a hot shower and a shave, he dressed, then meandered over to the motel's breakfast bar. When he arrived, he noted he was only the second customer so far and inspected the offerings, which consisted of coffee, juice, Danish and assorted cold cereals set up in a small room near the office. Marc poured himself a "to go" cup of coffee and selected a ripe banana from the fruit bowl to tide him over for the meeting with the Hubers.

57

As Marc passed the front desk, he spotted the same man that checked him in the prior evening. Despite appearing to be in his mid 60's, he looked muscular, like a retired rugby player.

Marc informed the clerk of his room number and was about to ask what the chances were of holding the room for another night, when the man said, "Ah, so you are Mr. LaRose. Well, let me introduce myself. I'm Hugh Jackson, the proprietor of this here establishment. My daughter mentioned you just this morning."

"So, that makes you Sophie's dad," Marc said, feebly.

"Happy to make your acquaintance," Hugh said, extending a 2X sized paw across the counter and giving Marc's hand a vigorous shaking.

"So you're a real live private investigator. I don't believe we've ever had a PI stay with us before, at least as far as I know. Hope you found our little motel to your liking, Mr. LaRose."

"It's Marc, and yes, everything's fine."

"Anything we can do, let me know."

"There is one thing. I have a few more people to talk to today and I may need the room for another night."

"Not a problem. It's yours. But, if you find you won't be needing it, let me know as soon as you can. Fair enough?"

"Fair enough, and thanks."

"My pleasure, and by the way it's just Hugh."

"Alright, Hugh. I'll hold on to the room key for now. If I find that I won't need the room, I can always leave the key with Sophie at the Inn.

Meanwhile, a couple of guests had come in and were standing behind Marc at the counter, apparently ready to check out.

"That'll be fine, Marc. Good luck with your investi…, uh, your work here. It's a pleasure to make your acquaintance," Jackson said as he glanced over Marc's shoulder at the next guest in line.

"Likewise," Marc answered, and with coffee in hand headed back to his room.

There were still a couple hours to kill before meeting the Hubers, so Marc watched the local news on the room TV. The big story was the preparations being made for the upcoming Winter Carnival and the approaching winter storm.

A little before ten, Marc loaded his overnight bag in his SUV and left for his rendezvous with the Hubers.

When he arrived at the Inn's guard gate, the same officer who was on duty the day before, greeted Marc with a professional grin.

"Still at it, I see," he said.

"Yeah, hopefully I can get this wrapped up today."

"OK, Mr. Emmanuel said to direct you to the main lodge. You are to meet Mr. Barris there. I'll let him know you're en-route."

"Have a good day," Marc said, and with a wave, continued up the winding road to the Inn.

As the guard had promised, Barris was waiting in the guest parking lot, and began waving his arms as soon as he saw Marc's SUV emerge from the tree-lined road. As Marc approached, he noticed Barris was wearing a full length tan coat, a red and black checked hunting cap with pull-down ear flaps ala Elmer Fudd, a green and yellow striped scarf, and a pair rubber boots with metal buckles.

Who dresses this guy?

"Good morning Mr. LaRose. Thanks for being punctual. The Hubers just sat down at their table."

"Well, let's not keep them waiting," Marc said as he alighted from the Explorer.

Barris led the way toward the dining room. Passing the concierge desk, Marc spotted Sophie rearranging the brochure display.

As he approached her counter, she smiled. "Good morning, Mr. LaRose. May I take your hat and coat? I'll keep them until you're ready to leave."

"That would be fine, thanks," Marc said, stuffing his knit cap and gloves into his coat pocket. He felt his face redden a bit and hoped it didn't show as he quickly turned to follow Barris.

When they entered the main dining room, Barris turned towards a corner table where Marc could see a middle-aged couple, drinking coffee and looking out the window toward the lake. The man had the cultivated good looks typical of those used to staying in high end places; stylish dark hair, grey at the temples, ruddy complexion, slim build, with a wardrobe to match. She appeared trim with short blond hair, chic in her European après-ski wear. A handsome black leather coat with a colorful wool lining was draped across the back of an extra chair.

As Barris approached, the man turned and rose from his chair. Barris made the introductions. Marc guessed Phillip Huber was a bit taller than he, a little over six feet. His handshake was quick and firm.

Bianca Huber remained seated and acknowledged Marc with a simple nod. After a polite exchange and a few pleasantries, Barris excused himself under the pretense of attending to other guests.

Phillip offered Marc a seat across the table from himself and Bianca.

Marc noticed that the Hubers each had coffee and were sharing a small basket of pastries.

A waiter appeared offering coffee and asked Marc if he wished to order breakfast. As it was obvious that the Hubers were eating light, Marc replied, "Just coffee, please."

The waiter instantly produced a cup and saucer, poured Marc's coffee and left the pot on their table.

As Marc stirred the cream in his coffee, he said, "My condolences regarding the passing of your friend, Mr. Al-Zeid." Both Phillip and Bianca Huber responded with a silent nod, nothing more.

"I assume Mr. Emmanuel has already informed you that I'm a private investigator hired by the Inn's insurance company to look into the circumstances of Mr. Al-Zeid's death."

Again, the nods.

"This is routine in these types of cases and I'll try to make this as brief and painless as possible. I just have a few questions," Marc said.

"I don't know what we could say that would help. We hardly knew Mr. Al-Zeid. Our relationship was mostly professional, however, I suppose it's the least we can do," Phillip said in his accented English.

Then, as an afterthought, he added, "I will do the talking as Bianca's English is not as good as her French or German, I'm sure you understand."

Marc opened his folder and made a pretense of referring to his notes, "So, you folks are also in the carpet business?"

Phillip appeared to be taken aback by the question, as he glanced toward Bianca, "No. Actually, we are in the hospitality business."

"I see. So, what brings you to Lake Placid?"

"We were visiting one of our properties in the New York City area and, as I said we've done some business with Jamal, ah, Mr. Al-Zeid, who told us about this wonderful Inn where there is great skiing. We thought we'd take him up on his offer to meet him here. It was supposed to be a combination business and pleasure meeting."

"Then, you don't live here, in the states?"

"No, we live in Austria. We use the property in New York City as our address while we are in the U.S.," Phillip said a little too defensively.

"How long do you plan to remain the U.S.?"

"Our visas allow us to stay up to 90 days, so we still have, about three weeks left before we have to return to Austria, but I don't think we will remain here that long."

"How long have you known Mr. Al-Zeid?" Marc asked as he made a note on his pad.

"Well, we started doing business together about two years ago."

Marc scribbled another notation, "And what sort of business relationship did you have with Mr. Al Zeid?"

Phillip seemed to shift uncomfortably in his seat. He sipped his coffee and appeared to ponder Marc's question. "We buy carpets from his firm in Montreal that we use in our property in New York. But tell me, Mr. LaRose, what does any of this have to do with what happened to Jamal?"

"Oh, probably very little. But information like this helps fill out the report that I have to make to the insurance company. Forgive me if I seem to pry."

Marc could see that questioning Phillip Huber about his relationship with Al-Zeid was beginning to annoy him.

"Can you remember Mr. Al-Zeid complaining about being ill the day that you went cross country skiing?"

"No, not really. I mean, he may have complained about being a little tired that morning, but there didn't seem anything really wrong with him," Phillip answered, stirring his coffee.

"Was taking this ski trip his idea, or yours?" Marc asked.

"He invited us up here because he knew that Bianca and I are avid skiers. Jamal admitted he didn't know how to downhill ski, but said he would try cross-country skiing if we would accompany him on a short ski trip. When he made the arrangements for us to stay at the Inn he was informed they would provide a guided ski tour complete with all the equipment."

Marc watched as Bianca glanced toward her husband.

"Could you tell if Jamal was enjoying the ski trip?"

"I really can't say. There was no doubt that Jamal was a novice. The guide had to help him with his equipment, and not long after we started, he began to fall behind. We actually had to slow down to allow him to keep up."

Marc noted Phillip's repeated use of Jamal's first name.

"Did the guide offer Jamal any instruction?"

"Yes, the basics are not that difficult. Cross-country skiing is a lot like walking, except you're wearing skis and using poles to push yourself across the snow. The trail was well groomed, so we just had to follow the tracks. Of course Bianca and I have skied all of our lives, so to us, it's as you Americans say, second nature."

"Were there other people on the ski trip?"

"No, just the three of us, plus the guide."

"Can you remember when you first discovered that Jamal was having difficulty?"

Marc noticed Bianca give her husband another glance as she seemed to fidget, stirring her coffee excessively and nibbling at the small bits on her plate.

She understands what we're saying.

"Well, let me think," Phillip started. "The guide was leading, of course, and it started snowing shortly after the trip began. Although Jamal stayed behind Bianca and me, we knew he was there as we talked to each other for at least the first part of the trip. But, I suppose that we must have lost track of him as the snowfall increased."

"You couldn't tell if he was still following you?"

"It's hard to explain. The snow was coming down very hard like...how do you say in English?"

"Like a whiteout?" Marc interjected.

"Yes, like that. It was blowing straight into our faces and we were all concentrating on just moving forward and following the trail. We didn't notice Jamal was missing until we arrived at the pickup point where the Inn's vehicle was waiting for us. We stayed there thinking Jamal would be along, but after a few minutes the guide began to worry. That's when he decided to retrace our tracks to find him. I offered to accompany him, but he insisted that Bianca and I remain with the Inn's vehicle. We waited there for about twenty minutes and, when the guide did not return, the driver phoned the lodge for further instructions. He was advised to return us to the Inn. It wasn't until later that evening that Mr. Barris informed us of Jamal's death. This whole business is so unfortunate."

Marc notice that Bianca was on her third cup of coffee, her

spoon wearing a hole in the bottom of her cup.

"I understand how you feel, but bear with me, I'm just about through," Marc said, then asked, "How much longer do you plan to remain in the area?"

"We are leaving for New York City very soon. It's about a six hour drive from here and we want to leave before it gets dark."

"Would you mind giving me your cell number so I may contact you if I have any further questions?" Marc asked.

Phillip removed a business card holder from his vest pocket, peeled off the top card and slid it over to Marc who studied it briefly. It showed an address in Aldrans, Austria, for Phillip and Bianca Huber and a set of phone numbers complete with international calling code.

Marc produced his own business card.

"You can leave a message at either my office or my cell number. I usually answer my cell phone day or night, provided I'm in an area with coverage." Marc handed the card to Phillip who slipped it into his trouser pocket, without as much as a glance and rose from his chair. This chat was coming to an end.

"I don't mean to sound rude, Mr. LaRose, but my wife and I have a long trip ahead of us."

Marc extended his hand, which Phillip took, saying with little expression, "Good luck with your investigation."

Marc then offered his hand to Bianca who had remained seated. She lightly took his hand and said, "Goodbye, Mr. LaRose."

Interesting, an English accent.

After wishing the Hubers a pleasant journey, Marc headed toward the lobby exit. He stopped by the concierge desk and seeing Sophie wasn't there, scribbled out a quick note.

'Thanks again for the lovely evening last night. I'm heading back to Plattsburgh. Tell your Dad I won't need the room tonight. Enclosed is my room key. Give me a call sometime, Marc.'

Marc folded the note and placed it, along with one of his business cards and the key, in an envelope he found on the concierge desk. He sealed it, wrote Sophie's name on the envelope, and left it on her computer keyboard. He collected his coat and hat and headed out to his SUV.

Before leaving the area however, Marc figured it would be a good time to speak to the guide, Larry Corbet, and maybe even check in with Jerry Garrant at the State Police barracks to see if he had learned anything more regarding Al-Zeid's cause of death.

As he made his way to his SUV, Marc was still nagged by the question of why the Hubers and Al-Zeid decided to meet in Lake Placid. Why not in New York City or Montreal?

The day was crisp and clear, allowing Marc to admire the grandeur of the Cascade Lakes off to his left. The narrow lakes, covered with a thick white blanket of snow, were framed on the far side by a face of jagged gray rock that shot up into the cloudless sky. It's times like these, Marc thought, that the sophistication of man and his language seemed insufficient to describe nature's beauty, especially in its most primitive, unspoiled form.

Marc opened his cell phone—two bars. He entered Larry Corbet's phone number that he got from Lucy Welch the day before. Through the scratchy connection, Corbet informed Marc he'd be home for another hour and gave Marc directions to his place.

Following the directions, Marc headed up the Mount Whitney Road, a paved town road running north from the village. After the houses ended and it looked as though he may have misunderstood Corbet's directions, the road narrowed to one lane, but Marc continued on.

After another ten minutes of slow going, Marc arrived at a small cottage set off the road, deep in the woods. It was neat, painted white with green trim, but the best part was the stunning view of Whiteface Mountain to the north.

As Marc parked behind an aging red Jeep Wrangler, a large German shepherd came bounding around the corner of the cottage, displaying a set of canines large enough to take down a full grown moose. Judging by the dog's unfriendly behavior, the sound of its growl and its obvious disdain for visitors, Marc figured it prudent to remain inside the protective confines of his Ford, windows rolled up and doors locked.

As he was about to give the Explorer's horn a tap, he heard a man's voice yell something that sounded like, "Waffles" and, as quickly as the dog had begun its frontal assault on Marc's tires, it ceased its attack and assumed a position directly in front of the vehicle, back on its haunches at sort of a doggie parade rest.

Waffles?

Marc shifted his gaze toward the cottage and saw the source of the command; a man standing on the front porch, sporting a thick dark beard, dressed in bib overalls, suspenders and a flannel shirt, ala Duck Dynasty, without the camo.

Marc's more of a cat guy and despite the presence of the dog's owner, he wasn't in a rush to remove his vehicle door from between himself and the dog, so he lowered his window just enough to communicate with the man on the porch in case ol' Waffles suddenly had a change of heart.

"Hello there. I'm looking for Larry Corbet?"

"You got him," the mountain man growled. "You must be the investigator that called. What'd you say your name was, Rosey, something like that?"

"Marc LaRose."

"Right. Had a hard time understanding you on the phone. Poor connection."

"No problem. Mind if I come in? I'd like to talk to you about that guy who died on the ski trail last week."

"Sure, come on in. Don't worry about Waffles. He won't bother you none. He's just a pussycat with a big dog's bark."

"Yeah right," Marc muttered to himself.

How many times have I heard that before.

As Marc cautiously left the safety of his Explorer and made his way up the driveway toward the cottage, he kept a wary eye on ol' Waffles, who remained at his post as if anxiously awaiting his master's next command. *Sic him Waffles!*

As Marc climbed the porch to where Corbet stood, he was confronted with an impressive assortment of downhill and cross-country ski equipment, as well as several sets of snow shoes, neatly secured to the side of the house. Corbet was obviously more than just your average outdoorsman.

After a brief introduction and handshake, Corbet invited Marc inside his cottage. On entering he was met with a soft pillow of warm air from the pot-bellied stove sitting in the center of the living room that served as dwelling's central heating system. The nearby wood box held a hefty supply of red oak logs, cut and split. A gun rack holding three rifles and a shotgun was mounted on a wall behind the wood box and, dangling from the barrel of the shotgun, Marc spotted what appeared to be an Olympic bronze medal.

Corbet walked past to stove into the kitchen area.

"You live out here alone?" Marc asked.

"Yeah. Married once, but that didn't work out too good. Thankfully, no kids."

He pulled out one of the chrome kitchen chairs from under the Formica-topped table, "Have a seat. Care for a cup of coffee? It'll only take a minute."

"Sure, if it's not any trouble." Marc said.

"If it was, I wouldn't have offered."

"OK," Marc said with a grin, taking a liking to this guy for his straightforward honesty and simple lifestyle. "As I said on the phone, I've been hired by a company that insures the Saranac Mountain Inn to look into the death of the gentleman that died on the cross country ski trip last Friday. As I understand, the Inn hired you as the guide for the excursion."

Corbet continued to prepare the coffee pot, seemingly oblivious to Marc's inquiry and set the percolator on the stove.

"Just be a few minutes," Corbet said and joined Marc at the table, setting down two mismatched coffee mugs.

"Yeah, the ski trip. Ya know, that was just my second job for them—the people at the Inn. The first time was about a week or so before. That one went off without a hitch, and there were six people on that tour. This last one though, that was kind of weird."

"How so?"

"Well, Lucy Welch from the Inn called me the week before and said they had booked this guided cross-country ski tour for the following Friday. I was supposed to meet up with these people at the Jack Rabbit trailhead at Mirror Lake, then take them down the trail to the Olympic Biathlon Center at Mount Van Hoevenberg. The Inn's vehicle would meet us there, take me back to Mirror Lake where I leave my Jeep, then return to the Inn with the guests. Ordinarily a trip like this takes three, three and half-hours, max. As Lucy explained it, the people involved in the trip were all experienced skiers. For a trip that short, I mean it's only about what, ten or twelve miles tops, I didn't think anything of it. Hell, I can do 30 miles a day by myself."

"Cream and sugar?" Corbet offered.

"Just cream, thanks. So what's the weird part?"

"Like I said, there were three people on the trip. There was this foreign couple that spoke French, but it wasn't like Quebec French that we hear all the time. It was kind of different. Then there was this other guy, dark looking. Had a peculiar name, Achmed or something."

"Jamal?"

"Yeah, something like that. I could tell right away he wasn't from the area, if you know what I mean. Anyway, this guy is supposed to be experienced, but he's wearing this light jacket, khaki pants, and a thin pair of gloves and it's only twenty degrees. What he's got on is what some guy might wear when he's putting the moves on some ski bunny in one of those bars up in Lake Placid."

Marc continued to listen as he sipped the strong brew.

"So, I tried to explain to this, Jamal fella, that he's dressed pretty light for the weather. Anyway, he tells me that he doesn't like to wear lots of heavy clothes because he gets too warm when he's skiing cross-country. So I said, 'suit yourself'. Then I had to help him with his boots and get him into his skis and, guess what, this guy's got no clue. I mean, I don't think he's ever been on a pair of skis before in his life. He stands up, tries to take a step forward by picking up the ski like he's walking through Walmart, and of course, falls face down in the snow."

"It sounds like he didn't know a ski pole from the North Pole," Marc said jokingly.

"You ain't just a shittin. All he did was fall down for the first fifteen minutes or so. I could see that the European couple was getting a little pissed. The lady was yelling something in French. I can't speak French, but by the way she was talking, I don't think she was impressed."

"Did you give him any instruction on how to ski?"

"Had to! By this time, the Inn's vehicle had left, and we were probably a quarter mile down the trail. So I gave him the basics, and he sorta got the hang of it after a while. Of course, that's when it started snowing. I did my best to keep them all together, and we were making good time until we got to where the trail crosses the road to the village reservoir. That's when the European couple said they wanted to stop and have a look at it, the reservoir, I mean. I told them that wasn't part of the trip and we'd have to keep to the trail, but they were pretty insistent. The man said something about him being an engineer and they really wanted to see it for themselves. It was just as well, this Jamal fella looked like he needed a break any way."

"How did the couple know that the reservoir was there? I mean are there any signs that say, 'Reservoir Ahead'?"

"Beats me. I think there's a sign out by the main road, and, of course, there's another next to the gate as you enter."

"Interesting," Marc said as he made a few notes. "So, what happened next?"

"Well, as I was saying, the reservoir's only a couple hundred yards up the road from the trail, and rather than stand there and argue with them, I took them up to where the gate is. There's a little break in the fence just to the right of the gate, and we went through it, then over to the treatment shed, past the pumping station right up to the pond. Of course it's all froze over this time of year. Anyway, when we got there, they seemed kinda interested in that reservoir. Couldn't really tell for sure 'cause they were all talking French. Even this Jamal feller."

Corbet paused for a sip of coffee.

"Anyway, we hung around there for about five minutes and that's when she starts taking pictures. I asked what she needed pictures of a pond for and her husband says that it's for their business or something and that they can write their trip off as a business expense by showing they were visiting this reservoir and pumping station. Sounded like bullshit to me. Anyway, after she got done taking her pictures, I told them we had to get going, because by then the snow is beginning to pile up. So, we headed back down to the trail and turned east toward the Craig Wood Country Club."

"What time was that?"

"Oh, I don't know, probably about three. We still had plenty of light, but with the snow picking up I wanted to keep them going. We got through Craig Wood and at first we were making good time. Of course, the European couple were no problem at all. I could tell they were in good shape, but the little guy, he was beginning to worry me some."

"How so?"

"Well, he looked pretty tired. I asked him if he was OK and he kept saying, 'I'm fine, I'm fine,' so we pushed on. The European couple stayed right behind me and I could hear them jabbering to each other in French. I just assumed that Jamal was right there with us, but when we got to the pick-up point at Mount Van Hoevenberg, that's about four miles from Craig Wood, Jamal wasn't with us. We waited for a few minutes and when he didn't show up, I told the Inn's driver that I was heading back to find him. The European guy wanted to go back with me, but I told him no, that he had to stay with the vehicle. I can travel a lot faster by myself."

"So where did you find Jamal?" Marc asked.

"I skied back toward Craig Wood and just about a half mile in, I spotted this young couple that looked to be helping someone. As I got closer, I could see they were tending to Jamal. He was lying in the snow, off to the side of the trail."

"How did he look then?"

"Not too good. He was lying there in the snow, shivering. The people that were trying to help him were from out of the area someplace, maybe Boston, by the way they talked. The man had taken off his coat and put it over Jamal and was rubbing his hands trying to get some circulation back in them. He told me that somebody had gone to call 911. About twenty minutes later, the Fire Department's all terrain vehicle made it to where we were. They loaded Jamal on a sled, covered him up real good and hauled him out of there. I picked up Jamal's skis and headed back down to the pick-up point. Of course by the time I got there, the Inn's vehicle was gone. I bummed a ride to Mirror Lake, got my vehicle started and came on back home."

"Did you contact anybody at the Inn?" Marc asked.

"Of course. I called the Inn as soon as I got home. Don't know who I talked to, but she, it was a woman, told me that the European couple had gotten back to the Inn, but she didn't know Jamal's condition. So, I told her he'd been taken to the Adirondack Medical Center by the Lake Placid rescue squad."

"How did you find out that Jamal had died?"

"It was later that evening. This state police trooper came up in his big SUV, with the lights and everything. Waffles went nuts, barking and growling and carrying on. Anyway, the trooper said he needed to talk to me about what happened on the ski trip and that's when he told me that Jamal was dead."

"Did he ask you to give him a written statement regarding what you knew about the incident?"

"Yes he did. I was a little uncomfortable with the idea of signing a paper. But what I told him was the truth. I got nothing to hide."

"Tell me Mr. Corbet. Do you have a license to be a guide?"

"Sure do. I renewed my New York State guide permit just this past September."

"And, do you carry insurance?"

"Costs me five hundred a year for a million dollars worth of liability. At first I thought the insurance was a waste of good money, but with what's happened, I thank the good Lord I have it. Ms. Welch has been bugging me for a copy of my policy. I called my insurance company and they said they would fax the Inn a copy but I guess they just haven't got around to doing that yet."

Corbet got up and went to a small roll-top desk in the corner of the living room. Mounted over the desk was the head of a white tail buck with a ten point rack. He pulled out one of the drawers and retrieved his insurance policy and his guide license and handed them to Marc.

Marc looked them over. The insurance policy was a standard business policy written specifically for tour guides, with errors and omissions included. He copied down the pertinent information including the guide permit number for his report.

"Thank you for your cooperation, Mr. Corbet. If you think of anything else, please give me a call," Marc said as he handed him his business card.

"Like I said, Mr. LaRose, I got nothing to hide. But I feel kinda bad about that poor Jamal fella. If something comes up, I'll be sure to let you know."

As Marc carefully made his way to his vehicle, Waffles was still at his post, lying in front of the Explorer.

"Good boy," Marc said, gingerly stepping past the dog. Finally seated inside his SUV, he exhaled a white plume of breath he'd been holding. As Marc slowly backed out of the driveway, he noticed the dog continued to watch the Explorer until he was out of sight.

Corbet has nothing to fear as long as ol' Waffles is on duty.

Curious to know if Jerry Garrant had received any news regarding Al-Zeid's autopsy, Marc continued on through Lake Placid, to the Ray Brook barracks, where he spotted Jerry's sedan parked in its usual spot.

After another cup of coffee, his fourth of the day, Marc got around to asking if there was anything new in the Al-Zeid matter.

"Not much really, other than some lawyer from Montreal who came in this morning. He and some other guy had court papers from the Quebec probate court showing they had legal authority to take Al-Zeid's body and his belongings back to Canada. I have his business card right here. If you want, I can make you a copy."

70

"You didn't just let him take the body did you?" Marc asked, incredulous.

"We can't hold onto it forever you know. Besides, we got what we needed and conducted a full autopsy, we just don't have all the results back yet."

"What about his belongings?" Marc asked, more forcefully than he intended.

"Oh, getting a little pushy, are we?"

"Sorry, Jerry. I'm just surprised that someone's showed up so soon," Marc said.

"Yeah, I hear you. First thing I did was call my captain and he called the State Police Division counsel's office in Albany. Counsel advised that we should release the body, but we have to hold onto his belongings pending the outcome of the lab results. Once we get the results back we can determine if there is any need to open a criminal case. If there's no evidence of foul play, we'll probably simply close the case as an unattended or accidental death and turn the property over to the estate."

"So, how did the lawyer take that bit of news?"

"Not well. He spoke with my captain for some time, then he and his assistant left for the morgue. We called over and advised the morgue to release the body to the attorney."

"You didn't happen to make a copy of the court papers by any chance?"

"Duh! Of course. I suppose you'd like a copy of those too?"

Marc sensed that Jerry was getting frustrated, so he thought he'd better ease off a bit, "Only if it won't get you in any trouble. Sorry, I don't mean to be a pain in the ass."

"No, not to worry," Jerry said, sounding more subdued.

"Like I've said, this is still an unattended death case, at least until something to the contrary comes to light, which, so far, hasn't. Have you come up with anything new?"

"Not much. I talked with the staff at the Inn and the guide, Larry Corbet, who seems all right. He told me he thought Al-Zeid wasn't prepared for the ski trip, didn't know how to ski, and seemed tired, but not much else. He did tell me one other thing, though, that I can't quite figure out."

"What's that?" Jerry said.

"He said Al-Zeid and the other two people on the ski trip were taking a particular interest in the Lake Placid reservoir."

"The reservoir? Why?"

"Beats me. Corbet said they insisted on deviating from the ski trail to look around the reservoir and take a few pictures."

"That's a little strange," Jerry said.

"According to Corbet, Phillip Huber gave him some line that he was an engineer back in Austria and that by visiting the reservoir and taking a few photographs, they could write part of their trip off their taxes for business purposes. It just seemed odd to me they would even know the reservoir was there in the first place."

"Yeah, I see what you mean. But you know, Marc, we've been in this business long enough to know that sometimes somebody's craziest ideas make sense to them and not to anyone else."

"Suppose you're right. But it's still kind of peculiar."

"Tell me, Marc, did you learn anything from Sophie Horton? Heard you guys were huddling over a couple of beers down at the Side Car last night. My informant tells me you two were having quite a cozy little chat."

Marc could feel his face flush.

"News travels fast around here, but before you get any crazy ideas, I'm sure you're aware that Miss Horton works at the Saranac Mountain Inn. She was kind enough to find me place to stay for the night and I ended up at her dad's motel," Marc said, defensively.

"Go on, I really want to hear about this," Jerry said.

"That's about it. We had a beer together at the Side Car and talked about the case. End of story."

"I see. So, just what did you learn from Ms. Horton at this 'business meeting'?" Jerry asked with a mischievous grin, making air quotes with his fingers.

"Not much really. Only that Al-Zeid was friends with the Hubers, and, this was not his first stay at the Inn, and huh, let me think, oh yeah, that he looked tired the day before he went on the ski trip."

"That's it?" Jerry asked.

"What'd you expect for two beers? The dead sea scrolls?"

Both men chuckled.

"So Jerry, your turn. Tell me about this lawyer that claimed Al-Zeid's body. Who was he representing?"

"According to the court papers he was representing the 'Estate of

72

Mr. Jamal Al-Zeid'. The papers didn't give an actual name of a person requesting the return of the body and belongings, just the Estate. I think to find that out we'd have to petition the probate court in Quebec, and, like I said, unless this case turns criminal we don't intend to do that."

"I see," Marc said, then remembering the car keys in his pocket, he retrieved them. "Before I forget, here are the keys to Al-Zeid's vehicle."

"Thanks, were you able to find anything in the car?"

"Not much. There was an address book in the center console with a few phone numbers, the same ones we found on his cell phone. There was also an address in Willsboro, somewhere on the Willsboro Point Road."

"Willsboro, huh? That's odd. I wonder who Al-Zeid knew in Willsboro, of all places?" Jerry asked.

"I was thinking the same thing. Look, not to beat a dead horse, but when do you think you might hear something from the lab regarding the autopsy results?"

"Any day now. Tell you what, while you're here, I'll give the lab a call and see if they have found anything."

Jerry gave his Rolodex a spin to locate the number for the State Police Laboratory and made the call. After a couple of minutes and a few, "uh huhs, and I sees," Jerry hung up and said, "Look's like they came to the about the same conclusion as the pathologist. A low blood count and signs of frostbite to his toes and ears. The fly in the ointment is the skin lesions. The lab tech indicated, off the record, that they are going with hypothermia as the cause of death, but are still waiting for more test results to come in before they can make it official."

Marc caught Jerry glancing at his watch and figured he had someplace else he needed to be.

"OK, looks like there's not much more we can do with this for now. I'll probably head back to Plattsburgh while the weather is still good, but I might detour to Willsboro to check on that place Al-Zeid mentioned in his address book. Anyway, I should file a preliminary report with the insurance company."

"If I hear anything new, I'll give you a call."

"I really appreciate your help, Jerry. Give Becky my best," Marc said and saw himself out to his car.

As Marc drove east on Route 73, past the Saranac Mountain Inn and Resort, his mind wandered again to thoughts of Sophie tending to her concierge duties. Those thoughts stayed with him while he drove to the hamlet of Willsboro.

It only took Marc a few minutes on the Willsboro Point Road to locate the residence and a mailbox next to the driveway with the number "1492".

The house was located on the Lake Champlain side of the road and was a typical two-story farmhouse that had been turned into a summer home. The snow covered driveway led around the side of the house about 100 feet from the road. Marc could see the shoreline of the ice covered lake about the same distance beyond the house. About midway between the lake and the residence was an out-building large enough to store a good-sized dock and a couple of boats with trailers.

The driveway had been plowed sometime in the past few days, but had since received an inch or two of new snow. There were fresh tire tracks in the driveway leading from the road to a white Jeep Grand Cherokee with New York registration. Marc couldn't tell for sure at this distance, but it looked like the Hubers' rental vehicle Marc had seen the day before. Next to the Jeep were two other vehicles. One apparently had been there for at least a couple of days and was completely covered with snow. The other was a dark-colored Mercedes Benz sedan, snow obscuring the license plate.

"Sure wish I could get a look at the license plate numbers," Marc muttered. To avoid drawing attention to himself, he continued past the house for another half mile before turning onto a side road, where he waited for a few minutes before returning to make another pass.

Not observing any activity, Marc figured it would be a good time to stop by the Willsboro town clerk's office and inquire who owned the place. By the time he arrived there, it was three thirty and, luckily for Marc, the clerk was still there. Deeds and tax maps are open to the public. One just has to hope that the clerk would be discreet enough not to let on to the owner that someone is nosing around.

The Town Clerk was a woman by the name of Thelma Recore. Marc remembered her from the days when he worked the area as a uniformed trooper. Back then she was the Town Justice court clerk, and she remembered Marc when he used to bring in speeders and the occasional drunken driver for arraignment. After chatting about how things had changed since then, Marc asked who owned the property on the Point Road.

Thelma gave Marc a puzzled glance, then pulled out a few drawers looking for the tax map in question. After locating the appropriate drawer, she pulled it out and started turning the oversized plot pages.

"Here we are. That place used to belong to George Paulig. It's been in the Paulig family for years. His wife passed about two years ago, if my memory serves me."

Thelma turned another page, "Yep, now I remember," she said, pointing to a line on the map. "He sold that house along with the outbuilding and two and a half acres of property just last year to a, let me see, um, oh yeah, Serge Remillard from Laval, Quebec, for four hundred and fifty thousand dollars. The property taxes are twenty-five thousand a year. That's probably why George sold it. He's been retired and on disability for well over three years now. He has no relatives living in the area and probably couldn't afford the taxes. Seems like he has a son in the south someplace. He probably went there to live."

"Are you familiar with Mr. Remillard?" Marc asked.

"Not really. I believe he came in the office once before he bought the place when he was doing just what you're doing now, inquiring about that piece of property before he actually bought it from George. Let me see, I think I have another address for Mr. Remillard."

Thelma grabbed a thick tax ledger and flipped a few more pages.

"Yes," she said, "Right here. He has his property tax bills sent to his home in Laval, Quebec. Thelma scribbled Remillard's Laval address along with a phone number and handed it to Marc."

"You interested in buying a piece of property on the Point, Marc?"

Small town clerks can be so nosey, which can sometimes be a blessing for a PI.

"Buy a house in Willsboro? Me? No, not really. I'm doing some claim work for an insurance company and I needed to compare property values. The Paulig place fits the comparison criteria that I'm working with," Marc fibbed.

Thelma gave Marc a doubtful look. "I see," she said, closing the tax book.

Marc knew that wouldn't satisfy her curiosity but it might keep her at bay for the time being.

"Well, Thelma, thanks for the info. Just one more thing. You wouldn't know if Mr. Remillard uses the old Paulig house himself, does he? Or does he rent it out?"

"I'm not sure, but I wouldn't be too surprised to hear he rents it out judging by the all the different cars I've seen parked in his driveway lately. Seems every time I go by, there's a different vehicle, and most have Quebec license plates."

Thelma's face colored, "Uh, I bring the mail to Curtis, the Town Supervisor. He's been laid up now for over two months because of that car accident he was involved in last November. You must remember him, Curtis Packwood, used to be on the town council. Anyway, Curtis lives just past the Paulig property and I drop off the office mail, board meeting minutes, stuff like that."

As Thelma was relating this last piece of information, she seemed to smile, but avoided direct eye contact with Marc.

"Sure, I remember Curtis. I haven't seen him in years. If I get around there, maybe I'll stop by and chat."

"I'm sure he'd like that."

"Well, thanks for all your help, Thelma," Marc said as he started for the door.

Thelma called out, "Anytime, Trooper LaRose."

Marc wanted to take another look at the Remillard house. This time, however, he figured he'd come in from the opposite direction to see if the vehicles he'd seen in the driveway were still there. The street lights had just come on and, as Marc passed the house, he could see the outline of all three.

Returning to the hamlet of Willsboro, Marc pulled into the parking lot of the local bank located where Point Road runs into Route 22. Anyone coming from the Remillard house would have to stop and turn at the intersection.

The lot was empty, so Marc chose a spot in an unlit corner. With the streetlight at the intersection, he could identify vehicles coming from the Point.

This is the part of a PI's job that Marc knows can get tedious…sitting, waiting and watching while trying not to be seen. If he could spot one of the vehicles parked at Remillard's coming through, Marc figured he would tail it to see where it went.

He killed his headlights and turned the engine off to eliminate the exhaust that, in the cold air, could give away his presence. He tuned the radio to a Burlington jazz station and pulled out a crossword puzzle book to kill the boredom.

It's been Marc's experience, that there is no reading while on surveillance…too distracting. But a quick glance at crossword clues helps keep one attentive without losing focus. There was very little traffic.

Sitting in the empty parking lot listening to Diana Krall on the radio, he reflected that chasing down an address left in Al-Zeid's notebook was probably outside the scope of the "accidental death" investigation the insurance company had hired him to look into. But his gut instinct was telling him that if he didn't do this, he'd regret it later.

Marc figured if anyone was going to move from the Remillard residence tonight, they would either do it just before, or just after dinner. Nighttime surveillance is good because the headlights alert you to the vehicles approaching and it's easy to follow someone's taillights on a dark road.

Marc was into his second crossword and his windshield was beginning to cloud over when he saw headlights approaching the intersection from the direction of the Point. First came the white Jeep, followed by the dark Mercedes that Marc had earlier observed in Remillard's driveway. Both turned right.

Looks like they're both heading toward the I-87 Interstate.

Marc paused to let the two vehicles get a safe distance away from the intersection, then eased the SUV out of the parking lot. Marc switched on his headlights and gave chase. As he accelerated, he caught a glimpse of the Mercedes' taillights just before they disappeared over a crest in the road ahead. The roadway was mostly bare save for a few scattered patches of ice and snow where the sun couldn't reach what the snowplow had left behind.

Route 22 leads over Willsboro Mountain, which isn't much of a mountain at all, really just a long incline with several hills and turns, then it descends to the I-87 Interstate highway, about ten miles distant.

Marc kept the taillights of both vehicles in sight, following at a discreet distance. He figured that they would probably take the Interstate south toward New York City, or north toward Montreal.

No sense of "spooking" them by tailing too close.

The road was pretty empty and only a few vehicles passed in the opposite direction. On a long straightaway, Marc could see the red taillights of both vehicles ahead, but they seemed to be catching up to a third vehicle, which, by the configuration of red lights, looked to be a tractor trailer.

"Probably a logger making its way toward I-87," Marc murmured to himself. He knew the truck would slow the progress of the two target vehicles because of all the hills and turns, so he dropped his speed. At the next long straightaway he could see the taillights of the Jeep were now in front of the truck and pulling away, but the those of the Mercedes were still behind. Marc figured that if the Mercedes got past the log truck, then he would pass the truck as well, or he would run the risk of losing the Mercedes. As it was, the Jeep was going to be out of sight by the time he got to the intersection, two miles away.

Continuing the chase, he slowly closed in on the Mercedes and the log truck. By the time the log truck arrived at the intersection, Marc was only a few hundred yards behind. As he crested the hill before the intersection, he could see that the log truck had made a right turn onto Route 9, which runs parallel to I-87, and was heading toward the village of Keeseville. The Mercedes continued across the intersection and turned north on Interstate 87. The Cherokee was nowhere in sight. Marc figured it could have also gone north on either Route 9 or I-87, or south towards New York City, a six-hour drive away. From the story Phillip Huber had given Marc, he could only assume that it had turned south.

But, everyone knows what happens when you assume, that's right, you make an ass out of you and me.

Marc turned right onto I-87 and followed the Mercedes.

In the darkness, Marc melted in with the few other vehicles, and concentrated on keeping the Mercedes' distinctive taillights in view, as it proceeded north at the speed limit, sixty-five miles per hour.

Marc watched as his quarry continued past the exit for Keeseville, then the exit for Peru five miles later.

As the Mercedes approached the Plattsburgh exit, Marc knew that if the car left the Interstate, following it would pose a challenge, despite his intimate knowledge of the city.

To his relief, the Mercedes continued north, toward the Canadian border, some twenty-five miles distant at the legal speed limit, fast enough to keep up with most of the traffic, but not so fast that it would attract the attention of law enforcement.

Marc had the distinct feeling that he might be in Canada before this night was over. The strip between Plattsburgh and the Canadian border is pretty straight and flat, so he eased off the gas pedal, putting a quarter mile between himself and the Mercedes. Only four exits left before the border.

As they passed the exit for Champlain and Rouses Point, Marc could see the glow from the Customs lights in the night sky. The Canadian Customs booths came into view, with a set of two green lights in the center, signaling they were the only open lanes.

Whatever lane the Mercedes got into, Marc figured he would get in the other and hope that he wouldn't be delayed getting past the Customs officer. The lines for each lane seemed about the same length, six or seven cars long. As the Mercedes got in the right lane, Marc pulled into the left.

Marc's lane moved faster, and as he inched his Explorer closer to the Mercedes he noted the license plate number, Quebec RGC9921. However, the Mercedes' side windows were tinted, preventing him from seeing its interior.

As the vehicle ahead of Marc's arrived at the Customs booth, Marc had inched ahead of the Mercedes, and he took this opportunity to adjust his passenger side mirror using its remote control.

Thanks to the glare of the security lighting, Marc could see the driver of the Mercedes...a mustachioed male wearing gloves, scarf, and a wool cap.

Keeping one eye on the car ahead, Marc continued to glance at his side view mirror. The driver appeared to be talking to a passenger, who was hidden from view. Just then, the car ahead of Marc cleared Customs, and he slowly pulled up to the booth.

The Canadian Customs officer, a youngish female with an obvious French Canadian accent, asked Marc, "Votre nom, s'il vous plait?"

Marc replied and at the same time handed her his enhanced driver's license, that for the purposes of crossing into Canada, acts like a passport. The customs officer proceeded to ask the standard questions; citizenship, where do you live, how long do you expect to be in Canada and the purpose of the trip.

Although Marc is loath to lying, especially to a border guard, he informed her that he was going to the Montreal Airport to pick up his wife who was returning from visiting family in Europe. This is a standard ruse that Marc uses, as it is pretty common for people from Plattsburgh to fly in and out of the Montreal Airport. After sliding Marc's drivers license through a scanner, and not finding any alerts, she returned Marc's document with a smile and a "Bon soiree".

As Marc slowly drove away from the customs booth, a glance in his side view mirror indicated the Mercedes was still the third vehicle from the booth.

Probably another five minutes before it clears.

A half mile north of the border, Marc noticed an exit for a souvenir shop that was still open. He pulled into the parking lot between a few other cars, dimmed his headlights, and waited for the Mercedes to pass.

A minute later, Marc saw the car that was in front of the Mercedes pass by, but it took another 10 long minutes for the Mercedes to come into view.

What took them so long to clear customs?

Again, Marc waited for the Mercedes to get down the road and out of sight before continuing the chase.

As Marc followed behind the Mercedes, he noted it was getting onto 8:00 p.m., and although the road was still clear, tiny ice crystals were beginning to fall, just visible in Marc's headlights, a warning that snow was on the way.

Five miles later, and just as Marc was settling in behind the Mercedes, he saw its right signal light illuminate, indicating it was exiting the Autoroute. The Mercedes turned east toward the village of Napierville.

Fortunately, Marc thought, there was still enough traffic to allow his SUV to blend in as he continued tailing the Mercedes.

As the car approached Napierville, however, it turned again, and headed north on another two lane road. Marc's headlights lit up a road sign, "St. Jean Sur Richelieu, 19 km".

"About 12 miles," Marc whispered to himself.

St. Jean is a city of about twenty thousand inhabitants, situated on the Richelieu River, connecting the St. Lawrence River in the north to Lake Champlain in the south.

Keeping the taillights of the Mercedes in sight, Marc noticed that the falling ice crystals had turned into snow-flakes, not a good sign, he thought.

The country lane was dark, save for the occasional farmhouse light, and Marc put some distance between him and his quarry.

Ten minutes later, the street lights of the city of St. Jean cast a muted glow as the Mercedes maintained its pace, then slowed a bit as it entered the first speed zone, 50 kilometers per hour. The city traffic was heavy, but the Mercedes continued on Highway 223 as it skirted the city's western edge, then back into the countryside. With the intensifying snowfall, it wasn't long before the Mercedes taillights were swallowed up by the storm.

Where the hell are you going?

Marc accelerated in an effort to bring the Mercedes back in view. Then, suddenly, as Marc passed another road sign announcing "Chambly 2 km", a ball of red appeared in the darkness ahead as the Mercedes brake lights reflected off the swirling wall of snow. The taillights veered to the right. As Marc slowed, he passed a driveway with a set of fresh tire tracks and the diminishing glow of the taillights at the other end. Marc noted a mailbox at the end of the driveway…it read, "Galarneau 2302".

Route 223 runs north and south right along the river's west bank, Marc thought to himself. Galarneau 2302 must be near the water.

Arriving in the village of Chambly a few minutes later, he found the streets mostly deserted. To verify that the Mercedes was still at the residence, Marc returned, and slowly passed the driveway. The single set of tracks had already begun to fill in with newly fallen snow, and from the street, Marc could see no other sign of life, no lights, nothing, for the short distance his headlights reached into the snowy darkness.

A whole evening's work and not much to show for it, except an address in Quebec and a half empty gas tank.

Oh well, Marc silently lamented, and continued south, back toward the U.S. Border.

At the Rouses Point crossing, a tired-looking Customs and Border Protection officer was reading a magazine as Marc stopped at his booth.

As the officer slid the window of his booth open, Marc said, "Good evening officer, nothing to declare," and handed the officer his ID."

Sliding Marc's license through his card reader, the officer asked in an bored voice, "Purpose of your trip, Mr. LaRose?"

With a straight face, Marc replied, "Just coming back from Chez Jo-Anna night club. Been there for a couple of hours."

Chez Jo-Anna, or 'The Chez', as it's referred to by the locals, is just north of the border near Clarenceville, and is well known for its exotic dancers. Although Marc has never been inside the place, he's heard that 'The Chez' is a common destination for single men. The CBP officer smirked as he handed Marc's ID back to him, and said, "Drive carefully, roads are pretty bad."

When Marc finally arrived back at his condo, Brandy and Rye met him at the door, meowing and following him underfoot as he kicked the snow off his boots and shed his coat. A check of their kitty dish and litter box showed they both needed his attention.

Marc opened the fridge, which still held two slices of pizza left from the previous Sunday night's takeout.

Only four days old, and no outward sign of mold.

"Perfect," Marc said to Brandy, who was busy licking the snow from his boot.

With Bud Light in hand, Marc fired up the computer to catch up on case notes for his report. A faint "beep" from his answering machine meant there were messages awaiting.

Too late to do anything about phone messages at this hour, they'll still be there in the morning.

It was after midnight when Marc finally finished his case journal. He poured a dish of milk for Rye who was splayed on his back with paws outstretched, then popped open another Bud and turned on the tube for a few minutes of late night TV. After finally turning in, Marc pulled the cool covers over his shoulders, and closed his eyes as the events of the day played over in his mind.

"What's the connection between the Hubers and the Mercedes that ended up in Chambly? What was Noah Emmanuel afraid of? What was the real cause of Al-Zeid's death? What was in that lousy pizza?"

DAY THREE

The following morning Marc was awakened by the sound of a snow plow thundering by his condo. He pulled a corner of his window curtain to reveal the outside thermometer, which registered a frigid 25 degrees. He glimpsed his neighbor across the street brushing snow off his car.

Marc's condo unit on the former Plattsburgh Air Force Base was once used to house military families. After the base closed, the units were sold off and Shirley and Marc bought one, intending to rent it out, which they did for a couple of years. After he and Shirley split, however, it became vacant, so Marc moved in. The unit is conveniently located near the center of town and it's just the right size for a divorced guy with two spoiled cats.

Brandy and Rye were already looking for their breakfast. Marc laid out sufficient cat food, water and litter to last them for the next three days.

After a hot shower, he poured his first cup of coffee, then scanned the *Plattsburgh Daily Standard* for anything of interest while downing a container of yogurt spread on wheat toast followed by a banana chaser.

"Looks like a slow news day," he murmured.

The storm was front-page news…six inches of snow complemented with a blast of cold Canadian air. A photo of some poor slob digging his car out of a snow bank after a city plow buried it next to the curb backed up the article.

Marc checked his answering machine. A 'click', followed by a dial tone.

"No message, your loss," Marc murmured. A check of the caller ID showed, 'Unknown number'.

Damn telemarketers.

Marc dialed the number for the flower shop and when Shirley answered he could her breathing into the phone.

"Hey lady, your flowers fresh?"

"Just finished shoveling the sidewalk."

"Uh, huh."

"Had to take Ann Marie to her classes. Her car is covered with snow."

"Uh, huh."

"Today's shipment of flowers was late because of the storm and I've got orders up the waa-zoo that need to get to the funeral parlor for the two o'clock showing."

"Uh, huh. Anything I can do to help?" Marc asked, meekly.

"Na, you'll just get in the way. You know how it is around here when the shit hits the fan. Controlled bedlam, but nothing I can't handle."

"You're always happiest when you're under stress."

"Yeah, well, I've got some help coming in around nine. I think we'll be fine. Look, hon, I don't mean to rush, but I'd better go."

"Me, too. Just wanted to check in, make sure everything's OK, talk to you later," Marc said as he hung up the phone, then reached for his coat.

It took ten minutes to brush last night's snow off the Explorer. After a brief warm-up, Marc put the SUV in four-wheel drive and blazed a path through the unplowed driveway out into the street.

After a stop at the local donut shop, he drove to his office. The Plattsburgh Public Works Department had done another fine job clearing the snow off the street, but in the process, had left a pile waist high along the curb. Marc gingerly scaled the snow bank to the sidewalk on the other side, and tramped up the steps to his office.

As usual, Norm had not yet made it in, so Marc set the bag with his coffee and jelly donut on his desk. The blinking light on Marc's office answering machine beckoned.

I have way too many answering machines.

Marc hit the play button. Two new messages.

It's so nice to be wanted.

The first was from Jerry Garrant asking him to call as he had some results from the lab regarding Al-Zeid's autopsy.

This could be promising.

Marc played the second message that sounded even more interesting. It was from Sophie. Her voice was halting, apparently uncomfortable talking to an unresponsive machine.

"Marc, uh, I'd like to, uh, see you again, if that's OK."

Whoa! Hope springs eternal.

Just then, Norm came through the door displaying his usual morning humor.

"Another beautiful fucking day in the north country," He bellowed, leaving a melting trail of snow in his wake.

84

"Well, good morning, Norman," Marc said, knowing Norm hated to be call by his proper name and which did nothing but add to his already surly demeanor.

"Took me an hour to get my frigging car out of a snow bank and another half an hour to get it cleaned off, just so I could make it down here to be humiliated by you," he groused.

But when he spied the familiar donut bag sitting atop his desk, his tone softened.

"Oh yeah, just what the doctor ordered," he said grabbing the bag. "Thanks for breakfast, Marky."

Enough of the morning office pleasantries.

"Say, Norm, do you have any contacts with the police in Chambly, Quebec?"

Norm slid the cup of coffee out of the bag while giving Marc's question some thought.

"Chambly? No, sorry. Don't you still have contacts with the Sûreté du Québec?" Norm asked, referring to the Quebec Provincial Police force, the equivalent of the State Police.

"Maybe, but the officers that I've worked with were along the border near Lacolle and Hemingford. Chambly's further north and I doubt if the Lacolle guys could be of any help."

"What are you looking for?" Norm asked.

"I need to find out who lives at a certain address up there."

"Well, I suppose I could reach out to one of my buddies in the Canadian Postal Service. I have a contact that I use when I'm trying to track down someone for a summons service. But, it's gonna cost you," Norm said as he stuffed half of the jelly donut into his mouth.

"Norm, since when do you serve court summonses in Canada?"

Norm swallowed and attempted to wipe the powdered sugar from his mouth with the back of his hand.

"Business disagreements, as well as matrimonial conflicts with their inevitable legal entanglements don't stop at the border. Anyway, I may have a friend up there that might help. Give me the address and I'll see what I can do, but it could take a couple of days."

"Couple of days would be fine," Marc said as he scribbled the address on a Post-it note.

"I suppose this means more coffee and donuts?"

"Donuts, my ass. This calls for a full breakfast."

"One big breakfast meal, coming up," Marc said with a grin.

"So, what've you got cooking up in Canada?" Norm asked.

"Not sure. It's more of a hunch. Probably nothing."

"Oooh. All sounds kinda hush hush. International intrigue?" Norm asked, flexing his eyebrows up and down, a smear of donut jelly stuck to the side of his mouth.

"Yeah, whatever. But if you want me to continue fetching your breakfast to pile onto your size 40 gut, you just get me that info!" Marc said, pointing to Norm's pouch.

"Fuck you," Norm said, grabbing his crotch.

As Norm slurped his coffee, Marc dialed Ray Brook and asked for Investigator Garrant. A moment later, Jerry came on the line with an officious, "Investigator Garrant speaking."

"Jerry, it's Marc. Got your message regarding the results of Al-Zeid's autopsy."

"Yeah, any chance you gonna be up in my neck of the woods anytime soon, like maybe, today?"

"Well, I suppose I could be."

Marc suspected there was something that Jerry did not want to discuss on the phone.

"Yeah, I'd like to look at those results with you," Jerry said.

What's he not telling me?

"OK, if you're going to be at the barracks later this morning, I could be up there by, eleven or so, if the roads are clear."

"We didn't get that much snow last night, not like you guys down in Plattsburgh. See you around eleven," Jerry said as he broke the connection.

It's not like Jerry to get so uptight, especially over an unattended death investigation, he thought.

Marc dialed the number for the concierge desk at the Inn. After a couple of rings, Sophie answered with her chirpy New Zealand accent.

"Saranac Mountain Inn and Lodge, concierge desk, Sophie speaking."

"Hey Sophie, it's Marc LaRose returning your call. What's up?"

"Nothing much, really. I missed you when you came to speak with the Hubers, and just wanted to see how you were doing."

"OK, I guess, why?"

After a short pause she said, " I just haven't heard from you, and, well…" Sophie let the sentence hang.

"Tell you what, I'll be up your way later today. I have something to check on, but I should be finished by three o'clock, four at the latest. If you're going to be free after that, maybe we can meet up," Marc offered.

"I don't get off until four. Why don't you call me when you're through doing whatever you've got to do?"

"That should work and if something comes up, I still have your cell number."

"Bye," Sophie said, cutting the connection.

Marc glanced toward Norm who was busy wiping some confectioner's sugar off his coat.

"Got a little something going on in Saranac Lake, big guy?" He asked with a sly grin.

"Just working one of my contacts," Marc said, feeling his face flush.

"Uh, huh. Sure. Wish I had a contact that could make me blush," Norm said, still grinning.

"The only contact you've got to worry about is the one at the Canadian Postal service," Marc said, as he stood and buttoned his coat. "I've got to run. If anyone is looking for me, I'll be in the Lake Placid area for the rest of the day."

"OK, big guy. And good luck with your contact."

It was a little past nine a.m. when Marc stepped out on the sidewalk. Cornelia Street was shiny wet with the rising sun and salt melting the residue from the overnight snow. The sounds of backup alarms from the army of privately owned snowplows could be heard coming from up and down the street.

Marc jumped behind the wheel of his Explorer and headed out of town, south on I-87 to the Keeseville exit, then drove west past Whiteface Mountain and up through the 'notch', his favorite route to Lake Placid.

When he arrived at the Ray Brook barracks, Jerry Garrant appeared to have been waiting for him and immediately buzzed him in.

"Come on back to my office, we need to talk," Jerry said, more of a command than a request.

Marc sensed something was wrong.

Jerry closed the door and pointed to a chair.

"Have a seat," he said, opening a case folder on his desk.

"Marc, I don't know what the hell's going on, but this Al-Zeid thing's got my captain's balls in an uproar."

"How's that?"

"First off, do you have any idea who this Al-Zeid character was?"

"We discussed this the other day. Now your captain mentions it and it's suddenly important?"

"Well, it seems things have changed."

"How's that?" Marc asked.

"For starters, we have this latest lab report to deal with. As we initially suspected, it says that Al-Zeid died of exposure."

"That's pretty much what we suspected all along Jerry. So, what's your point?" Marc asked, still puzzled at Jerry's line of questioning.

"I'm getting to that. You may remember, when a pathologist submits samples taken at an autopsy, a complete battery of tests is run. Some of them are standard and done for about every examination. They often support the preliminary findings but, they may show results that can change the focus of an investigation. That's the case here."

"Jerry, are you saying the lab tests confirmed Al-Zeid died from exposure, plus something else?"

Jerry referred to the open lab file on his desk.

"Not exactly, but you're close. There are some test results that the lab, the physician, nor I, can account for."

"Such as?" Marc asked, warily.

"Such as an acute inflammation of the larynx, for one."

"Well, he was out of shape. Maybe he got that from sucking in large amounts of cold air, trying to keep up with the group," Marc offered.

"That's what I figured at first, but the lab guys tell me that one exposure wouldn't have resulted in the severe inflammation Al-Zeid exhibited."

Jerry ran his finger down the report and continued, "Then there are the decreased plasma levels in his blood, decreased lymphocyte counts, decreased hemoglobin and chloride levels."

"Jerry, this is Marc. Speak English."

"Well, without putting too fine a point on it, the pathology results show that Al-Zeid was suffering from a severe inflammation of his entire gastrointestinal tract."

"Are you talking about his stomach, or his colon, or both?"

"Yep, that and everything in between. Small intestine, larynx, rectum, his whole insides appeared to be a fucking mess."

Marc paused as he digested what Jerry said.

"I sucked in biology class, but what do an inflamed stomach, and intestines have to do with hypothermia?" Marc asked.

"That's my point. A lot of these findings have nothing to do hypothermia. My captain is a mother hen when it comes to lab reports, and he's on my ass to explain these anomalies. On top of all that, there are these fucking ulcers that we found on his body."

"Did the lab provide you with any clues as to their cause?" Marc asked.

"No, nothing yet. The captain has been on the phone with the lab trying to get some kind of explanation, but so far they seem about as clueless as we are. The best they can come up with is that Al-Zeid died from complications of acute hypothermia, facilitated by grossly reduced gastrointestinal tract functions."

"I see your point. Sounds like you might have an open case, at least until you can get a definitive cause of death," Marc said.

"If you don't mind, Marc, I'd like to go over what you've come up with on this so far."

Marc suspected that Jerry was feeling the heat and needed answers. "I've talked to one of the EMT responders, Ned Barnes, and to Larry Corbet, the cross country ski guide, but I think you've also talked to both of them."

"We have, but I want to hear what they told you. And I also want to know what the people at the Inn who had contact with Al-Zeid told you."

Marc took out his notebook and went over his interview notes from Barnes and Corbet, then went on to describe his discussion with the Hubers, and their alleged business connection with Al-Zeid.

An hour later, Jerry suggested they continue their conversation at Ruthie's Restaurant over lunch.

At Ruthie's, Marc recounted his trip to Willsboro the past evening, his conversation with the town clerk and finding the Hubers' rental vehicle parked at the Willsboro address. He also told Jerry about following the car as it left Willsboro, then losing it before he got to the Interstate.

Marc left out the part about following the Mercedes into Canada, but he didn't feel it was necessary as there was no real connection with the black Mercedes and Al-Zeid, at least, not at this point.

It was almost three o'clock when Jerry and Marc arrived back the Ray Brook station.

"One more favor, any problem with making me a copy of that lab report?" Marc asked.

"You trying to get me fired?" Jerry said, feigning comic sincerity.

"Of course not, it's just that, for the purposes of civil litigation, it sounds like our friend Al-Zeid was suffering from a few other physical ailments that could have hastened the onset of hypothermia, which could mitigate charges of neglect that might be leveled against my client at trial."

"Hum, yeah, I see what you're saying, but I don't know. If my captain finds out…"

"You're not going to make me get a court order, are you Jerry?" Marc said, half jokingly.

"No, of course not. But look, if anybody…"

Marc interrupted, "I know, If anybody asks, I didn't get it from you."

"Or my ass is grass," Jerry said as he fired up the copy machine. "Oh, before I forget, the Montreal PD called, said they interviewed an employee at the Global Rug Importers who told them Al-Zeid was the manager, not the actual owner, and that they couldn't find any relatives living in Canada."

"No relatives in Canada? Where the hell is he from then?" Marc asked.

"According to the Montreal PD, he was a native of Iran."

"Iran, huh? I kinda figured he was Middle Eastern. That could be welcome news for the insurance company. No living relatives means less chance of a lawsuit," Marc said.

"One other thing. Remember the lawyer who showed up to claim Al-Zeid's body? Well, he was back yesterday to claim the SUV. He had a court order indicating he was handling all of Al-Zeid's personal arrangements. I'll make a copy of his business card for you, if you'd like," Jerry said.

"Sure, thanks."

Marc turned the lawyer's business card over.

"Jerry, don't you think it's kind of interesting that we have an attorney from Montreal, representing some sick Canadian from Iran, who has died from mysterious causes while cross country skiing, accompanied by couple of people from Austria?"

"Happens all the time!" Jerry said with a nervous laugh.

It was almost four in the afternoon when Marc left the barracks. As Marc was about to call Sophie, he received a call from Norm who said he had talked to his contact at the Canadian Postal Service who informed him that the address in question—Galarneau, 2302—was the address of one Jamal Al-Zeid.

"Great work, Norm," Marc said.

"No problemo, Marky."

"Yeah, yeah, thanks again, you prick. Before I forget, I probably won't be in the office tomorrow, so if anyone calls looking for me, have them leave a message. You know the routine."

"Yeah, sure, just don't forget, you owe me, big time, Marky," Norm said before cutting the connection.

As Marc set his cell on the front seat, the ring tone chimed again, and although he enjoyed the melodious tune of "The Pink Panther Theme", Marc's thought was, what did Norm forget?"

But a glance at the caller ID showed the call wasn't from Norm. "Hello?"

"Marc, it's Sophie. Did I catch you at a bad time?"

"Well, actually, I just finished talking with a police investigator and was going to give you a call."

"Well, now you don't have to. Are you still planning on stopping by today?" Sophie asked.

"I'm headed to Saranac Lake as we speak."

"Great! My dad has to go out tonight, so I have to stay home with Zoe. Why don't you come here for dinner? It'll give you an opportunity to meet Zoe and you can sample some New Zealand cooking."

"Sounds great, but I hate to see you go to so much trouble. I could always stop and pick up a pizza or something."

Sophie giggled. "I'm sure Zoe would like that, but I was planning to cook anyway, and I promise—no mutton stew."

"That's a relief," Marc said with a nervous laugh, "Is it too early to come over? I could be there in half an hour."

"That's perfect. See you then. Bye!"

Marc stopped at a wine store hoping to find a bottle of New Zealand wine, but had to settle for an Australian Sauvignon Blanc, and, although it was nicely chilled, he lamented that the bottle had a screw top cap.

Since when does the crack of a metal cap have the same effect a cork popping?

Sophie met Marc at the check-in desk and brought him back to their family living quarters in the rear of the motel. She introduced him to her six-year old daughter, and Marc was immediately struck by Zoe's blond curls and outgoing personality.

"Niyth to meet you, Mr. Laroth," she said, her speech somewhat impeded by the recent loss of two front teeth.

"Nice to meet you, too. Did you have a good day at school?"

"Oh yeth, thank you. Today our teather, Mith Anderthon, taught uth how to add by two. Two, four, thixth, eight and ten."

"Wow, that's pretty good. Do you know what comes after ten?" Marc asked.

"Yeth, twelve, fourteen, then thixthteen, then, ah maybe ith twenty, but Mith Anderthon theths not to thkip too far ahead of the clath."

"Oh, I see! Of course Miss Anderson is right, but it looks like you've been studying for the next lesson. Good work!"

"Thank you, Mithter Laroth."

Zoe turned toward Sophie, "Mommy, can I wath TV for a few minith. Juth one program. I promith."

"OK missy, just one program. Then be a good girl and get ready for supper."

"Hooray," she said and scampered to her room.

"That's quite a little lady you have there."

"Yeah, thanks. Kids can be a handful, but Zoe is special. She's so smart, just like her daddy," Sophie said as a blush returned to her face.

"Oh, I don't know, I can see a bit of mommy in her."

"Sure you do," Sophie said, unconvincingly.

"Would you like something while we're waiting for supper?"

"Maybe a cup of coffee, if you've got some started."

"Only take a minute," Sophie replied.

"Sorry your dad had to leave tonight. Hope everything's OK."

"Oh, dad's great. Tonight's his monthly Elks meeting. He likes being with the guys and it gives him something to look forward to besides taking care of the motel. He'll be back by nine thirty, ten at the latest. And speaking of supper, I hope you like roast chicken. I put it in the oven right after I called you. It probably needs another hour

92

or so."

"Sounds great," Marc paused, "Say, are you working at the Inn tomorrow?"

"No, thank God. I really need some time away from that place right now. Don't get me wrong, I like what I do and I get along with everyone there, but this latest incident with that guy dying on the ski trail has made the management a little edgy."

"I can understand. Do you think Mr. Emmanuel is taking heat from the main office?"

"Well, he hasn't confided in me personally, but my supervisor, Lucy Welch, told me he received a call from the owner, Mr. McKenzie. McKenzie calls almost every day, but this time, she said, they talked for quite a while. She said to expect some policy changes for events like the cross-country ski trips among other things."

"Yeah, I believe it's called limiting your exposure, to lawsuits, not the weather," Marc said.

"Very funny," Sophie said as she retrieved the pot and poured Marc a cup of the fresh brew.

"Cream and sugar?"

"Just cream, thanks. I'm sweet enough," Marc joked and immediately felt embarrassed for the lame comment.

"We'll just have to see about that," Sophie teased, again showing a hint of a color as the two held their glances for a moment.

"Did you learn anything new on your visit to the State Police station today?" Sophie asked.

"Let's just say, it's gotten a bit more complicated, but I don't want to bore you with the details."

"I don't get bored that easily. From the little bit I heard, it sounded to me like Mr. Al-Zeid, just got lost in the snow storm and basically froze to death."

"Well, that's what it appeared at first, but there are a few other things that seem to have complicated matters."

"Oh, and just what are these other things?" Sophie asked, teasingly.

"I don't think you'd understand. Besides, it's kind of confidential."

"What's so confidential about some poor guy dying on a ski trail? 'Enquiring minds want to know'," Sophie said, mimicking the old *National Enquirer* catchphrase.

Marc had the feeling that Sophie was not about to let this go.

"OK, but don't say I didn't warn you. First, during the autopsy, they discovered these weird sores, like ulcers, on his body. There weren't many of them, but enough that the pathologist noticed them right away."

"Sores, huh? That's strange," Sophie said, her tone reflecting an edge of concern.

"The pathologist didn't know what to make of them, so he took some tissue samples and sent them to the lab for further analysis. Standard procedure."

Marc took a long sip of coffee, then sat the cup on the counter. "Look, I really don't like discussing this with you right before supper. Maybe we can talk about it later, if you still want to."

"I understand, I guess." Sophie said with a pouting face. "Supper should be ready soon anyway, but you have to promise to tell me more later."

"Sure, but, it's not very exciting," he said, attempting to diminish her apparent interest.

Sophie smiled and rolled her eyes.

"Men," she said, and went to check on Zoe.

Alone, Marc was left to wonder how much of this he should be telling Sophie, when suddenly the oven timer sounded.

As Marc was awkwardly trying to figure out how to silence the buzzer, Sophie's arm suddenly brushed past him and pushed a button, quieting the offending clamor.

"Little oven timer got the world's greatest sleuth stumped?"

Marc smiled, a little embarrassed, "Your range is different than mine. Besides, I never use a timer."

"With the motel and customers coming in all hours of the day and night, I need a reminder when there's something in the oven."

"Yeah, I see what you mean. Anything I can do to help?"

"Why don't you go keep Zoe company for a while. I'll give you a call when everything's ready," she said and began setting the table.

"I can take a hint."

Marc found Zoe in the family room sitting in a child's chair watching a cartoon show. Marc sat on the floor next to her and they both watched the TV in silence. Marc thought how much cartoons had changed since he was a child.

Finally, Zoe looked up and said, "Do you like Thcamp the

Wonder Dog, Mr. Laroth?"

"Hmm, I've never seen him before, but I'll bet he's a really nice dog."

"Oh yeth. Heeth the greatesthed," Zoe said as she pressed the remote's off button.

"Mr. Laroth, can I athk you a quethton?"

"Sure, Zoe, what's on your mind?"

"Are you married?"

Marc was taken aback by the little girl's question. "Well, no Zoe, not at the moment."

"Oh, then you uthed to be married?"

"Well, yes I was, and do you know something? I once had a little girl just like you."

"You did?" Zoe said excitedly. "Whath her name?"

"Ann Marie."

"Maybe thee can come over and play with me thomtime."

"Well, Zoe, I don't know. She's all grown up now, and she works and goes to college in Plattsburgh."

"Oh, I thee," Zoe said, sounding disappointed.

After a moment of silence, she looked up at Marc and said, "Are you going to marry mommy?"

Marc was thinking how to best answer Zoe's question when Sophie called from the kitchen, "OK you two, supper's on the table."

"We're coming." Marc called back.

Zoe was still staring up at Marc, apparently waiting for him to answer.

"That's a tough question Zoe. I think right now, your mommy and I just want to be friends. Is that OK?"

"Oh, I gueth tho. Doeth that mean we are friendth too?"

"Well of course Zoe. You and I are special friends."

"Oh goody," she shouted, and scampered into the kitchen to give her mommy the good news.

Sophie served the chicken dinner and the three of them chatted about Zoe and her schooling, and the challenges of running a privately owned inn with so many national motel chains in town.

After dinner Sophie told Zoe to brush her teeth and get ready for bed. "I'll be in to help as soon I'm finished with the dishes."

"Good night, Zoe. It was nice talking with you," Marc said.

"Good night Mr. Laroth, it was nith talking to you too." Zoe said

95

as she padded toward her bedroom.

"She seems older than six. You've done really well bringing her up by yourself and all," Marc said.

"It hasn't been easy. My dad's been a big help."

When Sophie finished loading the dishwasher, she said, "I'm going to check on Zoe and tuck her in for the night. Would you be a dear and bring the bottle of wine you brought into the living room where we can talk. There are wine glasses on the counter."

"I can handle that, just as long as a timer's not involved."

"Very funny. I'll only be a sec."

While Marc sat on the couch waiting for Sophie to return, he contemplated just how much of this case he should reveal to her.

A minute later, he faintly heard Sophie's voice coming from the hallway, "Yes, I'll make sure to tell Mr. LaRose. Good night Zoe, I love you."

"Good night mommy," Marc heard Zoe say, as the bedroom door clicked shut.

Sophie joined Marc on the couch.

"Zoe wanted to be sure that you tell Ann Marie that she said 'Hi'. I think you have a new friend. She really likes you."

"She's a sweet girl."

"OK," Sophie said, lifting the bottle of wine off the coffee table, "It's time to sample that wine you brought. By the way, I really love these screw-off caps. A lot less fuss than messing around with a cork puller, wouldn't you say?"

"I suppose so," Marc agreed, grudgingly.

Marc raised his glass, "To Zoe, may she grow up to be as smart and as good looking as her mommy."

"Oh stop," Sophie said as their glasses clinked together.

They savored the wine in silence for a long moment.

"OK, you've stalled long enough. Out with it. What did you find out about our friend, Mr. Al-Zeid?" Sophie asked.

"Can't let it go, huh?" Marc exhaled deeply. "OK, I give up, what would you like to know?"

"Let's pick up where you left off. Something about the pathologist finding sores on his body?"

"That's the part that puzzles us. Like I was saying, the pathologist noted sores, or lesions as he called them, on his back, chest and legs. He took photos and sent tissue samples to the lab for analysis."

"Sores all over his body?" Sophie asked, concern returning to her voice. "That would certainly get my attention. Any other anomalies?"

"Well, let me think. There was an obvious lack of body hair. I suppose he could have shaven it off. A chronic inflammation of the larynx, you know, like a sore throat, only a lot worse."

"No body hair? Hmm, and the lab results on his organ specimens?" Sophie asked.

"You are a curious one," Marc said.

"Is that a problem?" she asked.

"Probably not, but before we continue, I want you to know, this is kind of confidential, so, whatever you hear has to stay between us."

"Of course, silly. Who would I tell? Certainly no one at the Inn."

"All right, but this is where it gets confusing, especially for a layperson like me."

Marc unfolded the copy of the lab report he had in his breast pocket and after a moment's hesitation, handed it to Sophie. Marc watched as Sophie looked it over. When she was done, she turned her gaze in Marc's direction, appearing deep in thought.

"Well, any ideas?" Marc asked.

"I don't have any conclusions. There's not enough information in this one report. However, with this and all you have told me so far, I do have a speculation."

"All right. Let's hear it," Marc said as he refilled their glasses.

Sophie took a slow sip of the wine.

"I believe I mentioned before that I used to work for the New Zealand Customs, intelligence branch. One of my duties was to look for people attempting to smuggle nuclear components into the country. My college degree was complimented with quite a bit of training in nuclear physics, courtesy of the government, and, part of that training included the physical signs of radiation sickness."

"Radiation sickness? OK, what's your point?"

"What I'm getting at, Mr. Detective, is that according to your pathologist's examination—the irritated larynx, ulcers, hair loss, overall rundown condition, and the blood analysis, could be signs of possible radiation poisoning."

"Radiation poisoning! Hell, this guy was a rug merchant, managing a carpet store in downtown Montreal. How can anyone get a dose of radiation poisoning from carpets unless they were the flying kind that used nuclear energy for lift-off?"

97

"Ha ha, you're a regular comedian," Sophie teased.

Although Marc was attempting to make light of Sophie's off-the-cuff diagnosis, some of his suspicions regarding Al-Zeid's presence in the Adirondacks were causing him to rethink what might be at play.

"Sorry, it's just my way of releasing tension I guess," he said.

"Marc, just because radiation sickness is not what you were expecting, don't blow it off too quickly. Radiation poisoning isn't all that common, especially up here in God's country where the closest nuclear reactor is someplace in southern Vermont. I can understand why a lab analyst might not pick it up, especially when the early signs of radiation sickness can be confused with other less serious illnesses, such as acid reflux, severe diarrhea, lower GI infection and so on. Looking at the totality of Al-Zeid's symptoms, I believe that advanced prolonged radiation poisoning should not be entirely ruled out."

"Radiation poisoning?" Marc said again, somewhat stunned.

Sophie continued, "Look, Marc, this is just my initial reaction to the report. I'm certainly not an expert and I'm sure if the lab suspected Al-Zeid had radiation poisoning they would have said so."

Marc considered what Sophie had said.

"Radiation poisoning just hadn't occurred to me, or apparently anyone else for that matter, and from the look of things, I'd say you are as close to an expert on radiation sickness as anyone who's had a chance to look at this report."

"Marc, not to change the subject, but why would the Inn be at fault because Al-Zeid died on the ski trip in the first place? I mean, it's not like he fell down the lobby steps or something."

"Now you're entering the complicated world of civil liability, which is the reason I was called in on this in the first place. To put it simply, the Inn could be exposed to a lawsuit for a number of reasons, mostly because the guide, Larry Corbet, lost track of Al-Zeid as they were making their way to the rendezvous area to meet up with the Inn's vehicle."

"I don't get it. Why would the Inn be at fault at all? I mean, it was Larry Corbet's job to provide the guide service and besides, he has his own insurance, doesn't he?"

"Yes, he does, however, the Inn hired Corbet to provide guide services. The act of hiring an outside contractor, in this case, Mr. Corbet, does not absolve the Inn from actions taken by him during the course of the trip."

"I'm still confused. The Inn insisted Mr. Corbet have his own liability insurance. You would think that his insurance would cover anyone getting hurt on the trip," Sophie said.

"To an extent, you're right, but civil law is not as simple as that. Let me try to explain. The Inn organized the ski trip, right?"

"Right," Sophie replied.

"The Inn provided transportation to and from the drop-off and pick-up locations, and through a subcontractor, in this case, Larry Corbet, provided guide service, right?"

"Right again."

Marc took a deep breath, "Corbet was hired by the Inn to provide a service so, in that capacity, he was acting as an agent of the Inn. For all the guests knew, Corbet could have been an employee of the Inn."

"But he isn't an employee," Sophie interjected. "He has his own guide business. We checked him out."

"True, but in the insurance world, this is referred to as *vicarious liability*, where one party, in this case, the Inn, can be held legally accountable for the actions or inactions of another party, in this case, Larry Corbet, the contracted ski guide."

"Does Mr. Al-Zeid have any family?" Sophie asked.

"Not that we know of. The Montreal police reported they could not find any family living in Canada. He's apparently an Iranian immigrant, so if he does have family, that's probably where they are."

"So, what do you intend to do now?" Sophie asked.

"Now? Well first, we should finish this fine bottle of Sauvignon Blanc," Marc said as he hoisted his glass.

"Oh Marc, you know what I mean. Like, what are you going to tell the insurance company?"

"The insurance company? I'll tell them what I've learned from the police report, the autopsy report and from interviews with witnesses. But, if what you say is a possibility, then the question is, what was he doing hanging around Lake Placid, and what was he doing with those people from Austria, the Hubers? This whole affair is looking more like a police matter than an insurance investigation."

"So, what's your next move?"

Marc hesitated before answering. "I don't think I've mentioned this to you before, but when I was looking through Al-Zeid's SUV at the Inn, I came across a notebook in the center console. In it, among other things, was an address in Willsboro."

"I don't think I've ever been to Willsboro, though I know it's somewhere on Lake Champlain. What's your point?"

"My point is, after I spoke with the Hubers, I decided to check it out. I located the house, but that's not all."

"Oh?" Sophie managed.

"I'm quite certain I saw the Hubers' Jeep parked there, along with another car, a Black Mercedes."

"Had the Hubers mentioned anything about going to Willsboro after they checked out of the Inn?" She asked.

"No, only something about some shopping in Lake Placid before returning to New York City. They said that they had about three weeks left on their visas, but thought they'd be returning to Austria before that."

"So, what else happened in Willsboro that's piqued your interest?"

"It was just after dark when I saw both cars leave the residence and head over to I-87. I guess Hubers' car turned south toward New York City, but because they got way ahead of the Mercedes, I couldn't confirm that. The Mercedes headed north and I followed it across the border into Canada where it eventually pulled into a residence in Chambly, Quebec."

"Chambly? Where's that?" Sophie asked.

"It's a small town on the Richelieu River just south of Montreal."

"I'm curious, why did you bother to follow the Mercedes to Canada? I mean, what does that have to do with your insurance investigation?" Sophie asked.

"I'm not sure yet, but I think that Al-Zeid and the Hubers were up to something more than carpet sales and his death is just the tip of the iceberg. Trouble is, nothing seems to fit, especially now, with your opinion, unverified as it may be, that Al-Zeid may have had radiation sickness."

They both sat in silence for a moment.

Sophie peered at Marc over her glass and said with a relaxed smile, "So, when are you heading back to Plattsburgh?"

"Tonight. Why, you trying to get rid of me?"

"Why don't you stay the night? Your room is still available. Then we can sit here for a while longer, enjoy this wine and decide how we can best proceed with this Al-Zeid thing."

100

"We? What's with the 'we' thing? I don't think you should get involved."

"Oh, but I think I'm already involved. Who provided you with the radiation diagnosis? Me. Besides, it appears you can use all the help you can get on this. Just call me your expert witness. Trust me, you can afford my rates, besides, like I said, I have the next couple of days off with not much to do." Sophie said, swirling the remaining wine in her glass.

Marc allowed a grin to creep across his face. "Well, when you put it that way, how can a helpless PI resist?"

Sophie looked as if she was about to say something a little more personal when they both heard the chime from the front office door.

"Sophie," Hugh Jackson called out. "Are you still up?"

"Yeah dad, we're in the living room. Oh, and there's a plate of food for you in the fridge."

"I had supper at the lodge, thanks," Hugh called back.

Hugh entered the room and saw Marc and Sophie on the couch, wine glasses in hand.

"Oops, looks like I'm interrupting. Sorry."

"You're not interrupting. Besides, it's getting late and I should be going," Marc said as he stood.

"Daddy, Marc is going to stay the night. I was just going to show him to his room."

As Hugh headed down the hallway toward his own room, he called back, "I think unit 12 is still available. That reminds me, would you mind turning the 'No Vacancy' sign on?"

"No problem Dad. Have a good night."

"Good night Mr. Jackson, uh, Hugh," Marc said as they heard the bedroom door close.

Sophie turned to Marc, "I'll get your room key."

"Sophie, let me pay you for the room. The insurance company's good for it, besides, they need the tax write off."

"Not necessary. Grab your coat and follow me. I'll show you to your room."

"I think I can remember where the room is."

"I don't want you to get lost," Sophie said with a sly grin.

She hit the switch and the red neon 'No' in front of the green 'Vacancy' buzzed to life on the sign outside. Sophie led Marc out the front entrance to the end unit where they both stopped in front of the

101

door marked with the number '12'. Sophie unlocked the door, pushed it open, then turned to Marc. "You look awfully tired, detective. I think what you need is our special Miss Saranac 'turndown' service."

"Well, it has been a long tiring day and after that wine I do feel a bit weary. A little turndown service would feel quite nice about now. By the way, what is a turndown service anyway?" Marc said playfully.

Sophie grinned, touched his cheek with her fingertips and said. "Follow me, Mr. Detective. I'll show you."

Sophie led Marc inside the room, and eased the door shut.

Later that evening, she silently returned to her own room, checked on Zoe, then slipped between the cool covers of her bed.

Sophie's attraction to Marc stemmed not only from her five- year self-imposed abstinence, but also from the exhilaration of meeting someone she finally felt good about, someone she felt she could trust.

However, while thoughts of her past, her little Zoe, Ian, her ex, and her dad, lingered on her sub consciousness, she was bothered by a mental itch, not unlike that of a healing insect sting, that delayed the onset of sleep. Sophie knew the signs of radiation poisoning, and from what Marc had told her, she was certain that that's what Al-Zeid had died of.

DAY FOUR

Early the following morning, Marc arrived back at the Miss Saranac Motel after a brisk walk around Lake Flower and found the motel's breakfast area open, with a few of the guests already enjoying breakfast before starting out on what was shaping up to be another clear, cold day in the Adirondacks. Marc opted for the instant oatmeal with a banana garnish. He found an empty table and, as he sat down, Sophie appeared with a basket of pastries and arranged them on the serving counter.

"Good Morning Mr. LaRose. Did you rest comfortably?" Her blushing cheeks were becoming a permanent feature.

"Like a baby, thanks for asking. Have you had your breakfast?"

"Oh yes. I've been up for an hour and a half helping dad with the buffet. I got Zoe ready for school and in between I grabbed something to eat. I could probably join you for coffee though."

"Please do." Marc said eagerly.

"So, what's up for today?" Sophie asked, eyeing Marc over the rim of her cup.

"I was thinking of returning to Willsboro where I saw the Hubers' Jeep parked. According to the town clerk, different vehicles park there quite often. She thinks maybe the owner, a Canadian by the name of Remillard, is renting the place out. That's not unusual, but I'd like to find out what attracted Al-Zeid and the Hubers to Willsboro."

"Yeah, I can understand why that would make you curious."

"Phillip Huber seemed a little evasive when I interviewed him at the Inn. His wife, Bianca, didn't say much. According to Phillip, she doesn't speak English, but I'm pretty sure she understood everything we were talking about. And there was something else."

"What's that?"

"Just a hunch, but I got the feeling that she's scared of something."

"Do you get these 'hunches' often?" She said teasingly.

Marc grinned, "My, aren't we feisty this morning!"

"No, I just get a kick out of listening to you, especially when you lose yourself in your own thoughts, like you did just then."

"Sorry, guess I don't mind talking to you. I mean, you probably know as much about this case as I do."

They both paused, taking sips of their coffee.

"So, like I mentioned last night, I have a couple of days off from the Inn. Any problem if I tag along? I promise not to get in the way."

Marc mimed indecision. "Only if I could get a warm-up," he said, pushing his cup toward Sophie.

"You're such a tease," she said, and slid out of the booth to retrieve the coffee pot.

Marc thought about the prospect of Sophie accompanying him to Willsboro. He liked working alone as it allowed him maximum flexibility. On the other hand, Sophie had expertise in a field where he had none.

"Fresh pot," she exclaimed as she refilled his cup.

"So, what do you think? Can I come along?"

Marc's expression turned serious. "Problem is, Sophie, I never know where a case will take me, and if we get on to something, well, we could be gone overnight, maybe even longer. What about Zoe?"

Sophie hesitated, "I can work it out with dad. He adores Zoe and I know he won't mind. Besides, he's always saying how it would be good for me to get away from the motel for a while."

"Well, I'll let you take care of that. Bring your passport in case we have to make a trip across the border and it wouldn't be a bad idea to pack a small overnight bag, just in case. You do have an American passport, don't you?"

"Of course, silly. I assume we're leaving this morning then?"

"Right after breakfast. I just need a few minutes to pack up. Just knock on my door when you're ready."

"Sounds like a plan. I have to help clean up the breakfast buffet, take about an hour," she said as she began collecting the discarded foam plates and utensils left on an adjoining table.

Marc drained his cup and returned to his room.

By 9:00 a.m., they were on the road. Marc drove through the Village of Lake Placid, then through the "Notch" along the Ausable River past Whiteface Mountain, alive with skiers zigzagging down the slopes.

"So Marc, when we get to Willsboro, what are we looking for?"

"I'd like to identify any vehicles parked at the residence where I saw the Hubers' vehicle."

They continued in silence for a while before Marc asked, "Sophie, we know Al-Zeid's symptoms, but how do you determine if a person has been over-exposed to a radiation source?"

"I suppose it's something like detective work. It's not just one symptom, or clue. Like in this case, you have the physical anomalies, lack of body hair, unexplained sores, overly irritated GI tract, and a run-down physical condition. Individually, these symptoms could mean anything, but taken together, they could be a prime indicator for something much worse. Of course, if the lab techs suspect radiation poisoning, they would have to do some pretty specific blood sampling. It's a little complicated and above my customs pay grade, but it's pretty definitive."

"So, if I understand you correctly, it's a process of elimination for an analyst to identify the cause of the sickness. Sounds like it could also be pretty time-consuming."

"It can be. As Customs officers, our branch was mainly interested in the illegal importation of nuclear components. We were trained to look for signs that someone could have been associated with that kind of activity. This might involve a person's travel to certain countries, ties to people known to be in the trade, unexplained transfers of cash as well as the persons overall physical health."

As Marc negotiated the Explorer through the Adirondack countryside and the villages of Ausable Forks and Jay, Sophie talked about her extensive training with the Customs Branch, as well as a few cases of attempted smuggling she had been involved in.

By the time she finished, they were approaching Willsboro. Marc turned onto the Point Road, remembering the Remillard house would be off to their right.

"Sophie, when we get near the house, I'll point it out to you. I'd like you to identify any cars parked in the driveway."

"As Marc's SUV approached the house, he nodded to his right, "It's the next white house—that one," he said.

Sophie strained to see past the mounds of snow piled on both sides of the driveway.

"There's a yellow van parked near the back of the house. I can just see the tail end, but I can't make out the license plate number."

Marc continued on, not wanting to attract undue attention by stopping. When they passed, he noticed smoke rising from the chimney.

"I'm pretty sure, there's someone there," he said.

They continued on to the end of the road which circled around to a marina located on the opposite side of the point.

Marc parked, with the SUV idling as he thought about his next move. As the wind blew off the lake, they watched the snow drift onto the docks that had been pulled up on shore. A row of boats, covered with shrink wrap to keep out the snow and moisture, sat behind the marina.

"OK, that was fun. What now?" Sophie said, half jokingly.

"I need to find out who's staying in that house."

After a moment's hesitation, he said, "The town clerk mentioned Curt Packwood, the town supervisor, lives next door. Maybe he's seen something."

"What are you thinking?" Sophie asked.

"I think now's a good time to pay him a visit. Do me a favor and jump into the back seat."

"I was wondering what kind of line you'd use to you get me into the back seat," she said playfully.

Marc ignored Sophie's banter, "My binoculars are in that duffle bag on the floor. When we get to Packwood's house, I want you to keep low, out of sight, and scan the Remillard house. See if you can read the van's license plate and look for any activity. You OK with that?"

"I think so." Sophie said. "Are you sure no one can see me inside the SUV?"

"The rear windows have a darker tint than the front. Just don't move around anymore than you have to."

"You're the boss," Sophie said as she took up her position in the back seat.

Marc retraced his route around the Point Road to the town supervisor's residence. As he drove to the end of Packwood's driveway, he estimated it to be a hundred yards across the snow-covered field to the Remillard house off to their right. At the end of the driveway, Marc saw a late model Chevrolet sedan that he assumed belonged to Curtis Packwood.

"OK Sophie, I'm going in to talk to Mr. Packwood. See what you can pick up with those binoculars. I'm going to turn the engine off, but I won't be long."

"I'll be fine, Marc. Stop worrying," Sophie called back from her position scrunched down behind the front seat.

Marc walked to the rear door of Packwood's house and gave the door a couple of sharp raps. He heard a voice call out, "Come on in, it's open."

As Marc opened the door, "Hello, Mr. Packwood, you there?"

"Well of course I'm here, who else would be yelling for you to come in?"

Marc entered the kitchen area and closed the door behind him.

"I'm in the living room. Just come on through."

Marc continued to the living room where he found Curtis Packwood sitting in a recliner next to a bay window with his feet propped up, his right leg in a cast. Although Marc hadn't seen Packwood for about ten years, he instantly recognized him, with his mane of neatly combed gray hair, sporting a pair of gold wire rimmed eye glasses that accented his fleshy red cheeks. He was attired in a long-sleeved flannel shirt, pajama bottoms and one wool lined bedroom slipper. A neatly folded blanket emblazoned with an American Indian pattern lay across his lap. A hand-hewn cane was hooked over the arm of his chair.

"Sorry, I couldn't greet you at the door. As you can see, I'm still recovering from that damn car accident I had a while back."

"No problem, Mr. Packwood. My name's Marc LaRose. You probably don't remember me. I used to be a state trooper a few years back."

"Of course I remember you. You were always bringing drunks and speeders into town court for arraignment. Yep, you sure had the locals excited for a while, but I've got to say you slowed them down a might. Other than a couple of extra pounds and a little gray in the temples, you don't seem to have changed much."

"Thanks, Mr. Packwood," Marc replied with a grin.

"Curt's what most folks call me," Packwood said pointing towards the couch with the tip of his cane. "Have a seat and take a load off."

Packwood continued, "Thelma, the Town Clerk, told me you were poking around the office the other day. Said you were interested in the old Paulig homestead next door. Says you gave her a story about looking for real estate price comparisons, but I don't think you convinced her."

Embarrassed that the cover story he'd given the town clerk didn't hold up, Marc decided to come clean, "I should have know that wouldn't fly. I have my own investigative business these days and right now I'm looking into an incident in Lake Placid where a fellow from Canada died, skiing up on the Jack Rabbit trail."

"Oh yeah, I remember reading something about that in the paper a few days ago. Too bad—a young feller dying like that. Must have been a pretty bad storm to get hypothermia on a cross country ski trip, but, tell me, what does that have to do with you coming down here to Willsboro?"

"Not sure, but it appears that the man who died might have ties with your neighbor," Marc said motioning toward the bay window that looked out onto the house next door. "So, I thought I'd drop by to ask if you'd met him or knew anything about him."

"Met him? Nope. I've been laid up for a couple of months now. Other than trips to the doctor, I don't get out hardly at all."

"I see." Marc said.

"As for the old Paulig house next door, I don't know what's going on," Packwood said as he motioned towards the bay window, "but there seems to be plenty of activity over there."

"Oh, really?" Marc replied.

"Say, would you like a cup of coffee or tea or something? I'd like a cup of tea myself," Packwood said, motioning toward the kitchen, again, with his cane. "All you have to do is set that teapot on the stove and turn it on high. It only takes a couple of minutes for the water to boil."

As Marc started for the kitchen, Packwood called out, "There are cups in the cupboard right above the stove and the teabags are in the tin on the counter."

"No problem," Marc called back. As he was retrieving the tea bags, he asked, "Mr. Packwood, would you mind telling me what you've seen next door? You mentioned you saw some activity."

"Be glad to. But first things first. Let's get that tea in here and don't forget to bring the pitcher of cream that's in the refrigerator, and the sugar too. That's on the counter next to the tea tin."

Marc brought in the two mugs of brewing tea, then returned for the cream and sugar and set them on the end table next to Curt Packwood's chair.

"Ah, that looks great. Now, you were asking about the goings-on next door. Well, I tell ya, it's like this. Right after Paulig sold his place to that Canadian feller late last summer, what's his name?"

"Remillard," Marc said.

"Anyway, it seemed like there was always someone around. I

heard that maybe this guy, you said his name was, Rembrandt?"

"Serge Remillard," Marc repeated, patiently.

"Yeah, anyway, I heard this guy was going to rent the place to summer visitors. Well, you know, I wasn't too happy when I first heard that. These summer people can be awfully annoying at times. Staying up to all hours of the night, drinking, playing loud music, you know."

Marc nodded in agreement.

"But I gotta say, despite all those cars coming and going, they didn't seem to cause much ruckus. Matter of fact, they're pretty darn quiet. I mean for so many cars in the yard all the time, you'd think you'd hear more noise. Most of what goes on seems to be centered around that old boat house down by the lake," Packwood said.

"A boat house, huh? When did you notice this?" Marc asked.

"Things seemed to pick up the beginning of September, right after school started back up. Look for yourself; you can see it from here." Packwood said, pointing at the bay window next to his chair.

Marc went to the window. As he pulled back a corner of the sheer curtain, his eyes followed the snow covered drive running behind the house about fifty yards to a small barn, situated on the shoreline of the ice covered lake. As he let the sheer fall back into place, he noticed a pair of binoculars setting on the windowsill within reach of Packwood's chair.

"Yeah, I can see the barn pretty clear from here," Marc said.

"That's where Paulig used to store his boats for the winter, kind of a boat house, sits up on blocks. He had a big pontoon boat and a good size fishing boat. Old Paulig used to drive his boats right into that barn and hoist them up out of the water. He had a workshop in there, too. I used to hear him clanging around inside. Not sure what he did with the boats after he sold the place though. Anyway, these new people, they brought a couple of big rental trucks down there. Looked to me like they were hauling in something to store in that barn. I mean, old Paulig, he cleaned it out before he left, so I guess there's plenty of room in there to do whatever."

"Could you see what these people brought into the barn?" Marc asked.

"Not really. But whatever it was, I think it must have been pretty heavy," Curt said.

"Oh, how's that?" Marc asked, his curiosity piqued.

"Well, these rental trucks, they were the boxy van types, you know the ones I mean. I think there were three in all, but there might have been more. They'd come, usually in the late afternoon just before dark and of course they had to back down the driveway to where the barn is. I thought for sure they'd get stuck the way they seemed to struggle to get down there, but they didn't. They keep one of those forklift things in the barn. That's what they'd use to off load with. Kind of a Bobcat, wasn't real big, but big enough. Anyway, whatever it was that they took off those trucks was packed in these big boxes."

"Big boxes, huh? How big?" Marc asked.

"Oh, I don't know. Probably about as long and wide as a sheet of paneling, maybe four by eight feet. Each box looked to be about a foot thick. I could tell the boxes had to be real heavy. That Bobcat thing would rock back and forth when it lifted one of them up, and the tires would sink right into the ground."

"Could you tell how many boxes there were?" Marc asked.

"Oh, hard to say for sure. Probably two or three in each of those trucks. I can't recall if the other trucks all carried the same boxes or not, but I know that at least one of them did. I think they had some other sized boxes, too, but it was kinda hard to see because it gets dark so quick in the fall. Sometimes it would take them an hour just to unload one of those trucks."

"Have you ever seen Serge Remillard, the new owner?"

"I don't think so." Curt said, stroking his chin. "You say, Serge Remillard? That's French, isn't it?"

"I believe it is," Marc said.

"Well, these fellers I seen over there, I don't think they're very French, if you know what I mean."

"No, what do you mean?" Marc asked.

"Well, they don't come out in the sunshine very much and they kinda stick to themselves. But once in a while you might see one or two coming or going and, like I said, they just looked different. Kinda dark skinned. Moustaches. Most of the time they wore hats and scarves and sunglasses and such. I thought they looked like a bunch of Mexicans, without the sombreros, but I don't think they were. Mexican, I mean."

"Could you tell if there is always someone at the house? I mean, is there ever a time when there's no one there?" Marc asked.

"Well, let me put it this way. I been laid up here now for the

110

better part of four and a half months. I don't get out very much anymore, outside of a trip to Plattsburgh to see the doctor every two weeks or so. Thelma takes me. Don't know what I'd do without her sometimes. Anyway, what I'm getting at is that outside of that and watching TV, I look to see what's going on next door. Sometimes, I think if I didn't have them to look at over there, I'd probably go a little daft. So, getting back to your question, to the best of my knowledge, there is somebody over there, twenty-four seven, as they say nowadays."

"Do you think the people that you've seen there lately are the same ones you saw late last summer?" Marc asked.

"Yeah, I think so. At least some of them. I can tell by the way they walk. I have my own way of identifying them. There's this one guy, for instance. He's taller than the rest, so I refer to him as Stretch. Then there's this other feller—always walks sorta bent over, looking down at the ground, so I call him Stoopy. And there's one other guy, he walks with a limp, seems to favor his right leg, he's Gimpy. Those three always seem to be walking back and forth between the house and that damn barn down by the lake, like their taking turns checking on it, or something."

"Is it just those three guys you see around, or are there others as well?"

"Yeah, there are others that come and go, don't stay long. Sometimes I see a car come in late in the afternoon or in the evening, but by then it's usually too dark to make out who they are, and they usually leave before morning."

Curt glanced up as Marc was finishing his tea and said, "Look Marc, if you want some more tea, please help yourself, you know where everything is."

"No, thanks," Marc said, as he thought about Sophie in the back seat of the Explorer with no heat.

"Look Curtis, I should be getting along, but I really appreciate you taking time to chat with me about this."

"Oh hell, time is what I got plenty of these days. Doc said it's going to be at least another couple months before I can get around on my own again."

Marc fished a business card from his wallet. "If you happen to see anything else, would you mind giving me a call?"

"Sure thing," he said, taking the card. "I hope you find whatever

111

it is you're after."

Marc picked up his empty cup. "I'll set this in the sink on my way out, and thanks again for everything."

"No problem, Marc. Thelma usually takes care the dishes. Remember now, the door's always open."

"I'll be in touch," Marc called back as he made his way out the back door to the SUV.

Sophie was still seated in the rear seat when Marc got in and started the engine. "Everything OK back there?" Marc asked.

"Not so bad. The cold was just starting to settle in. Find anything interesting?"

"A couple of things. I'll tell you about that later. For now, just stay low until I get us out of here."

Curt Packwood's driveway was well plowed and, as he made the turn to leave, he gave the horn a toot and waved to Curt who was still sitting near the window. Marc headed toward the Interstate.

"Did you see anything going on next door?" Marc asked.

"Not much, really. There was this one guy, kinda tall, he went out the back door and walked down to that barn by the lake. He went inside and then a different guy came up from the barn to the house. That's really about it. Oh, I found your camera in your duffle bag and I took a couple of photos of those guys as well as the van. I got the plate number right here," Sophie said as she handed Marc the note over his shoulder.

"Good job. I might make a detective out of you yet."

Marc looked at the note and saw the number was for a commercial New York registration.

"What did Mr. Packwood have to say?"

"Nothing specific. Packwood said he'd keep his eyes open and let me know if he see's anything new."

"So, where to now?" Sophie asked.

"I think it's time we paid a visit to that house up in Quebec where I followed that Mercedes the other night. I'd also like to visit that carpet store in Montreal where Al-Zeid worked, maybe talk to some of the employees there."

Marc headed north on I-87 to the Peru rest area where Sophie reclaimed her seat next to Marc. As they got back on the highway, Marc exclaimed, "Get your passport ready. Next stop, Quebec."

Rather than go through the main border crossing on I-87, Marc headed east, to one of the smaller ports of entry. The Canadian Customs officer asked for their identification and after glancing at their passports, asked the usual questions.

"Just a shopping trip to Montreal, officer, and possibly dinner afterwards. Nothing to declare now, but maybe on the way back," Marc replied. After a quick look inside the Explorer the customs officer returned their documents and waved them through.

Marc quietly relaxed. He didn't mention the H&K 40 caliber pistol in his overnight bag, a minor detail that could have become a major problem had the Customs officer searched his bag.

Marc easily located the address on the mailbox, Galarneau 2302, on the outskirts of Chambly, Quebec. As he slowed the Explorer, the house at the end of the drive came into view. The stately stone and wood Quebecois-style chalet, its steep pitched roof dripping with a thick layer of snow appeared quite innocent, if not picture postcard perfect. The frozen Richelieu River was clearly visible through a line of trees behind the house.

"What a pretty house," Sophie said.

"Isn't it, though," Marc said, as he quickly scanned the property.

The fieldstone house was trimmed with thick wooden beams that had been stained dark brown to match the slate roof, giving it the appearance of a gingerbread house on steroids. Marc estimated the plowed driveway ran about fifty yards from the road to the main house, where it divided. One branch turned left to a fieldstone garage, set perpendicular to the main house. The second branch veered right, past the main house towards the river for another twenty yards to another stone building.

A boathouse, perhaps? Marc silently asked himself.

Conifer trees dotted the spacious front yard and the tops of a few more trees could be seen poking up from the back of the main house. The stone chimney was pouring out billows of white smoke, a good sign that the house was occupied, Marc figured.

Marc slowly urged the Explorer back to the speed limit as he continued toward the village of Chambly, and asked, "How would you like to do some carpet shopping."

"I've never been to Montreal, and I love to look at carpets." Sophie said excitedly.

Marc smiled, "Don't get too excited, we're only looking. Try to keep your eyes and ears open for anything unusual."

"Unusual? What could I possibly see at a carpet store that would be 'unusual'?"

"You'll know when you see it," Marc said.

He pulled out his notebook and found Al-Zeid's business card. "Global Rug Importers, 44981 Sherbrooke St. NW, Montreal."

Marc's knowledge of Montreal dated back to when he travelled with his parents there as a child visiting great aunts and uncles, attending weddings and funerals, then liaising with the Montreal PD while working with the state police.

After crossing the St. Lawrence River using the 'Pont Champlain' and working their way up to Sherbrooke Street, Marc located Global Carpet Imports on the edge of the retail district surrounded by tenements and warehouses.

"Before we make our entrance, I want to look around the back of the store. Be on the lookout for security cameras," Marc said.

As he made the turn into the wide alleyway behind the storefront, Marc observed a black Mercedes and noted the plate number, a delivery van with Global Carpet Importers written on the sides, and a silver Audi parked near the loading dock.

"That's the Mercedes that I followed from Willsboro to Chambly night before last," Marc said, nodding toward the car.

"So, apparently, there is a connection," Sophie said.

Marc didn't respond as he continued down the alley, then turned right, back onto Sherbrooke Street and parked the SUV in the first available parking space.

"No cameras, at least none that I saw," Sophie said.

"Good, when we get inside I'll say we're interested in putting a new carpet in our home. Then, maybe we can find out more about our friend, Mr. Al-Zeid."

Marc produced a small digital camera from his coat pocket and handed it to Sophie, "Here, keep this out of sight. I'd like to get a photo of the salespeople."

"How am I going to do that without raising suspicion?" Sophie asked.

"As we're looking at carpets, ask a sales associate to hold up a corner, then snap his photo."

"You think that'll work?"

"I don't know. It's the best I can come up with right now. Besides, men are all the same. We'll do whatever a pretty woman tells us to do," Marc said with a playful grin.

Once inside the showroom, they could see several piles of carpets stacked and neatly arranged by size around the expansive interior. There were also display racks along the sidewalls holding more carpets. These, Marc noted, could be individually turned like giant pages of a book, allowing customers to inspect each carpet design, one at time.

As Marc and Sophie browsed along the piles of carpets, flipping the corners of a few and feigning interest, a salesman approached, seemingly out of nowhere.

"Bonjour. Puis-je vous aider?"

Understanding that the salesman had asked if he could be of service, Marc replied in English, "Yes, we're in the market for a carpet, preferably an oriental rug."

"Wonderful," replied the salesman, who immediately switched to English with an accent that was noticeable, but one that Marc couldn't place. The salesman's skin color appeared dark olive in the dim light of the showroom. He had a full head of curly black hair and a neatly trimmed moustache. He was neatly dressed in a light brown shirt, open collar, with tan slacks. His wardrobe was complete with a pair of brown oxford shoes badly in need of a shine.

"My name is Naveed and it would be my great pleasure to assist you," he announced.

Without waiting for a response, Naveed continued, "We, at Global Carpet Importers, have the grandest selection of Oriental and Persian carpets in all of Montreal. Now, tell me, monsieur, what is the size of the room?"

Marc responded, "Hmm, about eighteen by twenty. That's feet, not meters."

"Oui, monsieur, all of our carpets are measured in feet. So, to get started, I just need a little more information. What are the colors of the walls? How close would you like the carpet to come to the walls, and is this to go over a wood floor or vinyl?"

Marc began to respond, then hesitated.

Sophie, sensing Marc was struggling with questions of home décor, jumped in. "Let's see, we have oak flooring. On the eighteen foot wall, there is a gas fireplace. We would like the carpet to end about four feet from the fireplace and about two feet from other three walls. All the walls in the living room are painted an egg shell color,

115

which is an off white."

"Tres bien, madame, I am familiar with that color. Now, do you have a price range in mind?"

Again Sophie answered. "We're sort of open on that. I guess we'd like to see what you have in a carpet of that size and we could go from there."

"So, we'd be thinking of a carpet about twelve by sixteen. Let me see," Naveed said as he looked toward the carpets along the far wall. "We have many styles to choose from and several fabrics. All of our Persian carpets are hand knotted and colored with only natural dyes. Of course, they are made only in Iran. Otherwise, we couldn't call them Persian. We also have Oriental carpets made in other countries, but the Persian carpets are our specialty. If we don't have the exact size that you require in the style and color that you like, we can special order it for you."

"How long would it take to get a carpet that is special ordered?" Marc asked.

"Two to three months. All of our carpets are hand-made and one of a kind. Allow me to show you some carpets that I think would do very nicely. Please, right this way."

Naveed directed Marc and Sophie to a wall display that held a selection of carpets, and after dismissing the first few, he paused at a rather elegant one and took a moment to run his hand over the fabric.

"This is a Persian rug of the Tabriz style, which happens to be the city where my family is from." Naveed said, almost too proudly. "I believe that the reds and yellows of this carpet would go well with an oak wood floor as well as the eggshell of your walls."

"Exquisite!" Sophie exclaimed, as she played along, caressing the woolen fabric with the tips of her fingers.

Marc noticed that Naveed watched her closely, carefully brushing his moustache with his forefinger in the style of a used car salesman.

"What are its dimensions?" Sophie asked.

Naveed lifted a corner of the carpet and located a paper label stitched on the reverse side. "Ah yes, here it is. It's 11.85 by 16.06, quite close to your size requirements, don't you think?"

While Naveed was busy locating the size tag, Sophie had discreetly removed the camera Marc had given her.

"Naveed, if you could just hold that carpet open, I'd like to take a quick photo to help us make a decision when we get home."

Before he could protest, Naveed was momentarily blinded by the camera flash, while staring blankly back at Sophie.

Without missing a beat, Sophie continued, "That's a good possibility. What else do you have?"

"Uh, yes, I have a few more, right over here, I think," a flustered Naveed said as he guided Sophie to another display while glancing back toward the rear of the store.

As Naveed was showing Marc and Sophie a few other carpet choices, Marc saw a movement out of the corner of his eye. A second man had appeared, and was standing where Marc and Sophie had been, just moments before. The newcomer had the same olive skin, was a bit taller, and appeared to be slightly older than Naveed.

Naveed, now aware of the presence of the second man, paused from his sales pitch and called over to him in French, "What is it, Khaleed?"

"I saw a flash," he replied, also in French.

"Please excuse me for a moment," Naveed said to Marc, an edge of concern in his voice.

Naveed went to where Khaleed was standing and as the two moved slowly away, towards the back of the store, they began speaking rapidly in a language that Marc was unfamiliar with. It soon became obvious that Khaleed was the man in charge as he seemed to be scolding Naveed.

Marc whispered to Sophie, "Looks like Khaleed's camera shy."

The heated conversation continued for a full minute before Naveed returned to where Marc and Sophie waited.

"I apologize for the interruption, but I had to take a message," Naveed said, wiping his brow with a handkerchief.

"Not a problem. Tell me, if we decide on that first carpet you showed us, you know, the one from Tabuz, can you arrange for delivery?" Marc asked nonchalantly, purposely mispronouncing Tabriz.

Naveed, cleared his throat. "Actually, that carpet is a Tabriz, sir, and regarding delivery, yes. As soon as payment is made, we can arrange for delivery anywhere in the greater Montreal area, free of charge."

"That's a problem; we don't live in the Montreal area." Marc said.

"I see. We could still arrange to have the carpet delivered directly to your home, however, there may be a delivery charge depending on how far away you live. If you don't mind me asking, sir, where would that be?" Naveed said, the pitch of his voice rising almost imperceptivity.

"Actually, we live in Plattsburgh, New York."

"Plattsburgh? New York? That's in the United States," Naveed's tone rising again.

"Yeah, it was when we left there this morning," Marc said, half jokingly. "But it's only an hour's drive from here."

Naveed shot a glance to where his protégé Khaleed was last standing, and, cleared his throat again. "I'm sorry sir, but that would be out of the question. We do not deliver our carpets outside the country. If you were really interested in purchasing a carpet from us, you would have to make your own arrangements to transport it to the United States."

"Oh, that's too bad. When I talked to Jamal about buying a carpet, he didn't mention this delivery restriction."

A surprised Naveed looked back suddenly at Marc. "I'm sorry, did you say, Jamal?"

"Oh yes, I forgot to mention that I got the name of your store from this fellow I met while staying at an inn in Lake Placid, that's also in New York," Marc said with a patronizing tone. "His name is Jamal, Jamal Al-Zeid. Look, he gave me his business card. I have it right here." Marc produced the business card that Investigator Jerry Garrant had found in Al-Zeid's wallet.

Naveed paused as he stared at the card, "Well sir, ah, Mr. Al-Zeid is no longer with the firm."

"Oh really, what happened?" Marc taunted.

"It, ah, seems Mr. Al-Zeid has met with an unfortunate accident, I am sorry to say."

"Oh, that's too bad," Marc said in his best-surprised look. "When did this happen? I just talked with him not more than a month ago. Was it an automobile accident?"

"Oh no, nothing like that. Actually, ah, I'm not really sure of the circumstances," Naveed said as a fresh line of perspiration bubbled across his brow. "I am sorry if there was any confusion about our firm's delivery policy, but never the less, we cannot possibly deliver a carpet outside of Canada."

Marc got the feeling Naveed was looking for a way to end this conversation, and after an awkward pause, he continued, "If there is nothing else, I must excuse myself." He said as he attempted to steer Marc and Sophie toward the front door.

"That's really a shame about poor Jamal. He seemed like such a nice guy. Did he have family in the area?" Marc asked, standing his ground.

"Family? Uh, no, no family, at least not in Canada. Now, if you don't mind, I really must be…"

Marc, aware that Naveed was approaching panic level, decided to press further. "So, who is the store manager now, just so I know who to ask for when we return and you're not here?"

"The new store manager? Well, uh, I guess that would be Khaleed. Yes, of course, the new manager is Khaleed. Now if there is nothing else, I really must excuse myself."

"Sure thing, but if you don't mind, we'd like to take one last look at that carpet, you know the one, the, what was it, the Tabuz? We'll only be a minute," Marc said.

Not waiting for Naveed to answer, Marc led Sophie back to where the carpet was hanging and again examined it, leaving Naveed standing at the store's entrance.

Sophie whispered as she was peering up at the carpet. "Marc, these people want us out of here, don't you think it would be better for us to just leave?"

Marc replied under his breath, "Of course they'd like to be rid of us, but we might get more information by hanging around a little longer."

Glancing back, Marc noticed that Naveed was no longer near the entrance and assumed he had retreated to the rear of the store. Another five minutes passed with Marc and Sophie continuing their charade. Just when Marc was about to give it up, Khaleed reappeared wearing a strained smile.

"Hello, my good friends," he said, in very accented English. "I am sorry that Naveed had to leave you in such a hurry. He told me that you live in the United States and I'm sure he mentioned that we cannot make a delivery outside of Canada. It's not that we don't want to, but it's an issue with our insurance company. I'm sure you understand."

Insurance, my ass.

"We understand. I suppose we could make arrangements to pick the carpet up ourselves. However, one thing that Naveed didn't tell us about this carpet was the price. It's not marked on the tag."

Without looking at the carpet or the tag, Khaleed answered. "This carpet is very expensive. It costs fifteen thousand dollars. Canadian funds, naturally."

"That seems quite high, why so much?" Marc asked.

Continuing to stare, Khaleed responded, "It is a Tabriz, sir," he said, rolling the 'r' to give the name greater emphasis. "Some of the finest carpets in the world come from the city of Tabrreez." Khaleed's smile had turned to a sneer.

"We're going to have to give this purchase a little extra thought."

Again, Marc displayed Al-Zeid's business card.

"Like I was telling your Mr. Naveed, I have your store phone number right here on the business card that Jamal Al-Zeid gave me. Should I use this same number to contact you as well?"

Ignoring the business card in Marc's hand, Khaleed responded, "Yes, that is the store's number."

"I understand that Mr. Al-Zeid is no longer with the firm and that you're the new store manager. I believe Naveed mentioned your name. It is, Caleb, right?" Marc said, intentionally trying to provoke him using a name of Hebrew origin.

Khaleed's stare turned to a glare, as Marc felt Sophie's tug on his coat sleeve.

Khaleed said, "Is there anything more we can do for you, Mister...?" Khaleed left the question hang, in an apparent effort to glean Marc's name.

"No, that should do us for now. Thank you for your time. When you see Naveed, tell him thanks as well, you've both been very helpful."

Khaleed stood motionless continuing to give Marc the same icy stare as he and Sophie left the store.

When they got inside the Explorer, Sophie said, "I don't think Mister Khaleed will forget you anytime soon."

"Probably not. Did you see his expression when I mentioned Jamal's name? I think those two were more than just carpet-laying buddies."

"Possibly. So, what do you think we should do now?" Sophie asked.

"They're probably still watching us from the store. First, let's get away from here," Marc said as he pulled into traffic, joining the throng headed south on Sherbrooke Street.

"It's almost noon," Marc said glancing at his watch, "Hungry?"

"What do you have in mind?"

"Thought we'd head over to Place Jacques Cartier in the tourist section of Old Montreal. We should be able to find a cafe for a glass of wine and a light lunch.

"A glass of wine? I'm up for that."

****

Back at the carpet store, Khaleed approached his younger brother.

"What did you tell the American about Jamal?" Khaleed asked.

"I said nothing," Naveed pleaded. "He said Jamal gave him his business card when they met in Lake Placid. I only told him that Jamal no longer worked here."

"Did you tell him how Jamal died?" Khaleed asked.

"Of course not. I'm not a fool," Naveed answered defensively, "Just that he met with an unfortunate accident and you were now the store manager."

Alarm bells sounded in Khaleed's head, already on high alert due to the progress of the plan now in motion.

"Naveed, do you like living here in Canada?"

"Of course, Khaleed. Why do you ask?"

"It has been a long road for both of us. You, immigrating to Canada after claiming refugee status, and myself, smuggled here as well, aboard a filthy Liberian cargo ship. And do you know why, Naveed?"

"To serve the Mufti?"

"That is correct, to serve our supreme leader, Mufti Mangal Shakir. I'm sure you remember when we were growing up in Iran, in the slums of Zehedan. We faithfully attended evening prayers, and followed his teachings. He saved us from a life of useless poverty at the hands of the imperialist elite and taught us that to be true soldiers to our god, we have to destroy the Americans and their Zionist lackeys."

"Yes, Khaleed, I remember," Naveed said, unconvincingly, as he thought about his childhood days. Although they were indeed very poor, family and religion were what mattered, not the radicalized hatred of westerners espoused by the rogue Mufti Shakir, that had so emboldened his older brother.

"Although your knowledge of our mission here in Canada is limited, if you truly want to be helpful, you must continue to listen and learn the ways of these infidels. And above all, report to me, anything that you think looks suspicious."

Khaleed paused to calm himself to keep from showing his displeasure with this new situation. The fact that this American had met up with Jamal in Lake Placid, then, mysteriously appeared at the carpet store was troubling.

Naveed kept his eyes focused on the floor in front of him.

"I am very sorry, Khaleed. He had Jamal's business card. He said Jamal gave it to him," Naveed said, shrugging an apology.

"You did right," Khaleed said in a calming voice to quiet Naveed's fears. "There are many people at work right now doing great things in the name of Allah. Soon, you, will be called to take part. In the meantime, let me know if these Americans show up here again."

"I will, Khaleed. Thank you for understanding."

Khaleed returned to the back of the store. Inside his windowless office, he sat at his desk and glanced at the monitors with views from the security cameras positioned throughout the store as well as the loading dock. Khaleed would have to report this latest incident, but that would have to wait. Other things were happening that needed his immediate attention. He picked up his cell phone and dialed.

****

During the drive uptown, Sophie took in the sights of cosmopolitan Montreal with its modern office buildings and giant department stores, and noticed how they contrasted with the 'Vieux', or Old Port section of the city. She marveled at the distinctive French architecture of the oldest part of Montreal, Place Jacques Cartier. As Marc's Explorer rumbled down the narrow cobble stone streets past a line of sidewalk cafes, they dodged a line of horse-drawn carriages, their riders bundled up in heavy coats to ward off the chill.

Marc found a parking space on a narrow side street. A brisk two block walk later they spied an inviting appearing restaurant just off Rue Jacques Cartier.

"Let's try this one," Marc said as he scanned the French language menu posted outside the restaurant. The restaurant was a few steps below sidewalk level and once inside, they were seated at a table along the wall, away from the kitchen.

Marc could tell that a few of the diners were tourists, but he could also hear French being spoken by many of the patrons as well as the waitstaff. Marc always felt more comfortable in a strange restaurant patronized by 'locals'.

The waiter, a tall, thin man in his early thirties, wearing a long white apron over his black waiter's coat and trousers approached their table. Marc knew at a glance he was a typical Quebecois.

"Welcome to Le Restaurant Des Trois Soeurs," the waiter said in French and proceeded to announce the day's specials.

"Excusez-moi, monsieur," Marc interrupted the waiter and, in French, ordered French onion soup, a baguette, and two glasses of white wine.

The waiter nodded, and with a "Merci, tres-bien," left the two alone at the table.

"That was interesting, so, what are we having with our wine?" Sophie asked.

"Don't worry, you'll love it. It's one of my favorites."

"Ooh, I love surprises, I think," Sophie said, flexing her eyebrows upward.

"After lunch, I'd like to return to the carpet store and sit on it for awhile," Marc said.

"Sit on it? What do you mean?"

"We'll watch it from the street. If Naveed or Khaleed leave, we'll follow. See where they go. The store hours posted in the window said they are open from ten to seven, so we may be there for a while. Are you up to that?"

"Keep me well fed and I can do most anything," Sophie said with a wink.

Soon afterward, the soup arrived. The aroma of the hot cheese and onion soup filled the air and after a few sips, Sophie was hooked.

"Marc, this is truly delicious, and I love this crusty bread. What did you call it, a banquet, or something?"

"It's a baguette. The French have a way with food," Marc replied, revealing some of his private feelings about his heritage.

It was almost four o'clock by the time they left and made their way back to the carpet store. Marc found a parking space between two cars that provided him with a view of the front of the store as well the alleyway where they had observed the Mercedes parked earlier. They both slipped into the rear seat of the Explorer to continue their surveillance.

Taking turns manning the binoculars, they watched the storefront for activity with the intent of identifying those going into or leaving the store. In between customer sightings, of which there were very few, they chatted about their daughters, their previous jobs and, eventually, got around to talking about their failed marriages.

"When two people living together are passionate about their chosen careers that take them in different directions, the strain on the relationship is sometimes stronger than the desire to stay together. I think that's what happened to Shirley and me. Not that we stopped caring for one another. It's just our feelings for one another could not keep pace with our careers," Marc said.

Sophie remained silent as she continued to scan the front of the carpet store.

"None of my business, but do you think Zoe misses her daddy? I know that your dad is around and certainly seems to be helpful, but..." Marc trailed off.

Sophie exhaled, "Guess I'm still waiting for that proverbial Mr. Right. I'm sure he's out there somewhere. I've met lots of men, but like you just said, the Mr. Right that I have in mind has to be 'right' for Zoe as well as myself. In the meantime, dad isn't such a bad stand-in and besides he loves Zoe as much as I do and he's a great role model as well."

Just then, the silver Audi that they had seen parked behind the carpet store exited the alley and turned right onto Sherbrooke Street.

Marc motioned toward the Audi. "I think that's Khaleed leaving. Let's see where he goes!"

Marc slid into the driver's seat and pulled into traffic. By the time he got up to speed, there were several cars between them and Khaleed's car.

Sherbrooke Street is a four lane thoroughfare and Marc was able to pass a few cars, keeping the Audi in sight. At the intersection of University Street, the Audi stopped for a red light, which gave Marc a chance to catch up, but still left a couple of cars between him and the Audi. When the light changed, Khaleed made a left turn onto

University, which Marc remembered lead directly south to the Champlain Bridge and the West Island area near the Richelieu River.

Sophie asked. "Marc, is this the same way we came into Montreal?"

"Yes, and if my hunch is right, our Mr. Khaleed is taking us right back to that house in Chambly."

Marc followed the Audi over the Pont Champlain, then east on Autoroute 10 toward Chambly where they saw Khaleed's car exit the highway. They watched as it turned north onto Route 223.

"There's really no sense tailing him any further and risk being seen. He's obviously headed right back to the house at Galarneau 2302."

"So, what do we do now?" Sophie said.

"I'd like to get in that house, but outside of breaking the door down, I don't think that's going to happen. Outside of that, I'm really curious about that boathouse by the river. I doubt it's guarded."

"But Marc, how are we going to do that without being seen? We'd have to pass the main house to get to it."

"Not necessarily. The Richelieu River is frozen solid this time of year. In fact, the townspeople use it as a giant ice-skating rink. It runs through the village past the boat house, not far from the center of town. If we crossed the river after dark, we could get to the boathouse unseen."

Sophie remained silent, deep in thought, as she watched the snow-covered fields of the West Island whiz by.

Suddenly, she turned toward Marc and said, "Look, you've brought me here to Canada because you wanted to check out a few things regarding Al-Zeid's death. We've talked with the people who work at the carpet store. We know that at least one of those people, Khaleed, apparently stays in the house where the Mercedes led you during the snow storm. But so far it looks like the only thing you've accomplished is to piss Khaleed off. What do you hope to prove?"

Marc continued watching the road ahead for a few moments before he spoke.

"Have you ever been to a zoo where there's a crowd of people gathered in front of a cage that's supposed to hold some exotic animal, but you can't see it because it's hiding somewhere inside the cage, like behind a rock or a tree trunk?" Marc asked.

"Yes, but…"

"What do the people usually do?" Marc asked.

"I don't know, I guess sometimes they walk away. Sometimes they might yell, rattle its cage, or something," Sophie said.

"Exactly. When something is trying to remain hidden, you have to rattle its cage," Marc said.

"But do you think it's wise to draw attention to yourself? I mean, if these guys are up to something, who knows what they might do."

"I considered that, but I think they're intent is to stay out of sight. They already have to be worried that if Al-Zeid died from radiation poisoning, sooner or later the authorities are going to find out. Of course, this begs the question—if Al-Zeid was exposed to radiation, where and how was he exposed? Records show he was the owner of the house in Chambly. There's also been strange activity at the house in Willsboro, an address Al-Zeid had in a notebook. Associates of his, the Hubers were at the residence in Willsboro. Those houses are connected by a notorious smuggling corridor, the Richelieu River, which connects the St. Lawrence River with Lake Champlain, that is for all intents and purposes, practically unguarded. The possibilities are endless.

Marc took the next exit that led to a street running parallel to the Richelieu River, on the opposite side from Al-Zeid's house.

"Let's see if we can locate that house from this side," Marc said, glancing over the river off to his left.

Sophie, who seemed preoccupied by something that Marc had said, broke her silence. "What do you mean when you said that the water route between the Richelieu River in Canada and Lake Champlain is unguarded?"

"I said *practically* unguarded. Sure, customs have set up check-in stations for those coming from Canada to the U.S. by boat and occasionally they'll find some poor slob entering the country with a few marijuana cigarettes or an illegal alien stashed in the cabin somewhere. But countless boats simply float right on down the lake past the inspectors without ever stopping. The British used this same waterway to carry out the invasion of Plattsburgh during the War of 1812 with a small armada built just south of St. Jean. After that, it was the preferred route of smugglers to avoid tariffs and taxes in both directions, from liquor coming south during prohibition to cigarettes and drugs that are still being smuggled in today."

"Why doesn't the customs service have boats to stop everybody entering the country on the lake?" Sophie asked.

"The customs service inspects boats at the checkpoints only. The Border Patrol is tasked with inspecting the boats on the lake once they pass the inspection stations, but they only have so many patrols. At night the customs check point is unmanned. So, for much of the day, the lake is unguarded."

"You mean to say, no one watches the lake for smuggling activity at night? I thought that, with the increased presence of homeland security, all the borders would be watched twenty-four hours a day." Sophie said.

"That's what they'd like everyone to think. And, yes, there are a few cameras set up here and there to watch for activity on the lake near the border, but remember, someone has to be continually watching those monitors. Under cover of darkness, especially during cloudy or inclement weather, it's not hard to sneak something through on the lake. But the main problem is, everything coming into the U.S. from Canada in a car, bus, truck or train, has to pass through a radiation portal that detects even the minutest particle of radiation. When it does, it sets off all kinds of alarms. But there are no such radiation portals on any of the waterways."

As Marc was talking, they entered Chambly on a street aptly named "Chemin des Patriotes" or Patriots Trail. Marc noticed there were several boathouses along the opposite side of the river but had no trouble identifying the one that was part of the residence at Galarneau 2302, thanks to its fieldstone and brown wooden trim.

Marc noted that this section of the river was only 50 yards wide and was completely frozen and snow covered. Through the diminishing daylight, they could also see a half-dozen men wearing heavy parkas with hoods pulled over their heads sitting on the ice, huddled with their backs against the chilly late afternoon breeze.

"What are those men doing?" Sophie asked.

"Ice fishing. They bore a hole in the ice and drop their lines in to catch fish."

"Oh yeah, I've seen people doing it on Lake Flower. Doesn't look like much fun though…I mean, sitting there all day in the wind and cold just to catch a fish."

"Look at the bright side. There are no mosquitoes or black flies and you can drink all the beer you can drag out there with you," Marc chuckled.

It also means the ice is thick enough to hold our weight.

"Guess it must be a man thing," Sophie said with resignation.

"If I could find us a cozy inn, would you be up to hanging out here for the evening?" Marc asked.

"Yeah, I'm OK with that. I'd just have to check in with Dad and Zoe."

Sophie hardly had the words out when the SUV rounded a bend in the road and Marc spotted a painted sign off to their left, half covered with snow, that read, 'Auberge Richelieu'.

"Voila," Marc said, pointing toward the inn's sign.

Marc could see that the Auberge was a large Quebec style farmhouse that had been converted to an inn years before. Its small parking area held a few cars, and it was no more than a quarter mile north of the boathouse.

"Let's hope that they have a vacancy," Marc said as he pulled the SUV into an open space.

They grabbed their overnight bags and started down the partially cleared sidewalk that led to the inn's front entrance.

Sophie noticed the inn's faded brick had weathered over the years, lending it an authentic rustic charm. Strategically placed floodlights caught wisps of blowing powder snow and, even with the setting sun, they highlighted the inn's snow-covered gables as well as its large wrap-around wooden porch.

A bell attached to the front door sounded as Marc and Sophie entered, and as they approached the makeshift check-in desk, the aged wood floor creaked with each step. The walls were covered with a light floral wallpaper that flowed up to the white plaster ceiling.

As Marc and Sophie were surveying their surroundings, they heard the creaking of footsteps from the direction of a door behind the guest counter. A rotund elderly woman wearing a wide smile and a plain house dress covered with a white apron appeared, and said, "Bonjour, ça va bien?"

Marc replied, "Bonjour, très bien, merci."

Sensing that the woman could not speak English, Marc continued in French, asking if there was a room available for the evening.

The proprietress' smile grew as she informed Marc that, because this was a slow time of the year for business, she had three rooms to choose from.

Marc asked for a room that overlooked the river, preferably, one that looked toward the south, the direction of the boathouse, but of course, he didn't mention this.

The proprietress responded "Bien sur, monsieur," and handed Marc a registration card.

As Marc began writing, he could detect the aroma of food being prepared nearby and asked the woman if supper would be available at the inn.

She gave Marc a surprised look, saying, "Mais oui, monsieur, and went on to explain that supper is available from 6:00 p.m.

Marc looked at Sophie, then confirmed they would be having supper, adding that they wanted to take a walk along the river first.

After completing the check-in form, they followed the proprietress up the squeaky stairs to the second floor, then down a narrow hallway to their room.

The spacious corner room had two windows overlooking the river. One looked directly out on the river and the other faced south in the direction of the boat house. Through the lace curtains, Marc could see the streetlights on the other side of the river.

The proprietress handed Marc the room key and asked if the room was satisfactory, to which he replied, "Oui, madame, très bien."

Marc and Sophie listened in silence as the innkeeper retreated down the stairs.

"Sophie, why don't you touch base with your dad. I'm going down to the SUV, get my parka and toolkit and check out that boathouse. I won't be long. I just need to take a quick look inside."

"No way, buster. We've come this far together. If you're going to the boathouse, I'm going too."

Marc could see there was no use arguing, but he felt a pang of guilt for allowing her get so involved in this affair.

"Fine, call your dad. I'm just going down to get a few things, I'll be right back." Marc said.

"You've got five minutes, then I'll come looking for you," Sophie said playfully, but with enough edge that Marc knew she was serious.

After being routed through the local Canadian cell tower, Sophie reached her dad at the motel. Through a static-filled connection, she advised him that she was fine and would return home the following afternoon. Zoe then came on the line.

"Hi, Mommy. When are you coming home?"

"Sometime tomorrow. How's my big girl?"

"Oh, fine," Zoe said, sounding disappointed. "Pop Pop made dinner tonight, and I helped."

"Well, that's good. I miss you sweetheart," Sophie said.

"I misth you too Mommy. Goodnight."

"Goodnight Zoe," Sophie said and closed her phone.

Soon after, Marc returned with his tool kit, along with a parka for himself and heavy coat for Sophie. He also gave Sophie a pair of gaiters he had kept in the SUV. He knew her ankle high boots were fine for walking in a few inches of snow, but she would need the gaiters to keep the snow from working into her boots.

"Time to suit up," Marc announced.

Darkness had completely settled in by the time they left the inn. Their footsteps echoed in the stillness of the evening air as they crossed the parking lot and stepped onto the frozen river. They walked to the center of the river and turned toward the boathouse.

Lights from the homes that lined both sides of the river could be seen flickering through the trees. A cold blue, three-quarter moon was rising from the northeast and with the cloudless night, illuminated the expanse of the snow-covered river, giving it an appearance of a long, empty highway ahead of them.

After a ten minute trudge through the knee deep snow, they came across the path used by the ice fishermen who had since left for the warmth of their homes. Marc kept to this well trodden path in an attempt to disguise their own footprints that could trace them back to the inn. Soon, they were only a hundred yards from the boathouse, which appeared completely dark, but lights inside the main house, some distance beyond, were clearly visible.

Marc stopped as they were about even with the boathouse. The main house was now hidden from view by the boathouse and a stand of conifers in between. Aided by the moonlight reflecting off the snow, Marc could see there were a set of two sliding doors, each about four feet wide, their bottoms extending below the level of the snow on the river. They quietly approached the boathouse.

"I hope that those doors aren't frozen into the river," Marc said, as he began digging through the snow with his gloved hands in an attempt to reach the bottom of the doors. Sophie saw what Marc was up to and jumped in to help. It took the pair about five minutes of digging to reach the underside of the doors. A few more minutes of pawing through the powdery snow and they found that there was about a foot and a half space between the bottom of the boat doors and the frozen river below.

Just enough room to slide under doors and into the boathouse.

Marc grabbed his tool bag, and looping the handle around his foot, he said, "I'll pull myself in first. When I get through, follow me under the door."

Marc lay on his back, grabbed the bottom of the door and pulled himself through.

Once inside, he whispered, "OK, Sophie, your turn."

She quickly followed.

Inside the boathouse, it was pitch black. Marc felt around and found a large round pole and a ledge to his right.

Must be one of the side piers supporting the boathouse.

He looked toward the far end of the boathouse for any windows that might be in view of the main residence. With the moon's glow, he could barely make out the faint outline of two small quarter round windows near the top of the far wall. To lessen the reflection of his flashlight, Marc snapped on the red filter lens he'd kept in his tool bag.

"We'll use the light sparingly. Can't take the chance of alerting anyone of our presence," Marc whispered.

When he flicked the light on, both were surprised to see they were standing directly beneath a fairly large boat that had been hoisted up, hanging in place by a pair of wide boat straps.

Using the cross members that supported the piers, Marc climbed up onto the wooden floor of the boathouse with Sophie following his lead, bringing them level with the top of the boat. Using the flashlight's beam, Marc was amazed to discover that they were standing next to a large cigarette racing boat, about forty feet in length.

"This baby's built for speed. I've seen boats like this reach speeds of more than hundred miles per hour," Marc whispered.

The filtered lens showed the boat's black hull was devoid of registration numbers. A black canvas canopy covered the cockpit portion of the boat.

Marc scanned the expanse of the boathouse and saw that other than the boat, the section they were in appeared completely empty.

Sophie ran her bare hand along the side of the boat's hull, then

131

rubbed her thumb and fingertips together.

"Strange," she said in a whisper.

The high ceiling appeared open except for a motorized pulley lift mechanism attached to the heavy steel I-beam roof rafter. Marc followed the pulley cables with his flashlight and saw they were connected to the straps that held the boat out of the water. Toward the north side of the boathouse they could see a door that appeared to lead to a another room that had been partitioned off.

Marc carefully moved toward the door and held his breath as he slowly turned the door knob. It creaked open and, to his relief, no alarm bells, buzzers or lights went off, at least not that they were aware of. A quick peek inside revealed no windows, so he felt more at ease using his flashlight. Several rows of empty, heavy metal shelves lined the exterior wall. The remnants of packing crates, a few steel frame pieces and a pile of dark gray tarps, neatly stacked on the floor at the end of the room, were all they saw.

Marc lifted a corner of one of the tarps at the top of the pile. Sophie pointed to a corner of the tarp.

"What does that say?"

Using the flashlight they could barely make out the faint black letters, "Trans Arabian Logging Ltd." stenciled on the corner of the gray tarp.

Sophie whispered the name stenciled on the tarp as if reconfirming what she saw.

"What the hell?" Marc said, remembering the scrap of similar material bearing the initials "TA" that he had found in the back of Al-Zeid's SUV.

"What's the matter, Marc?"

"Probably nothing," he said, unconvincingly. Then added, "Nothing much else to see in here, let's go."

Leaving the store room, the two made their way back to where the boat hung on its hoist. Again, pointing his flashlight beam at the straps holding the boat, Marc noticed a second pulley mechanism suspended from the building's metal girder. This second crane appeared to run off the same motor that powered the boat hoist, but this one had a thick metal cable coiled around a winch assembly at one end. Following with his flashlight, he saw the opposite end of the cable was attached to an ominous metal hook dangling over the boat's forward deck.

"Whatever they're loading must be pretty heavy," Marc said.

Sophie, who still seemed distracted, stared up at the crane assembly and the heavy steel hook suspended above like a hangman's noose, as it swung lazily in a current of cold air. Silent since observing the stenciled tarps, she finally said, "Marc, I think we'd better leave. There's nothing else to see and there's no sense hanging around here and taking the risk of being caught inside this place."

"Right, I just need to look inside the boat."

Not waiting for Sophie to respond, Marc brought a stool he found leaning against the storage room partition and sat it next to the boat. As he climbed on the stool, he found it brought him chest high with the boat's cockpit. He loosened the snaps that secured the canvas covering, raising it so he could peer inside with his flashlight. The cockpit, protected by its heavy-duty windshield was fitted with three cushioned running chairs, two steering wheels and what appeared to be a state-of-the-art speed control mechanism. The dashboard, although unlit, looked more like the cockpit of a fighter jet with a myriad of switches and controls, as well as screens that apparently provided information about engine performance, and water depth, along with a separate screen that looked to be a GPS mapping system. But what intrigued Marc most of all was a red button on the throttle lever with the letters "H-U-D".

"Why would a boater on the Richelieu River need a 'Heads Up Display' function?" Marc muttered.

A small aluminum case was tucked between the hull and the driver's seat, apparently empty, but with an inscription on its side, 'Night Owl. See them before they see you.'

As he began re-securing the canvas enclosure, Marc spotted a folded map tucked in a pocket under the dash. Removing the map, he glanced at the cover, 'Le basin de Champlain la Carte Nautique' printed in French, which Marc translated, 'Champlain Basin Nautical Map'.

Marc stuffed the map in his coat pocket and continued to secure the canvas covering to the boat. Feeling a tap on his shoulder, he turned to find Sophie pointing toward the bow, "Any idea what that is?" She asked.

Marc directed his beam along the boat's extended prow and, for the first time, noticed a latching mechanism about midway between the cockpit and tip of the bow. Using the light's beam, they could just make out the faint outline of a rectangular hatch opening, about six foot long and four feet wide.

"Why would a speed boat have a cargo hold?" Marc whispered.

"Marc, please, can we go now?" Sophie pleaded.

"OK. Looks like we've seen about all there is to see."

After replacing the stool, they climbed down the side of the pier to the ice below and slid out underneath the boat house doors the way they came in. Before leaving, they refilled the void they had made earlier under the doors by brushing back the snow they had removed.

Keeping to the path made by the ice fishermen, the two made their way back up the river. To reduce the chance of someone tracing their footprints, they continued a short distance past the inn, then, followed another path leading to shore. Once on shore, they returned to the inn's parking lot via the street that had been scraped bare of snow. By then, the temperature had dropped another ten degrees and an icy breeze was picking up from the south.

It was after seven o'clock when they arrived back at the inn. They peeled off their heavy coats and Sophie removed her gaiters. Marc stowed the tool kit and heavy clothing in his SUV. Before going inside, he packed snow around his New York State license plate in an attempt to blend in with the Quebec plates of the other vehicles in the lot.

Once inside, they welcomed the warmth of the inn and were again met by the proprietress who was passing by the front desk with a armful of folded towels. Smiling at Marc, she asked in French, "Did you have a pleasant walk, monsieur?"

"Oui. Merci, Madame." Marc replied, and told her the walk in the cold night air had given them a good appetite and they were ready for dinner.

After setting the towels on the check-in counter, she led Marc and Sophie to a dining room table not far from the large corner fireplace, that was emitting waves of soft heat. Through the window next to their table, Marc could make out the frozen river and the row of houses on the other side. Above the village, the soft glow of the Montreal city lights some fifteen miles to the west reflected off a bank of low lying clouds.

After settling in their chairs, neither said anything for a few moments. Marc could see that Sophie's cheeks were still flushed with exertion, but her eyes seemed clouded with uncertainty.

134

Finally, Marc broke the silence, "I'm sorry if I made you uncomfortable back there, Sophie, but I felt we had to try to gather as much information as we could. I've probably said this before, but, it's been my experience that if you don't take advantage of an opportunity when it's presented to you, chances are there will never be a second."

Sophie, who still seemed distracted, glanced at Marc and rising from her chair said, "I need to go to the room a moment to freshen up. When the waiter comes, could you please order me a glass of white wine?"

Caught off guard, he handed Sophie the room key and watched as she carefully made her way around the other tables back toward the entrance to the connecting hallway, then turned to go up the stairs.

I wonder what's got her so anxious.

When Sophie returned a few minutes later, a bottle of Quebec Provencal Sauvignon Blanc wine was chilling in an ice bucket on a stand next to their table.

As she seated herself, the waiter, appeared, as if on cue, and poured a dollop of wine the into Marc's glass, and waited for his approval. Marc signaled to continue pouring.

After the waiter left, Marc said, "Hope you don't mind, but I've already taken the liberty of ordering dinner."

"Fine," she replied, then, after taking a sip of the wine and examining the label, her otherwise cloudy mood seemed to soften. "I've never heard of a Quebec wine. This is actually quite good."

Before Marc could comment, the waiter returned with their salads and producing a pepper grinder the length of a Louisville slugger from under his arm, proceeded to crank off the desired amount on each salad plate before retreating back toward the kitchen.

As the two began eating in silence, Sophie said, "Marc, I'm a bit concerned over something we saw back there in the boathouse."

"Yeah, me too. Why would anyone have a boat that big, outfitted with all that gear unless they were up to something?"

"That's part of it," She replied, "Do you remember that stack of canvas tarps in the room next to the boat?"

"Yeah, the tarps. They had the name of a company on them, Trans Arabian Logging, or something."

"Trans Arabian Logging Ltd.," Sophie said in an assured tone.

"Yeah, what's up with that? Kind of weird don't you think? An Arabian logging business?"

"No Marc. I don't think…"

Before Sophie could finish her thought, Marc continued, "I suspect that boat is used for smuggling. Sort of reminds me of the speed boats they use over by the Indian reservation along the St. Lawrence River for smuggling drugs and cigarettes, but this one is even bigger."

"Marc, I…" Sophie began, but Marc again interrupted.

"Remember that map I found in the boat? I had a chance to look at it while I was stowing the gear into the SUV. It's a nautical map of Lake Champlain and its tributaries covering the continuous waterway from the St. Lawrence down through the Richelieu River and Lake Champlain all the way to the Hudson River. It shows the water depth all along the lake, locations of the maritime buoys, bridges, locks, the usual nautical stuff. Funny thing, I also saw that someone has inked in the location of the house in Willsboro including the water depth just off shore, and…"

Sophie placed her glass on the table and held up an index finger indicating she wanted to make a point, "Marc, that's interesting, but if you would just let me finish."

Marc stopped in mid-sentence, "What?"

"I agree with you that these people are smuggling something, but I doubt its drugs, or cigarettes."

"What do you mean?"

Sophie took a breath. "Trans Arabian Logging Ltd. hasn't anything to do with trees."

"OK, what then?"

"I believe the name refers to a business involved in geological logging."

Marc sipped his wine. "I'll bite, what the hell is geological logging."

"It's kind of complicated, but put simply, it's a process of drilling into the earth to sample rocks for analysis."

"So, why would a smuggling operation be interested in rock samples?" Marc asked.

Before Sophie could answer the waiter returned with their entrees, moved their unfinished salad plates off to one side and set the heaping dishes of steaming food in front of them. After the waiter repeated the pepper mill ritual and went on to another table, Sophie cut off a small bite of pork, looked over at Marc and said in a lowered voice. "Not all geological logging is the same. Some companies use long bores to drill holes hundreds of feet into the earth, then retrieve the bore samples and examine them, usually to determine if there are minerals or oil in the area. But, some other companies specialize in the search for desired minerals using a method called 'nuclear logging'."

"Nuclear logging? You mean actually looking for radioactive material by drilling holes in the ground?"

"No, silly," Sophie said, rolling her eyes in exasperation. "Nuclear logging refers to a method of searching for the existence of minerals, usually hydrocarbons, or oil deposits deep underground by placing a known quantity of a nuclear material, usually cesium 137 or iridium 192, into a deep bore hole, often an existing oil well. From what I remember, measurements of the returning radiation are analyzed to determine if oil is present and estimate the quantity of the oil deposit. Obviously, it's all kind of technical and I'm not familiar with the specifics. I just know that, when I was working for customs we had to monitor for this kind of activity."

"Iridium and what was that other one, cesium? Never heard of them," Marc said.

"Well, believe me, they're both highly radioactive materials and most definitely something you don't want to be around unless you're well protected."

"How would something like that be transported?" Marc asked.

"Usually radioactive material has to be encapsulated in a lead-lined container often referred to as a 'pig'. The higher the level of radiation, the thicker and heavier the 'pig'."

Marc paused as he finished chewing his last bite, "That could explain the heavy duty shelving back at the boathouse."

"Yes, and the hoist with the thick wire cable used to raise and lower objects into that boat, like heavy lead-lined containers. Now do you see why I was so concerned back there? The way I see it, Al-Zeid could have contracted radiation poisoning from some of this smuggled material."

Again, Marc recalled the scrap of material he'd found in Al-Zeid's SUV with the letters "TA" on it.

"But where did these guys get this stuff and just who is Trans Arabian Logging?"

"Trans Arabian Logging? Who knows? My guess is that it is, or was, a legitimate business using nuclear material for this kind of oil

137

exploration as it has been done for years. The material has served its purpose but apparently was never properly documented or disposed of. This used to happen a lot, especially in third world countries and particularly after the break-up of the old Soviet Union. Unfortunately, there are still tons of this stuff floating around out there. And with the advent of terrorism, it's on the black market and available to the highest bidder."

"Shit!" Marc said, a little louder than he meant too.

"Shush, not so loud," Sophie said as she glanced around at the other diners who appeared to be interested in their own conversations.

"So do you think you have enough to turn this over to the police now?" she continued in a lowered whisper.

Marc, lost in thought, picked at his food.

I suppose we could just leave in the morning and report what we've found to Jerry Garrant and let him decide how to best handle this. Of course, he'll think I'm crazy.

After a long silence, Marc said, "Did I mention that the man who bought the house in Willsboro lives in Montreal? I have his home address in my notes. I wonder what he knows about his tenants."

"What are you thinking?" Sophie asked.

"Just that before we head back to the states, we could call on him and see what he has to say."

Sophie finished another bite. "OK, but do you think you could get me home before Zoe finishes school tomorrow?"

"It's settled then. Tomorrow we pay a visit to Mr. Remillard, but tonight, let's just enjoy the rest of the evening. I'll have you back in Saranac Lake before school's out. I promise."

"Be careful what you promise, I might hold you to it," Sophie said with a mischievous smile.

They continued the dinner with light conversation. After a serving of cream-filled profiteroles, they spent the rest of the evening enjoying the ambiance of the inn. A second bottle of wine was ordered which was enjoyed in the comfort of their room.

Sleep overtook both of them quickly, due to the effects of the meal, the wine, and the trek through the snow to the boat house. Sophie awoke several times during the night however, as she thought about what she had seen in the boathouse, the mysterious-looking boat and the ominous perils that may lay ahead.

138

DAY FIVE

The following morning, Marc and Sophie were awake by 6:30, and after showering, made their way to the dining room for breakfast. Following a hearty meal of omelets, sausages, beans and liver pate (a breakfast staple the Quebecois refer to as 'creton'), they checked out of the inn and left for the city of Laval, just north of Montreal.

Using the address provided by the Willsboro town clerk and his GPS, Marc located the residence of Serge Remillard located in an upscale Quebecois neighborhood.

The house appeared to be a typical French style city residence, two-story, red brick with a sloping slate roof dating from the turn of the nineteenth century.

Marc parked on the opposite side of the street. "Sophie, stay here while I see if anyone's home. Keep your eyes open for anything suspicious."

"Suspicious? Like what would be suspicious?"

"You'll know when you see it," was Marc's pat answer as he made his way toward the front entrance of the house.

Marc used the ornate 'fleur-de-lis' shaped door knocker to announce his presence and, after a second series of raps on the immense wooden portal, the lady of the maison, already well dressed and coiffed, appeared through one of the door's side lights.

She opened the door just enough to be heard as she asked Marc in French, "May I help you?"

"Oui, Madame." Please pardon my intrusion, but is Monsieur Remillard about this morning?" He asked in French.

Madame looked concerned at the inquiry.

"May I ask why you wish to speak with my husband?"

"I was hoping to inquire about the lakefront property that Monsieur Remillard owns in Willsboro, New York. I understand it may be for rent."

The woman's expression changed from concerned annoyance to a pleasant smile, and, satisfied that Marc did not appear to be a mugger or worse, a door-to-door salesman, she opened the door a little wider.

"I'm sorry, but Monsieur Remillard is away on business and I'm not sure exactly when to expect him."

Marc explained that he was in Montreal for the day on another

139

matter and thought he would stop by on the off chance that Monsieur Remillard might be available. Seeing the woman relaxing, he added that he might try another time when it would be more convenient, unless there was a phone number or a work address where her husband could be contacted.

Madame Remillard paused, "Momente, s'il vous plait." She retreated from the door, leaving it partly open with Marc standing in the portico. Marc glanced back at the SUV with Sophie watching and shrugged his shoulders.

Shortly, she returned and handed Marc a business card explaining that he could try to contact Monsieur Remillard at one of the numbers on the card. However, she added that he was out of the country for a few days and was not expected to return until the following Monday.

Marc accepted the card, thanking Madame for her patience, bid her "bonjour" and rejoined Sophie in the SUV. After securing his seat belt, Marc studied the card.

Serge Remillard
Logistics Coordinator
"Majestic Freight Systems Ltd."
Montreal Office
1225 Avenue Pierre Dupuy, Montreal PQ, Canada
514-236-7290

Pointing to the card, Marc said, "I think that address is near the city's south shore. Madame Remillard told me her husband is out of town and won't be back until Monday, but she sounded unsure. I don't think it would hurt to give him a try at his office."

"Marc, don't forget your promise. Saranac Lake before school gets out."

"Don't worry. We'll make it quick, my dear." Marc said teasingly.

He turned the SUV back toward Autoroute 15, and maneuvered through the city to the south side of town known as Ville Marie. As they approached the waterfront, they could see the long shipping piers jutting out into the partially frozen St. Lawrence River. Probably because of the ice in the river, there were only two small freighters tied up with a few longshoremen working near the ships. Marc and Sophie looked for the address listed on the business card and found it situated between two abandoned warehouses. Remillard's office building appeared to have been recently refurbished.

"Is this the right address?" Sophie asked.

"There's only one way to find out for sure," Marc replied.

He parked on the street in front of one of the abandoned structures, and turned toward Sophie, "This could be tricky. Sure you want to come along?"

"Try to stop me," she said and the two headed for the office building about a block away.

When they arrived inside the building's street entrance, an office directory opposite the elevator indicated that Majestic Freight Systems Ltd. was located on the seventh floor. The ride was smooth and on the seventh floor, the elevator opened onto a large windowed foyer with a view of the St. Lawrence River. From this vantage point they looked north toward the city of Montreal with the Victoria Bridge in the foreground and the Jacques Cartier Bridge in the distance.

Surprisingly the foyer contained no furniture or receptionist, simply a locked door next to a wall phone, with another directory listing various Majestic Freight Systems Ltd. personnel and an extension number for each. Marc eyed the two security camera domes in the ceiling, one by the elevator and another over the office door. He tried the door, confirming it was locked, then dialed the extension number for Serge Remillard. After a few rings, a recorded message clicked on—a man with a pronounced nasally voice identified himself as Serge Remillard, and in French, then in English, apologized for not personally taking the call, but said that if the caller would leave a contact number, he would reply at his earliest convenience, "Yeah, right," Marc whispered.

At the tone, Marc left a short message indicating that Madame Remillard had given him the office address and that he wanted to speak with him regarding the rental property in Willsboro. After waiting a few minutes on the oft chance that someone might venture outside the locked offices, Marc decided it was time to leave. Rather than take the elevator back down, however, he told Sophie that they would use the stairs. The pair descended to the sixth floor and tried the door that presumably led to another foyer. It was locked, as were the remaining stairwell doors, except, the ground floor door that took them back to the original entrance room and the building's office directory.

A security measure, perhaps?

Giving the directory another scan, Sophie exclaimed, "Oh my, why didn't I see this before?"

"What's that?"

"Here's a listing for 'The McKenzie Group Ltd'. That's the name of the company that owns the Saranac Mountain Inn and Resort."

"You think it could be one and the same?"

"I don't know. Like you say, there's one way to find out. It's on the fourth floor."

They took the elevator back up to the fourth floor, and when the elevator door opened, found a view similar to the one they had seen on the seventh floor. And like the seventh floor, there was a directory of the different offices on the floor under the banner "The McKenzie Group Ltd." with a phone extension listed for each. The only difference was a huge map of North America, Europe and Asia adorning the wall next to the office directory. The location of each property owned and managed by the McKenzie Group was listed on the map and marked with a gold star, followed by the name and address for each one.

Sophie used her index finger to trace the locations of the properties. Sure enough, the Saranac Mountain Inn and Resort in upstate New York was indicated as well as other properties including those in Thunder Bay, Ontario; Banff, Alberta; Vancouver Island, British Columbia; Hot Springs, Arizona; and Napa Valley, California. There were two in Asia; one in China; another in South Korea, and another in Europe near Innsbruck, Austria. The Beijing and the Innsbruck properties included a notation "Future Development" after their star.

Sophie said, "I was aware that McKenzie owned other inns in Canada and the U.S., but this is the first I've heard that the company had interests in Europe and Asia."

Marc said teasingly, "His extension number is right there, pointing to his name at the top of the listing. Maybe you should just buzz him and ask him about it."

"I don't think so. I'm sure we would only get another recorded message. Besides, this place is starting to give me the creeps. Let's get out of here."

They took the elevator back to the ground floor and as they made their way to the SUV, Marc said, "I didn't want to say anything back in the office building because I didn't know who could be listening, but don't you find it kind of ironic that of all the office buildings in Montreal, this one just happens to house the head offices of the Saranac Mountain Inn and Resort and the Majestic Freight Systems, which is headed by the man who owns the house in Willsboro?"

"Yeah, I was thinking the same thing. That's what was giving me the creeps."

"It's getting late. If we're gonna get to Saranac Lake before Zoe gets home from school, we'd better get going."

Marc headed the Explorer across the Pont Victoria, then south on Autoroute 15 toward the U.S. border. The half-hour ride was fairly mundane with its flat landscape and occasional "tourist trap" stores selling last minute souvenirs and fireworks to the returning American visitors.

As they approached the border, Marc pulled into the Canadian duty free shop.

"What are you stopping here for? Duty free cigarettes?" Sophie teased.

"No, but there's something else I'd like to pick up. Don't worry, I'll only be a sec."

A few minutes later he returned, carrying a plastic bag with the duty free shop logo emblazoned on the outside.

"I thought I'd pick up something for Zoe. It's just a little souvenir from Canada."

Sophie peered inside the bag and saw Marc had bought a stuffed bear wearing an RCMP hat.

Sophie said, "Oh Marc, that's so sweet of you. You really shouldn't have."

Crossing the border was uneventful, with Marc making sure to claim the stuffed bear. Traveling south on the Interstate, Marc took Route 3 toward Bloomingdale. The crisp clear day allowed Marc and Sophie to see the western slopes of Whiteface Mountain.

Another twenty minutes and they arrived at the Miss Saranac Motel a few minutes before 2 p.m.

Marc turned to Sophie and said, "There you are, back home all safe and sound and on time, as promised."

Sophie smiled, then hesitated, somewhat reluctant to leave Marc's SUV, not quite ready for this trip to end.

Marc sensed her anxiety, "Look Sophie, I can't thank you enough for all your help. You're a brave girl, but I especially want to thank

143

you for your company. It's been fun. Right now, though, I have a lot to discuss with Jerry Garrant. Please tell Zoe I said "Hi" and I hope she likes her Canadian bear."

"I'm sure she will. Thanks for letting me tag along and for the guided tour of Montreal. Let's do this again, maybe with a little less stress next time."

"Sounds like a date." Marc said as he leaned over to give Sophie a peck on the cheek.

Sophie turned to Marc and kissed him on the lips, holding his face in her hands. As she slid toward the passenger door, she looked back at him. "You have my number. Call anytime."

Marc pulled out of the parking lot, turned left, and, with a quick wave, headed toward Lake Placid.

It was still early enough to try to catch Jerry Garrant. A call to Garrant's cell number was answered by voice mail and, without leaving a message, Marc stopped at the barracks to see if he was in. No sign of Garrant's car in its usual spot. The desk trooper advised Marc that Jerry was out on a camp burglary investigation in the Star Lake area and was not expected back until the next day.

Marc asked the trooper to leave Jerry a message that he had some information regarding the Al-Zeid investigation.

Leaving the trooper barracks, Marc continued east toward Lake Placid. Not quite sure what to do next, he decided to take the Military Turnpike Road that skirts around the southern edge of the village and connects with Route 73, toward the Saranac Inn.

Still about two hours of daylight, so while I'm here, why not give the area another quick look?

As Marc drove past the village reservoir road, he noted a set of fresh tire tracks leading in from the main road.

Wonder who would be driving to the reservoir now?

The tire tracks looked to have been made by a fairly large truck or a van, Marc assumed.

Could be just a water department truck, I suppose, but why would they be turning in from the south, Lake Placid is just north.

As Marc continued on, he passed the entrance to the Craig Wood Golf Course. The diminishing daylight cast an orange glint on the pine trees drooping with a heavy layer of snow. A few miles further, the entrance to the Mount Van Hoevenberg bobsled run veered off to Marc's right and he could see cars leaving the sports complex, some with cross country skis tied to their tops. There were still a few vehicles left in the parking lot, mostly SUVs, perfect in this kind of terrain with their four wheel drive capability. Marc reflected again on how perfect this area was suited for winter sports. Continuing toward Keene, he thought about something else he'd just seen. He hadn't given it much thought, thinking only that it looked out of place. But a black Mercedes had been parked alone off to one side of the parking lot he'd passed. He drove on for another mile before finding a place to turn around, then headed back toward the parking lot.

When he arrived back at Mount Van Hoevenberg, he pulled in and drove past the black Mercedes as though he was headed for the Olympic bobsled run beyond. He eyed the license plate number. Sure enough, there it was—Quebec RGC-9921, the same one he had tailed from Willsboro to Chambly, then seen again yesterday parked behind Global Rug Importers. The tinted windows prevented him from seeing who or how many people were inside, but the exhaust coming from the tail pipe indicated the car was running.

"What the fuck would they be doing here?" Marc muttered out loud.

He continued further into the lot until he was around the corner and out of sight of the Mercedes, then parked the SUV and thought about his next move.

What could the Mercedes be doing here? Could it have anything to do with those fresh tire tracks back on the village reservoir road?

As he sat with his engine running considering his options, he spotted Larry Corbet, the ski guide, walking through the lot toward his red Jeep Cherokee. Marc suddenly had an idea.

"Hey, wait up Larry!" Marc called out and jogged over to where Corbet had parked his Jeep.

Corbet turned and saw Marc approaching.

"Oh, hi there, Mr. Rose?"

"Yeah, hi Larry, I'm Marc LaRose. We talked a couple of days ago." Marc said, extending his hand.

"Yeah, I remember. I can't think of anything else to tell you about that incident we were talking about, though," Corbet said as the two shook hands.

"That's OK. Look, I'm in kind of a tight spot and wondered if you could help me out."

"Sure. What'd you do, run out of gas or something?"

145

"No, nothing like that," Marc said. I think something's going on down by the reservoir and there's a black Mercedes in the parking lot down by the main road that maybe involved. I'm afraid if they see me hanging around, they might get suspicious and I'll blow what little cover I have."

"Yeah, so, how can I help? I ain't no investigator you know," Corbet said, a bit apprehensive.

"Do you have your cross country skis with you?"

"Well sure. I got about three or four pairs in the back of my Jeep. I always keep a couple of extra sets on hand, you never know when you might need' em."

"Larry, this is what I'd like to do."

Marc explained that he wanted Larry to accompany him to the Jack Rabbit Trail where it crosses the Reservoir Road. Marc told him about the set of suspicious tire tracks that he had observed leading in toward the reservoir.

"Look Larry, I'm not going to mess with you. This could be dangerous if these guys are up to no good. If you don't want to do this, I'll understand. It's just that I don't have many options right now."

"Those tire tracks you saw may just be a village water department truck checking on things. Although, I gotta say, they usually don't go up there much in the winter, especially this time of day."

Marc agreed, "Yeah, that, and why would a truck enter the reservoir road from the south, from Keene, rather than Lake Placid?"

"Good point," Larry said as he glanced at his wristwatch. "Look, it should only take an hour for us to get up there, but there's not much day light left, so if we're going to do it, we'd better get going. You got a set of skis?"

"Sure do." Marc said. "Let's get started."

As Larry opened the Jeep's hatch and began hauling out his cross-country skiing equipment, Marc returned to the Explorer and retrieved his H&K from under the front seat and clipped it to his belt. He stepped into his ski boots, adjusted the bindings, tugged on his ski jacket, pulled on his knitted cap and grabbed his ski poles. Within three minutes, the two men were heading toward the Jack Rabbit Ski Trail.

Larry led the way, taking Marc around the rear of the parking lot, keeping out of sight of whoever might be watching from inside the

146

Mercedes. Through a break in the trees, Marc caught a glimpse of the car, still parked where he had last observed it, with a steady plume of white smoke drifting up from the exhaust.

After crossing to the north side of Route 73, Larry picked up the pace, following the trail where it led uphill in the direction of the golf course.

"It's about four miles to the golf course, then two more to the reservoir." Corbet called back as they started the uphill climb.

Despite the fact that it had been more than ten years since Corbet won the bronze Olympic Medal in Salt Lake, it was obvious he was still in good physical shape. Marc, no stranger to cross country skiing himself, envied Corbet's natural ability as he expertly propelled himself forward on one ski while pushing with opposite pole, then with a minimum of wasted effort that only comes with years of experience, repeat the same powerful stroke with the opposite ski.

"You OK, Marc?" Larry called back.

"I'm fine for now. Just don't get too far ahead of me."

The trail was easy to follow in the waning sunlight with its grey ribbon of snow cutting though the thick forest on either side. Marc drew on all his strength and stamina to keep up with Corbet, while making a silent pledge that in the future he would try harder to stay in shape.

No more deep-fried jelly-filled crullers covered with powdered sugar for me.

The trail was not a straight up or down run, but cut through a stretch of rolling terrain known as the McKenzie Wilderness. After ascending one knoll, they experienced a brief respite coasting down the other side, only to be confronted with the upward push of another climb, all the while ascending generally upward toward the Lake Placid reservoir.

As Marc continued his labored efforts to keep pace, he thought he heard an eerie, high-pitched sound. First dismissing the noise as a ringing in his ears possibly due to his exertion, he soon realized the noise seemed to build in intensity.

Marc got Corbet's attention by tapping him on the leg with one of his poles.

When Corbet turned, Marc put a finger to his lips and the two slid to a stop, standing motionless in the middle of the trail. They had met no one since leaving the trailhead at Mount Van Hoevenberg. Marc removed his knit cap to help him hear more clearly.

147

Dead silence, save for the whisper of wind hissing through the tree tops.

"Thought I heard something," Marc said.

"Probably just the wind. Happens a lot at these higher altitudes, especially if you're out of shape," Corbet joked with a wry smile.

Just as the pair turned to continue their trek, however, the sound returned, and this time they both heard it. Although it was still faint, it had a piercing high pitch, not unlike a dentist's drill.

Corbet whispered, "Whoa, that's definitely not the wind." The smile left his face.

Suddenly, a heavy movement and the sound of snapping branches coming from the right side of the trail startled the men. Marc instinctively pulled his H&K from under his jacket and took dead aim at the fast-moving mass emerging from the wall of trees and onto the trail twenty yards ahead.

Corbet quickly turned to Marc and motioned to him to put the gun down. "Deer," he whispered.

A whitetail deer, sensing a potential threat, froze in the middle of the trail. The buck, with its massive rack of horns, stood perfectly still, instantly sizing up these two invaders to his domain. Then, in the next breath, it bounded off to the left, and was quickly swallowed up in the dark shadows of the Adirondack forest.

Marc slowly returned the pistol to his waistband. He and Larry stood silently, listening to the fading sounds of the buck as it moved away through the brush. With nothing left but the breeze sighing above them, they continued their push towards the Reservoir Road.

Another mile and the pair broke out of the forest onto the wide expanse of the golf course, an area that Marc recognized as the tricky par four third hole.

How many of my golf balls are still hidden somewhere under all this snow?

They followed the trail as it turned into the woods for another arduous two miles before they arrived at the spot where the trail crossed Reservoir Road.

Larry turned to Marc and, with his ski pole, pointed off to his right.

"Reservoir's this way, not far," he said and pushed off, continuing to lead the way on the snow covered road.

As they headed toward the reservoir, Marc could feel through his skis the staccato ripples of what he suspected to be caterpillar-like tracks pressed into the snow. The piercing high-pitched sound, so evident before, had long been absent and the tread marks, packed down hard onto the road made a soft puttering sound as their skis slid over them.

"Stay with these tread marks, Larry. I want to find where they lead."

Aided by the half light of the rising moon, Larry and Marc could see that, just before the gate, the caterpillar tracks veered off to the left, through a clearing that circled around toward the back side of the reservoir. They followed the tread marks, keeping the reservoir to their right and soon, Marc could make out the dark face of a sheer rock wall looming ahead. The moonlight reflected off patches of snow caught on a few of the rock's outcroppings and along its top. The two followed the tracks for another hundred yards until they stopped abruptly at the base of the rock wall. Marc flashed his light around the area where the tracks ended, but all they found were a few limbs and branches of dead trees that lay atop rubble that Marc assumed had slid down the sheer rock face.

"I suppose we could chase after..." Before Larry could finish his thought, they both heard the sound of a diesel truck engine starting up somewhere from the direction of the main road.

The two stood motionless and listened as the diesel engine revved up, then, as the pitch of the engine changed with the driver going through its gears. As the engine continued to accelerate, the sound of its motor faded as it slowly headed away from them, until eventually, the only noise to be heard was the familiar sighing of the breeze buffeting the thick coniferous forest. Marc had a sinking feeling as he glanced back at the pile of limbs and rocks.

"Shit. Looks like we missed them, whoever they were," Marc said.

Just then, however, something else caught Marc's attention. He again aimed his flashlight at the base of the rock wall.

"Larry, you notice anything peculiar about those tree limbs?"

Larry looked in the direction where Marc's light was bouncing off the pile of limbs at the bottom of the rock face.

"Hmm, I see what you mean. No snow. Looks like maybe someone was in a hurry and left them pretty much uncovered. Wonder what that's about?"

"I'm not sure, but I'd say those limbs were just recently piled

149

there, like someone's trying to hide something." Marc said, moving the flashlight's beam around the heap of branches.

Corbet looked at the pile, then back to Marc, deeply exhaled and said, "I suppose you're suggesting that we gotta dig through those limbs and find it."

Without answering, Marc placed his flashlight on a fallen log, aimed the beam at the pile and began pulling the limbs off the top. Soon, Larry jumped in, and the two began pushing and rolling away the heavy rocks underneath.

After ten minutes of picking, throwing, and rolling the rocks away, Corbet stopped, stood back a moment. He pointed to a darker shadow that was about level with the top of the rock fill they were removing. "What do you think that is?" he asked.

"Don't know, but the area around it feels pretty warm," Marc said, touching the wall with an ungloved hand.

Without answering, both men continued to pull more rocks away from the area around the shadow, feeling the warmth intensify as they did so.

Marc's flashlight batteries were running low, but in its weakening beam, he could see a round object, like a plug, about six inches in diameter that looked as though it had been pounded into the face of the rock wall.

Marc brought his light in closer where they could see that the plug appeared to be made of a thick, soft metal. The edges had been rounded a bit from the pounding it took to get it seated into the rock face.

"Probably made out of lead. You ever see anything like this around here before Larry?"

"Hell no, you kidding, who would want to plug up a rock?"

Marc attempted to turn the plug with his gloved hands, but to no avail.

"That thing's not coming out without the proper tools," Larry said.

"Yeah, I guess you're right. Just as well, no telling what's behind that thing." Marc said, thinking about his next move.

"You know, hate to say this, but I think we should leave this place as we found it, in case whoever put this in there should happen to return." Marc said.

"You mean, put all this shit back?" Corbet asked pointing at the pile of rocks and limbs that they had just removed, rolling his eyes in exasperation.

Marc turned the flashlight with its weakening beam back on the log pile.

"Well, I suppose we'd better get to it then," Larry said.

After replacing the rocks and limbs, Larry used some tree branches to brush out their footprints as best he could.

After attaching their skis, the pair headed back out the way they came in, and to Marc's relief, the mostly downhill return trip to the Mount Van Hoevenberg parking lot was much less grueling.

It was almost eight o'clock by the time they arrived there, and as Marc expected, the black Mercedes was nowhere in sight.

After removing his cross-country gear, Marc turned toward Corbet.

"So, what do I owe you for the guided tour and your labor?"

Corbet smiled, running his fingers through his beard, "The tour's on me, but the labor's gonna cost you. I'm kinda partial to Jack Daniels and the old jug's about empty."

"Man, you drive a hard bargain," Marc said with a smile, retrieved his wallet and handed him five twenties. If that's not enough, let me know. But do me a favor. What we saw tonight's just between us. Deal?"

"Didn't see a thing." Corbet said as he slammed the Jeep's door shut and with a wave, he sped off.

Marc sat in his SUV and letting the engine warm up, contemplated what he had seen during the past few hours.

What the hell is going on here?

He mulled over some possible explanations.

Maybe it was something legitimate like a contractor testing the rock for a construction project? Possibly Lake Placid was thinking of building a water tower and had hired a geological testing company to determine if the rock was strong enough to hold it. Or maybe I've been working too much.

Marc was searching for answers and wasn't coming up with anything that made sense. If this was a legitimate operation, why would someone try to hide the fact they were here by covering that metal plug in the rock face with tree limbs and debris?

Still pondering what to do next, he started the SUV and headed back toward Lake Placid. As he slowly passed the entrance to the reservoir, he noticed another set of fresh tire tracks, exiting this time, tracking the snow back onto Route 73 and turning left, away from the village.

Whoever they were, they had turned toward Keene, Marc surmised.

As he drove, he let his mind replay the events of the last few hours.

What was the black Mercedes doing in the parking lot? What's up with a track vehicle by the reservoir? Why had someone drilled a hole in the rock face, then seal it shut and try to hide it?

Marc turned his SUV around and headed south on Route 73, passed the Mount Van Hoevenberg parking lot, through the hamlet of Keene and Elizabethtown, arriving in Willsboro just before nine o'clock.

When Marc drove passed the Remillard house, lights were still on inside. Clouds had rolled in and, without the moonlight he couldn't see any vehicles in the driveway. But he did notice what appeared to be fresh tire tracks in the snow-covered driveway. Lights were also on at the house next door.

What the heck, Marc thought, and turned into Packwood's driveway. The Chevy was still parked at the far end of the drive and he pulled around it, to the back of the house. Marc got out of his SUV, and stood in the darkness for a moment, listening for any sounds. Nothing. Only the crackling of his engine as it cooled in the night air. He went to the back door of Packwood's home and rapped.

"It's open," Packwood bellowed from within.

Marc stepped inside and called out. "Curt, it's me, Marc LaRose."

"Well come on in. Don't just stand there with the door wide open. Can't afford to heat the whole outdoors, you know."

Marc closed the door.

"Never mind your shoes," Packwood said, "it's just snow. Come on in. I'm in the parlor. Wondered when you'd be back."

Marc wiped his boots on the braided rug by the door and found Packwood, still in his recliner in front of the TV.

"Sorry to barge in on you, Mr. Packwood."

"What do you mean, barge in? He said as he turned the TV off. And what's up with this 'Mister Packwood' shit? It's Curt, and like I said last time you were here, you're welcome anytime. You must be looking for an update on what's going on over there at the old Paulig place."

"Well, I was in the area and saw your lights were still on, so I thought I'd stop by to see if you'd noticed anything new."

"It's kinda funny you asked. Actually, I was thinking of calling you."

"Oh? Why's that?"

"There seems to have been an increase in activity over there lately."

"What kind of activity?" Marc asked.

"Couple more of those rental vans came in, then left. One late last night and another sometime before I got up this morning."

"Any idea what they were up to?" Marc asked.

"Yeah, but I'm not sure how to explain it."

"What do you mean?"

"Well, it was last night, right during the rerun of The Beverly Hillbillies, the one where Jed's sister-in-law, Pearl, comes to visit. She and Granny never got along too well. Anyway, it was about then when the first van arrived. It was pretty dark out, but those fellers over there sure seemed set on bringing something out of that boathouse. I mean, it's pretty quiet here at night with the lake frozen over and there was hardly any wind. I even hobbled over by the back door and stuck my head out for a minute. I swear I could hear sounds coming from over there, like people walking around, footsteps crunching on the snow."

"Could you see any lights?" Marc asked.

"Funny thing, no lights on at all, but I could hear voices. They were talking kinda low, couldn't make out a word though. And every once in awhile I heard a scraping or shuffling noise, sorta sounded like there was something being slid into the back of a truck, or maybe that van."

"You said that another van arrived early this morning?"

"Around four o'clock. I was sleeping right here in my chair. Woke me up when I heard it come down the driveway, tires crunching away. Same thing as before. Lots of commotion, feet shuffling over that frozen path coming from the boathouse, more hushed voices, but no lights. And with the cloud cover, they were operating in pitch dark."

"Or maybe with the help of night vision goggles," Marc said, thinking out loud.

"What's that you say—night fishing goggles? I seriously doubt those fellers are ice fishing."

153

"Sorry Curt. I was just thinking out loud."

Marc noticed Packwood glance at his watch, then at the blank screen of his TV.

Marc took the cue. "It's getting late, Curt. I should get going. Thanks for taking the time to talk to me tonight."

"Like I have such a tight schedule." Packwood replied with a chuckle. "I'm happy for the diversion. Sorta reminds me of that old Jimmy Stewart movie, *Rear Window*. 'Cept this is my side window and I don't think anybody over there has buried their old lady, at least not as far as I can tell."

"Let's hope not," Marc said.

"Sure I can't interest you in a cup of tea? Only take a minute."

"No thanks. Maybe next time."

"Stop in anytime."

As Marc passed through the kitchen, he heard the TV come to life with the whistling of the Andy Griffith theme song.

It was after eleven p.m. when Marc arrived at his condo. Despite the late hour, he dialed the number for Jerry's home phone.

When he answered on the first ring, Marc suspected he must be on call.

"Jerry, it's Marc, hope I didn't wake you up."

"No problem, I'm on call tonight. What's up?"

"It's this Al-Zeid thing, Jerry. It's getting a little weird. I just got back from Willsboro and thought we'd better talk."

"Must be really weird for you to call me at this hour."

"Let me pass a few things by you, then you can be the judge, OK?"

"Sounds like you're going to tell me whether I want to hear it or not, so shoot, what have you got?"

"It's not just one thing, it's a couple of things. Remember the lab report on Al-Zeid—sores on his body, inflamed GI tract and overall rundown physical condition?"

"Yeah?"

"I took the liberty of showing the report to a friend who told me Al-Zeid's symptoms were consistent with radiation poisoning."

"Oh, who's your expert?"

"You remember Sophie Horton?"

"That chick you met at the Inn? Come on Marc, it's too late for this."

"Before immigrating to the U.S., Sophie worked with the New Zealand Customs Department, and nuclear materials smuggling was her specialty.

Jerry's end of the line was silent, so Marc continued.

"Also, the Hubers, you remember them, the couple staying at the Inn who were with Al-Zeid on the ski trip when he died?"

"How do we get from Al-Zeid's lab report to the Hubers?" Jerry asked.

"Hang on. The same day I interviewed the Hubers, I found their car parked at a house in Willsboro, out on the Point Road right on the lake. Funny thing is that, during the interview, they never said anything about going to Willsboro, just that they intended to return to New York City before flying back to Austria."

"Marc, have you been drinking? You've already told me about the Hubers going to Willsboro."

"I know, but there are a few things I neglected to mention. Later that evening Hubers' Jeep left the house in Willsboro along with another car. I followed them both to Route 87 where I lost the Hubers because they got too far ahead, so I followed this other car, a black Mercedes that led me to a house up in Chambly, Quebec, that happens to be located on the Richelieu River."

"So, someone who stays in a house on Lake Champlain also has a house on the Richelieu River. Big fucking deal."

Knowing Jerry's patience was wearing thin, Marc continued.

"After a little nosing around in Chambly, I discovered the people who live there keep a high-powered speed boat, equipped with night vision goggles in their boat house. Also, I found evidence that they may have access to nuclear materials."

"Nuclear materials? Maybe you need a rest."

"I haven't got to the best part yet. While I was in the Montreal area, I decided to check out the rug store where Al-Zeid worked. I talked to these two guys, both Iranian immigrants who work there. They were pretty cagey and I couldn't get much out of them directly. But later I found out that at least one of them lives at that same house in Chambly. Then, just tonight, I saw what appeared to be something suspicious going on at the Lake Placid reservoir."

"Hold on Marc, what the hell are you doing at the Lake Placid water reservoir? You were talking about some speed boat in Chambly just a second ago."

"Like I said, it's all kind of weird, and everything seems to be happening so fast, just let me finish." Marc took a breath. "This afternoon, I dropped Sophie off at her dad's motel and when I was going to head back to Plattsburgh, I thought I'd check on Curtis Packwood. He's the Willsboro town supervisor who lives next door to the house where the Hubers went. Anyway, as I was heading down Route 73 toward Keene, I noticed fresh tire tracks that turned into the Reservoir Road coming from the south. I thought it was a little peculiar and as I continued on towards Keene I noticed this car, a black Mercedes in the parking lot at Mount Van Hoevenberg. It turns out this Mercedes is the same one I followed to the house in Chambly with the speedboat I mentioned before."

Marc half expected another retort, but Jerry's end of the line remained silent.

"Anyway, Larry Corbet, remember him? The Olympic Medalist guide that was with Al-Zeid and the Hubers when Al-Zeid died on the trail? He happened to be in the parking lot at Mount Van Hoevenberg finishing with a ski trip, so the two of us trekked up from the parking lot to the Reservoir Road where we discovered someone, using what must have been a commercial high speed drill, had bored a large hole into the rock shear that faces the reservoir. I mean this hole is at least six inches in diameter."

"Could you see if anything was inside the hole?" A suddenly interested Jerry asked.

"No, it was plugged with what looks like a piece of lead. It was just done because the area around the hole was still warm to the touch and whoever's done this didn't want anyone to find it right away. They covered it up with a pile of stones and brush in an effort to hide it."

"If someone tried to hide it, then how did you find it?" Jerry asked.

"Corbet and I found ruts in the snow on the Reservoir Road that looked to have been made by some kind of a tracked vehicle, you know, like the kind a small bulldozer might make. We also found where it had been loaded onto the back of a truck, the same one that made the tire tracks I noticed out at the end of the Reservoir Road. Anyway, Corbet and I followed the tracks in the snow to where we found the hole in the rock face. By the time we got back to the Mount Van Hoevenberg parking lot, the black Mercedes was gone."

Marc stopped to take a breath.

"Now I know that was quick, but like I said, it's kind of a long story and I didn't want you to hang up on me before I told you the whole thing."

No response.

"Jerry, you still there? Jerry?"

Another moment passed and just when Marc thought he'd been disconnected, Jerry said, "Yeah, I'm still here. Just trying to make some sense out of what you've told me. If I didn't know you, Marc, I'd think you'd been drinking, or smoking something, or both."

Marc started to protest but Jerry cut him off.

"Marc, tell me again. Just where did you see this hole that was supposedly drilled into the rocks by the reservoir?"

Marc ignored the 'supposedly', and gave Jerry the directions to the location of the rock face.

"I'm going to call the superintendent of the Lake Placid water department. Hopefully he can shed some light on this. There's got to be a rational explanation. We can talk about the rest of your ramblings later." Jerry said before cutting the connection.

Marc thought he'd probably be pissed, too, if someone called at, what time is it? He glanced at his watch. Oh shit, it was almost midnight.

The investigative log will wait until tomorrow.

As Marc's head hit the pillow he heard the faint "thump, thump, thump" of the Homeland Security helicopter taking off from the air strip at the old Plattsburgh Air Force Base runway as it started out on its routine nightly patrol along the U.S./Canadian border. As the sound of the helicopter's rotors faded in the distance, so did Marc, exhausted from the day's excitement.

DAY SIX

Marc and Sophie were enjoying a clear day on the slopes of Whiteface Mountain. Suddenly, he glanced over his shoulder and saw the Hubers were also on the ski trail, following them. Phillip was wearing a bright red ski jacket and a white hat with a large black tassel on top. Bianca had on a pink ski parka with a white scarf flowing about her neck. For some unexplainable reason however, Marc had a creepy feeling that he and Sophie should get away from the Hubers and urged Sophie to go faster. When he looked back up the trail, he saw Phillip was pointing something at him. It was a gun. Phillip and Bianca were chasing them, and Phillip was shooting. But when he discharged his gun, it sounded odd, more like a loud bell. Marc and Sophie increased their speed, but the Hubers were better skiers. Phillip continued to shoot at Marc, and the bell got louder. Phillip and Bianca had closed in on them. Suddenly Phillip was right behind Marc, his gun had flames coming from the barrel and the bell got louder and louder.

Marc awoke in a sweat, the room pitch dark. The bedside telephone was ringing incessantly. Blurry-eyed, he looked at his alarm clock. The green numbers read "4:33". Half asleep, he found the bedside lamp's switch and, momentarily dazed by its light, rubbed his eyes with one hand and fumbled for the phone with the other.

"Marc, you there?"

He recognized the voice.

"Yeah, Jerry. I'm here, sorta."

"Well, wake up old buddy. All hell's breaking loose. How quick can you get your ass over to the Plattsburgh State Police barracks?"

"What, why?" Marc said, still trying to push the strange dream away.

"Someone will fill you in as soon as you can get there. For now, let's just say that that hole you found in the rock on the Reservoir Road is hotter than you thought."

"Yeah, I know. I told you before it felt warm," Marc said, still rubbing his eyes.

"Not that kind of hot, Marc, I'm talking hot, like in radioactive hot. Low level, but, it's got our attention."

Although the statement came as a surprise, Marc was not shocked, especially with the death of Al-Zeid and Sophie's diagnosis.

"OK, give me a few minutes to get my bearings," Marc said huskily as he tried to clear his throat.

"Good. When you get there, ask for Senior Investigator Tim

Golden. He'll be expecting you. Got that?"

"Timmy? Sure. I worked with Tim back when he was a junior road trooper."

"Golden will fill you in on what's going on. He has a few more questions and you'll probably have to give him a written statement."

"OK, I'll be on my way just as soon as I get cleaned up."

"You're clean enough. Just get your ass over there ASAP. Got to go, talk to you later." Marc heard a click followed by a dial tone.

Making his way to the bathroom, he splashed cold water on his face and combed his hair, all the while thinking of what Garrant had told him about the rock face and the radioactivity.

"What have I got myself mixed up in now?" Marc asked himself as he put on a change of fresh clothes. A quick check on the cats' fountain showed they still had plenty of water, but he refilled their food dish.

"Better leave an extra bowl for you guys," Marc said to them, half expecting a reply.

"Meow," was the best Brandy could summon as the cat rolled over on his back looking for a belly rub.

"Sorry old boy, no time for that," Marc said as he slipped into his parka.

As Marc was about to open the front door, his phone rang again. Expecting it to be Jerry, he picked up the receiver. "Yeah, yeah, hold your horses, I'm on my way."

A moment of silence followed. Marc said, "Jerry, did you hear me?"

A female's voice, "Mr. LaRose?"

Puzzled, Marc looked at the receiver. The voice with the slight accent seemed vaguely familiar, but he couldn't make the connection.

"Yes, this is Marc LaRose, who's this?"

"Bianca Huber. Do you remember me, Mr. LaRose?"

Marc remembered her all right. He had dreamed about her and her husband chasing him down Whiteface Mountain. Marc also remembered Bianca as the one who supposedly did not understand English.

Without waiting for Marc to answer, Bianca continued. "Mr. LaRose, forgive me for calling at such an early hour, but it is very urgent that I speak to you." Her accented voice was calm, but edged with intensity.

"Mrs. Huber, this wouldn't have anything to do with Mr. Al-Zeid dying on the cross country ski trail, would it?"

A pause.

"Mr. LaRose, what I have to tell you will make that problem pale in comparison to what may happen unless some urgent action is taken."

"Look, Mrs. Huber, I think you should really be speaking to the police if you have information that important."

"Mr. LaRose, if I go to the police, I will be killed. If anyone finds out that I'm speaking to you, I will be killed. My life is in danger as we speak. You are the only one I know who is familiar with this situation and can help. Please, Mr. LaRose, you must believe me." Bianca said, her voice beginning to quiver.

"Where are you now?" Marc asked, hesitantly.

"I am calling you from a house on the Lake Shore Road in Chazy, but I cannot meet you here. It's not safe."

"Lake Shore Road? That's on Lake Champlain about seven miles south of the Canadian border," Marc said.

"Your knowledge of the area is very good, but that is unimportant right now. The important thing is that I speak with you privately and in person as soon as possible. There is not much time."

"All right," Marc said. "If you can get to Plattsburgh, I will meet you in the parking lot of the Holiday Inn just off Exit 37. Are you familiar with that location?"

"Yes, I am," Bianca replied. I'm driving a white Jeep Grand Cherokee. I will be there in one-half hour." Then, there was a click. Bianca had cut the connection.

Marc stared at the phone as it emitted its monotonous tone. He thought for a moment, then dialed the number for the Plattsburgh State Police barracks.

"State Police, Plattsburgh." A female trooper answered on the first ring.

"Senior Investigator Golden," Marc said.

"Investigator Golden is in a meeting right now. Can I take a message?"

"Tell him that Marc LaRose is on the line and it's urgent, please."

"Hold on sir," Marc heard as he was put on hold.

Within five seconds there was a click on the line, "Marc, where the hell are you? We're waiting for you to get over here."

"I know, but something new has come up. I just received a call from Bianca Huber. I'm supposed to meet her in the parking lot at the Holiday Inn in half an hour."

"Who the hell is Bianca Huber?" Tim Golden asked.

"She is Phillip Huber's wife and I believe they are people of interest in this affair in Lake Placid. We don't have much time. If you can meet me at the Holiday Inn parking lot, I can explain while we wait for her to arrive. I'll be in a green Ford Explorer."

"Be there in five minutes," Golden said and ended the call.

Marc grabbed his case folder and headed out to his SUV. As he stepped outside, he was met with the freezing chill of the still morning air. The crusty snow exploded underfoot as he made his way down the front steps and onto his driveway. Marc unlocked the SUV but, because of the layer of ice that had formed overnight, he had to tug on the driver's door to get it open. He retrieved an ice scraper from the door's side pocket and proceeded to scratch a hole through the thick layer of ice that had formed on the windshield. After a minute of steady etching, Marc managed a six inch square of clear windshield to peer through.

"That should hold me until the defroster kicks in," he muttered to himself, bemoaning the lack of a heated garage.

After a reluctant few turns, the engine revved to life and Marc forced the shifting lever to 'Drive'. The power steering growled from the cold as he maneuvered the vehicle onto the street in the direction of the Holiday Inn, located on the opposite side of town.

Plattsburgh is a sleepy town at five a.m. especially in January with the thermometer pegged at zero. A few energetic high school kids, bundled up in heavy coats, their faces hidden by the wrapping of protective scarves, and with white puffs of frozen breath coming through, could be seen lugging large canvas bags containing copies of *The Plattsburgh Standard* newspaper for delivery.

Guess I shouldn't bitch about not having a heated garage, Marc thought, as the Explorer passed.

About halfway to the Holiday Inn, Marc stopped by the Dunkin' Donuts drive thru and picked up coffees and a few plain donuts.

Old habits are hard to break.

At the Holiday Inn, he scanned the parking lot for Golden's car. The windows of the cars looked frozen over, except for one, a tan sedan parked to the right of the entrance, with a telltale plume of exhaust coming from up the tailpipe. A flick of the sedan's headlights confirmed Marc's suspicions and he pulled into the empty space next to it. Through the partially cleared driver's side window Marc could see Golden behind the wheel. He grabbed his notes and the warm donut sack and crunched his way over to the unmarked sedan. The two shook hands and after a minute of 'haven't seen you in ages' and 'cream and sugar,' etc., Golden said to Marc, "OK, what have you got so far, before this, Bianca, gets here?"

"What do you need?"

"Everything. How you came to find that hole in the rock face at the reservoir, who you think may be involved, who you've talked to, everything. I'm going to record it and take a few notes as you go."

"OK, Marc said, but before we start, do me a favor and cut your engine, the exhaust is a giveaway in this cold air."

Golden turned off the engine, then pushed a button on his dash that was apparently hooked up to a recorder. Using his official monotone voice, he said, "This is Senior Investigator Timothy Golden. The date is January 20, and the time is 5:00 a.m. I am in my troop car sitting in the parking lot of the Holiday Inn, Route 3, Plattsburgh, New York, interviewing Marc LaRose of Plattsburgh, a licensed private detective regarding an apparent radiation incident at the Lake Placid reservoir. Mr. LaRose has been advised that his statement is being electronically recorded."

"OK Marc, would you please identify yourself and for the recording, lay out the facts of your investigation as you know them so far."

Marc referred to his case notes, as briefly and as succinctly as he could. As he finished the synopsis of his investigation, a white Jeep Cherokee pulled into the lot.

"I think that's Bianca Huber coming now," he said pointing toward the Jeep as it slowly wound its way past the rows of parked cars.

Golden spoke into the car's dictation device stating there had been a break in the interview and switched it off.

"Look, Tim. She doesn't want to talk to the police. She's pretty scared. If you don't mind, let me talk to her alone, at least for now. I think we'll get more out of her that way."

"Fine with me," Golden said, "but we're running out of time here. I'll hang close for a while."

Marc exited Golden's car and headed for the Jeep Cherokee that had stopped near the motel's front door.

As he approached, he could see that Bianca Huber was alone and appeared to be agitated. When he tapped on the rear door, Bianca whipped her head around to see who was there. Seeing Marc, she unlocked the passenger door and motioned for him to get in.

Although it had only been four days since Marc last saw her, she looked as though she had aged five years. The knitted hat that was pulled over her blond hair, so meticulously coifed when he last saw her at the resort, only partially hid the straggled ends sticking out from the bottom of the hat.

"Where can we go, Mr. LaRose? "We have to talk, but we cannot be seen," Bianca said, sniffling and wiping the tears with the back of her hand.

"Drive back out onto Route 3, turn left and head toward downtown."

When Bianca and Marc arrived at the corner of Clinton and Cornelia Streets, Marc pointed toward a building on the corner.

"Just pull around to the back," Marc said.

"What's this place, Shirley's Flowers?"

"It's OK. I know the owner."

At the back of the shop, Marc pointed to the rear entrance, "Park next to that door. No one will look for you here."

Marc led Bianca to the back door of the flower shop. Before entering, he glanced around to confirm they hadn't been followed. Using the key he kept to the shop, he unlocked the door and held it open for Bianca, then relocked it after they were inside. The front window flower display case emitted enough light for them to see each other. Marc pulled two stools to the workbench used for arranging flowers.

"Sit here, Mrs. Huber. Would you like some coffee?"

"Yes, that would be good and please, it's Bianca."

Although Bianca was still apprehensive, she appeared to have regained her composure. Marc went to where Shirley kept the coffee maker and prepared a full pot, then brought cups and spoons to where Bianca was sitting.

"We shouldn't be disturbed here. The owner doesn't come in for at least another hour and a half. So, tell me, Bianca, what's this all about?"

She paused, the coffee maker softly burbling in the next room.

"It's all so complicated, Mr. LaRose."

She inhaled deeply and stared down at the ceramic tile floor.

"Take your time. We're in no rush here," Marc said.

"Lake Placid and Innsbruck are competing to host the 2026 Winter Olympics. As I'm sure you are aware, Lake Placid last hosted the winter games in 1980 as Innsbruck did in 1976, so naturally, each feels that it's their turn to hold them again. Lake Placid has powerful influences within the World Olympic committee and has made strong overtures to host the games. An Olympic event brings lots of money to the host community, not just from the people who attend the games, but also from the massive government subsidies, as well as corporate monies that go into bringing the different venues to world class status. Then, there's the building and refurbishing of infrastructure, roadways, airports, housing, and, of course, the games themselves with all the marketing. We're talking about hundreds of millions of dollars, Mr. LaRose."

"I understand, but what did Al-Zeid have to do with all this?"

"I'm coming to that, but if you don't mind, could I get a cup of that coffee now?" Bianca said.

"Thought you'd never ask," Marc said, and slid off his stool to retrieve the pot.

A moment later he returned and filled their cups with the fresh brew. "Now, where were we?"

Bianca, cradling her cup in both hands, took a long, slow sip. She set the cup on the workbench, and though she was still shaking, appeared more composed.

"You were asking me about Al-Zeid. He is, er, was, a Canadian citizen, although I believe he was born somewhere in the Middle East, Iran, I think. He was the contact person that Phillip was working with to bring certain items across the border from Canada to the United States. Items that would help insure that Lake Placid would fail in its bid for the games."

"What do you mean by 'certain items'? I get the feeling we're not talking about carpets," Marc said.

"No, not carpets, Mr. LaRose," she said with a hint of exasperation. "Other items, things that ordinarily people cannot bring across any border without special authorization."

Marc, thinking back to what he'd seen at the boat house in

Chambly, the connection with the house in Willsboro and Sophie's diagnosis of Al-Zeid's symptoms of radiation poisoning, was beginning to get the uneasy feeling that things were about to get worse.

"Bianca, what are you talking about?"

She took another deep swallow of coffee, "Let me try to explain it to you this way, Mr. LaRose. My husband, Phillip works with a consortium of people who are intent on returning the Olympic Games to Innsbruck. I know them. There is a lot at stake, and they will stop at nothing to insure that the games are awarded to Innsbruck."

"Consortium? What kind of consortium?"

"Mostly Europeans, as well as interested parties from other countries whose aim is to remove Lake Placid as a contender. Certain steps have already been taken in this regard."

"I see, go on," Marc said, gently coaxing Bianca to continue her story.

"Phillip is the coordinator, the go-between, if you will, which unfortunately included working with the smugglers who were to supply him with the radioactive material."

"Smuggling radioactive material? How?" Marc asked, although he already suspected what Bianca was about to say.

"Quite simple. As you probably know, since 9/11 and the events that followed, shipments of everything coming into the United States by air are thoroughly checked before they are put on the plane. Likewise, all cargo coming into the United States across the border from Canada or Mexico by truck, car or train has to pass through a radiation sensing device. Even the major seaports are guarded with radiation detectors. But there are hundreds of miles of unguarded waterways around the United States, and Lake Champlain with its direct connection to the St. Lawrence River is ideal. As long as Al-Zeid's boat does not come in contact with a Customs or Border Patrol agent, his men and their cargo can easily elude detection."

Marc's mind raced back yet again to the boathouse in Chambly where he'd seen the cigarette boat, the night vision goggles, and the navigation map. He also thought about the tarp he and Sophie had seen with "Trans Arabian Logging" stenciled on it.

"What about the Customs Officers at the boat piers in Rouses Point? They inspect every boat that passes, coming south from

Canada on Lake Champlain," Marc asked.

"True, but Al-Zeid's men travel at night, after the Customs inspectors have left for the day, and then only during inclement weather, usually rain or fog. This way they avoid detection by the cameras that scan the lake in the area of the border."

"And the Homeland Security helicopters?"

"Al-Zeid worked out a system of alerts using a spy who lives near the old Plattsburgh Air Force base where the helicopters are stationed. He simply alerts the men in Chambly when he hears a Customs helicopter take off. If a shipment is en route and they get an alert that the helicopter is heading north toward the border, they dock the boat at the safe house at Chazy Landing and wait for it to pass before continuing to Willsboro."

"Ah, the house in Willsboro," Marc said, mentally arranging the pieces of this puzzle in his mind.

"But what did your husband plan to do with the radioactive material once it got to Willsboro?" Marc asked.

She took another deep swallow from her mug.

"Do you know anything about a dirty bomb, Mr. LaRose?"

"Dirty bomb? Yes, I think so," Marc said warily, thinking back to the events of the past evening at the Lake Placid reservoir. "I read somewhere that it's an inexpensive way to spread radiation over a given area without actually exploding a thermonuclear device."

"Very good, Mr. LaRose. It's a terrorist's dream come true. A simple, effective method of causing widespread panic, fear and disruption. All one needs is a decent source of radioactive material, medical or industrial waste, and an explosive charge, powerful enough to get the radioactivity airborne. Not much physical damage, but the psychological damage could be enormous."

"What you're saying is that the plug in the rock face at the reservoir in Lake Placid is concealing a dirty bomb? But why there?" Marc continued, thinking out loud, "Unless the radiation would contaminate the Lake Placid water supply? Is that it?"

"So you've already found it." Bianca said with a stunned look on her face. "Then I suppose I'm not telling you anything you don't already know." Tears again welled up in her eyes.

"But there is still time to act," she continued. "Nothing is supposed to happen until the ice on the reservoir melts in the spring."

"Why are they waiting until spring? I don't understand."

166

"You see, it wouldn't be as effective to detonate the device now. Yes, there would be some initial panic, but after the authorities figured out what happened, the effects could be quickly mitigated by removing the snow containing the radiation from the top of the ice covering the reservoir. The reservoir is spring fed, so there is little runoff from the snowmelt. No, they are waiting until the ice begins to thaw, then when they explode it, the melting ice will carry the radiation right into the water supply. Of course radiation won't stay in the water indefinitely, but long enough to create panic, with the intent that it will eliminate Lake Placid from hosting any future Olympic event."

Marc, sorting out what he had just heard, sat in silence for a long moment.

"Bianca, we're going to have to go to the police with this. If what you're telling me is true, there's still time to stop this crazy scheme from going forward."

Bianca drained her cup, and said, "I'm not so sure."

"What do you mean? You just said that nothing's going to happen until spring, and that's three months from now," Marc said, as he refilled their cups.

"I'm afraid there is more to this plan that even my husband did not foresee," Bianca whispered.

"What? How much worse can this get? I mean, if they contaminate Lake Placid's water supply, that should accomplish what they set out to do, don't you think?"

"I think it's out of Phillip's hands now, Mr. LaRose."

"Out of his hands! I thought you said Phillip was running the show for this, this consortium, or whatever," Marc said, bracing himself for more bad news.

"Well, he is, or was, I guess. But I'm afraid that something's going to happen to Phillip, if it hasn't already. You see, he left two days ago. He said he was attending a meeting. He didn't say with whom, probably the 'Arabs', as he calls them."

"Arabs?"

"That's what he calls Al-Zeid and his organization. They do the dirty work, you know, smuggling the components in from Canada and then setting them into place. They've got the experience and besides, if something goes wrong, who best to blame? Anyway, Phillip was worried. The Arabs were demanding more money, millions more. He

167

doesn't trust them, and now he's got the consortium to deal with. He's always so thorough in everything he does. But I haven't heard from him," she said, tears running down her cheeks.

"I assume you've tried his cell number?" Marc asked.

"Countless times. Always the same, no answer. I've left him messages, still nothing."

"Bianca, when you called me this morning, you said that the situation in Lake Placid would pale to what you believed is really being planned. Do you remember that?"

"Yes," Bianca replied. Her hands shaking as she set her cup on the counter. "Phillip didn't elaborate, only that he suspected the Arabs may have other plans, plans that go well beyond Lake Placid."

Bianca dabbed her eyes with her handkerchief.

"The police have to know about all of this. I think we should go to them right now and tell them everything you know," Marc said.

"Mr. LaRose, I'm not privy to all of the details, I only get bits and pieces from Phillip and what I overhear from time to time. I'm talking to you because you're the only person I feel that I can trust and are familiar with this situation. It's just, with Phillip suddenly disappearing, I'm sure that something has gone terribly wrong. If I go to the police and they find out, what will they do to Phillip? I feel so lost and helpless, and I'm so ashamed."

Bianca buried her face into her sodden handkerchief.

"Bianca, listen to me. I have friends in the State Police. They are already looking into this and they are very good at what they do. No one will have to know that you talked to them, but we're going to have to do something and very soon."

As Marc was talking he could hear the crunching of a car's tires on the ice-covered parking lot in back of the flower shop.

"The police already know?" Bianca said, peering over her handkerchief.

Ignoring Bianca's question, Marc walked to the rear door and opened it a crack. Through the open slit he could see Tim Golden parking his car next to the Cherokee. Marc opened the door a little wider so Golden could see him, then motioned him to come in.

"Thought this is where I'd find you," an anxious Golden said.

Marc locked the door after him.

Bianca looked up from her handkerchief and, seeing Golden, she began to slide off her stool, her flight instinct taking effect. Marc gently took her by the arm, "Bianca, relax, this is a friend of mine. He can help us," he said, trying to calm her.

"I want you to meet Tim Golden of the New York State Police."

Bianca's eyes bulged as she first stared at Golden then back at Marc. "You tricked me. I trusted you Mr. LaRose," she said in a loud whisper, her eyes darting back and forth between the two men.

Golden surveyed the situation and immediately attempted to calm Bianca saying, "The best way to help your husband is to cooperate with us."

Bianca seemed too shocked to respond at first, but after a few moments, Marc could see the resignation in her eyes and she slowly nodded.

"Mrs. Huber, this situation is very serious and we want to help you, but to do that you must first cooperate with us and tell us what you know," Golden said. He continued to calmly speak to Bianca and within minutes, she appeared to realize she had no alternative.

"What choice do I have?" Bianca finally said, directing her gaze toward Marc.

Marc took her hand and squeezed it, "Bianca, we won't let anything happen to you."

Golden turned to Marc, "I'll take her back to the trooper barracks. Would you mind securing her car somewhere where it will be safe and out of sight?"

"No problem," Marc said as he slid the keys to Bianca's Jeep off the counter.

"Mrs. Huber, we're leaving now. Do you have something you could put over your head?" Golden asked.

She removed the knit cap from her coat pocket and pulled it low.

Golden led her out the rear entrance of the flower shop. Marc watched as he secured her in the rear seat of his car. Following Golden's instructions, she lay across the seat, out of view.

As he watched them from his position behind the partially opened flower shop door, Marc hesitated a moment, waiting to see if they were being followed, but he saw no one.

After relocking the door, Marc sat alone inside the shop and finished the last of the coffee as he waited for Shirley, who he figured would be in shortly to open the shop.

I'll ask her to follow me to Walt's Auto Parts where I can store Bianca's Jeep, then have her give me a lift to the Holiday Inn to retrieve my SUV.

Marc welcomed this quiet respite, giving him some time alone to think about what he would do next.

Shirley arrived a half hour later and was understandably surprised to find Marc sitting alone in the flower shop work room.

"So, to what do I owe this honor so early in the morning?" She said, teasingly.

"It's kind of complicated. I was hoping you could give me a lift to the Holiday Inn, if you're not too busy."

"OK, I guess," Shirley said sounding confused.

After securing Bianca's Jeep at Walt's garage, the two drove back across town to the Holiday Inn.

"I know you're busy, Marc, but I could really use a hand with Ann Marie. She needs a father, or at least her father's guidance."

Marc, still thinking about the morning events, said, "Huh? Oh, Ann Marie. Sorry, my mind is somewhere else right now. What seems to be the problem?"

"It's more like a pattern, not caring about school work, coming home at all hours, always late for work. I've tried to talk to her, but she blows me off, says I make a big deal of everything. And lately, she's even mentioned something about getting a tattoo. That's just not like her."

"Probably just trying to fit in. A tattoo's not exactly the end of the world. Wouldn't be my choice, but…" Marc said, leaving his unfinished thought hang in the air.

They rode the rest of the way in silence. As Shirley turned into the Holiday Inn, Marc turned to face her.

"I'll have a talk with her. Could be a boyfriend problem, who knows? Look, I'm sorry I've been so out of touch lately. I've been working on this case and now the cops are involved. I'll have a sit-down with her as soon as I can, I promise."

Although encouraged, she's heard these promises before. "Just take care of yourself and call when you can," she said with a wave as Marc got out and closed the door.

Marc retrieved his Explorer and for the fourth time in three hours headed across town, back to his shared office space on Margaret Street.

As he entered the office he was again greeted with the blinking light from the answering machine.

There were ten messages; two from Lateesha at Humbolt

Insurance looking for an update on Mr. Al-Zeid, and two from Shirley; a few inquires, mostly suspicious wives or girlfriends asking about his rates for domestic investigations; one from Sophie wanting Marc to return her call as soon as he could; but it was last message that was most troubling. According to the caller ID, it was from a phone with an unusual, but familiar prefix, placed earlier in the morning. "Mr. LaRose, this is Naveed, call me."

The voice, in a low whisper, sounded strained, like he was afraid someone might overhear him.

How the hell did he get my name and phone number?

Marc looked at the caller ID again. He retrieved his note pad and scanned the first few pages. Found it. The number matched one Marc had copied from Al-Zeid's address book and was similar to those assigned to a prepaid phone.

Difficult to trace, especially if the phone was paid for with cash.

Marc knew that any GPS feature that could lead to the location of the caller would probably be disengaged, and as far as triangulation of cell towers, there just aren't that many in the North Country.

I should let Tim Golden or Jerry Garrant know about this.

"Fuck it," Marc muttered as he dialed the number. After a few clicks Marc could hear the phone ringing. Seven, eight, nine rings, and as Marc was about to disconnect, a voice answered, "Hello".

Marc recognized Naveed's voice.

"Naveed, this is Marc LaRose. I got your message." Silence.

"Naveed, are you there?"

Another pause.

"I can't talk right now, Mr. LaRose. I'll wait for you in the parking lot of the old Keeseville Civic Center in one hour. Come alone."

"Naveed, what's this all about?"

A click, then a dial tone. The connection had been broken.

Well fuck me. This is getting weirder by the minute.

Marc thought about the phone call from Naveed.

How could Naveed get across the U.S./Canada border to meet him in Keeseville, given his apparent status as an Iranian immigrant without attracting the attention of Customs? With his Iranian citizenship, he'd be automatically flagged as a person of special interest. Unless, of course, he didn't go through Customs. And what would he want to talk to me about anyway? He wants to meet me at the old Keeseville Civic Center, alone. Could this be a set up?

171

Marc remembered Naveed as the more timid of the two men he'd met at the Global Rug Importers. He also recalled that Naveed had seemed nervous, especially when he was around Khaleed, the more aggressive and obviously the person in charge.

Definitely a good time to call Golden or Garrant and tell them about Naveed's call.

"They're the cops. It's their job. Let them handle it." Marc muttered to himself.

But the clock's ticking. Tim's tied up with Bianca Huber and Jerry's somewhere up in Lake Placid, probably still at the reservoir. To try to contact them and explain this new twist would take too long and I doubt if Naveed would talk to them anyway.

Marc quickly decided the best way to handle this would be to follow Naveed's instructions and get to the Keeseville Civic Center before Naveed.

It's a twenty minute ride south. No time to waste.

Marc grabbed his notes, locked the office door and headed out to his Explorer. His 'emergency kit' with extra clothes and the 40 caliber H&K was still packed in the SUV. Removing his handgun, he attached it to his belt, under his jacket.

The early morning ride would have been pleasant under different circumstances. Heading toward Keeseville, Marc glanced over at Lake Champlain and the wide open expanse known to locals as the "broad lake" section. Across the lake were the Green Mountains of Vermont, now white with snow.

Fifteen minutes later, Marc passed over the Ausable Chasm Bridge and through the outskirts of Keeseville, a village of about fifteen hundred inhabitants straddling the Ausable River.

He is familiar with the Keeseville Civic Center, which is housed in what used to be the local high school.

Marc entered the parking lot about a half hour ahead of Naveed's scheduled meeting time. As this was Sunday, the lot was mostly empty except for a few government vehicles parked in their assigned spaces. Locating an empty space at the far end of the lot next to a van with "Clinton County Meals on Wheels" stenciled on the side of it, he backed into the space, cut the engine and slid over the center console, taking up a position in the passenger side rear seat which gave him a clear view of anyone entering the parking lot from Main Street.

As the minutes ticked by Marc could see the parking lot across

172

the street begin to fill up for the Sunday morning mass at St. John's Church. Soon the church bells began pealing, alerting parishioners it was time for the nine a.m. mass and a few last minute stragglers hurried in to hear the Sunday sermon.

Another ten minutes of waiting in the increasingly colder SUV with still no sign of Naveed. Marc began to think he'd been stood up. An additional ten minutes that seemed more like thirty and Marc was pretty sure that Naveed was a no show.

As Marc was about to reclaim his position behind the steering wheel, he saw a movement in another parked vehicle three spaces away.

It was a grey van, no printing on its side. The rear door opened and a bundled figure exited. Marc couldn't see the man's face because he was wearing a heavy anorak with the fur lined hood pulled over his head. The bundled figure closed the van door and headed in the direction of Marc's SUV, his hands pushed deep into the parka's pockets and his hood bent downwards against the wind.

As the figure approached the passenger side of the Explorer, he suddenly looked up and Marc could see that the 'he' was apparently a 'she'. Although much of her face was still wrapped in the anorak's hood, he could make out the olive complexion, dark hair and the feminine features of this surprising visitor.

The woman motioned for Marc to unlock the passenger door.

Marc, unsure what to make of this development, hesitated at first, and then unlocked the door.

As the woman got into the SUV Marc said, "Sorry, I was expecting someone else."

"Naveed couldn't make it. I'm a messenger and I've been instructed to tell you this," she said with a thick accent. Then the woman pulled an automatic pistol equipped with a silencer from her parka pocket and pointed it at Marc.

"No funny business, Mr. LaRose, one false move and I'll put a bullet through your head." The way she handled the pistol left no doubt to Marc's trained eye that she was familiar with its operation and was not afraid to use it.

Marc had dealt with aggressive females in the past, but he had never met one with such determined, unblinking eyes. It was those eyes that bothered Marc as much as the gun she was holding. They held no emotion, no feeling, just a lifeless cold stare. Marc hadn't seen eyes like these since he came across a timber rattlesnake while hunting years ago. Now, it seemed to Marc that those same eyes were focusing in on him, and for the first time in a long time, he was frightened.

"Look, there must be some mistake. "I was at the carpet store in Montreal a couple of days ago talking to Naveed about buying some Persian carpets. When he called just this morning, he said he would meet me here," Marc said, stalling for time. "I must say you folks sure have a funny way of following up on a sales lead."

"Forget about Naveed." The woman snarled, grim-faced and paying no attention to Marc's feeble attempt at humor.

"There are more than twenty pounds of C4 explosives in that van," she said, motioning with the gun in the direction of the gray van she had exited from. "If you try anything foolish that is enough to level everything in this fucking parking lot, Mister LaRose. One signal from me, and, boom!"

"But you would be killed too," Marc managed.

"I am not important, besides, my rewards are awaiting me somewhere else, but you would know nothing about that. We know where you live, Mr. LaRose. I am here to advise you...no, warn you to stay out of our way and to stop nosing around. We are aware of some inquiries you have been conducting lately, inquiries into certain matters that are of no concern to you."

"Look, I'm a private investigator. I look into lots of matters. Who are you and what's this all about anyway?"

"You know very well of what I speak, Mr. LaRose. You've been out of the country the last couple of days digging around in business that is of no concern of yours. You and your little friend, Ms. Sophie Horton."

"How do you know..." before Marc could finish, snake eyes continued.

"I should just kill you right now, but this is your one and final warning, a break for both you and your little friend. Stay out of this and keep your mouth shut. Believe me, our patience with you has run out."

"Look, miss, whoever you are, if this is about the Jamal Al-Zeid thing up in Lake Placid, I talked to Phillip Huber just a few days ago. Huber knows what I'm doing. He and Al-Zeid were business associates. Why haven't you talked to him?"

The lifeless eyes shifted back toward Marc. "You can soon forget

Phillip Huber, Mr. LaRose. He will be, how do you Americans say, 'out of the picture'." She paused, letting this statement hang between them for a few moments.

"You've had your warning. My business with you is now finished, providing you do as I have instructed. I will now return to my vehicle and you will remain in yours and if you're lucky, you'll never see me again."

With that the woman opened the passenger door and slid out of Marc's SUV. She glanced around, then, stepping back a couple of paces, fired a single muffled shot into the right front tire of Marc's SUV. She glanced back at him with a twisted grin and stuffed the gun into her parka pocket, then slowly shuffled sideways towards her van, all the while keeping those dead eyes focused on Marc. He could feel the front of his Explorer sink as the air rushed out of the ruined tire.

When the woman reached her van, she started the engine and drove out of the parking lot, then, turned left toward downtown and disappeared.

Marc remained seated.

Sit tight Marc, you're not going anywhere until that tire's fixed.

He had driven to Keeseville thinking he would meet with Naveed and get some information about what was going on in Willsboro and Chambly as well as the situation at the Lake Placid reservoir. Instead he had been confronted by a new character, this female with the eyes of a serpent and an attitude to match, and given a very clear ultimatum that he cease and desist from his investigatory activities concerning what Marc now believed could be a severe risk to the North Country and possibly beyond.

Wonder how she knows about Sophie? I was careful not to use our names when we signed the register at the Inn in Chambly.

Marc was brought back to the moment by the pealing of church bells indicating that the morning mass was over. He could see parishioners begin to file out of the church, all bundled up in their heavy coats as they trundled toward their waiting vehicles.

Marc got out of his SUV, and began the process of removing the spare tire from the back. He couldn't help but wonder about the messenger, who she represented and how she knew about him and Sophie and the fact that they'd been to Montreal. He was still haunted by the woman's attitude and the intensity in which she delivered those threats against him.   Although he was accustomed to being threatened, he knew this woman was someone to be feared and that he and Sophie were in danger.

And what had happened to Naveed? Had he set Marc up for this meeting with the 'serpent girl', or had something happened to him? Then there was Phillip Huber. Perhaps Bianca's fears were well founded. Too many questions with no answers.

After Marc exchanged the shot-out tire with the spare, he eased the Explorer out of the parking lot onto Main Street. He was relieved to find the gray van nowhere in sight, but he was not convinced that someone, either the 'serpent girl' or someone else wasn't watching him. He drove to the post office parking lot, waited for a few minutes, then headed south on Route 9, all the while scanning the streets in front as well as behind to see if he could pick out anyone that might be tailing him.

After a half hour and about five miles of driving through the town and doubling back, Marc had not detected a tail. Either there was no one following him or they were real good at being invisible, something that Marc had practiced many times in his years of surveillance.

It was almost eleven a.m., and as Marc started back out of town he was thinking he should get in contact with Investigator Golden. He was certain Jerry Garrant and Golden were wondering why he hadn't appeared at the barracks yet. But before he talked to either of them, Marc wanted to check with Sophie to make sure she was safe. He was regretting his decision to allow Sophie to get involved in this affair.

Marc pulled into a restaurant parking lot and dug his cell phone out of his emergency bag. As usual, it was turned off, as he used it mainly for outgoing calls. Marc wasn't big on leaving his cell phone on to have it go off in the middle of a surveillance. He punched the number for the Miss Saranac Motel. Hugh picked up on the second ring.

"Hugh, it's Marc LaRose. Is Sophie around?"

After an initial hesitation, Hugh responded, "Uh, yeah, hold on Marc."

Marc could hear the muffled sound as Hugh apparently held his hand over the receiver and called for Sophie. After a few anxious moments, Sophie's voice came over the line.

"Marc, is that you?"

"Yeah, hey, I got a message on my machine that you called."

"Um yeah, look Marc, we need to talk. Something's come up and maybe we shouldn't discuss this over the phone. Any chance you'd be coming back up to Saranac Lake anytime soon?"

Marc could detect apprehension in Sophie's voice. Had the 'serpent girl' talked to Sophie as well?

"Uh, I don't know Sophie," Marc said, his mind racing as he tried to sort out what Sophie just said regarding her suspicion that someone might be listening in on the call, coupled with this morning's meeting with the messenger.

Marc chose his words with care, "I'm heading back to Plattsburgh. At one o'clock, I have to talk to a guy who got side swiped at the railroad station. I'll call you later. Is that OK?" Marc hoped that Sophie caught his veiled reference to meet him at the Side Car Restaurant at 1:00 p.m.

"Oh, ah, yeah, sure Marc. I'll be here most of the day. I'll talk to you then."

Marc was pretty certain that Sophie caught on.

He glanced at his watch.

Plenty of time to get to the Sidecar Bar.

Marc left Keeseville and headed back toward Plattsburgh. Exiting the Northway he passed by the State Police barracks, and noticed more cars than usual around the side of the building where the investigators usually park.

They must still be talking with Bianca Huber.

Figuring that Golden and Garrant would be looking for him, he knew he couldn't just go home or to his office just yet. He decided it was more important to talk with Sophie to find out why she suspected someone could be listening in on her phone.

Marc returned to Walt's Auto Parts store to check on Bianca Huber's car, and after verifying it was still there and no one had been around asking about it, he had his damaged tire replaced with a new one.

Wonder what Humbolt Insurance will think when they get a bill for the repair of a tire with a bullet hole?

Marc drove by Shirley's Flower Shop to see if everything looked normal. He recognized the wholesale flower truck parked outside.

Nothing seemed out of the ordinary. He resisted the notion of speaking with Shirley about what had occurred in Keeseville. Mentioning anything to her about the possibility of her being watched

177

would only complicate matters and beside, the 'serpent girl' had made no mention of her or Ann Marie.

As Marc set out toward Saranac Lake, a trip he usually looked forward to, he was too distracted about the morning's events to take in the scenery. Among the things that weighed heavy on his mind were the safety of his family, Sophie, and the impending disaster of a dirty bomb set to explode.

It was almost twelve thirty by the time he arrived in Saranac Lake, and, rather than go directly to the Side Car to wait for Sophie, Marc found a parking space on the street about a half block away and decided to wait for her there. Ten minutes later, he spotted Sophie making her way toward the restaurant on foot. He watched from his position on the opposite side of the street, trying to see if she was being followed. Nothing seemed unusual, and as she was about to pass on the opposite side of the street, Marc got her attention by tapping the vehicle's horn and motioning to her. Her facial expression was serious.

"Marc, I'm so glad you could make it up here today."

"Good to see you, too. Let's find someplace else for lunch, if you don't mind."

"Oh, I don't mind. Got any suggestions?"

"I know a place over near Paul Smiths called the Wagon Wheel Restaurant. That's a few miles out of town and no one should bother us there."

"Sounds good," she said.

Still mindful that someone could be following them, Marc looped around the block once before heading south out of town toward the hamlet of Gabriels.

"Why are you going back around this way?" She asked.

I'll tell you later. What did you want to talk to me about?"

"Well, it's..." Sophie paused, exhaled, and continued, "I don't know for sure, but I think there's something strange going on at the Saranac Mountain Inn."

"Really, like what?"

"Well, it started last night when I got a call from the Inn's manager, Noah Emmanuel."

"Oh?" Marc answered, cautiously.

"He called me ten o'clock last night and said they've had to make some changes at the Inn and that I'm not to report for work as

178

scheduled tomorrow. He also said not to call him, that he would advise me when I was needed again. I asked him what was going on and he said he couldn't talk right then and that he would be in touch."

"Has this ever happened before?" Marc asked.

"Never. And it's just too odd."

"How's that?"

"Emmanuel never calls me. If there are any scheduling changes, and there are from time to time, Mr. Barris, or sometimes, Lucy Welch, might call, but never Mr. Emmanuel."

"I don't see why you should be too concerned. Sophie. I'm sure there must be a logical explanation," Marc said.

"I hope you're right, but I have my doubts. You see, there is a strict protocol for instructions at the Inn. Mr. Mackenzie, the Inn's owner, only deals with Mr. Emmanuel and he, only deals with Lucy or Mr. Barris who disseminate instructions to the staff. I mean, if I saw Mr. Emmanuel around the Inn, he would say "Hi", and maybe ask about Zoe, you know, small talk, but all official direction follows a tight chain of command, starting with Mr. Mackenzie, who as you remember has his office in Montreal."

"Sophie, have you heard anything about an incident at the Lake Placid reservoir, something that might have happened there last night?"

"The Lake Placid Reservoir?" Sophie said, perplexed. "I know that's just a couple of miles from the Inn, but no, I don't recall anything about an incident there. As far as I know, the Inn doesn't even get its water from the reservoir. The Inn has its own well. So, what happened?"

Marc thought for a moment. He didn't want to alarm Sophie unnecessarily, but he felt that she should know what he knew.

"Somebody drilled a pretty good-sized hole into the rock wall face overlooking the reservoir."

"Oh," Sophie said, "Sounds kind of mysterious, but what's the big deal with that?"

"After they drilled this hole, they put something inside it, then sealed it up with a lead plug."

"Why would anyone do something like that? And what did they put in the hole? You're not making sense, Marc."

"I know it sounds weird, but someone did and whatever they stuck in that hole was radioactive."

179

"Radioactive! Marc, you've got to be kidding me." She studied Marc's face hoping for a sign that this might be a practical joke, but she could tell he was deadly serious.

"I wish I was. Jerry Garrant called and told me this morning. Which reminds me, I should get back to him. He's probably mad as hell," Marc said as they approached Gabriels.

"How did Jerry learn about the hole?"

"I called him last night and told him that there had been some suspicious activity up there. I'll tell you more about that later. Anyway, he apparently checked it out and, I don't know, someone must have had access to a Geiger counter or radiation detector or something."

"So, the question is, how do you think this situation at the reservoir ties in with Al-Zeid having radiation sickness?" Sophie asked.

"Well, it's obvious they're somehow related, I just haven't connected the dots, but there's a few other things that have happened since the last time we met."

"A few other things? What kind of things?"

"Ah, there's the Wagon Wheel coming up on the right. I'll fill you in over lunch."

As Marc pulled the Explorer into the parking lot, he was relieved to see a limited number of parked cars which meant a light lunch crowd.

Upon entering, Marc chose a booth along the far wall, out of earshot of other customers.

As the waitress approached their table, Marc noticed that her brown eyebrows seemed inconsistent with her black shoulder length hairdo, streaked with pink and blue highlights.

She plopped a grease-smeared menu on the table and retrieved an order pad from her apron pocket, "The day's lunch special is two Michigan hot dogs and fries," she lisped as a stainless steel tongue stud clattered against her smoke-stained cuspids.

"I'm sorry, but did you say today's special is two Michigan hot dogs and fries?" Marc asked.

"That's right," she said, impatiently tapping her order pad with an oversized pencil that could have been mistaken for a piece of kindling if it weren't for the artificial pink daisy wired to the eraser.

"Could you give us a minute to look over the menu, please?" Marc asked.

The waitress rolled her eyes and retreated back toward the kitchen.

Marc shook his head and said, "Don't take this the wrong way, but I can understand Zoe easier than our waitress."

It was Sophie's turn to roll her eyes. "OK Marc, I'm anxious to hear what you discovered from your conversation with Bianca Huber, but first, what the heck is a Michigan hot dog?"

"Sorry, I thought you knew. It's simply a hot dog on a bun, covered with a spicy hamburger chili sauce, and covered with diced onions. I grew up eating Michigans."

"Sounds great," Sophie said with an affected grimace, flipping the menu over to read the reverse side.

Marc shrugged. "Suit yourself, but you'll never know until you've tried one."

The two perused the menu in silence for a minute before the waitress returned to take their orders.

"Grilled cheese sandwich, a cup of tomato soup, and a glass of water, please," Sophie said.

"Chic-ken," Marc taunted.

"Chicken salad sir?" The waitress lisped once again.

"Oh, no, sorry. I was talking to her," Marc said, motioning toward Sophie.

The waitress gave another eye roll accompanied by a loud sigh.

"I'll have the Michigan special, buried, and a diet Coke."

"Uh huh," The waitress grunted as she ambled off, the pink daisy aflutter as she scribbled down the order.

"Buried?" Sophie asked, raising a brow in Marc's direction.

"It's a Plattsburgh thing," Marc said, with a wry smile and no explanation.

"So, tell me about this hole you found up at the reservoir. What's up with that? And what in the world were you doing there in the first place?"

Marc placed a finger to his lips, and in a hushed tone, related the circumstances that had brought him to the reservoir the previous evening.

"So you followed the tracks up to the reservoir all by yourself?"

"No, I ran into Larry Corbet and asked him to guide me. I'm glad I did. He was really helpful."

Marc went on to tell how he and Corbet had made the ski trek to

181

the reservoir and located the freshly drilled hole in the rock face.

"That's all kind of interesting, but how does this tie in with Mr. Al-Zeid contracting radiation sickness?"

Marc filled Sophie in about his meeting with Bianca Huber earlier that morning and her revelation that a dirty bomb had been placed inside the rock face along with a high explosive charge.

"Ah, so Al-Zeid was somehow involved with that. But why would anyone would want to explode a dirty bomb near the reservoir?" She asked.

"The intention, according to Bianca, was to detonate the dirty bomb and contaminate the reservoir, leaving Lake Placid with no usable water supply for the foreseeable future."

"But, why?"

"Because there are people who want to prevent Lake Placid from hosting the 2026 winter Olympics. By polluting the only viable source of water for the town and the Olympic village, Lake Placid would be removed from any possibility of ever hosting the Olympics again."

Sophie contemplated what Marc had said, quietly stirring her soup.

"So who would benefit, and why?"

"This is where it gets a little complicated. According to Bianca, her husband, Phillip is involved in a conspiracy with a consortium, whose ultimate goal is to ensure that the 2026 Olympics are staged at Innsbruck. This consortium feels that, right now, Lake Placid has the upper hand in getting the winter games to return here."

"But Marc, if the Austrians try to pull this off, don't they realize that it could all backfire on them?"

"I suspect that they do. That's why they've hired a bunch of Muslim extremists to carry out their bidding. That way if something goes wrong, they'll take the blame."

"Marc, come on, be real. For something like this, you'd need people with an expertise in bomb-making, as well as radioactive materials handling. That's a pretty tall order, don't you think?"

"Hang on. I'm coming to that part. It's no secret that Canada with its liberal immigration laws has a ready supply of people from Muslim countries, and as with any culture, there are always a few extremists."

"Marc, I remember how the customs service works. There's no way these people are going to be allowed into the U.S without the proper credentials, and even then, there would be intelligence reports. Sharing the longest common border in the world, I'm sure the U.S. and Canadian customs work closely to keep tabs on suspected terrorists."

"Sure they do, but it's not that easy. Immigrants come to Canada all the time and most become productive members of society, as they work toward Canadian citizenship. Extremists know this. They also know that a Canadian passport opens the door to travel to the states. All they have to do is keep out of trouble, stay below the radar and not do anything that would get their names on a terrorist watch list. Like you just said, it's a pretty long border and if they have to, they could get themselves smuggled across, happens all the time."

"So, you said you met with Bianca Huber this morning. Where was her husband?"

"That's a good question. Bianca said she hasn't seen or heard from Phillip for a few days now, and is worried something's happened. His apparent disappearance was the main reason for her reaching out to me. She doesn't seem to have anybody else around to turn to, at least anybody she feels she can trust. I got the impression that she's pretty well up on what's going on at the reservoir but I don't believe she took an active part."

Marc spotted the waitress heading towards them with their orders.

After she set their lunches on the table and was turning to leave, Marc said, "uh, Miss, I ordered onions with my Michigans." The waitress turned with another eye roll and said, "You ordered them buried, sir."

"You're right, my mistake, sorry." Marc said sheepishly as the waitress turned on her crocs and clogged back toward the counter."

"So, buried means the onions are under the sauce? Why, may I ask?"

"To prevent them from falling off the top of the dog when they are eaten. It's just not fashionable to wander around the North Country with diced onions stuck to the front of one's hunting shirt," Marc said with his patented grin.

"Oh, brother," Sophie said with some exasperation.

"Can we get back to what we were talking about before we got distracted with your onions?"

"Sure," Marc said, squirting a line of mustard on top of his

183

Michigan.

"I get that what Bianca Huber said has caused some excitement, but how can you tie Canadian immigrants and hired terrorists into this whole thing without any other evidence?" Sophie asked.

"I was coming to that," Marc said as he took a bite of the Michigan Red Hot, pausing to enjoy this North Country staple. "Remember that guy up in Montreal at the carpet store, not the boss, but the first one, the salesman, Naveed?"

Sophie nodded while blowing on her soup.

"He called me this morning. Said he wanted to meet me at the Keeseville Civic Center. He sounded kind of nervous. I'd already spent the morning talking with Bianca Huber, so I figured it was something to do with this Al-Zeid thing and maybe he could shed some light on what was going on."

"You met with Naveed this morning? What did he have to say?"

"Well that's just it, I didn't meet him. I went to the civic center and got there a little early because I wanted to see if anyone else was with him, or if maybe I was being set up."

Between bites of fries, Marc related how surprised he was when this woman, the 'Serpent Girl', as he described her, approached him with a gun.

"A gun? You've got to be kidding," a startled Sophie said a little too loudly as she was about to take another spoonful of soup.

"Shhh," Marc warned as he glanced toward the counter.

"At first I figured it was Naveed wearing a parka, but as 'he' came up to my car, I could see it was a woman. Anyway, she motioned for me to open my passenger door, climbed in and, like that, she pulled out this gun fitted with a silencer and pointed it at me."

"Holy crap," Sophie whispered. "Then what happened?"

"Well, she warned me that she knew that you and I...she mentioned you by name by the way...that we were in Montreal yesterday, poking around, asking questions. She said that we should mind our own business, and that she knew where we lived. Then she said if I tried anything, she had explosives in her van that on her signal would ignite and blow up everything and everyone in the parking lot."

"You said, she knows about me? My name?" Sophie asked with obvious concern.

"That's what she said. I was thinking about that on the way up here. I'm still not sure how she got your name. I used false names

184

when we registered at the B&B in Chambly. The only other thing I could think of was when we visited the offices of the McKenzie Group in Montreal yesterday. Remember all those cameras?"

"Shit, those cameras. Someone must have recognized me from the security camera in the lobby. I wonder if that had anything to do with Mr. Emmanuel calling me last night and telling me not to come to work."

"That's a possible explanation, I guess."

"But that would mean that Mr. McKenzie, the McKenzie Group and possibly Mr. Emmanuel could also be involved in this scheme to pollute the reservoir's water supply."

"I wouldn't count that out either."

Marc could see this news had caused Sophie to lose her appetite as she sat motionless and stared out the window, ignoring the remains of her lunch.

"Sophie, I've been thinking. Maybe you and Zoe should go somewhere for a while. Who knows what these crazy bastards are up to or what they might try next. I got you into this mess so I'm willing to pay, plane tickets, whatever, to get you someplace where you will be safe, at least until this is settled."

Sophie sat speechless, continuing to stare out the window at the snow bank that ringed the restaurant's parking lot.

Marc started to say something else, but the waitress returned.

"How was everything? Oh you didn't finish your soup," she said as she looked at Sophie's half empty cup.

"Everything was fine," Marc said. "We just weren't as hungry as we thought, thank you."

"Are you ready for the check then?" She asked.

"Yes please."

She tore the bill from her pad, dropped it on the table and left.

Sophie looked at Marc. "I'm not going anywhere. Zoe and I are fine, thanks just the same. You didn't get me into this. I went with you of my own free will. I'm just pissed at myself for not being more aware. I should have known something was wrong at the Inn before."

"What do you mean by that?" Marc asked.

"Oh, they seemed like little things then, but now when I look back, it all makes sense."

"What little things?"

"Well, for one, Al-Zeid was not the first ethnic Arab we've had as a guest at the Inn lately. There were others, not many, but at least five or six since the start of the fall season. Seems like they usually came in groups of two and always stayed in the same room. This was about the same time that the Inn initiated the policy of taking more advanced bookings. We used to book for up to a year in advance, but about mid-September, just after the first of these Arab guests arrived, a new booking policy went into effect, which allowed a guest to book up to five years in advance."

"Five years," Marc exclaimed. "That seems a little excessive."

"Actually, the industry standard is three years. When the word came down that we were taking five-year advance bookings, I thought that it was a long time out, but you know, these advanced reservations started coming in pretty steady to the point we are just about booked up for the whole five years."

"Interesting," Marc exclaimed. "Tell me, if the Inn raises the room rates in the meantime, does the guest get the room for the rate he originally reserved it for, or will he have to pay the new rate?"

"The new rate, of course. They even published a disclaimer," Sophie said.

"The reason why I asked is, in the insurance business, a fire or other catastrophic event that would preclude honoring a guest's reservation, may entitle the Inn to a loss of business coverage. I'm getting the feeling that the Inn could be setting the groundwork for a major insurance claim."

"I'm not following you, Marc. The Inn has the latest in fire protection. It even has its own mini fire department right on the premises. Outside of an earthquake or a massive rock slide, I can't even imagine..." Sophie stopped speaking for a moment as though a light clicked on inside her head. "Or a terrorist attack. Is that what you're getting at?"

"Well, for argument's sake, let's suppose that a dirty bomb was exploded somewhere in the area, at the reservoir, for instance. How far away is that, two or three miles? The physical damage would be negligible, maybe nothing depending on the size of the explosion, but the psychological damage would be devastating. It could take years for the radiation to be mitigated to a level where it would be safe to return. Imagine the financial impact of that. By the way, how much does the Inn gross a year?" Marc asked.

"I'm not sure, but I'll bet it's pretty substantial," Sophie said.

"What are there, twelve rooms plus the cabins averaging sixteen or eighteen hundred a night? I'd need a calculator to be sure, but I'd guess we're somewhere in the three million a year range."

"And for five years," Sophie said. "Plus the income derived from the sales of alcohol, wine at a hundred dollars a pop, massages, facials, ski excursions, snowmobile trips, boat trips and sight-seeing tours. Add another million a year."

"That's a lot of tax free dollars," Marc said.

"The best part is, the Inn would still be there, intact and ready to use after the 'scare' is past. Mr. McKenzie would still have his Inn and twenty million or so to use in the meantime."

They sat in silence, as they mentally assessed this possibility.

"So, Mister PI. What do we do next?"

"We?" Marc asked. "We, are going to get you back to the Miss Saranac Motel. I think you're in enough trouble already. That little excursion to Montreal yesterday may have cost you your job and who knows what else. Let's not push our luck. As far as what I intend on doing, I haven't decided."

"We'll have to see about that," Sophie said stubbornly.

Marc paid the bill and feeling somewhat sorry for the waitress, left her a hefty tip.

The sunny day the two had enjoyed on the way to the restaurant had turned to clouds and a light south wind, which usually meant more snow was on the way. They returned to Saranac Lake without as much as a sentence passing between them.

When Marc pulled into the Motel, Hugh could be seen sweeping sand and snow off the front sidewalk. Spotting Marc's SUV, he stopped his sweeping and made his way toward the Explorer. The look on his face said he had something on his mind.

Sophie rolled her side window down, "Everything OK dad?"

"There you are," Hugh said as he approached Sophie's side of the SUV. I tried your cell, got no answer so I left you a message. You said you were going to the Side Car to meet Marc for lunch. When you didn't get back, I called, but they said that they hadn't seen you. I was beginning to get concerned."

"I'm sorry, daddy. We decided afterwards to have lunch someplace else. What's up?"

"You've got a couple phone messages. One is from a State Police Investigator. I think he said his name is Garrant or Garrand,

187

something like that. He said he wants you to call him as soon as you get in. Sounded kind of important."

"I think I know what that's about. You said there was another message."

"Yeah, Lucy Welch from the Inn. Said she needed to talk to you. When I told her you weren't in, she became annoyed. I told her you'd call as soon as you returned. She said not to call her at the Inn because she doesn't work there any longer and wanted you to call her at home. Her phone number's right on the pad beneath the Investigator's number. Some days I get the feeling I'm running a messenger service rather than a motel."

As Hugh went back to his sweeping, Sophie turned to Marc. "Why don't you come inside while I make those calls? What they have to say may interest you as well."

"OK, but I can't stay long. I've got to call Garrant myself, then I should get back to Plattsburgh."

Marc parked the SUV, and as the two walked to the Motel office, he noticed the sprinkling of snowflakes in the air.

Once inside, Sophie located the pad with the phone numbers.

"Which one should I call first?" She said, more to herself.

"Why don't you try Lucy? She might have some new information that could be helpful when you talk to Garrant," Marc suggested.

"Good idea. Besides, I'm a little concerned about what she told daddy, not working at the Inn any more. She's been there for years."

Lucy Welch answered on the first ring, "Sophie, I'm so glad you called back. I hope your dad isn't mad, I was just so upset when I called earlier and I really wanted to speak with you."

"No problem. Daddy said you're not working at the Inn any longer? What happened?"

"Oh, Sophie. I'm so confused. I don't know what's going on up there."

"I'm sure it can't be that bad. It's probably just some kind of mistake. Who told you that you were being let go?"

"Mr. Emmanuel called me this morning and told me that he was sorry, but that the Inn was going through a reorganization. Can you believe that? He said he got word from the main office to begin downsizing, some hooey about slow economic times. They won't even let me go back to pick up my last paycheck. They're supposed to ship my personal belongings to me by UPS. I don't get it. Our bookings are better than ever. I feel so bad for Walter, too. His wife just had a baby girl and they bought that new house over on Ampersand Avenue last fall."

Sophie could hear Lucy begin to cry.

"Walter? Walter Barris, the assistant manager? He was let go as well?" Sophie asked in amazement.

"Yes," Lucy said between sobs. "He called me shortly after I got the call from Mr. Emmanuel and said he was let go for the same reason I was. Apparently a bunch of the staff was fired too. Have you heard anything?"

"Sort of. Mr. Emmanuel called me and said not to come in until I heard from him. At the time, I didn't think it sounded permanent, but now I'm not so sure. How can they let Walter and you go? Who's going to run the Inn? Mr. Emmanuel can't do it all by himself and now with the staff gone, that's just too weird."

"Not quite all the staff. Walter said a few of the security guards are about the only ones still working. And this is the week that big group is coming and they've booked the entire Inn. I'm so upset," Lucy said.

"Oh, you're right, I almost forgot about them." Sophie thought, "Aren't they the 'Epee' group from Europe?"

"I think so, but it doesn't make any difference now. Mr. Emmanuel will have to take care of things without us. Look, Sophie, I'm sorry to have bothered you with this. If I hear anything more, I'll let you know, and you do the same, OK?"

"Sure thing, Lucy. In the mean time, hang in there. Talk to you soon." Sophie said, breaking the connection.

Marc had heard Sophie's side of the conversation, "That didn't sound good. Lucy and Barris both got the axe?"

"That's right. I don't know how much you caught, but according to what Mr. Barris told Lucy, most of the staff has been let go. This whole mess sounds fishy, Marc. Things just are not adding up."

"What's this you mentioned to Lucy about an 'Epee'?"

"Oh, nothing. We were talking about a large group who had booked the Inn this week. Some kind of business meeting, I guess. I told her they reserved under the group name, 'Epee', or something like that. That's French, I think."

"Interesting, 'Epee' is a French word meaning sword." Marc said.

"Great, just what they need at the Inn—a fencing match,"

Sophie said with a nervous giggle.

"Are you up to returning Garrant's call?" Marc asked.

"Sure, might as well get that over with," Sophie said as she dialed his number. After a few rings, the call was put through to his voice mail.

Sophie left a short message and turned back to Marc, "His cell must either be off or he's in an area with no coverage. Not much more I can do until we hear back from him, I guess."

Marc was silent, as he stood staring at the pad with Garrant's phone number.

"Hello, earth to Marc."

"Oh sorry, what'd you say?" Marc said, trying to refocus his attention.

"What are you going to do now?" She asked, sounding impatient.

Slowly, Marc said, "I was just thinking about this 'Epee' group renting the Inn for the week. Isn't that a bit unusual for the Inn? I didn't think it hosted conventions."

"It is a bit unusual. We've had small groups stay in the past, usually six or eight people for a couple of nights, but never the entire Inn and certainly not for a whole week. The Inn's just not set up for conventions. Besides its pretty pricey. This 'Epee' group, whoever they are, must have some serious bucks."

"Sophie, I know there's a security guard at the main gate. What other kinds of security does the Inn have?"

"What are you thinking about? You're not going to try to sneak up there, are you?"

"Uh, no, I was, uh, thinking." Marc said, unconvincingly.

"Bullshit, Marc! You're thinking about sneaking up to the Inn and checking it out yourself, aren't you?"

"Well, maybe. It would depend."

"Depend on what?"

"Uh, on what I thought I could find," he said, feebly.

"Ah ha, I knew it," Sophie exclaimed.

"Marc, you can't go up there alone. I have to go with you. You have no idea how to get in or where to go once you get there."

"That's out of the question. You're already in enough shit over this as it is. I'm probably responsible for you losing your job and I told you what that serpent bitch said to me in Keeseville this morning. They suspect that we know something. You've got your daughter and your dad to think of."

"Oh, right. Like what happens to you doesn't mean anything either?"

Marc could see that Sophie was beginning to tear up. He pulled her close and held her.

Marc could feel Sophie's sobbing. He kissed her forehead and, as he pulled back, he saw her cheeks were moist with tears.

"Sophie, I just can't allow you to come with me on this. It's too risky."

She pulled a tissue from the box on the counter, softly blew her nose and wiped away the tears.

"OK," she snuffled. "If you're bent on going, I can't stop you. But at least let me draw you a map of the place. No, wait, actually I have a map that we give to the guests."

Sophie retrieved a brochure for the Saranac Mountain Inn she had kept in a kitchen drawer.

Unfolding the brochure, Marc could see it contained a stylized map depicting some of the buildings, the main road into the Inn with the location of the guard gate, and directions for visitors to get to the Inn's check-in desk. Sophie smoothed the glossy brochure on the counter and pointed to the road with the guard gate.

"You can forget about trying to get onto the grounds by driving up the main entrance. Remember, the gate is right here," she said, tapping her finger on the map. "It's manned 24/7 and there are cameras and sensors all along the road. You can't see them, but they're there. The guards will know you're there the minute you pull in from the main road. Best way for you to get up to the main lodge without being seen is to use an old walking path across from Upper Cascade Lake. Do you know about where that is?"

"I think it's a mile or so past the main entrance, isn't it?"

"Close," Sophie said. "It's not marked, but there's a small opening in the woods across the road from the lake. It's hard to see, but there's a length of chain across the entrance. There's also a 'POSTED' sign with 'McKenzie Properties' on it, if it hasn't rotted away by now. It's hardly used anymore, hasn't been for years. From there, it's a two mile hike straight uphill to the backside of the Inn. There are a lot of downed trees, thick brush, and boulders, but the trail is there. I know because I've walked it myself a few times, but never in the winter. They don't clear this trail because they don't want

191

anyone using it. You're going to need snow shoes. Also, you should leave your Explorer down at the picnic grounds at the end of the lake. That's another half mile further down the road."

"I know where the picnic grounds are, but won't that be covered with snow this time of year?" Marc asked.

"Not necessarily. It's right on the town line of North Elba and Keene. The town's snow plows use the parking lot as a turn-around."

Sophie filled Marc in on where Noah Emmanuel's living quarters were located, as well as the route the night security guards took to do their checks. She also pointed out the locations of the main administrative offices, and the security office.

Marc asked, "You think I'd need a master key to get inside?"

"Hmm, that could be a problem. We use key cards. I'd give you mine, but I'm sure they've changed the codes by now," Sophie said, pausing a moment as she thought.

"There is this window, though," she continued, pointing to the Inn's building diagram. "This corner, right here, is where the bookkeeper's office is. She...her name is Samantha...is a smoker. We're not allowed to smoke inside any of the buildings, but I've been in there and I could smell cigarette smoke. I've often seen it opened a crack, and sometimes she forgets to close the window. It faces the woods on the other side of the parking lot so hardly anyone goes by there, but you'll need something to stand on to get up to it."

"Thanks. This gives me something to start with."

He glanced at his watch. "I'd better be leaving while there is still daylight."

"Sure I can't come along? Maybe I could wait for you in the SUV?" Sophie pleaded softly.

"We've been through this. If I get in a jam, I'll get to a landline and call you. Meanwhile, you've got plenty to take care of right here."

"I suppose, if you're sure there's nothing more I can do to help."

"Well, maybe one thing. Looks like I'll need a set of snow shoes."

"Daddy has a set and I'm sure he won't be using them today."

"Let's go ask him just to be sure," Marc said.

"Alright, I'll go look for them. I think he keeps them in the garage."

As Marc left the office, he spotted Hugh still working on the sidewalk.

"I guess there's always something to do around here," Marc said.

"You don't know the half of it," Hugh responded as he paused from his sweeping. "I don't know how I could manage without Sophie's help. Speaking of which, is everything all right with you two? I thought I heard her crying a little while ago."

"Oh, everything's fine. She's upset because she wanted to come with me on this matter I'm looking into. I told her that it would be better if she stayed here with you and Zoe. I think she understands, but, you know how women can be sometimes," Marc said, somewhat embarrassed.

An uncomfortable silence fell between the two men as Hugh continued brushing an already cleared section of the sidewalk.

Hugh gave a soft cough and opened his mouth to say something, when Sophie came out the office door holding a pair of snowshoes.

"Daddy, I told Marc it would be OK if he borrowed these for a day or two."

"Well, I was fixing to climb Noon Mark Mountain right after I finished morning chores, but what the heck, Noon Mark will still be there tomorrow," Hugh said, giving Marc a conspiratorial wink.

"I told you daddy wouldn't mind."

"Thanks Hugh, I'll return them when I get back."

"No rush, I got plenty to keep me busy."

Sophie handed Marc the snowshoes and they walked to where his SUV was parked. Placing them in the back, he closed the hatch. When he turned to face Sophie, he saw tears again welling up in her eyes.

"I'll talk to you soon," he said, and turned to open the driver's door.

She stopped him and put her arms around him, "Please be careful Marc. I'm afraid something bad is happening up there," she said, then kissed him tenderly.

"Not to worry," he said with a forced smile.

As he wiped her tears from his cheeks, she turned and quickly ran past her father, disappearing back inside the motel.

Hugh watched Sophie run by, turned toward Marc, and with a wave yelled, "Good luck, Marc."

"Talk to you soon." Marc called back, and with a wave, headed his SUV toward Lake Placid.

During the eighteen-mile drive past Lake Placid and south on Route 73, the snowfall increased in intensity. As Marc passed the entrance to the Inn, he noticed the road had not been recently plowed and was void of any fresh tire tracks.

Continuing on another mile and a half, he arrived at Upper Cascade Lake. With the intensifying snowstorm and diminishing daylight, Marc almost missed the chain across the entrance to the trail that Sophie said would lead to the backside of the Inn. Another half mile took him to the picnic area, now used as a turnaround for the town plows, and he parked his SUV. Before locking up, he double-checked his H&K to make sure it was fully loaded, then slid an extra magazine in his pants pocket. Marc pulled on his parka, grabbed his flashlight, and, with the borrowed snowshoes over one shoulder, set a brisk pace to where the trail met the road.

Marc found the weathered "POSTED" sign Sophie had mentioned tacked to a tree a few yards in from the road. He figured there should be enough daylight left to make it up to the Inn, but he knew it could be dark by the time he got there.

After fastening the borrowed snowshoes, Marc began his uphill trek. He surmised that this long abandoned path to the Inn was originally cut as a logging trail, used by woodsmen and their mules before the advent of mechanized equipment. Over the years, however, the brush had thickened and wash outs had cut away much of the soil on the steeper portions, exposing boulders along its route. This, coupled with more than two feet of snow, made for arduous climbing and, without snowshoes, almost impossible.

The blowing snow cut through the trees and made a hissing sound as the snow crystals collided with pine needles. Occasionally clumps of freshly fallen snow that collected on tree branches would fall making a soft thumping sound. Marc stirred up the occasional ruffled grouse or snowshoe rabbit that had taken refuge from the storm in thickets of snow covered bushes. Their sudden and noisy outbursts as they fled from perceived danger kept Marc on edge and each time he would stop and crouch down expecting the worst.

By the time Marc finally glimpsed lights from the Inn, it was almost four thirty and the setting sun, obliterated by the heavy snowfall, provided a eerie veil over the landscape. He kept to the shadows of the forest as he worked his way around the Inn to the parking lot, trying to get a feel for the kind of activity he might expect. To his surprise, the guest parking lot held fewer than half a dozen vehicles, all of them covered with about four inches of the freshly fallen snow.

Still using the woods for cover, Marc continued past the parking lot until he came to a large garage that he suspected was used to house the Inn's vehicles. It's interior was dark, but two outside floodlights illuminated the entrance to the six overhead doors. He located a side window and used his flashlight to peer inside. A small dump truck with a snow plow blade and sander attached occupied one of the bays. Another bay housed a van body truck that appeared to have a hydraulic slide that would allow the body to be tilted and lowered for easy on and off loading.

Interesting that the snowplow should be sitting idle in this storm. Perhaps the 'Epee' group decided to cancel.

Although the breeze and hissing of the heavy snowfall covered most of his movements, Marc was careful not to make any more noise than was necessary as he continued toward the employee parking area. There, he observed a few more vehicles, three of the Inn's Chevrolet Tahoes, and a SUV Land Rover.

Referring to Sophie's map, Marc located the Inn's administrative offices at the far end of the main lodge, just past the parking lot. The only lights from inside the Inn were coming from the dining room area.

Marc's leg muscles burned from the arduous trek up the logging trail. He removed his borrowed snowshoes and secreted them in an unlit corner of the administrative building. Sophie hadn't mentioned any surveillance cameras, but he scanned the rooftops and light poles just in case.

At one end of the administrative building, Marc located the bookkeeper's office window. He could see that it was indeed slightly open, a dark slit visible at the bottom of the sash. The window appeared to be about six feet off the ground. He pushed up on the window and opened it a little further, but, found it was too high for him to pull himself through without the aid of a step. Marc retraced his tracks to the garage and the side window that he had peered through before.

After checking the window casing to confirm it was not wired for a burglar alarm, he tried to open it, but it was locked from the inside. Using his gloved hand, he broke the pane nearest the inside latch and, reaching inside, unlocked and opened the window and pulled himself through. Once inside, he closed the window and hastily kicked the shards of glass against the garage wall. A quick flick of his flashlight revealed a stack of white five-gallon buckets, piled against the back wall near the van body truck and a pair of snowmobiles. After removing one of the pails from its nested stack, he walked to the rear of the truck and raised its overhead door about two feet so he could peek inside.

At first he didn't know what to make of the small tracked vehicle parked inside the van. Marc raised the overhead door another couple of feet to reveal a compact machine, like a mini bull-dozer. He aimed his flashlight at the front of the machine, thinking it could be a small earthmover, but instead he saw a hydraulic arm folded into its cradle. It appeared the arm could be unfolded, then raised or lowered to fit the need. At the very end of the arm was attached a large screw-like bit, similar to ones Marc had used in the past to drill holes in concrete or masonry, only this one had a much larger diameter–about six inches.

Is this what was used to drill the hole in the rock face at the reservoir?

Marc quickly closed the van's overhead door, and with the 'borrowed' pail, climbed back out the window, closing it behind him. Retracing his steps to the bookkeeper's window, he removed one of his boot laces and tied one end to the handle of the bucket. Turning the bucket upside down so he could stand on it, he opened window and pulled himself through, carefully holding onto to the shoelace. Once inside, he pulled the bucket up and through the window, closed it, and slid the locking hasp in place.

The computer screen atop the bookkeeper's desk emitted a dim glow and as he laced his boot, he took in the surroundings. The desktop was neat and tidy. A photograph of a young girl, probably five or six years old, dressed up and posing with her arms wrapped around a stuffed teddy bear with palm trees in the background, the kind of photo one gets taken at a department store, was the only personal thing Marc observed. Apparently Samantha the bookkeeper was either a single parent, or just didn't want to keep a photo of daddy at the office. A tug on the desk drawers confirmed they were locked.

Marc knew it would be foolhardy to try to access the computer. Without a password, any attempt to access the Inn's computerized business records could send off an alarm signal. He sat in the bookkeeper's chair assessing his next move, listening to the low hum of the computer and the soft ticking of snowflakes against the outside window.

196

Marc eased over to the office door that he assumed led into the hallway. A turn of the handle showed it was locked from the inside, probably by the bookkeeper as she left for home. Marc slowly pushed it open. Cautiously, he peered down the darkened hallway. Finding it all clear he silently closed the door behind him, making sure he could re-enter the office if he had to.

Remembering his tour of the Inn just days before, he turned left and carefully made his way toward the stairwell, grimacing with every small squeak, the floorboards under the carpeting protesting his weight. Noises that were barely noticeable under daytime circumstances now sounded like claps of thunder as he edged forward. He slipped past office doors with the names of Lucy Welch and Walter Barris inscribed on their windows, backlit with the faint glow of computer monitors left on inside.

Marc remembered that Noah Emmanuel's office was located further down the hallway past the stairs, and as Marc inched closer, he heard the murmur of voices coming from somewhere above. Deciding to investigate, he crept up the stairwell while the voices, punctuated with occasional bursts of laughter, grew louder. Continuing his ascent, he remained alert for the sounds of staff personnel, night watchmen, or anyone else that might happen upon him.

As Marc approached the dining room level, he spotted a partition and grinned at this piece of luck. As long as he stayed behind the partition, he could continue to the top floor unnoticed by anyone in the dining room.

His leg muscles ached with tension as he finally reached the top floor, where he heard the muffled sound of footsteps on the carpeted hallway coming from the direction of the guest rooms. Stepping into the shadow of a doorway marked 'housekeeping', Marc held his breath and stood dead still. Years of surveillance taught him to become one with the background. Movement, no matter how slight, attracts attention.

A tall, middle-aged man, smartly dressed in dinner attire, passed by no more than three feet away; his eau du toilette leaving a wake of cloying fragrance hanging in the hallway. Only Marc's eyes moved as he watched the man turn onto the landing, then disappear down the stairwell. Seconds later, he heard the shuffling of chairs as the gathering below rose to greet this latest addition to their group with a smattering of applause.

When the welcome finally subsided, someone, perhaps the fragrant newcomer, said, in accented English, "Gentlemen, gentlemen, please. Thank you for the warm welcome, but as you know, we have much to discuss."

Again the chairs scuffed on the wooden floor as those in attendance casually reclaimed their seats.

Keeping to the shadows, Marc inched forward where he could actually see many of those seated below. It was like looking down at a meeting of a local Chamber of Commerce. Through the haze of cigarette smoke, he could see about a dozen men, ranging in age from early forties to late sixties, seated around two large dining tables. Marc eased around the partition to get a complete view of the gathering, while remaining hidden in the shadows of the alcove.

The newcomer had taken his position in front of the tables, commanding the full attention of the gathering, and with his back toward Marc he began to speak. "First, I want to thank you all for taking time out of your busy schedules to attend this very important conference on such short notice. I know many have had to travel long distances, but thanks to modern transportation as well as America's lax border policy, your attendance here insures a successful meeting."

Is this the consortium that Bianca was talking about?

"Phase one of our plan to host the 2026 Winter Olympic Games in our Austrian homeland is already well under way. With the help of our associates, a radioactive device has been installed very near the Lake Placid water reservoir. However, I have just received some rather unfortunate and untimely news."

With the announcement of impending bad news, the speaker had the full attention of his audience.

"We have, just this afternoon, learned that the local authorities have become aware of the presence of the device. For reasons yet unknown to us, they have remained silent about this discovery. Either they do not know what they have, or perhaps they want to avoid undue publicity and panic."

Suddenly, the previous air of congeniality was replaced with anxiety as murmurs of discontent billowed up from those sitting around the tables.

Marc observed an elderly white haired gentleman rising from the center of the crowd, tapping his cane on the wooden floor as he did

198

so. Although his accented voice boomed, Marc had to hang on his every word.

"Herr Heitmeyer, I can only speak for myself, but there are others in this room who, I believe, feel as I do. Everyone here has a vested interest in having the Olympic Games returned to Austria. You have summoned us to this place to hear what we assumed was news of progress in this endeavor, but now we learn that we are a mere five kilometers from an explosive device that could spread radioactive fallout over the entire area. With respect, I feel very uncomfortable with this arrangement and certainly would not have come here had I known this was the case."

Marc watched as several members of the gathering nodded in agreement as the white haired attendee slowly reclaimed his seat.

Heitmeyer must be the key man.

"My dear Otto, I share your concern. However, the local authorities do not have the means of extracting the device without prematurely exploding it, thus, through their own incompetence, completing our immediate goal themselves. As you are aware, despite Lake Placid's favored status, just the hint of radioactive pollution either in the air, on the land, or worse, in the water supply, will ultimately eliminate its bid to host an Olympic event.

Despite Heitmeyers's assurances, it was apparent that the news had a disquieting effect on the listeners, and, as if on cue, another attendee, sporting a pair of thick horn-rimmed glasses, a dark ascot and a bare pate, rose to speak. Clearing his throat, he spoke in an accent that Marc did not recognize.

"Herr Heitmeyer, surely, you must understand our concern. Given this latest turn of events, what are your plans to mitigate this problem to provide a more positive outcome for the investors?"

Again, several attendees nodded in agreement as the curious-looking man reclaimed his seat.

"Nicolai, your feelings of apprehension are completely understandable. This revelation was as much a shock to me as it is to you. Unfortunately, our Arab friends were not as careful with implanting the device as we had hoped; however, there is no need to panic."

Heitmeyer paused for a slow sip of water, possibly gathering his thoughts as he did so, Marc figured.

"As you are aware, my seat on the International Olympic

199

Committee's executive board carries substantial weight in determining the location of the winter games. Once word gets out that there is even the potential of radioactivity anywhere around Lake Placid, it will not be hard to sell the selection of Innsbruck as the preferred site for the 2026 winter games."

This seemed to mollify the gathering as the rumbling receded to a few whispers. This change was not lost on Heitmeyer as he charged ahead.

"In the first place, the device is not timed to explode for another month. Obviously, the authorities will not wait around that long to see what happens. I assume they may endeavor to disarm it and they may be able to do so, but in the meantime, we are here, close to ground zero. Think about it. We are attending the annual meeting of L'epee Argentee. Who could possibly suspect a prestigious group of philanthropists deciding on worthy causes that need our support? Besides, the device that has been installed can only spread low level radioactivity limited to the reservoir area."

Again, the white haired gentleman rose from his seat.

"Herr Heitmeyer, I hesitate to ask, but feel that it is my duty. What if this device that, as you say, our Arab friends have installed, fails to explode, or is somehow deactivated by the local authorities? Won't that jeopardize our whole plan? Might it not even backfire and rouse sympathy for the cause to have the games held in Lake Placid?"

Again, a few heads nodded in agreement. Heitmeyer, who had appeared to regain the upper ground, answered with an icy edge to his voice, "My dear Otto, we have known each other a long time and you know that I am a serious man. As I have indicated to you before, this device is practically foolproof and any attempt to neutralize it will simply cause it to prematurely explode. Of course, we would rather that it exploded at the proper time when the ice on the reservoir is melting. But, even in a worst case scenario, the news that radioactive material is spread out over the frozen reservoir will have much the same psychological impact as it would have if it were in the water. As I said before, this discovery by the local civilian authorities is unfortunate, but should not preclude us from going ahead with our plans."

He continued, "As for us, we are simply guests of Mr. McKenzie. The snowstorm that we are experiencing could not have come at a better time. The roads to the Inn are completely snowed over and we intend to leave them that way. No one can leave or enter, so we should not be disturbed. We are above suspicion. Our Arab friends have been paid for their services and they have begun the process of leaving the area."

Another sip of water as an obviously confident Herr Heitmeyer continued.

"What we now require, gentlemen, are your assurances and agreed-upon commitments for funding the consortium that is charged with preparing the winter games to be held in Innsbruck, as that decision, thanks to the discovery of the device, should now only be a formality."

With this announcement, on the heels of the revelation of the device being discovered, the mood of the assembly changed to uncertainty. No one seemed to dare move or be the first to speak. The hum of an unseen furnace fan was the only sound. The silence hung over the gathering in tandem with the cigarette smoke and seemed to drag on for minutes.

Was there reluctance on the part of the conspirators to commit to the cause? Was there a rebellion brewing?

Then, after a few hushed whispers and turning of heads, Otto, the man who had only moments before challenged Heitmeyer, slowly rose and faced both the speaker as well as his fellow conspirators. In his accented baritone voice, Otto boomed, "I am proud to announce to all that the Fatherland's Front Party, formerly known as the Vaterlandische Front of Austria, stands ready to support the consortium in its efforts to bring the 2026 winter Olympics to Austria, where it rightfully belongs, with five million Euros on the condition that Innsbruck is awarded the games. We will hold another five million in reserve."

Otto had everyone's attention and Marc saw that from the deference the others paid him, he was held in high regard.

"As many of you are aware, the Vaterlandische Front of Austria has been lying in wait since the 1940's, slowly rebuilding and consolidating power. We plan to use our political network to convince those in the present government who may be hesitant to cooperate with us. We expect the games to generate the appropriate interest and enthusiasm among our aspiring political candidates for the re-emergence of a proud Austrian fatherland and a return to a strong central government. This will be accomplished by the placement of appropriate political party banners and slogans on all official advertising for the games, including TV and print advertisements, internet, and social media sites, as well on all official Olympic communications."

"Thank you, Otto, my old friend," an obviously relieved Herr Heitmeyer said.

Marc watched as Otto looked around at the others, then carefully reclaimed his chair. Again, heads turned, each waiting to see who would speak next. This time, it was Nicolai, his heavy glasses perched on his nose, who stood to address the gathering.

"Herr Heitmeyer. As the representative of the European syndication of family-run businesses that, despite what Interpol says, has only the best interests of the games at heart..." he hesitated, allowing the smattering of chuckles from the gathering to subside before continuing, "Along with other organized affiliations in the European Union, we have pooled twelve million Euros. I have been authorized to transfer six million to the consortium's bank account in Geneva. The balance will be made available upon the announcement that Innsbrook has been successfully awarded the games. As you know, in return, all we ask for is a small percentage of the gross receipts, which should cover the costs of any risk we should encounter in this endeavor.

"Thank you Nicolai. You will not be disappointed."

With these two organizations having pledged their support, the pace of the meeting picked up, and no sooner had Nicolai sat down, then another quickly rose.

"Herr Heitmeyer, the Austrian Federation of Trade Union workers is proud to commit twelve million Euros, with the understanding that contracts awarded for refurbishing the roads, bridges and tunnels will include workers from our unions."

One after another, each of these men, representing an assortment of nefarious groups with strange-sounding names rose to pledge support to the consortium. As Marc listened, he recognized these men were hardly philanthropists, each demanding a return on their investment, which ranged from public relations and marketing exposure, labor management, security, a percentage of hotel room rentals to downright skimming.

Marc jotted down as many of the men's names and the organizations they represented as he could on a piece of the Inn's stationary that he found next to one of the house phones.

The last of the group was finishing with its pledges and demands, when Marc figured it was time for him to make his exit. As he was retreating down the stairwell, he heard Heitmeyer announce, "Gentlemen, thank you for your support. This concludes the business portion of the meeting and now it is time to enjoy ourselves. The bar is open and dinner will be served shortly." This was followed by shouts of approval and scattered applause.

Continuing his descent past the main floor, Marc heard the sound of a cart being rolled down the corridor above. He glanced up in time to see the Inn's general manager, Noah Emmanuel, pushing a steam tray loaded with bins of food heading for the main dining room.

So, Emmanuel is in on this. That must be why he let the employees go, leaving himself alone to take care of the guests.

When Marc reached the ground floor, he eased around the stairwell and crept back toward the bookkeeper's office where he was surprised to find the door ajar. His heart rate jumped as he was sure that he had previously closed the door.

Has someone discovered my footprints in the snow outside the window?

Marc backtracked down the dark corridor toward Emmanuel's office, passed the stairwell. His eyes strained to locate the exit he remembered was at the far end, now concealed in the darkness. The muffled sounds of chairs being rearranged could be heard from the floor above, coupled with the din of the men talking. As he crept toward the far end of the hallway, he stopped every few feet and listened for footsteps, continually glancing back in the direction of the bookkeeper's office.

A floor board creaked somewhere in the passageway behind him. Marc turned and dropped to one knee, his left shoulder pressed against the wall as he grasped his H&K automatic in both hands, scanning the blackness.

Was that a flicker of movement back by the stairwell? Got to keep moving, find a way out of here.

Looking forward he could see a pinpoint of light in the exit door's glass made by the reflection of an exterior floodlight. Marc's knees burned in this crouching position, as he slowly worked his way down the hallway. Finally, the outline of the exit door came into focus, its doorknob just a few feet away. Marc could feel cold air seeping in from under the door. As he reached up for the doorknob, however, he was jolted by a whispered voice that came out of the darkness, somewhere behind him; "Don't touch that."

Marc again whipped around, the muzzle of his automatic pointed in the direction of the voice. Expecting the glare of overhead florescent lights at any moment, he crouched further down near the doorway, his heart pounding. For a long moment, he remained frozen, the pad of his index finger pressed against the gun's trigger, its muzzle vibrating with tension as he waited for whoever it was to reveal himself.

I know I'm not hearing things.

As if answering his thought, the same whispered voice came again from the darkness, closer this time, and worse, it sounded too familiar, "Marc, back this way, hurry."

It can't be.

"Sophie, is that you?" Marc whispered, lowering the firearm.

"Over here, in Emmanuel's office doorway. If you open that exit door, you'll set off the alarm."

As Marc's eyes slowly focused on the figure crouched in the office doorway, a mere four feet away, he could see it was Sophie, dressed in dark cross-country ski pants, coat and a knitted wool toque as she emerged from the shadow. Marc crept to where she was kneeling, reached out, and as he touched her arm, he felt the cool wetness of melting snow on the fabric of her coat.

"What the hell are you doing here? I told you, this could be dangerous."

"Shhh. Look, we can argue about this later, but if you've found what you came for, I think we'd better find another way out of here."

"How did you get in?" Marc asked.

"Through the service entrance. The outside door was open and I snuck through the kitchen and down the stairwell. When I went to the bookkeeper's office I caught a glimpse of you in the hallway. I think our best chance of getting out without being discovered is to leave the way I came in."

Without waiting for Marc to respond, Sophie turned and led the way back up the stairwell. Arriving at the kitchen's swinging doors, she peeked through the small glass window in its center. Seeing no one, she pushed through with Marc close behind. His eyes blinked as they adjusted to the kitchen's bright halogen lights. The two rushed past a wall of stainless steel appliances, fryers, refrigerators and a curtain of polished pots and pans suspended like Christmas ornaments over a cooking island. The aroma of freshly prepared food lingered in the air.

Sophie continued to the opposite end of the kitchen toward the service entrance. However, upon reaching the exit door, she saw that it was now firmly shut.

"Shit." Marc heard her say.

Before he could ask what the problem was, she slammed down on the door's crash bar, and using the forward motion of her body, shoved the metal door wide open. Immediately, the stillness of the deserted kitchen was shattered with the blaring of a klaxon alarm, its deafening staccato pitch reverberated off the banks of steel cupboards and appliances. Outside, on the loading dock, the alarm's unnatural blast jolted the frozen night air.

Shit is right! Someone's probably checking the alarm panel now. No time to lose.

Sophie retrieved her snowshoes from the rear of a dumpster where she had stashed them before entering the Inn.

Marc yelled over the piercing alarm, "Forget the snowshoes! This way!"

With Marc now in the lead, the pair slogged their way through the freshly fallen snow past the bookkeeper's office back to the Inn's garage with its broken side window. Aware that they had only a minute or so before someone found their footprints, Marc threw open the window sash and they both climbed through.

"Marc, we can't hide in here. Someone will find us and, believe me, they won't be long in coming."

"I know, but I have an idea," Marc said, as he made his way toward the back of the garage.

Sophie followed him to the pair of snowmobiles that Marc had previously noticed parked in the far corner. Hopping on the seat of the closest sled, he fumbled around to locate the ignition key.

"Damn, no keys."

"Hold on," Sophie said. Sprinting to a wall cabinet, she picked off a key ring with a tag 'snow sled'. "I think this is what you're looking for," she said, handing Marc the key.

"Open one of those overhead doors!" He shouted.

Sophie slammed her palm against the automatic door opener, but as one of the center doors slowly rose, she could see the bobbing reflection of a flashlight beam heading toward them from around the corner of the Inn.

Marc revved the snowmobile's powerful engine, "Hop on and hold tight."

Sophie jumped onto the rear passenger seat, wrapped her arms around Marc, and yelled, "Go!"

Marc turned the accelerator to full throttle and the snow sled shot out of the garage and onto the snow-covered parking lot. With the bouncing flashlight beam closing in, Marc veered away and headed toward the guest parking lot. When he glanced over his shoulder, he saw a series of bright flashes accompanied with the muffled pops of automatic gunfire.

"Keep low," he yelled, and held the throttle at full bore. Heading across the parking lot, the Skandic snowmobile skimmed over the layer of fresh powder snow throwing up a rooster tail in its wake, helping to obscure Marc and Sophie from their pursuers. Making the wide turn out of the lot, he glanced back toward the Inn. Through the dining room windows he could see the heads of a few of the Inn's guests peering out, probably wondering what this flurry of commotion was all about.

The snowmobile screamed down the Inn's main road, its bright twin headlights lighting the way between snow banks piled high on either side. Marc pushed low behind the windscreen and Sophie's grip tightened around his waist.

As successful as they had been so far, their escape was hardly a sure thing. Marc knew the guard at the main gate would have been instantly notified and waiting for them.

Sophie, however, was already thinking ahead and tapped Marc on the shoulder, "Turn left onto the nature path. It should be coming up any moment."

"Where does it go?"

"Never mind. Just don't miss it because we probably won't be able to turn this thing around if you do."

Marc throttled the engine down and squinted to see through the heavy wall of falling snow. Soon he saw a narrow opening through the trees. As he leaned to the left and steered the sled toward the opening, its halogen lights shone on a small wooden sign that was almost buried in the snow, 'Saranac Mountain Inn Nature Trail'.

As the sled's skis reached the bottom of the snow bank, he yelled,

"Hang on," and gunned the engine, sending the sled over the snow bank and onto the unplowed nature trail.

With Sophie's guidance, Marc carefully navigated the sled down the narrow trail and away from the Inn's main road.

So far, so good. No sign of any pursuers since those gunshots back at the parking lot.

A quarter of a mile further and the pair arrived at a frozen pond Marc vaguely remembered seeing on the map Sophie had given him.

Sophie yelled over the noise of the engine, "Head straight across the pond. There's another trail at the other side that will take us back to the Inn's main road. Route 73 is just beyond that."

The intensifying snow storm made navigating difficult. With few reference points and everything around the sled a wall of white, Marc had to refer to the sled's compass built into the dashboard.

Gotta keep this thing heading due south or with these white-out conditions we could be going in circles.

The sled quickly covered the four hundred yards to the opposite side of the pond where Marc could see the snow-covered branches of trees lining the shore.

"Turn left. The trail should be off to our right," Sophie yelled, motioning toward the shoreline.

Marc turned the machine and strained to see through the heavy flakes of snow. As the sled approached the shoreline, Marc could see groupings of overturned aluminum canoes and kayaks stacked neatly on their racks. Easing the sled onto the shore, Marc quickly found where the trail continued through another opening in the woods.

A minute later, they came to a section that seemed to be cleared of trees on either side and Marc cut the sled's engine.

"What's the matter? Why are you stopping?"

"Shhh, let's try to hear if anyone is pursuing us."

As the two sat in the cold silence, the soft patter of falling snowflakes and the crackling of the sled's heated engine was all they heard.

No other sounds.

Finally, Sophie said, "Just stay on the trail. It's only a quarter mile or so and we'll come back out on the main road, past the guard shack. Then it's just a short distance to Route 73."

Five minutes later Marc maneuvered the sled onto the Inn's road. He half expected a greeting party from the Inn's security to meet them there, but to his pleasant surprise, there was no one. As he turned left toward Route 73, he let himself relax, knowing it was a just short distance to the highway that would take them to the Cascade Lake parking lot and his SUV.

Another quarter mile and Marc could see the reflection of a streetlight through the trees ahead. Just one more corner to get around, then they would be on the main road. He briefly considered hitting the throttle and speeding up, but then thought better of it.

Patience, Marc. No sense in taking chances now. We're almost out of here.

Through the snowfall, the black surface of the recently plowed tarmac on Route 73 came into view.

As they reached the intersection, Marc slowed the sled to check for traffic when suddenly they were bathed in high intensity light coming from several directions at once. Red and blue flashing lights lit up both sides of the intersection. A police vehicle was driven onto the Inn's main road behind them blocking off any return. A voice on a loudspeaker boomed, "This is the State Police. Release the throttle and raise your hands." Sophie yelled, "Marc, stop, it's the police."

Although Marc was still in flight mode, there seemed nowhere else to go. Besides, as Sophie had just said, they were safely in the hands of the State Police. As he brought snowmobile to a halt, Marc could see past the spotlights that the entire roadway was blocked with a sea flashing emergency lights.

Suddenly, Marc heard Sophie scream and felt himself being grabbed, pulled from the sled and pushed forcefully to the pavement. Powerful hands pinned both of his arms in back of him and he felt the ratcheting handcuffs biting into his wrists.

"Don't move," was the terse command from one of his abductors.

Marc felt someone grab his ankles and probe upwards as he was frisked for weapons.

"I have a permit for that," Marc yelled, as he felt another hand yank the back of his parka up and remove the H&K from its holster secured in the small of his back.

Then, a familiar voice.

"Stand him up, guys. Let's see who we have here."

As Marc was helped up off the pavement by two large uniformed State Troopers, he came face to face with Investigator Jerry Garrant.

"Jerry," an astonished Marc said, "Thank god it's you! We've got a lot to talk about."

"Yeah, we certainly do," Jerry said, his voice tinged with frustration. Then, pointing to one of the unmarked police cars, he said, "Boys, remove the cuffs and put Mr. LaRose and the young lady in my car."

As Marc was helped into the rear seat of the car, he could hear Garrant directing other troopers to secure the snow sled and make arrangements for it to be transported to the Ray Brook barracks.

Sitting in the back seat, Marc and Sophie could see that, in addition to the troop cars parked along the highway, a State highway department snowplow was being positioned on the entrance to the Inn with its wing plows fully extended, virtually blocking the road from both directions so that no one could enter or leave via the Inn's main road.

Sophie looked over at Marc, "I haven't had time to tell you, but after you left for the Inn this afternoon, I called Jerry Garrant. I told him what you and I had talked about, you know, the woman with the gun in Keeseville, the explosives and what you found up at the reservoir. I also told him that you were coming to the Inn tonight to check things out. I'm sorry Marc, but I was afraid...afraid something would happen to you."

Sophie leaned her head on Marc's shoulder, sniffling back tears.

"You did the right thing. I'm glad you told Jerry what I told you, but now there's a lot more he should know."

Suddenly, both front doors of the vehicle opened almost at once. Garrant got in behind the wheel and Tim Golden climbed in on the passenger side. Before Marc could say a word, they both turned back toward him and Sophie. Golden spoke first, "Look Marc, I thought we had an agreement. You were asked to come to the Plattsburgh barracks and talk to us about this situation, but for whatever reason, you had other plans. We're getting pretty sick of picking through your shit and cleaning up after you."

"Guys, I know how this looks, but...," Marc started to explain, but Garrant cut him off.

"Marc, first you had this theory about what killed Al-Zeid. Then there was that hole you found in the rocks by the reservoir. This morning you bring us this Austrian broad blubbering about her missing husband. And twenty minutes ago we were notified of a burglary in progress at the Inn. Of course, with the information

Sophie gave me this afternoon, we figured you had to be involved."

"Let me explain. You're right, I was at the Inn, and while I was there, I witnessed a meeting that was taking place and I overheard what was being said. There are people up there who represent various underworld organizations. They were pledging their assistance, mostly financial support, with the aim of getting Lake Placid eliminated from hosting the 2026 winter Olympics."

"Marc, this shit's getting deeper by the minute." Jerry exclaimed. "Everyone knows that the decision on where the 2026 winter games will be held has not been made."

As Jerry was talking, Marc heard what he thought was a thumping noise coming from somewhere outside.

"Besides Lake Placid and Innsbruck, there's Santiago, Chile as well as Reykjavik, Iceland," Jerry explained.

Marc replied, "True, but it's no secret that Lake Placid is favored to get the nod. The intent of these people at the Inn is to get Lake Placid knocked out of contention by polluting the water supply. That's where the hole in the rock face comes in."

Marc noticed the thumping noise was getting louder.

"Is that a State Police helicopter I hear, or is it Custom and Border Protection's?" Marc asked.

"It's definitely not ours," Jerry said, peering up out the windshield as the noise continued to increase in intensity.

Jerry and Tim got out of the car and looked skyward. The snowstorm was passing and the moon was faintly visible through the thin cloud cover. The heavy thumping of a helicopter's rotary blades seemed to come from the direction of the Inn, but as suddenly as the noise had started, it grew quiet again.

"It sounds like the Inn's visitors, the ones I was just talking about, have an alternate escape plan," Marc said, still seated in the back seat of the troop car.

"What do you mean by that?" Tim asked.

"They left the Inn's road unplowed to dissuade outsiders from snooping around, except they didn't plan on a frustrated PI working an insurance claim to come snooping around. Now, that their presence has been discovered, they've called in the cavalry to whisk them off, probably back over the Canadian border."

Jerry seemed to consider what Marc had said, then turned to the trooper who was preparing the snowmobile to be transported to the

Ray Brook headquarters, "Trooper, change of plans, we're going to need that." Then turning to back toward the troop car, he yelled, "Come on Marc, you know how to drive that thing, take me up to the Inn, I want to meet these people."

Marc handed Sophie his car keys, "You're going to need a ride home. It looks like I might be busy here for a while."

As Jerry and Marc made their way to the snowmobile, Jerry reached under his coat and brought out Marc's handgun. "Here, take this. Just don't get cute with it." He then yelled to his partner, "Tim. Take charge down here. I'll be on the air with my portable radio. Have headquarters call the Homeland Security air branch in Plattsburgh and ask if they can send their chopper to help us out." He then waved to the snow plow driver to move from its position across the Inn's road and yelled instructions to three of the uniformed troopers to follow him and Marc in their State Police Yukon SUV's.

Marc started the sled's engine and when he felt Jerry hop on behind him, gunned the engine and cut around the snow plow, heading up the Inn's main road. Using the sled's twin halogen lights, he followed his earlier tracks in the snow until they got to the nature path where they veered off to the right.

Jerry yelled at Marc over the noise of the sled, "Keep going straight up the main road to the Inn. If there's someone still at the gate, we'll deal with them."

When Marc glanced behind, he saw the headlights of the State Police SUV's following, but, his sled was losing them fast in the deep snow.

As the road curved, Marc could see lights from the guard shack flickering through the trees ahead. Getting closer, he noticed that the entrance gate arm was down, and without slowing, cut the sled to the left around the building into the lane designated for departing guests. Suddenly the road ahead was awash in a blaze of bright light as the gate guard hit the light switch.

I just hope the troopers can deal with the guard before he has a chance to warn anyone of our approach.

Knowing that time was of the essence, Marc continued at full throttle toward the Inn with Jerry tightening his grip around his waist. The darkened guest check-in building flew by in a blur.

Two hundred yards from the main parking area, Marc sensed as much as heard, a high pitched shrill noise, accompanied by that same thumping he'd heard before.

"That's got to be the helicopter," he yelled, urging the sled on at maximum speed.

Soon, Marc caught flashes of the parking lot lights blinking through the forest of trees. As the entrance to the parking lot came into view, he could see the air was alive with the flurry of powder snow blowing wildly in all directions, and at its center, a set of flashing red lights.

When the sled burst into the lot, Marc was stunned by the dark outline of a Huey helicopter coming straight toward him, its nose pointed downward in a forward cyclic as the pilot was attempting to gain speed and altitude as quickly as possible. The helicopter passed overhead, its jet-powered turbine screaming at full throttle to clear the wall of pines surrounding the parking lot. As Marc brought the sled to a halt, he was mesmerized by the helicopter's slow labored climb. Its exterior spot light frantically searching for a channel through the trees to make its escape.

Just when it appeared that the pilot had succeeded in powering his craft over the pine trees, it mysteriously hesitated, then heaved forward. One of its landing skids had become entangled in a branch near the top of the trees. The craft slowly pitched forward as it strained to free itself of this last tentacle, the pilot holding at full throttle. Suddenly, the tips of its spinning rotary blades made contact with the top of the tallest pine within reach. The contact between metal blades and pine sent a shower of bark and shavings into the parking lot, not unlike a giant wood chipper. The combination of screaming jet turbines and twenty-four foot composite blades chopping pine branches into bits was deafening. Then, with a loud bang, one of the helicopter's blades shattered.

Marc and Jerry watched in horror as the doomed craft pitched to the right, the stubborn pine branch clutching like a hawk's talon, held tight to the entangled skid. As the helicopter body twisted sideways, the remaining blade whirled in an off-balanced arc. Finally, the offending branch, sensing its job completed, reluctantly gave up the helicopter's skid, allowing gravity to complete the task.

As the helicopter descended, it rolled over, down the side of the pines until it hit the pavement with a loud crash. With its engine still at full throttle and laden with jet fuel, it exploded in a giant fire ball. The force of the blast blew Marc and Jerry from their sled.

212

Moments later, Marc slowly stood, shaken and dazed by the blast. From far away he could hear someone speaking. Slowly, the voice grew louder. "Gotta see if anyone's alive," Jerry shouted as he ran towards the inferno.

Marc instinctively staggered after his friend, and slowly, the shock from the blast began to dissipate. As they approached the burning helicopter the intense heat forced them to retreat. Marc thought he heard screams coming from the burning remains.

Must be my ears are still ringing; no one could have survived that blast.

A police SUV arrived and Marc heard Jerry yell for the trooper to notify fire and rescue. Using his portable radio, he called to the troopers that were manning the road block to have the snow plow clear the Inn's road for the rescue vehicles.

While Jerry was busy with the task of setting up a perimeter around the helicopter and assigning troopers to cordon off the area, Marc got back on the snowmobile to see if any of the conspirators had stayed behind at the Inn. He drove around to the service entrance where he and Sophie had made their escape a mere forty minutes before. The service door was still open.

Marc got off the sled and cautiously made his way up the stairs to the loading dock. As he was about to peek inside, he heard the noise of another snowmobile engine starting up somewhere behind the Inn.

Who else would be using a sled tonight? Unless…

Marc ran back to the corner of the building just in time to observe the remaining Skandic snowmobile erupt from the open door of the garage. There appeared to be two people on the sled as it veered to the right, away from the main parking lot.

I guess someone's missed their flight.

Marc quickly recovered his sled and took off after the second Skandic. Locating its tracks in the snow, he followed them around the back of the Inn toward the logging trail that he'd hiked up earlier in the evening.

Marc could see the fleeing sled's track cut deep in the powder snow, probably because of the extra weight of carrying two people. He positioned his sled directly in the track blazed by the fleeing Skandic, allowing him to speed up and soon he caught sight of its red taillight.

As Marc pressed on he could see that the driver was trying to maneuver the sled around some fallen trees as it started down a steep rock cut. It wouldn't be long before they'd know he was behind them, but it was too dangerous to cut his headlights.

Marc got to within a hundred feet, suddenly there was a bright flash coming from the lead sled, then another.

Oh fuck, gunshots, time to back off.

But before he could react, the red taillight ahead seemed to just disappear. *Must have gone around a corner or down a ravine.*

Marc slowed, careful not to drive into an ambush.

Following the tracks over a rise in the trail Marc inched his sled forward to the top of a ridge guarded on both sides by huge boulders. He remembered this part of the steep climb where he had to carefully pick his way up to the Inn. Still, no taillight, no sign of the sled ahead.

Bringing his sled to an idle, he positioned its headlights down to the trail below. The track of the fleeing sled had vanished. At the bottom of the ravine, however, he saw an object next to a boulder. He swung the nose of his sled to focus its powerful beam on the object. Apparently the fleeing machine had become airborne as it crested the ridge and made a direct hit on a jagged boulder at the bottom of the gorge. The sled's crumpled remains lay on its side with its skis and rubber track torn away.

Holding his H&K in one hand and adjusting the sled's beam with the other, Marc quickly scanned the area for the passengers, keenly aware they were armed. A slight movement caught his eye and as he glanced upwards over the wreckage he focused on an dark shape in a birch tree, about eye level, but ten feet above the gorge. His sled's headlight illuminated the body of a man, wearing a dinner jacket, dangling from a tree limb. The broken end of a thick branch glistened in the beam's light as it protruded from the man's back. His stocking feet were still twitching as if continuing his attempt to escape.

Gives new meaning to the term 'Tree Hugger'.

Marc dismounted and carefully picked his way down the ravine toward the sled's wrecked remains. As he got closer, he heard a gurgling inhale from the shoeless victim as he struggled to breathe, his body bouncing lightly as it dangled from the tree branch above. A dark stain on the snow beneath him appeared to expand outward. Anxiously, Marc continued to scan the area for the other rider as he was sure there had been two on the sled and at least one of them had a gun.

Through the receding light from his sled, Marc noticed another movement beyond the destroyed sled further down the ravine. Holding onto saplings for support, he continued his descent through the knee-deep snow toward what appeared to be the figure of another man lying among the rocks and downed trees, one of his legs laying at a peculiar angle, obviously broken.

As Marc crept closer, he noticed the second man was wearing a waiter's jacket. He bent down and brushed the snow covering the man's face and immediately recognized Noah Emmanuel. He had a large gash on his forehead, and when Marc touched him, he moaned in pain. Marc removed his own parka and laid it over him. "Noah, don't try to move. I'm going for help."

Emmanuel, his weakened voice barely audible said, "Got to stop the Arabs."

"What? Noah, what about the Arabs?"

Emmanuel opened his exposed eye and tried to look toward Marc's voice, "Shit, I can't move my head. I can't move at all."

Marc surmised that Emmanuel's neck or back might be broken.

"Noah, I'm going for help, but first, tell me, what about the Arabs? We know they planted the explosive device up at the reservoir."

"Forget that, that's nothing." Emmanuel struggled to say.

"Forget about it? What do you mean?" Marc shouted.

"Nothing there, just a diversion to…to fool the consortium. The Arabs only wanted the money so they could fund their stupid Jihad against the New York City Jews."

"Noah, who was with you on that sled?"

"Who? Oh…Hub," Noah started to say, then faded off.

"Noah, who was that with you," Marc yelled again.

"Huber. He's as crazy as those fucking Arabs…" Was all that Emmanuel could get out before he slipped into unconsciousness.

He's going into shock. Got to get some help.

Marc passed back under the lifeless body of Phillip Huber and climbed up the rock cut to his snowmobile. After restarting the engine he reversed the machine and followed his tracks back to the Inn. Without his parka, the cold air bit through Marc's sweater. He figured it was around twenty degrees above zero, but cruising along in the open air on the sled made the night air feel much colder.

When Marc returned to the Inn's parking lot, he found it ablaze with flashing red, blue, and white lights from the vast assortment of

215

emergency vehicles. Ned Barnes was standing with a few other volunteers from the Lake Placid rescue squad watching as the fire department sprayed fire-retarding foam on the still flaming hulk of the helicopter, which was, by now, barely recognizable, as it had melted into a red hot glob of metal and plastic.

"Ned, there are two people on the old logging trail around back of the Inn. They were thrown off their snowmobile. I think one's dead, but the other, Noah Emmanuel, is still alive, but he looks pretty bad."

"Well, it doesn't look like we're going to be needed here, poor devils." Ned said, motioning towards the inferno.

Marc gave Ned instructions to where he would find Emmanuel and what remained of Phillip Huber skewered by the tree limb. The EMTs hastily hooked up a makeshift stretcher and body board to the snow sled that Marc had commandeered.

Ned asked Marc to return with him.

"Sorry Ned, I've got to locate Jerry Garrant. Just follow the snowmobile tracks. When you get to the crest of the ravine, that's where you'll find them."

Marc looked for Jerry, but he was nowhere in sight. When asked, a trooper informed him that Garrant had gone to set up a command center at the guest check-in building.

Marc started off toward the guest check-in, then hesitated.

Jerry's busy getting things set up down there. Before I lay more bad news on him, maybe now would be a good time to take another look inside the Inn.

Entering the kitchen area, Marc found the remains of the supper that had been served to the men of the consortium earlier in the evening. Dinner plates were piled onto transport carts along with drinking glasses and half-empty serving baskets of bread and rolls. Apparently the dinner meeting had ended abruptly, probably when he and Sophie made their clamorous departure on the snowmobile, Marc figured.

This place is beginning to creep me out. Not a soul around and all that commotion outside.

When he entered the main dining room with its giant antler chandelier still fully lit, he saw that the dining tables had been only partially cleared.

Lights are on but nobody's home.

It was apparent that everyone had cleared out in a hurry.

216

He checked the guest registry. No names had been listed for the past two days. Apparently, the meeting of the 'L'Epee Argentee' was meant to be a non-event, Marc figured, as he looked around the main desk for room keys. Beneath the check-in desk he found a box of plastic key cards, emblazoned with the Inn's name and a color photo, probably taken from the center of the lake, he surmised.

As he passed back through the dining room, he spotted a key card lying on the carpet behind the podium where Herr Heitmeyer had been speaking. Marc slipped the card in his pocket and took the stairs two at time up to the guest rooms on the upper floor. With no room number on the key card, Marc tried the card on each of the guest room doors he came to in an attempt to access one of the locked rooms.

On the third try, at the guest room with "Haystack Mountain" printed above the door, a green light came on followed by a clicking sound as the door's internal locking device deactivated, allowing him access to the room. Inside, the dresser lamp was still on. The bed, although still made up, appeared to have been laid on by the occupant, probably resting up before the dinner, Marc surmised.

On the coffee table, Marc observed a wine glass with remnants of red wine pooled at the bottom. He pulled back the bedcovers exposing the bottom sheet, then threw them off to one side, revealing only a bare Serta Sleeper.

A check of the nightstand and bureau drawers showed nothing but the Inn's Gideon bible in a relatively unused condition.

The flat screen TV yawned back at him in grey silence.

In the bathroom, he saw a half empty plastic bottle of perfumed shampoo and the remnants of a bar of herbal soap. A towel on the bathroom floor had been used as a bathmat and its matching washcloth looped over the shower rod.

"A shower before supper, perhaps?" Marc muttered to himself, as he returned to the bedroom.

He opened the closet door. The top shelf held an extra pillow, blanket, and a few plastic bags for items to be sent out for cleaning, but that was not what interested Marc. His attention focused on the full-length black leather coat hanging to one side. Marc removed the coat and spread it out on the bed's bare mattress. He could tell by the feel that the leather was good quality. The wool lining had an unusual color pattern. The label read, "Fabrique au France" and was a size

"Grand taille," indicating that the owner was at least an average-sized man, probably taller.

Marc remembered seeing this coat hanging off the back of a chair the day he interviewed the Hubers in the Inn's dining room.

This must be Phillip Huber's room.

Marc checked the coat's side pockets and found an empty chewing gum wrapper and a book of matches from a disco bar on Crescent Street in Montreal. When he flipped the coat open and examined the inner breast pocket he located a travel brochure with, "Teitelbaum Transit Company," emblazoned across the top. Underneath the name of the company was a photograph of a white tour bus with the company's logo printed in blue, "*One People, Two Countries.*"

Flipping through the brochure, Marc came to the company's tour schedule that indicated Teitelbaum provided direct transit service between Montreal and New York City on Thursdays and Sundays. The schedule also indicated dates and times for special sightseeing tours of Montreal, New York as well as Lake Placid.

What would Phillip Huber want with a Jewish bus schedule?

He stuffed the schedule in his shirt pocket and returned the coat to its hanger. After finishing with Huber's room, he checked the other guest rooms. Most were still locked and the few unlocked ones appeared unused.

When Marc peered out a window on the second floor he saw that the helicopter fire had been extinguished. The police ID section had arrived and officers were busy taking photos and measurements while the rescue people appeared anxious to begin the grizzly process of recovering the charred remains of its occupants.

As Marc made his way down to the dining room area, he heard the sound of a snowmobile coming around from the back of the Inn. Exiting the kitchen door he saw Ned Barnes driving the sled pulling the body board with Noah Emmanuel lashed down, his head and neck fitted with a brace for transport. They were headed toward one of the ambulances in the parking lot.

The body in the tree would become another crime scene for the police to handle, as if they didn't already have enough to do, Marc thought to himself.

Marc got to the ambulance as the EMTs were loading Emmanuel on a stretcher. Ned Barnes eyed Marc and handed him his parka, "I guess this belongs to you, Marc. Good thing you covered him up. He's gone into shock. Keeping him warm was a good idea."

"How bad is he?"

"Possible broken back and a few other fractures as well. Really too early to tell, but I think he stands a good chance of making it."

Without waiting for Marc to reply, Ned yelled to the ambulance driver. "OK Tom, the hospital has been alerted that they have a severe trauma case coming in. I'll see you back at the office."

As Emmanuel was secured inside the ambulance and as its rear doors slammed shut, Barnes turned back toward Marc, "Guess I should get going too, see you around sometime."

"Thanks for returning my coat," Marc said as he gave Ned a wave.

Marc slipped into his parka, and despite the blood smears, he was grateful for its return.

As he watched Ned drive away he was surprised to see Sophie and a uniformed trooper standing in the middle of the parking lot looking toward the crash site.

Marc waved, catching her attention. She returned the wave and ran to where he was standing.

"What are you doing back up here?" He asked.

"Investigator Garrant said I might be of some assistance, showing him where things were located around the Inn. He said he had to go to Lake Placid, something about getting a search warrant. He had me drive your SUV up from the Cascade Lake parking lot. I think he wants you to stay here and wait for him to return."

Dismissing Garrant's message with a wave, he asked, "Have you ever run across a bus company by the name of Teitelbaum, maybe here at the Inn or in Lake Placid?

"Teitelbaum?" "Well, not here for sure, I mean, the Inn doesn't cater to tour buses, but, that name does sound familiar. Why do you ask?"

As Marc started to explain, Sophie interrupted, "Wait, now I remember. I've seen buses with that name parked at the Mount Van Hoevenberg Ski Center."

"I wonder if they lay over somewhere in town while their touring the area?" Marc asked.

"I'd assume so. I'm not sure where, but if I had to guess, I'd say they would stay at one of the chains, or the Olympic Arena Motel in

Lake Placid. I've seen other tour buses parked there from time to time."

Marc retrieved the bus schedule from his shirt pocket. Scanning it again, he saw there were listings for direct bus service several days a week from Montreal to Monsey, New York, and on to Borough Park in Brooklyn.

About half way down the page, Marc read, "Tour Lake Placid and the 1980 Olympic Region, ski Whiteface Mountain followed with a night's stay at the Olympic Arena Motel."

Marc looked at his watch, "Shit, according to this schedule, Teitelbaum Transit has a bus in Lake Placid right now!"

"OK, Marc but…"

"Come on Sophie, let's get into town. I want to find that bus."

"Well, alright," Sophie said hesitantly. "Maybe I wasn't clear, but I believe Investigator Garrant wants you to wait for him here. Are you sure you want to piss him off again?"

"When we get closer to town, I'll try him on his cell."

"OK, but don't say I didn't warn you."

"I can handle Jerry. Let's get going," Marc said motioning toward the SUV.

Sophie reluctantly handed Marc his keys and they climbed into the Explorer. The Inn's parking lot was still full of emergency vehicles and a second mobile generator had been set up near the crash site, its powerful floodlights further illuminating the area.   Marc motioned towards an unmarked police vehicle as it arrived with its red grill lights flashing. "That looks like the Troop B Commander. He'll be taking charge of the scene," Marc said. "Now's a good a time to make our exit."

He eased his SUV out of the parking lot and down the Inn's main road past the now deserted guard shack.

When they reached the intersection with Route 73, they could see the snowplow that had been blocking the road to the Inn was replaced by single troop car and two troopers directing responders onto the Inn's roadway. Intent on keeping unauthorized people out, they gave Marc's SUV scant attention as he turned right toward the Village of Lake Placid.

Route 73 had been cleared of snow and, although the moon was visible, it was encircled with a hazy ring, an omen of more inclement weather to come. Two red beacons high up off to their left marked the presence of the Olympic ski jump towers.

Marc retrieved his phone from the center console, and pressed the number for Jerry's cell, but after a few rings he was directed to his voice mail.

"Shit, he must still be busy getting that search warrant."

Marc left a message that he and Sophie were en-route to Lake Placid and he'd found something in the Inn that he needed to share with him.

"The Olympic Arena Motel is on Main Street toward the north side of town. I want to first check their parking lot and see if Teitelbaum's bus is parked there," Marc said.

"Jerry's gonna be pissed," Sophie said, her tone implicating they should have waited for him at the Inn.

The evening's storm had left Lake Placid's narrow Main Street even narrower. Snow had been plowed to either side where it was piled up along the curbs forcing the parked cars closer toward the center of the street. At this late hour, the myriad of boutique shops were shuttered, but the bars and restaurants were booming as groups of revelers filled the sidewalks in search of more excitement. Marc took his time maneuvering past the lines of parked cars, on the lookout for the wayward partygoer attempting to dash across the slippery roadway.

"The motel you're looking for is just past the arena. There's a restaurant right across the street called the Bark Eater. Odd name for a restaurant, don't you think? Wonder if they serve tree bark," Sophie said with a giggle.

"Lore has it that the Mohawk Indians referred to their hated enemy, the Algonquins as "bark eaters" given their penchant for eating berries and young shoots during the winter when food was scarce." Marc said.

"OK, I'm impressed," Sophie said.

"I'm sure there are things you know about the Maori people of New Zealand that I'm not aware of either," Marc said.

"The Maoris? You know about them? Now, I am impressed," Sophie said in mock earnest.

Before Marc could respond, The Olympic Arena Motel came into view off to their right. Marc had passed by the motel many times before, but he'd never given it much notice. It was situated at a right angle so that its front office faced Main Street, but its two floors of rooms ran perpendicular, away from the street. A large parking lot to the right was shared with a real estate office next door, which ironically, displayed a "For Sale" sign in the window. The left side of the motel butted up against a wooded lot that ran another hundred feet along Main Street before meeting the open expanse of the Lake Placid Golf and Country Club.

Marc made a left turn into the half-full parking lot of the Bark Eater Restaurant and slipped the SUV into a space between two cars facing the road with the motel across the street. He dimmed his headlights and cut the engine.

They could see that the motel's parking lot, which also appeared to be half-full of cars, had been recently cleared as evidenced by a large pile of snow to the right of the real estate office. Another mound in the middle of the lot surrounding a cluster of light poles, effectively blocked the view of any vehicles that might be parked toward the rear of the lot. There were no tour buses in sight.

"It's still early. Let's sit here and see if that bus shows up," Marc said.

"Sure, I guess," Sophie said unconvincingly.

A few minutes into the surveillance, a group of patrons left the restaurant, driving off in the cars that were parked on either side of the SUV, and Marc could see that his cover was slowly disappearing.

As the evening lingered on and the temperature continued to drop, Marc began to doubt his decision to hang out in a cold car to watch a parking lot when suddenly they heard a diesel engine. From the direction of Whiteface Mountain, a large white touring bus lumbered into view. Sophie poked Marc, "I think that's your bus."

As the bus passed "Teitelbaum Tours" was plainly visible along its side. With its left turn signal blinking, the bus turned into the motel's lot, then made a wide arc around the back of the real estate office, pulled up alongside the motel entrance and stopped to the hissing of its air brakes.

The bus's four way flashers lit up the side of the motel with staccato bursts of amber light. The doors opened and passengers began to straggle off. Most seemed to be in good spirits laughing and shouting to one another, an indication they had probably visited an après ski party.

It took about ten minutes for the passengers to disembark. Most went straight to the motel while the remaining few headed downtown,

222

not quite ready to call it a night. Marc and Sophie watched as the bus was driven back around the real estate office where it parked—out of their sight. A few minutes later, the bus driver, obviously weary from a long day of chauffeuring the load of boisterous party goers, made the slow walk to his own room in the motel, the wheels of his rolling suitcase etching two lines in the thin remnants of snow as he dragged it along.

"Well, that was exciting," Sophie said, still annoyed that Marc hadn't waited for Jerry back at the Inn.

"Jerry's still in court and probably hasn't checked his voice mail. We'll hold up here for a while longer. The fact that Huber was carrying that bus brochure on the same night he got himself killed and the fact that the bus is now parked right here is just too much of a coincidence to overlook."

"Whatever," Sophie said with a ting of resignation. "I should give my dad a call. He didn't want me trekking up to the Inn by myself tonight and he's probably worried."

"Sure, just keep the phone below the dash. I don't want to alert anyone that we're sitting here."

As Sophie finished her call, Marc caught sight of couple coming out of the restaurant. Although Marc and Sophie sat still in the darkness of the SUV, the couple glanced toward them as they passed. Marc already had his arm around Sophie and he hugged her closer whispering, "Pretend were lovers."

"What's to pretend?" She whispered as the couple got to their car.

They embraced each other until they heard the crunching of the car's tires on the snow as it pulled out of the lot. Marc was still thinking of how to reply to Sophie when his cell buzzed. He kept his head low as he flipped his phone open. Jerry's cell number was displayed.

"Jerry," Marc said.

"Where the hell are you now?" Jerry's voice was filled with exasperation.

"I guess you got my message."

"I thought I was clear when I told Sophie you were to remain at the Inn.

"Yeah, but…" Before Marc could explain, Jerry continued his rant.

"Look, I'm on my way back to the Inn with a search warrant. My captain's been in touch with the duty officer in Albany, again. I don't know how much more of your help I can stand, old buddy." Marc had the feeling that their friendship was wearing thin.

"First of all, don't blame Sophie. She gave me your message, but a few things have come up since then."

"Marc, this better be good. You know what I'm up against here and I don't know how much longer I can cover for you."

"I understand your frustration, Jerry, but listen for a moment. After I found Huber dangling from that tree, I had a chance to look inside his guest room where I came across a tour bus schedule."

"That's nice. You planning a trip?"

Ignoring the jab, Marc continued.

"I'm sitting in front of the Olympic Arena Motel looking at the tour bus. I think there's a connection with the helicopter crash and this bus."

Marc could hear Jerry exhale. "Tell you what. I don't have time to babysit a tour bus. You do whatever it is you think you need to do. I have a search warrant and a forensic detail waiting for me at the Inn. We're going through that place top to bottom. For now, you stay put, take notes, and keep me posted. I have enough dead bodies to deal with. I don't need any more."

Marc started to respond, but Jerry cut the connection.

"That went well," Sophie said, "So, who can we piss off next?"

"He'll get over it. Jerry's a perfectionist and all I've done lately is cause him problems."

"Well, I wouldn't say that it's been all your doing. I mean, you didn't cause any of this. You just have a peculiar knack of showing up when shit happens."

"Shh…listen," Marc said, glancing at his side mirror. Another group of diners left the restaurant and were starting across the street.

"Looks like they're staying over at the motel." Marc turned to Sophie. "Look, I know it's a drag, sitting here in the cold, but I need to hang out here, see what happens with that bus."

"If we're staying here all night, you're going to have to either start the engine and heat this thing up, or find another way to keep me warm." She said with a sly grin.

Marc grabbed a blanket that he kept on the back seat and spread it out over her.

"Is this what you had in mind?"

"It'll do, at least for now, but it's big enough for two," she said, spreading the blanket across the seat.

They huddled in silence, watching the motel and warmed by nothing more than the thin blanket and the combined heat of their bodies. Diners continued to trickle out of the restaurant. One by one the cars left the parking lot, leaving Marc's Explorer alone and exposed, its windows frosting over.

Midnight passed with no activity and, although the motel parking lot seemed full, the red neon 'Vacancy' sign continued to sputter away in the frozen stillness. As time dragged on, Marc sensed Sophie's growing uneasiness as they waited for something…anything…to happen. The blanket slowly lost its warming effect as the cold seeped into the SUV. It wasn't long before the windshield was almost completely frosted over, save for a clear slit just above the dash vents. Marc fought the temptation to doze off and strained to keep watch.

Except for the occasional police patrol, traffic on the Main Street had thinned to a trickle and Marc was bothered by an uneasy feeling. He couldn't help but think that he was missing something right in front of him.

Whoa, was that a flicker of light coming from inside the real estate office?

He nudged Sophie to ask if she had seen it, too.

"Huh?" She answered, having given in to the creeping onset of drowsiness.

Marc focused on the office windows, straining to see through the slit of clear windshield.

"Probably just a reflection from a car headlight," Marc said.

Then another flash.

"Was that what you're referring to?" Sophie asked, now fully awake.

"You saw it too? Good, at least I'm not totally losing it."

"Looks like someone's inside the office using matches or a lighter." Sophie said.

"OK, but what the hell would they be doing in there this time of night?"

"What, so you think it's too late for a home tour? Rates are pretty low, you know," she joked.

Before Marc could answer, a movement in the shadows beyond the real estate office caught his attention.

225

"I need to see what's going on over there," Marc said.

"Hate to sound redundant here, but don't you think you should call Jerry first?"

"He knows where to find us."

"Yeah, I know, Marc, but..." Her thoughts were cut short as, this time, they both saw movement.

"Sophie, sit tight. I'm going around the back side of the motel to see what's going on."

Marc grabbed his flashlight and instinctively felt for his gun.

"Hold on, big boy. You think you're leaving me alone in this icebox on wheels? I'm right behind you."

Exiting the SUV, they silently pushed their doors shut. Then, mimicking the late night crowd, they casually walked arm in arm past the motel on the opposite side of the road. Once they were out of view of the real estate office, Marc led Sophie across the street, then cut through the adjacent wooded lot, keeping the motel between them and the office. The knee deep snow and thick brush made for slow going. Beyond the street lights, they were guided by the stray flickering of blue TV light that seeped through a few of the motel room curtains.

As they came around the back of the building, they walked into the rear parking area, but Marc kept close to the motel wall. They could see each unit had a small patio with two plastic lawn chairs covered in snow. A line of vehicles, mostly mini vans and SUVs with ski racks were parked in a long row, facing in toward the units. From where they stood however, the real estate office was blocked by another mound of plowed snow.

In the stillness of the cold night air, Marc heard a shuffling sound coming from the direction of the real estate office, but to see anything, he would have to work his way around the snow bank, which could leave him exposed.

Think Marc, think.

"Sophie, I need you to hang here a moment," Marc whispered as he crouched down in front of the row of parked cars.

Using the vehicles for cover, Marc crept forward and, as he passed each one, glanced in the direction of the real estate office before coming to a stop behind a van at the end of the row. He signaled for Sophie to join him.

She slipped past the line of vehicles and crouched next to Marc.

The mound of plowed snow no longer shielded the real estate office from view.

The reflection of the parking lot lights gave the scene an eerie appearance and Marc scrunched his face in an attempt to discern the peculiar scene before them. The tour bus parked alongside the real estate office was plainly visible. As his eyes slowly adjusted, he could see that a long table, or skid, had been extended down a short flight of stairs from the office directly into the rear cargo door of the bus.

"Looks like someone's planning on loading something into that bus. But, why at two o'clock in the morning?" Marc whispered.

Before Sophie could answer, the figure of man dressed in a snowmobile suit appeared at the office door. He seemed to struggle as he pushed a crate along the skid towards the bus. A moment later, another man emerged from the office door to assist, and with one on each end, they slowly moved the box toward the bus.

"Curious," Sophie muttered.

Although the bulky suits the men were wearing looked oddly familiar, Marc's attention was focused on the crate.

Several moments passed before the men finally made it to the landing with their cargo. Then, from the shadow of the bus, two more similarly clad men emerged. The second pair took over and continued to guide the crate down the conveyor to the bus while the first two turned back toward the real estate office.

From over Sophie's shoulder, Marc watched as the first two men headed back to the office. Something about the way these two walked looked vaguely familiar to him.

Shit. That's Stretch and Stoopy from the house in Willsboro.

"Whatever's in that box must be pretty heavy," Sophie whispered. When the two finally arrived at the bus's cargo bay, a pair of arms reached out from inside the bus, helping to pull the crate inside.

Sophie and Marc continued to watch as the men brought one container after another down the conveyer to the waiting bus, when unexpectedly, a flash of red light came from somewhere inside the cargo hold, reflecting off a face shield on one of the men.

Face shield? That's odd, Sophie thought. Why would anyone need a face shield? Unless, whoa, wait a minute; they're wearing air tanks, with face shields.

"Oh shit, those aren't snowmobile suits, they're hazmat suits," she whispered.

"What?" Marc said.

"Marc, we should clear out now and call the cops. State cops, locals, any cops. But first we've got to get the hell away from here," she whispered loudly and with panic in her voice as she started to crawl back toward the corner of the motel.

"Sophie, where are you going? We can't just leave now."

"The hell we can't. If those guys are handling what I think they are, we may have already been exposed."

"Exposed to what?" Marc asked incredulously.

"Marc, I don't have the time or patience to figure a safe distance equation, I just know that if those crates are radioactive, we need to get some distance between them and us as quickly as we can."

By now, Sophie was half upright, retreating toward the corner of the motel. Marc gave one last look toward the bus and noticed that one of the suited men had stopped what he was doing and seemed to be looking in his direction.

She's right, time to leave, Marc thought to himself as he turned to follow Sophie, who, by this time had rounded the back of the motel. Minutes later they cut through the wooded lot the way they had come in and back onto Main Street.

"Let's cross the road out of sight of the real estate office and circle around the back of the restaurant. Hopefully no one will see us getting into the Explorer," Marc said.

As they crossed the restaurant's deserted parking lot, each step they took made an unnervingly loud crunching sound on the thin layer of the snow that covered pavement.

Before they rounded the back of the restaurant, Marc peered around the corner of the building toward the motel parking lot to check for any movement. The view was eerily serene—the only movements were white puffs of chimney smoke from nearby buildings, lazily curling upwards in the still, cold night air.

No one's coming, so far, so good.

"Come on!" He said pulling Sophie along toward the SUV, that now looked like a block of ice with its windows completely frosted over.

Sophie, opened the passenger door as quietly as she could, slid in on the frozen leather seat and slowly pulled on the door until it clicked shut behind her.

Marc grabbed a credit card from his wallet and using its edge as an ice scraper, began chipping the frost from the driver's side of the windshield.

Suddenly the sound of an engine starting came from somewhere across the street. In the shadows he could see a van slowly rounding the back of the real estate office with its lights off, turning in his direction. A few more quick swipes with the credit card and he slid in behind the wheel. Even in the darkness, there was something about that van that made Marc feel uneasy. He nervously fumbled in the pockets of his parka to locate the vehicle's keys.

Valuable time wasted.

The SUV's engine stubbornly turned over a few times before it fired into life. To keep it from flooding, Marc tapped the accelerator gently and it settled into a slow idle.

More time wasted.

Peering through the hole in the frost-covered windshield, Marc could see the silhouette of the van backlit by the parking lot lights. It had crossed the motel's parking lot and had stopped on the opposite side of the street facing the SUV.

It was then that Marc recognized the van as the one he had seen in the Keeseville Civic Center just a day before when its driver had threatened his life.

"Fasten your seat belt," Marc said as he rammed the gear shift into drive and revved the motor. The engine coughed as though it might stall, but recovered and Marc swung the wheel sharply to the left onto Main Street. Not taking any chances on flooding the motor, he eased down on the accelerator, letting the engine speed up slowly. A glance in his side mirror revealed a set of high beams right behind him.

Marc handed Sophie his cell phone, "Give Jerry a try. Just hit redial."

Cautiously, Marc eased up to fifty miles an hour, heading north out of town toward Whiteface Mountain. The two lane roadway had been plowed and sanded, but with the frigid temperature, it was still partially covered with snow and ice. Despite the approaching threat from behind him, Marc preferred to err on the side of caution rather than end up in a snow bank, or worse yet, against the rocks that bordered both sides of the road.

Marc prodded the SUV as they passed the white expanse of the

Lake Placid golf course, steadily increasing speed as the Explorer headed down a long stretch of road, a mile or so before it crossed the Ausable River bridge.

"No luck," Sophie said. "We're already too far out of town to access a cell tower."

"That van looks very familiar, and if it's who I think it is, it's not good news," Marc whispered, almost to himself.

"Those guys had to be loading something hazardous into that bus. But I don't get it. I mean, what's up with putting radioactive material on a bus bound for Monsey, New York?" Sophie said, oblivious to the threat behind them.

"Remember what I told you about my encounter with the woman who I called the 'serpent girl'?" Marc asked, glancing into the side mirror.

"How can I forget?"

"After she shot a hole in my tire, she warned me to stop my investigation into Al-Zeid's death. I think she's driving the van behind us."

Sophie looked apprehensively in her side view mirror, "Oh, shit."

With a downhill curve coming up, Marc let off on the accelerator and noticed that the van's headlights were closing in on them.

Picking up speed after the curve, Marc could see they were fast approaching the intersection that lay just beyond the bridge, its reflective hazard markers coming into view. Marc briefly thought of making the sharp right hand turn that would take them back towards the ski jumps, but to do that, he would have to slow his Explorer and risk the van ramming them from behind. Marc pressed the SUV faster as it seemed to fly over the bridge.

Suddenly, in the darkness, just beyond the reach of his headlights, Marc noticed what appeared to be two tiny yellow dots hovering in the roadway, directly his path.

"Oh fuck," he yelled as he recognized the points of light for what they were.

"At the same moment, Sophie yelled, "Watch out for the deer," as she, too, realized what was just ahead.

Rather than slam on the brakes, Marc pressed down on the accelerator and eased the SUV into the left-hand lane. He glanced at the passenger side mirror and saw the van's headlights begin to pull up alongside the Explorer.

Marc's SUV barely missed the large buck as it seemed to fly by the right side of his vehicle. He let off on the gas in preparation for a long right-hand curve he knew would be coming up fast.

As he maneuvered his vehicle into the curve, he could feel the rear of the SUV begin to slide. He avoided the temptation to touch the brakes, which he knew would throw his vehicle into a skid. A patch of bare road caught the rear tires and whipped the SUV back in line. Not sure if he was still being pursued, he continued to speed down the mountain road.

Suddenly, the snow-covered pine trees lining both sides of the road ahead lit up with a flash of bright light from somewhere behind them.

"Do you think that was the van?" Sophie asked.

"Yeah, too bad. That was a good-looking buck," Marc said derisively.

Although the van's lights had disappeared from his mirror shortly after passing the buck, Marc continued on, taking no chances that the threat from behind had been abated.

Two miles further down the road, Marc passed a sign for High Falls Gorge, a seasonal tourist attraction, coming up on their left. With still no sign of headlights behind them, Marc slowed the SUV, relaxed his grip on the wheel, and pulled into the cleared parking lot.

"Nobody's been behind us since that flash, but let's sit here for a few minutes just to make sure," Marc said, as he cut the SUV's headlights.

"Good idea," Sophie said as she looked back up the road apprehensively.

"What do you think happened back there, Marc?"

"Your guess is as good as mine, but I doubt it was good news for anyone inside the van," Marc said, the darkness hiding a cautious smirk.

Five minutes crept by with no sign of traffic.

Finally, Marc said, "What do you think? You up to heading back up there and finding out what happened?"

"Just as well, we can't sit here all night."

When they got back to the curve where Marc had last seen the van's headlights, they were greeted by the flashing amber lights of a state DOT sand truck parked alongside the roadway. Marc could see the truck's crew was busy setting out a line of traffic flares along a stretch of ripped-up guard rail. In the truck's headlights, they could see pieces of burning wreckage spread over the snow off the road near the river.

Marc maneuvered past the sand truck and with his four-way flashers on, parked the SUV between the line of flares. He called out to one of the crewmen, "Need any help?"

"Nothing you can do for them now. Looks like one person's dead, but it's kinda hard to tell how many were in the vehicle. My guess is they hit a deer. There's body parts and fur and shit all over the place."

"We're heading up to Lake Placid. Want me to notify the police when we get there?" Marc asked.

"Naw. We've already contacted our dispatcher on our two- way radio. He's called the troopers. We're gonna stand by until they get here."

Just then, Marc heard another one of the crewman call out, "Hey, here's another one. Looks like he's still alive!"

Marc looked to where the DOT worker was shining his flashlight. Along the river's shoreline, he could see the dark form of a body lying in the snow.

Sophie, overhearing what the crewman had said, caught up to Marc, and the two trudged through the snow to where the body lay.

As they approached, they could see a man lying face down in about a foot of powder snow. Curiously, both of his arms were extended out in front of him. His jacket was badly ripped and just like Phillip Huber dangling in the tree, he too was shoeless, apparently the result of being thrown from the van by the blast.

"Another three feet and he'd have made the river. Probably been swept away in those icy rapids," the crewman said, pointing his flashlight toward the Ausable River rushing by.

The crewman grabbed hold of one of the man's arms and was about to roll him over when Marc yelled, "Don't do that, you might injure him further. Do you have a blanket or something to cover him up with?"

"Yeah, I think so. Let me check," the crewman said hesitantly, before scurrying back to his truck.

As Marc knelt next to the body, he pointed his flashlight beam toward the man's face. Brushing the snow away, he immediately recognized him from their meeting at the carpet store in Montreal.

"Naveed, can you hear me?" Marc yelled above the noise of the rapids.

A muffled groan, then the man said something in a language that neither Marc nor Sophie could understand.

"Sounds like he's speaking Farsi or something," Sophie said.

Marc saw that Naveed's wrists were bound together with plastic flex ties, the kind that plumbers use to secure water pipes, or cops to restrain a prisoner. He turned toward the crewman who was still making his way to his truck, "Hey buddy, we'll need a set of wire cutters too."

"Naveed! Hold on. Help is coming," Marc said.

Upon hearing Marc's voice, Naveed attempted to lift his head, but was unable to do so.

"Who are you?" Naveed cried out. "Where am I? Where's Nousha?"

"Naveed, this is Marc LaRose. You called me yesterday. You said you were going to meet me in Keeseville, but you never showed up. A woman came instead."

"Mr. LaRose?" Naveed asked, sounding confused.

"Yes, Naveed, I'm right here."

"Oh, Mr. LaRose, please help me. I can't feel my legs, my hands are tied and I can't see anything. Please help me up," he said as he attempted to raise his arms.

"Naveed, you've been in a bad accident. Just lay still. Help is on the way."

The crewman returned with an emergency blanket and wire cutters. They spread the blanket over Naveed and Marc carefully snipped the plastic flex ties from his wrists, then Sophie gently rubbed them in an attempt to restore the circulation.

"Mr. LaRose, I tried to call you. I wanted to talk to you, but Nousha was suspicious. She would have killed me but for my brother. She tied me up on the floor of the van, said she would deal with me after the bus left for New York City."

"Naveed, tell me, what's on that bus? I saw some men dressed in protective suits. It looked like they were loading something very heavy into the cargo hold."

"What? I'm not sure. None of us are supposed to know what the others are doing," Naveed said, his voice weakening.

"Naveed, this is important. What were they loading into that bus?" Marc said, very firmly.

"Uh…yeah…I…I heard Khaleed say something about polluting New York City's water supply, the…Kensico Reservoir, I think. All of the City's water goes through there," he said, barely audible.

"How? How was he going to pollute the water supply, Naveed? Come on, talk to me!" Marc shouted.

"With radioactivity…My job was…just to help Nousha bring in the C4…Khaleed will do…anything that the Mufti…asks him to do…and so will that…fucking Nousha."

Naveed's comments confirmed what Marc and Sophie had already suspected, that the Teitelbaum bus was carrying a dirty bomb destined for the New York City watershed.

"Khaleed…brought me to…Canada." Naveed continued weakly. Said he would…get me a job and a…new life…but I didn't want this…I never wanted to hurt anyone."

"I understand, Naveed. Look, try to rest; the ambulance will be here soon."

"I told…that stupid bitch...she was driving too fast," he gasped. "She wouldn't listen…said she had…warned you and…" His voice trailed off.

Marc could hear sirens in the distance coming down the notch from Lake Placid.

"Come on, Sophie, the ambulance is on its way. We've got to get back to Lake Placid and find Jerry," Marc said.

As they left the scene, they passed a State Police patrol, an ambulance, and a fire truck. It took another ten minutes of hard driving before Marc and Sophie arrived back in Lake Placid.

"Try Jerry again," Marc said, handing Sophie his phone. Sophie hit the redial button and, when it started ringing, handed it back.

"Did you have anything to do with that accident down in the notch?" Jerry yelled.

"Well it's about time you answered you're phone. Been trying to call you for almost an hour, and, no, we were not involved in any accident," Marc said, unconvincingly.

"That's not what I asked. Where the hell are you two anyway?"

"We're in the village, hoping to catch you before you left to serve that search warrant. I have some critical information to discuss with you, A-S-A-P."

"Marc, I've just pulled into the Inn's parking lot with the warrant.

If you've got information, you're gonna have to meet me up here."

"Fine, but look, there's a tour bus involved in this mess and we believe it's still at the Olympic Arena Motel. Do you have a patrol that can go there and hold onto it until you're through at the Inn?"

"Are you shitting me? We're up to our asses in alligators with all that's gone on up here. If you want to mess around with some fucking bus, you do it. I'll catch up with you later," Jerry said, his voice filled with exasperation as he cut the connection.

"I've got a feeling that our favorite investigator is pissed," Marc said as they passed the "Entering Lake Placid" sign, barely visible above the snow bank alongside the roadway.

As they approached the Olympic Arena Motel, Marc slowed the SUV, and scanned the parking lot for the tour bus. From the street, it was impossible to see if it was still there.

"I'm not trudging back through the woods again," Marc said.

"Marc, I don't remember seeing those tracks before," Sophie said, pointing to a set of tire tracks that led from the parking lot into the street.

"That makes two of us," Marc said as he cut his headlights and wheeled into the lot. He maneuvered the Explorer around the rows of parked cars and snow banks hoping to find the Teitelbaum bus parked where they last saw it.

"Fuck, it's gone," Marc said.

"Yeah, and those tire tracks where the bus was parked look suspiciously like the ones crossing back onto Main Street, Sophie said, pointing to the tracks next to the real estate office.

"Sonofabitch," Marc said, bringing the Explorer to a stop at the rear the real estate office. He ran to the back door where they had observed the men in the hazmat suits an hour before. The door was locked, and a glance through door's glass window revealed nothing…no lights left on…no movement inside…nothing.

"They couldn't have left that long ago," Marc shouted as he hurried back to his SUV.

"OK, but where do we start looking?" Sophie asked.

"We know it turned left out of the parking lot, and assuming it's headed toward New York City, it's either got to go east past the Inn or south toward Saranac Lake." Marc answered, his mind mapping out the most likely route.

Marc wheeled his SUV back onto Main Street and a minute later they arrived at the main intersection near the center of town.

From here, Marc knew that continuing straight ahead would take them to Saranac Lake and deeper into the Adirondacks, while a left turn would lead them past the Inn and to the Interstate, Route 87. Marc slowed his vehicle and concentrated on the road ahead, scanning for the bus's tire tracks.

Again, it was Sophie who spotted them, "Look there," she said, pointing to a set of dual wheel tire tracks that had crossed over the accumulation of snow in the middle of the intersection. "They're heading toward the Olympic Ski Jumps and Route 73."

As Marc made the left turn, he said, "Makes sense, from here the Big Apple's about six hours south. Whoever's driving the bus is probably in panic mode after the helicopter crash and now with this Nousha woman gone, they have nothing to lose."

Marc handed Sophie his cell phone, "Try raising Jerry and ask him if they're still manning the roadblock at the entrance to the Inn. They may be able to stop the bus if it hasn't already passed."

After a couple of tries, Sophie said, "No luck. Cell phone reception at the Inn is spotty at best and if Jerry's somewhere inside, forget it."

Marc was vaguely aware of the tiny ice crystals pinging off his windshield as he pushed the Explorer to over sixty miles an hour. Minutes later, they were on the Cascade Road, then Route 73 leading out of town, with still no sign of the tour bus.

"I don't know, Marc. Maybe they didn't come this way after all, seems like we should have seen something by now."

Marc, sensing the anxious note in Sophie's voice, pressed on. Passing the entrance to the Craig Wood golf course they came over a rise, then a long downhill stretch of road spotted with patches of ice. In the SUV's headlights, they could see wisps of snow from the impending squall snaking across the highway in front of them as a cold breeze picked up from the north. Then, faintly visible through a break in flurries, Marc saw a set of tail lights at the far end of the straightaway.

"There it is! See the red clearance lamps above the tail lights. That's got to be our bus," Marc said just before its lights disappeared around another bend in the road.

Marc pressed on at over seventy miles an hour, slowing only as he approached the curve.

As they passed the darkened entrance to the Saranac Mountain Inn, Marc saw Sophie glance back apprehensively.

"Sorry if this speed makes you nervous, but we've got to finish this," he said.

"Don't slow down on my account. I was just hoping the troopers would still be manning the roadblock, but obviously they've all left."

A minute later, the snow flurries morphed into larger flakes that coated the roadway. A road sign indicated 'Sharp Curve Ahead', and Marc eased off on the accelerator.

"Careful with this next curve, Marc, there's a hundred foot drop into the lake just on the other side of the guard rail," Sophie said as he brought the SUV into the slippery curve.

Marc suddenly felt the rear of the Explorer begin to slide toward the snow bank guarding the right side of the roadway. Gripping the wheel firmly, he eased the SUV ever so slightly in an attempt to prevent it from crashing into the looming snow bank. *Always turn towards the skid*, the words of his high school drivers ed teacher flashed through his mind, as he desperately fought to keep the Explorer from plowing into the looming wall of snow whizzing past Sophie's side window, mere inches away.

Sophie instinctively grabbed the dash in an attempt to hold on, then screamed as they both felt the SUV's right rear bumper strike something hard.

As Marc braced for the impending collision, the Explorer's rear wheels caught on some sand spread earlier by a passing road crew.

"Did we just hit something?" Sophie asked, nearly hysterical.

"I don't know, may have been the guard rail," Marc answered, still concentrating on the road ahead.

Having regained control of his vehicle, Marc continued the pursuit, but with renewed respect for the quickly deteriorating road conditions, hopeful that the taillights of the tour bus would reappear around the next bend in the road.

After another mile, the road straightened and Marc continued to follow its descent toward the hamlet of Keene, two miles distant.

Surely, we should catch the bus before then.

Sophie, having regained her composure, said, "Where'd that freaking bus go?"

As they continued toward Keene however, the storm increased in both intensity and volume. The light from the Explorer's high beams

237

reflected off the wall of falling snow, and the dizzying display of swirling flakes appeared to hang in the air before exploding onto the windshield. In the short space of a quarter mile, everything around the vehicle had turned to a sheet of solid white, making it almost impossible for Marc to see where the roadway ended and the snow banks on either side began. Without visual cues to judge his speed, he was shocked when he noticed the speedometer registered a mere twenty miles per hour.

"What we have here is a classic whiteout." Marc murmured, blinking his eyes in an effort to keep his concentration. Switching his head lights to low-beams helped reduce the glare as he continued down the winding road toward Keene.

After a few minutes, Sophie asked, "Marc, haven't you noticed something peculiar?"

"Yeah, it's snowing, hard," Marc joked, as he focused on keeping his vehicle between the guard rails hidden beneath long berms of snow on either side of the road.

"If that bus was somewhere ahead of us, shouldn't we be seeing its tire tracks in the snow?"

There was hardly any snow on the road when they left Lake Placid, and after striking the guard rail and the sudden whiteout, Marc hadn't given much thought to the bus's tire tracks.

Marc slowed as he concentrated on the road. He figured there was at least five inches of new snow, and Sophie was right, there were no tire tracks.

"This storm came up kinda quick, but I can't imagine how the bus could have gotten so far ahead of us that the snow filled in its tracks."

"Right, and besides, we were beginning to close in on it. So, where could it have gone?" A bewildered Sophie asked.

"I don't know, but we sure as hell didn't pass it. It's gotta be up ahead somewhere."

Finally arriving in Keene with its streetlights barely visible through the storm, Marc stopped at the only intersection in town. The snow was piling up and at this rate, Marc knew it could be twice as deep in less than an hour. Still not willing to give up, he turned the Explorer south, toward the Interstate. Ten minutes and another half mile later, there was still no trace of the bus's tire tracks and the storm continued its fury.

"Marc, I think we should give this up and start back toward Lake Placid. Maybe Jerry is still at the Inn. We could try and catch up with him there."

"I suppose you're right," Marc said, as feelings of frustration and fatigue began to take their toll.

Reluctantly, he engaged the vehicle's four-wheel drive and turned around at the next intersection, "I know there's not much more we can do in this storm, I just wish I knew what happened to that damn bus. Tour busses just don't vanish into thin air."

It took them almost an hour to make the ten-mile trip back to the Inn. When they finally arrived, they found the parking lot was still illuminated with portable emergency lighting and two state police SUV's were parked near the remnants of the burned-out helicopter. Marc parked near one of the police vehicles. The trooper, who appeared to have been reading a book, pulled himself upright and Marc heard the hum of the driver's side window being lowered.

"Hey, Mister LaRose, Investigator Garrant's been looking for you. He told me to give you a message."

"Shit, you mean he's not here?" Marc asked, exasperated.

"Left over an hour ago."

"Damn. Well, what'd he say?"

"Uh, let me see, how do I put this?" He said frowning, "It was something about getting your butt over to the Ray Brook barracks tomorrow morning bright and early or he was thinking of arresting your ass!"

"Arresting me? What for?"

"He said he'd think of something," The trooper said, grinning at this inside joke. "Anyway, he said he'd been working for over two days straight and was going home for a nap and was not to be disturbed."

Marc was sure that the "not to be disturbed" part was for his benefit.

"So, what else's is going on? You guys gotta baby sit this thing all night?" Marc asked, pointing to the steaming remnants, hissing as the snowflakes came in contact with it.

"Yeah, well, seeing it's already past four a.m., there's not much of 'this night' left, and this is still a crime scene. All the bodies, well, all they could find, have been recovered. They're going to remove what's left of the helicopter and take it back to the barracks after the FAA guys have had a chance to look at it, hopefully, sometime tomorrow. Garrant and a bunch of the Bureau of Criminal Investigation guys went through the Inn with a search warrant, but I understand they came out empty. A total cluster!"

"Thanks for the message," Marc said, and waved good night to the trooper, who slid his window shut and resumed his position, slumped down behind the steering wheel. Marc returned to his SUV and gave Sophie the message that he was to report to Jerry in the morning.

"Marc, there's no sense in driving to Saranac Lake in this storm. There's plenty of room at the Inn, no pun intended. What do you say we just bunk down there for the rest of the night?"

Marc had been up since 4:00 a.m. the day before and hadn't had a good night's sleep in over seventy-two hours, and coupled with the intensity of the evening's events, he knew he'd hit a wall.

"You know, Sophie, ordinarily, the idea of spending a night in this Inn, after all that's happened, would creep me out. But right now, I am so bushed. And besides, that's the best offer I've had all day. Where do we check in?"

Inside, Sophie retrieved a key from behind her concierge desk and led Marc, not to one of the guest rooms, but to another room not far from the Inn's lounge. Although not as nicely appointed as a guest room, it was a bit larger, with two double beds, a couch, a few overstuffed chairs, fridge and a flat screened TV.

"This is sometimes used by employees who have to stay over due to a quick turnaround or inclement weather. I'd say this storm rates as pretty inclement, don't you?"

"So, which bed would you like?" Marc asked as he dropped his coat on the floor.

"The one you're standing next to will do just fine," Sophie said with a tired grin.

THE LAST DAY

The storm was violent. The racks of his delivery van were full with vases of arranged roses, some red, some yellow, some pink. Oddly however, all of them were to be delivered to the same person, but the directions were vague. Marc has knocked on several doors, but it's always the same; a young girl answers and when Marc asks if her mommy is home, he's told that he must have the wrong address because her mommy doesn't live there anymore. Marc is getting desperate to make the delivery because the roses are beginning to wilt.

Suddenly, his van begins to rock from side to side, gently at first, then more violently. One of the vases tips over spilling roses and water onto the floor of the van, then another, and another. Marc pushes down on the brake pedal in an effort to stop the rocking, but the van continues, even more violently. Then, from somewhere outside the van he hears someone calling his name, "Marc, Marc, Marc darling. Hello. Earth to Marc!"

Marc opened his eyes, blinked a few times, and looked around the room. Slowly he focused on Sophie standing over him with her hand on his shoulder.

"Where the hell am I? Oh yeah. The Inn." Marc muttered as the lingering dream began to fade.

"Sorry to wake you, but you said Jerry wanted to talk to you this morning. No sense pissing him off any more than he is. It's already after nine."

Marc swung his legs out from under the covers and sat at the edge of the bed. The floor felt cold on his bare feet.

"Sorry, guess I was really out. Just having a weird dream. Is it still snowing?" Marc asked, pushing the clouds of the dream from his mind.

"No, it stopped, not long after we went to bed. I woke up once when I heard snowplows out in the parking lot. Last time I looked, they were loading what's left of the helicopter onto a flatbed wrecker."

"They'll be keeping it for evidence until the case is closed," Marc said.

"Why don't you take a shower? It might help you get your bearings. In the meantime, I'll forage around the kitchen and see if Mr. Emmanuel left us anything for breakfast." Sophie said as she turned to leave.

Marc remained perched on the edge of the bed, letting his head clear. "There's a towel and a package of courtesy toiletries on the chair next to the sink," Sophie yelled over her shoulder as she closed the door.

By the time he finished his shower, Sophie was returning from the kitchen, pushing a serving tray with a pot of coffee and a two plates piled with scrambled eggs.

"There wasn't much left in the refrigerator, but I think this should hold us for now," Sophie said as she set the plates on a table in front of the TV.

"Smells great. Have you talked to your dad?"

"I finally got through just before I woke you. The lines were down earlier. Everything's OK at home, but I think he was relieved to hear from me. Quite a storm we had after all. Zoe said to tell Mr. LaRose she said 'Hi'."

Marc just smiled as he hungrily started in on the breakfast.

When they finished eating, he poured himself a second cup of coffee. "Before I talk to Garrant, I'll drop you off at the motel. I'm sure Zoe will be glad to see you."

"What? No way. I want to see Jerry's face when you tell him what went on last night. Besides, Zoe will be in school by the time I get home."

"I suppose you're right. Garrant will probably want to talk to you, too."

By the time they arrived at the Ray Brook barracks it was almost ten o'clock. They were met by a young trooper at the front desk, one that Marc had not seen before.

"Yes sir. May I help you?" He said quite crisply.

"Marc LaRose to see Investigator Garrant. I think he's expecting us." Marc said as he presented his State Police 'Retired' ID card and shield.

The trooper gave it a quick glance, "Just have a seat, folks. I'll let him know you're here."

A few moments later, the door to the interior offices suddenly opened. Jerry Garrant appeared and motioned for Marc and Sophie to follow him inside. Although freshly shaved and smartly dressed, Marc could see that he had not slept well.

"Morning," Marc said, as he and Sophie walked past.

Jerry grunted a terse reply and led the two down the hallway.

No small talk, not a good sign.

242

When they arrived at Jerry's office, he again held the door open, and motioned Marc and Sophie inside. As they entered, Marc recognized another man seated behind Jerry's desk, someone Marc had intentionally tried to forget. He hadn't been one of Marc's favorites five years ago and there wasn't any reason to believe that their relationship was about to get better.

When Marc retired, Amos Welch was a senior investigator who had somehow passed the lieutenant's exam. Since then, Amos had risen in the ranks to Bureau Captain, putting him in charge of all investigative matters occurring in Troop B. His reputation as a hard-charging detective, who let nothing get in his way, including three wives and numerous official misconduct charges, was well-known in the law enforcement community.

Marc was not surprised to see that Amos had put on a few pounds since he'd last seen him, as evidenced by the fact that his wrinkled sports jacket failed to reach around his rotund potbelly. He also noted Amos was cultivating an alcoholic's red face complete with spider veins and bumpy rosacea scars covering his bulbous nose, giving him a comical, W.C. Fields-like appearance. However, Marc doubted that today, Captain Welch would be in the mood for any slap stick.

"Have a seat." Jerry said tersely, directing Marc and Sophie to the two remaining chairs on the opposite side of the desk.

"You remember Captain Welch?"

"How you been Amos?" Marc asked.

Welch simply shifted his gaze between Sophie and Marc.

"Marc, we have a few questions regarding your activities over past few days and particularly last night," Jerry said.

"Sure." And without waiting, Marc began to relate the results of his investigation. "Like I've mentioned before Jerry, I'd been pursuing leads regarding the death of Mister Jamal Al-Zeid at the request of my client when…"

Marc was suddenly interrupted by Captain Welch, who pushed back from the desk and bellowed, "Pursuing leads, my ass. First you take a simple unattended death case, and, with your little sidekick here," he nodded toward Sophie, "come up with some cockamamie bullshit about radiation poisoning. Then you call us regarding an Austrian woman who claimed her husband may have been offed by a bunch of Arabs. Now, normally, one would think that would be enough mayhem for one week, but nooo…" Welch dragged out the vowel, accentuating his sarcasm. "Next we get a 911 call regarding trespassers at the Saranac Mountain Inn, and, surprise, it's none other than you two characters, up there nosing around."

"Captain, I can explain," Marc began, but was again cut off as Amos Welch held up his hand for him to stop.

"Then, just when Investigator Garrant has you two in custody, a helicopter crashes right there at the Inn, killing all ten people on board. That's ten fucking people, LaRose! And do you know who these people were? They weren't just any ten jerk-off's from Tupper Lake. Some were well known and highly connected, some badly connected, but before they had the misfortune of crossing your paths, they were at least connected to their lives. Now we've got the State Department on our ass, a few federal agencies including the FBI, FAA and the Department of Homeland Security and, let's see, who'd I leave out? Oh yeah, almost forgot, Interpol, how could I forget fucking Interpol?"

Welch gulped from his mug, coffee dripping down his chin. Marc knew it would do no good to interrupt Welch's tirade. He was on a roll.

Amos Welch wiped his mouth with the back of his hand, "Now, let's see, what else?" He opened his note pad and made a point of flipping through a few of the pages.

"Oh yeah, here we are. Shit. How could I forget?" He said, as he zeroed in on a page. "After you wiggle away from Investigator Garrant, taking advantage of his preoccupation with those people roasting in the helicopter crash, you come across a fatal snowmobile accident out behind the Inn, involving none other than the husband of the Austrian woman you called about earlier, except now this guy is dangling from the end of a tree limb that's been shoved clear through his chest."

"But even with all this, could you two call it a night? Hell no. Next, you decide it's time to take a late night cruise down toward Whiteface Mountain where you happen onto a fatal car crash involving a couple of people who oddly enough hail from Iran. Fucking Iran, of all places! And naturally, they just happened to have a crate full of highly explosive C4 in their vehicle."

Sophie shot Marc a nervous glance.

No sense arguing with this fool, better to let him finish.

Welch snapped his note book shut and jammed it in his inside coat pocket. As he slowly leaned back in his office chair with his hands clasped around the back of his neck, the gaps between the buttons of his coffee-stained shirt opened to reveal a dingy tee shirt. He held the pose for half a minute, readying himself for his next barrage.

"I hesitate to ask, Mr. LaRose, is there anything I haven't mentioned? Was there something else that only you, a small town piss pot PI, with your vast network of international informants, have picked up that the ineffectual resources of the governments of the U.S. and Canada have somehow overlooked?"

"Well Amos…er, Captain, there is the matter of a Jewish tour bus that we observed over at the…"

"Stop right there!" Welch bellowed, then turned toward Jerry, "Investigator Garrant, do you know anything about this Jewish tour bus he's yammering about?"

"Not really," Jerry stammered, "I mean, I think he might have mentioned something about a tour bus as we were beginning to conduct our search of the Inn, but…"

"How would he know?" Marc interrupted, struggling to keep his voice under control. "We made several attempts to contact Investigator Garrant, but between the lack of cell phone coverage, the snow storm, and the helicopter crash, we kept missing each other. Besides, it turns out that the Jewish tour bus thing is probably immaterial; we couldn't verify that it ever left Lake Placid or where it went. It just sort of disappeared."

Welch exhaled and rubbed a beefy hand across his face, further irritating his rosacea-infected nose.

"Are you playing games with me, LaRose?"

Again, Marc thought it better not to answer.

"I'm almost afraid to ask, but what the fuck does a Jewish tour bus have to do with everything else that's been going on around here?"

Marc chose his words carefully so as not to further jeopardize his relationship with Jerry. "The evening before the helicopter crash, Ms. Horton mentioned that things weren't going well at the Saranac Mountain Inn with Mr. Emmanuel, the manager, letting everyone go so suddenly. As you have pointed out, I did visit the Inn last night. But what you may not know is while I was scouting around inside, I overheard a presentation that was attended by several of those who later died in the helicopter crash. In brief, these people were conspiring to sabotage Lake Placid's chances of hosting the 2026 Winter Olympics."

Marc expected Welch to explode again, but to his surprise, he remained silent, so he continued, "Then, after the helicopter crash, I had the opportunity to look into the room previously occupied by the deceased, Phillip Huber, where I found a brochure put out by the Teitelbaum Transit Company." Marc reached in his shirt pocket and handed Welch the brochure.

"As you can see, they advertise excursions from New York to Montreal, then to Lake Placid before returning to New York City. One of the buses listed on the brochure arrived at the Olympic Arena Motel last night for its scheduled overnight stay. I thought the coincidence of finding a brochure featuring a Jewish tour bus package in Huber's room, along with the presence of the bus in the village on the night he was killed, was enough reason to place the bus under surveillance. It was during the course of the surveillance last night that we observed men in hazmat suits loading something into the cargo hold of the bus."

"Stop right there!" Welch bellowed again. "Have you lost your fucking mind, LaRose? First, you go digging around inside the Inn without the owner's permission. That sounds like burglary. You listen in on private conversations. You go rifling through guest rooms removing whatever you want. And on top of that you steal a snow mobile. I think we have enough to lock you up at least until we figure out what the hell happened without you meddling any further into an ongoing police investigation."

Jerry interrupted, "Captain, I've known Marc over twenty years. I know how this looks, but I'm certain he would not intentionally break the law without good reason. I really think we need to hear him out on this."

Welch stood and stared at Jerry, "You better be right on this, Garrant, or you'll be looking at a demotion, plus a transfer to Shitsville."

Returning his attention to Marc, Welch said, "Before we continue with this fantasy tour you've been taking us on, LaRose, do we need to read you your Miranda rights, or does the rest of your investigation rely on legal means of inquiry?"

Marc glanced at Sophie and saw the concerned look on her face, "Before I continue, Captain, there is one thing I need you to understand. What you do to me when this is over is up to you, but Sophie Horton's role in this matter was solely at my direction."

"I'll be the judge of that. Now, let's get back to what you were saying about men loading something into the tour bus wearing what 'appeared' to be hazmat suits," Welch said, making quote signs in the air and perching himself on a corner of the desk.

Although Marc's throat felt dry with tension, he continued, "The Olympic Arena Motel shares a parking lot with the vacant real estate office next door. Early last evening, we observed the tour bus in question park behind the office. From our position across the street, we continued to watch the parking lot for signs of movement, then, around midnight, we saw strange flashes of light coming from inside the office, so we decided to investigate. We made our way around the opposite side of the motel, and that's when we saw these men dressed in hazmat suits loading what appeared to be heavy containers into the bus's cargo hold." Marc paused and brought his cupped hand to his mouth, giving Jerry the signal that he needed a drink of water.

"Is that it? You saw what you thought were a few men loading something into the cargo hold of a bus? Well, excuse me, but where else do you load shit into a bus, under the hood? Come on LaRose, get to the point, if you indeed have one."

"I'm trying to, sir," Marc said testily. "Like I was saying, after we watched the men struggle, loading those containers, we returned to my vehicle, and as we were leaving to alert Investigator Garrant, we saw a van come around the other side of the real estate office and head straight toward us. It was then that I recognized this van as the same one that was driven by the woman who shot my tire out the day before.

"Shot your tire out!" Welch yelled, his rosacea seemed to take on an added glow as he threw his arms up in exasperation. "Tell me, Mr. LaRose, did you bother to report this detail, or was this just another trifling occurrence that you face on a daily basis?"

Ignoring the dig, Marc continued. "I figured this woman was some kind of fanatic because after putting a bullet hole in my tire, she warned me to stop my investigation into Al-Zeid's death, or the next time, it wouldn't be my tire she'd be shooting at."

Welch continued to glare at Marc, "Go on," he demanded.

"So, when I spotted her van last night, I knew we were in danger. The quickest way out of there was to head north toward Whiteface. When I did, the van caught up to us, shots were fired, and, at one point, she tried to run us off the road. When we were about six miles out of Lake Placid, I swerved to avoid a large buck in the middle of the highway, but I guess she didn't. That put an end to the chase, because the van's headlights disappeared and we saw a brilliant flash of light coming from behind us."

"I see. Then what?"

"After the flash, we figured the van had crashed and maybe exploded. When we came back to investigate, about ten minutes later, a state DOT truck was on the scene. We assisted, giving aid to the lone survivor, then returned to the Olympic Arena Motel's parking lot. Finding the tour bus gone, we followed its tire tracks in the snow out to Main Street and even spotted it heading east on Route 73, but before we could catch up to it, we ran into a heavy snow squall. We lost sight of it on the sharp curve overlooking Cascade Lake."

"Uh huh, go on," Welch grunted.

"There's really not much left to tell. We continued to look for the bus all the way to Keene, but by then, the storm had turned into a full blown white-out, and we never saw it again. By the time we returned to the Inn to report to Investigator Garrant, the trooper told us he had left for the night then gave us the message that we were to meet him here this morning, and here we are."

Welch continued to stare at Marc, and after a long moment, he got up, walked around the desk, and said, "Your tale sounds so fucking far-fetched that I doubt even a person with your active an imagination could actually make this shit up. But, if you would be so kind, just who the hell was this guy in the accident that the EMT's dragged into to the ER last night?"

"His name is Naveed Hashemi, how's he doing?"

"He's beat up pretty bad, but he should make it. We tried to talk to him, but, for some god-forsaken reason, he keeps asking for you. No wallet, no ID. Nothing. We're pretty sure he and the girl, what's left of her, are in the country illegally, but we're holding off calling the border patrol until we've had a chance to talk to him. Which begs the question, how do you know this Naveed guy anyway? And please, just the short version."

Just then, Jerry returned with two bottles of water and handed one to Marc.

"Captain, I'm afraid there is no short version," Marc said as he cracked the cap off a water bottle.

"Well then, do the best you can without making a fucking trilogy out of this mess."

After a long swallow, Marc again related the results of his investigation: starting with the interview with the Hubers at the Inn, and finally ending with the search for the Teitelbaum tour bus the previous night. In the meantime, Welch had reseated himself behind the desk with his note pad. By the time Marc finished it was almost noon. Welch silently scanned the notes he had taken, the only sound in the room, the steady hum of the florescent lighting above. When Welch next spoke, his voice was almost devoid of sarcasm.

"OK. Tell you what. We're going to need a full written statement from both of you. Of course you can call an attorney if you want, but understand, I'm going to check out your stories, and if I think you're feeding us a line of shit, LaRose, I'll personally run your sorry ass up that flag post out in front of the barracks."

"Captain, I won't need a lawyer, but I can't speak for Sophie."

"Suit yourself, but I want this done right away, as in now."

Jerry, who had previously left the room to locate a stenographer to take the statements, returned, wearing a puzzled look on his face, "Captain, something's come up that I think you should know about."

"Investigator Garrant, can't you see I'm busy?"

"Yes sir, but I just overheard a report from the Department of Transportation. Seems they were clearing a large snow drift down on Route 73 when their plow struck what looks like a rear axle assembly from a large vehicle buried in the snow bank on the curve overlooking Cascade Lake."

Still trying to sort through Marc's explanation of events, Welch blurted out, "So what? How does that concern…?" He glanced over at Marc and Sophie, hesitated, and then nodded in Sophie's direction. "Garrant, you remain here and start on her statement," Then turning toward Marc, he said, "LaRose, you come with me. I'll need you to verify just where you lost sight of that bus last night. I'm gonna get to the bottom of this even if I have to miss happy hour for the rest of the week."

Sophie turned toward Marc, "Do you really think I need a lawyer?"

Jerry interrupted, "I don't know, but it looks like we're going to need all the help we can get."

"Marc, when will I see you again?" Sophie asked.

As he pulled on his parka, Marc reached over and touched her arm, "I shouldn't be long. Don't worry; things will be OK."

"If you two love birds are through cooing, we've got work to do. Come on, LaRose, we ain't got all day," growled Welch as he started for the door.

"I'll make sure Sophie gets home after we're finished taking her statement," Jerry said.

"Thanks Jerry," Marc said, as he gave Sophie a wink and followed Captain Welch out of the office.

Following the directions supplied by the desk sergeant, Marc and Amos Welch soon located the flashing lights of the DOT snow plow. Flares had been set out to warn oncoming traffic of the hazard.

"This is where we felt a bump last night as we skidded toward that snow drift," Marc said, pointing to the snow bank off to the right side of the road. "At the time, I figured we might have hit the guard rail."

"And you're sure this was the curve?" asked Welch.

"No doubt about it," Marc said assuredly.

Welch parked the car a short distance away and the two approached the scene on foot. Having investigated his share of auto accidents, Marc associated the familiar acrid smell of burning sulfur from the traffic flares as a foreboding sign of tragedy.

One of the crewmen recognized Captain Welch and motioned him to where he was working with a shovel. As they got closer, Marc could see the men were busy clearing snow around a large axle assembly still half buried in the snow drift. There was also a collection of guard rail posts and cable strewn about near the axle.

"It looks like a truck, or maybe a bus axle, not sure which," the crewman said. "They must have missed the curve, then the rear wheels got caught up in the guide cable, ripping the axle right off its chassis."

"So, where's the rest of the vehicle?" Welch asked.

"Went over that bank, I recon. Take a look for yourself." The crewman said, motioning toward the embankment with his thumb.

Welch and Marc trudged up the snow bank at the end of the curve to where they could see the snow-covered expanse of Cascade

Lake, a hundred feet below. As Marc scanned down the rocky embankment beneath him, he saw what looked like a round skating rink on the ice just off shore.

"Looks like your bus missed the curve and plunged into the lake. The hole it made in the ice has since frozen over. The scuba team is gonna love this," Welch quipped, as he started back to the troop car.

By the time State Police divers arrived later that afternoon, dusk had settled in, and because of the impending darkness and extreme depth of the lake, the dive was put off until the following day. That evening, Marc gave Amos Welch a detailed written statement of his investigation.

Subsequent examination of the axle revealed a VIN number and a computer check confirmed it was registered to a bus owned by the Teitelbaum Bus Company.

As he was leaving the police barracks, Marc's plan to return to Saranac Lake was abruptly cut short when he received a frantic call from his ex, Shirley. Their daughter, Ann Marie was again threatening to quit school and move in with, as Shirley described, "An out-of-work loser ten years older."

So, with a feeling of guilt, Marc returned to Plattsburgh to convince his daughter to stay in school and end this relationship. He spent the night and a case of Kleenex tissue with Shirley and a tearful Ann Marie.

*****

Early the following day, Marc received a call from Sophie. "I understand you and Captain Welch were busy with the accident scene, but I thought I'd hear from you when you finished up," she said. "What happened?"

"It's complicated. The bus is apparently at the bottom of the lake. The divers are supposed to start looking this morning. I wanted to see you last night, but then I got a call from Shirley. She needed to see me right away."

"I see," Sophie said, warily.

"No, it's not like that. It was about our daughter, Ann Marie. A little family problem, but I think it's been taken care of," Marc said.

"So, what are you up to today?" She asked.

"Well, let's see. Where do I start. There are a few people with

251

funny initials who want to talk to me about what we saw, as in FBI, ATF and FAA. Give me a couple of days. Think you can hold out?" Marc asked teasingly.

No answer.

"Sophie? You still there?"

"It's ironic. You got a call from your ex yesterday, then I get one this morning."

"What do you mean?" Marc asked.

"Ian called."

"Oh." Marc replied.

"His prostate cancer's come back with a vengeance, stage four. Says he wants to see Zoe again before it's too late. He's too sick to travel and he's asked me to fly Zoe over to see him."

"Sorry to hear about Ian, but, what do you intend to do?"

"We're leaving this afternoon from the Lake Clear airport, then on down to Logan. Probably be gone for at least a week or two, maybe longer, I'm not sure."

"Wow, that's kind of short notice," Marc said, caught off guard.

"Yeah, I know, but, Ian doesn't have much time."

"Sophie, if I left right now, I could be in Saranac Lake before noon."

"Oh Marc, that sounds tempting, but I've got a lot of packing to do, plus some last minute stuff for dad. Besides, it sounds like your plate's pretty full as well."

"If I didn't know any better, I might suspect that I just got dumped," Marc said.

"Fat chance on that happening. Look, as soon as I get back, let's plan on picking up where we left off," she said, hopefully.

"Sounds good, but next time we could do without a bunch of crazies shooting at us and trying to run us off the road."

"Marc, I have a feeling that the crazies of this world have you on speed dial. I can put up with them, if you can put up with me."

"Let me know when you get back, and give Zoe my best."

"You take care too, Marc."

As Marc cut the connection, he swung his chair around and absently stared out his office window down onto a snow-covered Margaret Street. He thought of Sophie and when he would see her again.

"OK Marc, time to get to work," he said to his own image,

reflected in the window.

He scanned his notepad at the contact numbers of the agencies that had earlier left frantic messages for him to call.

What I wouldn't give for a nice simple domestic case right now.

Just then, his office phone rang.

Maybe Sophie's changed her mind.

"Is this the private detective, Marc LaRose?" A woman asked, snuffling back tears.

"Depends. What's the problem?" Marc asked, hopefully.

"It's my husband, I think he's seeing another woman."

"Sorry to hear that," Marc answered, trying not to let the grin he was wearing show in his voice. "What can I do for you?"

EPILOGUE

The following day, the *Plattsburgh Daily Standard* headline read, "Spate of Tragedies Hits Lake Placid Area."

The lead story, big on headlines but short on details, advised that the Ray Brook State Police reported their busiest night ever as they continued their investigation into a string of incidents, including a deadly helicopter crash, a snowmobile tragedy, a stolen bus believed to be at the bottom of Cascade Lake, and a fatal car/deer accident. A police spokesman would not confirm the rumor that the incidents were somehow connected.

Facts of the case were released piecemeal over the following weeks and months as various investigating agencies struggled to connect the dots. Attempts by the FBI laboratory to confirm the identity of the remains of those aboard the helicopter were inconclusive, due to the incineration of the craft and the absence of any flight manifest.

A confidential intelligence report presented by the International Criminal Police Organization of Lyon, France, also known as Interpol, stated although it suspects the sudden disappearance of many of Europe's top organized crime figures may have been linked to the crash, most were quickly replaced by a cast of younger, ambitious upstarts, eager to make their way to the top of the European organized crime heap. The void left by Wolfgang Heitmeyer, the prestigious member of the International Olympic Committee's Executive Board was discreetly filled a few months later by an interim selectee, who has chosen to remain anonymous pending a permanent appointment to the committee.

At the coroner's inquest held the following spring in Elizabethtown, Marc testified regarding the events surrounding the terrorist attack, including being first threatened, then pursued by the woman later identified as Nousha Asgari, a radical Islamist recruited by Khaleed Hashemi, as well as his knowledge of the snowmobile accident that resulted in the death of Phillip Huber. While at the hearing, Marc learned that, of the bodies that were eventually recovered from the murky depths of Lower Cascade Lake, only the corpse of Khaleed Hashemi was identified by his brother, Naveed.

About two hundred pounds of C4 blocks were found enclosed in the bus's overhead luggage compartment, but no radioactive material was located. An accident reconstruction specialist theorized that contents of the bus may have spilled out while being raised, and maybe buried in the thick mud at the bottom of the lake.

At the hearing, Naveed Hashemi asked for political asylum status in the United States, stating he feared persecution if returned to Iran. In return, he has promised to cooperate with investigators and has provided information concerning the Mufti Mangal Shakir's terrorist network in Canada. He remains in protective custody at an undisclosed location.

A State Police forensic specialist testified that further tests of the tissue samples taken from Jamal Al-Zeid during his autopsy confirmed Sophie's diagnosis of radiation poisoning.

After a day of testifying, Marc and Jerry met at the Deer Tale Inn, a Elizabethtown eatery. Over dinner, Marc asked what had become of Noah Emmanuel after the snowmobile accident.

"He'll be testifying, tomorrow. From the statement he gave us while he was hospitalized in Burlington, we expect him to tell the coroner that Phillip Huber forced him to drive the snowmobile during his escape from the hotel and that Angus McKenzie had directed him to clear the hotel of all but the security staff prior to the meeting of the European consortium the night of the helicopter crash."

"What's going to happen to him?" Marc asked.

"In return for his cooperation, he's been offered immunity from prosecution. Word is, he'll return to his hometown, Charleston, South Carolina, where he'll probably become a ward of the state."

"Sounds like his injuries were pretty serious," Marc said.

"Crushed L3 and L4. There's no way he can take care of himself; he'll probably be in a wheelchair the rest of his life."

"And Bianca Huber?"

"Although she lost her husband in the snowmobile crash, she's remained cooperative. Her allegations regarding the consortium's efforts to terrorize the Lake Placid community were substantiated, plus, she was able to corroborate Naveed Hashemi's claim that the Montreal-based arm of the Iranian terrorist group used the European consortium to fund the terrorist desires of the Mufti Mangal Shakir. From here, she'll have a hearing in front of a U.S. Immigration judge, where, I'm told, she'll be deported to Austria for her association with known terrorists."

"So, what's with this Mangal Shakir guy? Sounds like he's

255

someone the U.S. should be interested in finding."

"Good luck with that. Word is, he's still holed up somewhere in Iran," Jerry said.

"Did the police check out Global Rug Importers in Montreal?"

"Yeah, the RCMP got a search warrant. There's no doubt that the store was a front for the Iranian terror cell, but because of the Islamic (Sharia) money transfer system known as Hawala, no written records were found connecting the store to any terrorist organization."

"Any word about the owner of the Inn, Angus McKenzie, or Serge Remillard, the guy the owned the house in Willsboro? You'd think we'd be able to get those assholes to talk," Marc said.

"Another dead end, I'm afraid," Jerry said, almost apologetically. "Efforts to extradite them to the United States have been futile due to the lack of evidence linking them with the terrorist conspiracy.

"Interesting. I wonder what will happen to the Inn?" Marc asked.

"Supposedly, it's been sold to a nature conservancy group, who, according to the paper, intend to reopen it in the fall, under a new name."

"A new name? What's the point?"

* * * * *

The International Olympic Committee has yet to decide on the location for the 2026 Olympic Winter Games, but it is rumored that an unidentified European country is at the top of the list.

Captain Amos Welch quietly retired from the state police a month after the incident, claiming health concerns. A retirement party was initially proposed, but was canceled due to lack of interest.

Investigator Jerry Garrant was promoted to the rank of Senior Investigator and is still stationed at the Ray Brook barracks.

Although Sophie has yet to return to the U.S. from New Zealand due to her estranged husband's lingering illness, she and Marc remain in contact.

The adventures of Marc LaRose continue in his upcoming thriller, *Southbound Terror*. Agreeing to take a missing person assignment, Marc ultimately joins forces with a Quebec police detective, Sylvie Champagne.

From the border town of Plattsburgh, New York to the seamier side of Montreal's criminal underworld, the pair soon find themselves involved in the world of drug dealing, money laundering and a labyrinth of kidnapping, international intrigue, murder, and state sponsored terrorism.

Thank you for reading and I sincerely hope you enjoyed *Borderline Terror*. As an independently published author, I rely on you, the reader, to spread the word.

If you like what you've read, please consider reviewing *Borderline Terror* on the Amazon.com website. Just a few short sentences are all it takes to make a huge difference.

Also, please say hello through my website, rgeorgeclark.com, or my Facebook page, R. George Clark. I love to hear from my readers.

ACKNOWLEDGMENTS

First of all, I owe a big thank you to the New York State Police and the U.S. Customs and Border Protection for providing me the platform I drew on to write this book, the first in a series of Marc LaRose mysteries.

Without the guidance of my fellow writers at the Aiken Chapter of the South Carolina Writers Association, as well as a dear friend, Carolee Smith, this book, most assuredly, would be less readable.

I will always be indebted to my daughter, Elaine Kehew, for her cover design and Lori Darlow, for her trust and faith that I could see this project through to a successful completion.

Over the course of writing this book, I received words of encouragement by a list of friends, much too long to mention on this page. You know who you are. Thank you.

Lastly, I am most grateful to have as my best friend, and life-long soul mate, my lovely Delena, whose inspiration and reassurance helped me to weave the tapestry of this story.